The Anvil's Whisper

Jaime Rodriguez

JR Publishing LLC

To my wife,
my greatest supporter.
Thank you for everything.

Pronunciations

The following terms are rather unique and I thought to provide a pronunciation in order to help all readers with saying them in their heads or out loud.

Anakuatl
Pronunciation: Ah-nah-KWAH-tuhl
Breakdown: "Ah-nah" (like "Anna"), "KWAH" (like "quad"), "tuhl" (like "tool" but softer).

Ojtlists
Pronunciation: Ohk-tlees
Breakdown: "Ohk" (like "oak"), "tlees" (like "fleets" without the 'f').

Sitlali
Pronunciation: Seet-LAH-lee
Breakdown: "Seet" (like "seat"), "LAH" (like "la"), "lee" (like "Lee").

Akeskauiya

Pronunciation: Ah-kehs-KAH-wee-yah

Breakdown: "Ah" (like "father"), "kehs" (like "guess"), "KAH" (like "car"), "wee-yah" (like "we-yah").

Tlanextli

Pronunciation: Tlah-NESH-tlee

Breakdown: "Tlah" (like "claw" but with a 'T'), "NESH" (like "mesh"), "tlee" (like "flee").

Taurtepetl

Pronunciation: Towr-TEH-peht-l

Breakdown: "Towr" (like "tower"), "TEH" (like "ten"), "peht" (like "pet"), "l" (soft 'l').

Ueuejtlakatl

Pronunciation: Way-way-tlah-KAH-tuhl

Breakdown: "Way-way" (like repeating "way"), "tlah" (like "claw" with a 'T'), "KAH" (like "car"), "tuhl" (like "tool" but softer).

Tzilkarit

Pronunciation: Tseel-KAH-reet

Breakdown: "Tseel" (like "seal" with a slight 'ts' sound at the beginning), "KAH" (like "car"), "reet" (like "read" with a 't').

Preface

This story you are about to read began as an impromptu children's tale, spun late at night for campers I watched over at a summer camp when I was seventeen. Back then, it was nothing more than a fun bedtime adventure, a simple story to lull campers to sleep beneath a canopy of stars. Years later, after I'd gotten married and found myself unexpectedly unemployed, I attempted to reshape that old story into a modern dystopia. The effort lasted about a chapter and a half before it felt forced, and I eventually set it aside.

Several years passed before the spark reignited. While on vacation, I found myself reflecting on stories I had loved and imagined, and the idea returned—this time transformed. I envisioned a world called Anakuatl (pronounced *Ah-nah-KWA-tul*), a land of sweeping valleys, hidden forests, ancient gods, and the harsh realities of tyranny. Hours were spent building this world before I wrote the first sentence. As the story grew, it drifted far from my original outline. Characters changed, the journey twisted, and the ending remains a mystery even to me. But

I am grateful to have finally set this hero on his path, and I hope his journey speaks to you.

Chapter One

Yordan Arano remembered the passage from the Revelations of Light as if it were etched into his very soul. His mother's voice, gentle yet firm, echoed in his mind. "The light within you shall guide your path, even when darkness surrounds. Trust in the luminescence of your heart, my son, for it will lead you to your true destiny."

He had been only nine years old when she had told him this, her eyes filled with a mixture of hope and sadness. Now, nearly ten years later, those words held a weight he was only beginning to understand. Yordan stood at the anvil, sweat dripping from his brow, the heat of the forge enveloping him. The sounds of him hammering on steel were a familiar symphony, one he had been part of since he was ten years old. His hands, strong and calloused, worked with precision born from years of practice. His mentor's forge was his sanctuary, nestled at the edge of Aralonis, in the fertile Valley of Akeskauiya in the land of Anakuatl.

The forge was a modest establishment, built from study stone and timber. The forge itself was the heart of the workshop, a large, roaring furnace, that cast a warm, flickering glow over everything. Trade

1

tools were neatly organized on the walls: hammers, tongs, chisels, and various molds for shaping steel. The air was thick with the smell of burning coal and hot iron, a scent that had become as familiar to Yordan as the breath in his lungs.

Outside Aralonis' walls, the valley stretched out in a lush expanse of green, dotted with vibrant wildflowers and crisscrossed by meandering streams that sparkled in the sunlight. The River Lumina flowed nearby, its gentle currents a constant reminder of life's ever-moving nature. The sounds of the Artisan's Quarter of the city near the river, merchants haggling, children running towards the river to swim and test their wooden toy boats.

Despite the beauty and tranquility of his surroundings, Yordan felt restless. The teachings of the Aralonic Codex, a sacred text he had kept close to his heart since his mother's passing often occupied his thoughts. The Codex spoke of unity, compassion, and a light that connected all beings—a light that Yordan struggled to find within himself.

"Yordan, you're going to chip that piece if you're not careful," warned Ferran, his mentor and the owner of the forge. Ferran was a burly man standing about that was slimer than you would expect from a man approaching seventy. He often wore his leather apron unless he decided to go for a swim in the river. His patience and guidance often helped Yordan when he would get frustrated in his early days of becoming a blacksmith.

"Sorry, Ferran." Yordan replied, shaking off his thoughts. He adjusted his grip on the tongs, carefully heating the metal to the right temperature before hammering it into shape. Finding a good rhythm always centered Yordan's thoughts, but the unease remained.

As he worked, his mind wandered back to the passage his mother recited. He often wondered if the light she spoke of truly existed within him. He was nearing his nineteenth birthday, and despite the years of learning and labor, he felt as though he had yet to truly find his purpose.

Standing in the doorway to the forge was Saamael, or Sam as he preferred to be called. Sam's dark skin and tall, muscular frame were familiar sights in Artisan's quarter. Though blind from a young age, Sam possessed an uncanny perception that often made it seem like he saw more than those who could see with their eyes.

"Yordan, are you daydreaming again?" Sam teased, yet there was an underlying concern. "You know, the metal won't shape itself."

Yordan managed to smile. "Just thinking, Sam. Have you ever got the feeling you're meant for something more?"

"Every day," Sam replied, leaning against the doorframe. "But that's why we keep moving forward, right? To find out what that 'more' is."

Yordan nodded, the weight of the hammer in his hand, a comforting reminder of his present reality. Yet, the words of the Revelations of Light and the teachings of the Aralonic Codex lingered in his mind, urging him to seek the luminescence within.

As the sun began to set, casting long shadows over the valley, Yordan finished his work for the day. He wiped the sweat from his brow and carefully set his tools aside. The forge's glow dimmed, but his restless mind continued to wander.

Stepping outside, he looked towards the distant horizon, where the Sitlali Mountains loomed, their peaks bathed in the golden light of dusk.

As he cleaned himself up at the well outside the forge, the cold water was a stark contrast to the heat inside, refreshing his tired body. He couldn't help but think about Katherine. She had always been a bright spot in his life, her presence a soothing balm to his often-restless soul.

"Yordan!" Katherine's voice rang out, pulling him from his thoughts. She approached with her usual graceful stride, her auburn hair catching the last rays of the setting sun. Her green eyes sparkled with a mix of amusement and concern.

"Hey, Katherine," Yordan said, smiling despite himself. He felt the tension in his shoulders ease just a bit.

"Have you been working non-stop again?" she asked, hands on her hips. "You smell like iron."

"That's what I keep telling him," Sam chimed in, grinning as he leaned against the well. "But he doesn't listen. I told him you'd blame me for not warning him."

Katherine shook her head, a soft smile playing on her lips. "Well, I do appreciate the heads-up, Sam. But Yordan, you need to take better care of yourself. You're not made of steel, you know."

Yordan laughed. "I know, I know. I just get lost in the work sometimes."

"Sometimes?" Katherine raised an eyebrow, clearly not buying his nonchalant attitude. "You need to find a balance, Yordan. Promise me you'll try."

He nodded, feeling a warmth spread through him at her concern. "I promise."

They spent the evening together, talking and sharing stories. Katherine's laughter was infectious, and even Sam couldn't resist joining in. As the night wore on, Yordan felt a sense of contentment he hadn't felt in a long time. As the evening grew late and the stars began to twinkle in the night sky, Sam stretched and stood up. "Well, I should probably get going. Early morning tomorrow," he said with a grin. "You two behave now. Don't do anything I wouldn't do!"

Katherine laughed and playfully swatted at Sam. "Oh shush, you scoundrel. Get out of here before I tell Yordan about that time with the barmaid and the goat."

Sam held up his hands in mock surrender, chuckling. "Alright, alright, I know when I'm not wanted. Goodnight, you two." With a final wink that seemed uncannily accurate for a blind man, Sam headed off into the night.

Yordan and Katherine sat in comfortable silence for a moment, the crackling of the fire and the chirping of crickets the only sounds. Katherine scooted closer, resting her head on Yordan's shoulder. He wrapped an arm around her, savoring her warmth and the sweet scent of her hair.

"I've missed this," Katherine murmured, her fingers tracing idle patterns on Yordan's thigh. "Just being with you, away from all the noise and expectations."

Yordan hummed in agreement, pressing a kiss to the top of her head. "Me too. I feel like I can breathe when I'm with you. Like the weight of the world isn't quite so heavy."

Katherine tilted her head up to look at him, her green eyes shimmering in the firelight. "You know you can always share your burdens with me, right? You don't have to carry everything alone."

Yordan cupped her cheek, his thumb gently caressing her soft skin. "I know. And I'm grateful for that, more than you know." He leaned in, his lips meeting hers in a tender kiss that quickly deepened, sparking a familiar hunger between them.

Katherine shifted, straddling his lap as her hands tangled in his dark curls. She pressed herself against him, the heat of her body igniting a fire in his veins. Yordan's hands roamed her back, pulling her closer, needing to feel her skin on his.

Breaking the kiss, Katherine stood and took Yordan's hand, leading him towards his humble home. Once inside, she pushed him against the closed door, her lips finding his neck, nipping and sucking at the sensitive skin. Yordan groaned, his hands gripping her waist as he ground his hips against hers.

They stumbled towards the bed, shedding clothes as they went. Yordan laid Katherine down on the soft furs, taking a moment to admire her beauty in the warm glow of the hearth. Her skin was like cream, smooth and inviting. He trailed his fingers down her body, marveling at the way she arched into his touch.

Yordan trailed his lips down Katherine's neck, savoring the taste of her soft skin. She arched beneath him, a breathy moan escaping her as his hands roamed her curves, mapping every dip and swell. He took his time, worshipping her body with reverent touches and heated kisses.

Katherine's fingers tangled in his hair, tugging gently as she guided him lower. Yordan obliged, his mouth blazing a path down her chest, pausing to lavish attention on her breasts. He swirled his tongue around a pert nipple, delighting in the way she gasped and writhed under him.

"Yordan, please," Katherine panted, her hips rocking against his hips in a silent plea.

He smirked against her skin, continuing his leisurely exploration despite her urgency. His hand dipped between her thighs, finding her slick and ready. Katherine cried out as he stroked her, his fingers gliding through her wet heat with practiced ease.

Yordan knew her body as well as his own, attuned to every shiver and sigh. He circled her sensitive bud with his thumb, applying just the right pressure to make her back bow off the bed. Katherine clutched at his shoulders, her nails digging deliciously into his skin as she chased her pleasure.

Unable to hold back any longer, Yordan settled between her thighs, the hard length of him pressing insistently against her core Yordan paused, his body hovering over Katherine's, their heated skin barely touching. He gazed down at her, drinking in the sight of her flushed cheeks, kiss-swollen lips, and emerald eyes dark with desire. A sense of awe washed over him, marveling at the depth of love and passion he felt for this incredible woman.

Katherine smiled at him, her fingers tracing the contours of his face with a tender touch. "I love you," she whispered, the words a sacred vow in the intimate space between them.

"I love you too," Yordan breathed, capturing her lips in a searing kiss. As their tongues danced, he slowly pushed into her welcoming heat, their bodies joining as one.

Katherine moaned into his mouth, her legs wrapping around his waist to pull him deeper. Yordan began to move, his thrust was slow and deliberate, savoring the exquisite feeling of her velvet walls gripping him tight.

He broke the kiss to trail his lips along her jaw and down the column of her throat, his tongue flicking out to taste the salt of her skin. Katherine tilted her head back, giving him better access as her fingers raked through his hair.

"Yordan," she gasped, her back arching as he hit a particularly sensitive spot. "Don't stop..."

Yordan increased the speed of his thrusts, driving into Katherine with building urgency. Her moans grew louder, echoing off the cottage walls as she met him stroke for stroke, her hips rolling in perfect sync with his.

"Yes, Yordan, right there," she panted, her nails digging into the firm muscles of his back. The slight sting only spurred him on, his rhythm growing more intense, more primal.

Sweat glistened on their entwined bodies, the flickering firelight casting sensual shadows across their passion-flushed skin. The air was thick with the heady scent of their arousal, an intoxicating perfume that filled Yordan's senses and fueled his desire.

He could feel the pressure building to an almost unbearable peak. Katherine was close too, her inner walls fluttering around him, gripping him like a velvet vice. Yordan slipped a hand between their straining bodies, his fingers finding her sensitive pearl and rubbing in firm circles.

"Oh, don't fucking stop Yordan!" Katherine cried out, her back bowing off the bed as her climax crashed over her. Her release triggered his own, and with a low groan, Yordan pulled out just in time, his seed spurting hot and thick across Katherine's heaving breasts.

Yordan watched, transfixed, as his seed painted Katherine's soft mounds, a primal sense of satisfaction surging through him at the erotic sight. She looked up at him through heavy-lidded eyes, a sated smile playing on her lips as she slowly trailed a finger through the pearly essence, bringing it to her mouth for a taste.

"Mmm," she purred, her pink tongue darting out to lick her finger clean. "You always make me feel so good, Yordan."

He grinned, leaning down to capture her lips in a deep, languid kiss, tasting himself on her tongue. As the kiss gradually softened, he rolled to the side, pulling Katherine into his strong arms. She nuzzled into his chest, her fingers idly tracing the defined lines of his muscles.

They lay like that for a while, basking in the afterglow of their lovemaking, their bodies intertwined and their heartbeats slowly returning to normal. The warm glow of the hearth bathed their skin in a soft, intimate light, casting sensual shadows that danced across the cottage walls.

Eventually, Katherine stirred, pressing a tender kiss to Yordan's chest before sitting up. "I should probably clean up and head home," she said, a note of reluctance in her voice. "As much as I'd love to stay here in your arms all night."

Yordan propped himself up on an elbow, watching appreciatively as Katherine slid gracefully out of bed, the flickering firelight dancing across her bare skin as she padded over to the washbasin. Yordan watched, transfixed, as she dipped a soft cloth into the water and began to clean his seed from her breasts with gentle, circular motions.

The intimacy of the moment struck him - the easy familiarity and comfort they shared with each other's bodies born from countless passionate nights spent exploring and pleasuring one another. Katherine glanced over, catching him staring at her with undisguised desire and adoration. A coy smile played at her kiss-swollen lips.

Yordan grinned wolfishly. "Always. You're a vision, Katherine. Sometimes I can scarcely believe you're real."

She laughed, the melodic sound sending pleasant shivers down his spine. Finishing her ablutions, Katherine sauntered back to the bed, crawling up Yordan's body to straddle his lap. The tantalizing press of her soft curves against him reignited the embers of desire low in his belly.

Katherine leaned down, her chestnut locks forming a curtain around their faces as she captured Yordan's lips in a deep, sensual kiss. He groaned into her mouth, his large hands roaming the silky expanse of her back to grip the supple globes of her rear. As their passionate kiss gradually softened, Katherine pulled back, gazing down at Yordan with a tender smile. Her fingers traced the chiseled lines of his face, committing every beloved detail to memory. With a sigh of reluctance, she slid off his lap and padded over to where her dress lay in a forgotten heap on the floor.

Yordan propped himself up on his elbows, watching with undisguised appreciation as Katherine stepped into the soft fabric, the firelight casting a warm glow on her creamy skin. She pulled the dress up over her curves, the material whispering against her body like a lover's caress. Turning her back to him, she gathered her long chestnut tresses and swept them over one shoulder, exposing the elegant line of her neck.

"Help me with the laces?" she asked, glancing coyly over her shoulder at Yordan.

He rose from the bed, the furs falling away to reveal his muscular form. Crossing the room in a few strides, he stood behind Katherine, his rough hands gentle as they grasped the delicate laces of her bodice. Yordan took his time, savoring the intimacy of dressing his lover, his fingers brushing against the smooth skin of her back with each crisscross of the laces.

Katherine leaned back into his touch, a contented hum escaping her lips. She closed her eyes briefly, as if offering silent gratitude to Toteko who watched over them, for granting her this fleeting serenity. As Yordan finished tying the laces, he wrapped his arms around Katherine's waist, pulling her back against his chest. He nuzzled into the crook of her neck, inhaling the intoxicating scent of her skin - jasmine and honey, with a hint of their shared passion.

"Stay with me tonight," he murmured, his lips brushing the shell of her ear. "I sleep so much better with you in my arms."

Katherine sighed, melting into his embrace. "You know I want to, Yordan. But people will talk if I'm seen leaving your cottage in the morning. Aralonis may be a progressive city, but certain proprieties are still expected of unmarried women."

Yordan turned Katherine in his arms so he could gaze into her striking green eyes. "Then let's get married. Make this our home together."

His voice was low and earnest, his hazel eyes shimmering with hopeful intensity in the warm light of the hearth.

Katherine's breath caught in her throat. She reached up to cup Yordan's face, her thumb tenderly caressing his cheekbone. "Oh Yordan, I am truly flattered. You know how much I care for you. But I'm just not ready to settle down and become a wife. There's still so much I want to learn and experience."

Yordan tried to mask the flicker of disappointment in his eyes, but Katherine knew him too well. He managed a small, understanding smile, pressing a kiss to her palm. "I know, my love. And I would never want to hold you back from pursuing your dreams. I just can't help but imagine a future with you by my side, partners in every sense of the word."

Katherine's eyes softened, a wistful smile playing on her lips. "It's a beautiful dream, Yordan. And perhaps one day, when we're both ready, we can make it a reality. But for now, let's cherish what we have - this deep connection, this incredible passion that we share."

She leaned in, capturing his lips in a tender kiss that gradually deepened, their tongues dancing in a sensual caress. Yordan's hands roamed her back, pulling her flush against him, the evidence of his renewed arousal pressing insistently against her belly.

Breaking the kiss, Katherine grinned up at him, her eyes sparkling with mischief. "I thought you wanted me to stay so we could sleep?"

Yordan chuckled, nipping playfully at her lower lip. "Sleep is overrated. I can think of much more pleasurable ways to spend our time together."

As he began to walk her backwards towards the bed, Katherine placed a hand on his chest, halting his progress. "As tempting as that sounds, my love, I really should be going. We both have early mornings ahead of us."

Yordan sighed, resting his forehead against hers. "I know, you're right," Yordan conceded reluctantly. "As always." He pressed a lingering kiss to Katherine's forehead before stepping back, allowing her space to finish dressing.

As she smoothed her dress and gathered her shawl, Katherine glanced up at Yordan, a thoughtful expression on her face. "You know, Yordan, I've been with my fair share of men over the years. Dalliances and flirtations, passionate affairs and comfortable companions. Each one taught me something about myself, about what I want and need in a partner."

Yordan leaned against the sturdy wooden bedpost, his eyes never leaving Katherine's. "I understand that well. I've had my own experiences, ever since I was a gangly youth fumbling in the hayloft with the farmer's daughter." A wry smile tugged at his lips at the memory. "Those early explorations, the rush of desire and the thrill of learning someone's body...they were formative, in their own way."

Katherine nodded, a knowing glint in her eye. "Ah yes, the fumbling of youth. I remember my own early trysts - stolen kisses in the orchards, clumsy but enthusiastic explorations in the cool shade of the forest. Each encounter, a new discovery about the delights of the flesh."

Katherine's fingers continued their sensual path along Yordan's chest as she gazed up at him with an intensity that made his breath catch. "In all my experiences, Yordan, I've never felt a connection as deep and profound as the one I share with you. It's not just the incredible passion between us, though the gods know that's unlike anything I've ever known."

A sultry smile played on her lips as memories of their countless heated encounters danced in her eyes. "It's the way you see me, truly see me, like no one else ever has. The way we can bare our souls to each other, sharing our hopes and fears and dreams without judgement or reservation."

Yordan's heart swelled with emotion at her words, the sincerity in her voice wrapping around him like a warm embrace. He thought back on his own romantic history - the awkward but eager explorations with the miller's daughter in his youth, the intense but fleeting affairs with travelers passing through the village, the comfortable dalliances with women he considered friends but not great loves.

Each experience had taught him something about himself, his desires, what he needed in a partner. But it wasn't until Katherine that everything crystallized into perfect clarity. She challenged him, inspired him, understood him in a way that made him feel both thrilled and utterly at peace.

"I feel the same way, Katherine," he said softly, his rough hands gentle as they cradled her face. "I've cared for others, desired others, but I've never loved anyone the way I love you. It's as if all those other experiences were preparing me, leading me to you. To this profound connection we share on every level - mind, body and soul."

Katherine leaned into his touch, turning her head to press a tender kiss to his calloused palm. "I don't know what the future holds, Yordan. The world is vast and ever-changing, and my own path is still unfolding before me. But I do know that whatever adventures lie ahead, whatever twists and turns our journeys take, you will always hold a special place in my heart. A piece of me will forever be yours."

Yordan swallowed past the lump of emotion in his throat, his eyes shining with adoration and gratitude. "And you in mine, my love. Always and forever." He drew her into his arms, holding her close as he breathed in her familiar scent, committing this perfect moment to memory.

They stayed like that for a long while, simply savoring the comfort and rightness of being in each other's embrace. The fire crackled softly in the hearth, the dancing flames casting a warm, intimate glow over their entwined forms.

Eventually, Katherine pulled back just enough to gaze at Yordan, a soft smile on her kiss-swollen lips. "As much as I wish I could stay in your arms all night, I really should be going. The hour grows late, and we both need our rest."

Yordan sighed, knowing she was right but loathe to let her go. "I know, my love. As much as I wish we could shut out the world and lose ourselves in each other, duty calls." He pressed a lingering kiss to her forehead before reluctantly releasing her from his embrace.

Katherine gathered her shawl, draping it around her shoulders as she made her way to the door. Yordan followed, his hand resting lightly on the small of her back, savoring these last moments of closeness before they parted.

At the threshold, Katherine turned to face him, her hand coming up to cup his cheek. "Until next time, my heart," she whispered, rising on her toes to brush a soft, sweet kiss against his lips.

"Until next time," Yordan echoed, his voice rough with emotion. He watched as she disappeared into the night, her form slowly swallowed by the shadows until even her silhouette had faded from view.

With a heavy sigh, Yordan closed the door, the cottage suddenly feeling emptier without Katherine's vibrant presence. He made his way to the bed, his body sinking into the furs that still held a trace of her scent.

As Yordan drifted off to sleep, his thoughts were a jumble of the day's events - the hours spent at the forge, the laughter shared with Sam and Katherine, the profound intimacy and connection he had experienced with his beloved.

Somewhere in the hazy realm between wakefulness and slumber, tendrils of dreams began to weave through Yordan's mind, ethereal and elusive. Images flickered behind his closed eyelids, sporadic flashes that seemed to dance just out of reach, taunting him with their obscurity.

In the shifting dreamscape, Yordan found himself standing at his forge, the familiar heat of the flames licking at his skin. His hands moved with a surety born of years of practice, gripping the hammer as he brought it down upon the glowing metal before him. Each strike sent a shower of sparks cascading through the air, their fiery trails painting ephemeral patterns in the darkness.

As he worked, the metal began to take shape beneath his skilled hands, elongating and twisting into a form that seemed both familiar and wholly unknown. It was a weapon, that much he could discern - a sword, perhaps, or a spear. But there was something different about this creation, an aura of power that thrummed through the metal, setting his nerves alight with a strange, exhilarating energy.

The scene shifted, blurring at the edges as the dreamscape morphed and changed. Yordan now stood in a vast, open field, the lush green grass rippling in a gentle breeze. As Yordan drifted deeper into the realm of dreams, the ethereal landscape shifted once more. He found himself standing at the edge of a shimmering lake, its placid surface reflecting the luminous, ever-changing sky above. The air hummed with a palpable energy, a sense of anticipation that set his heart racing and his skin tingling.

In the distance, a figure emerged from the misty veil that shrouded the far shore. It was a being of pure light, its form both indistinct and radiant, as if woven from the very fabric of the celestial heavens. As the figure drew closer, Yordan felt an overwhelming sense of awe and reverence wash over him, his knees threatening to buckle beneath the weight of the divine presence.

The angelic being hovered above the surface of the lake, its luminous wings unfurling like gossamer curtains caught in a gentle breeze. Yordan squinted against the brilliance, trying to make out the details of the figure's face, but it remained frustratingly obscured, a mystery just beyond his grasp.

In a voice that seemed to resonate from within Yordan's very soul, the angel spoke, its words a melodic whisper that filled the air with a haunting, unearthly beauty. "Yordan Arano a great destiny awaits you, a path that will lead you to the very heart of the divine mystery."

Yordan's breath caught in his mouth as he woke up a little disoriented. Looking around, getting familiar with his room and the sunlight began to peak through his window. As he rubbed his face, waking up, he opened his eyes and came across a stray lock from Katherine's hair, bringing a smile to his face.

Chapter Two

Yordan awoke as the first rays of dawn filtered through the small window of his humble quarters. He rose from his simple mattress, stretching his strong, lean frame. Today was an important day - the sword commissioned by his Aralonic master Ferran was finally complete, and Yordan needed to deliver it to the prince's palace.

He washed his face in the basin of cool water, letting the droplets trickle down his warm brown skin. After dressing in his simple tunic and breeches, Yordan made his way to the forge where he had labored for weeks on the exquisite blade.

The sword gleamed in the early morning light, its polished steel reflecting Yordan's reverent expression. The blade was a masterpiece of craftsmanship - perfectly balanced, razor sharp, with an elegant fuller running down its center. Intricate swirling patterns were etched into the steel, intertwining with ancient Aralonic runes that spoke of courage, justice, and the eternal wisdom of Toteko.

The hilt was wrapped in the finest leather, dyed a rich crimson and embossed with golden filigree. The pommel bore the sigil of Aralonis - a radiant sun cradling a crescent moon, symbolizing the union of divine illumination and earthly reflection. As Yordan hefted the sword, feeling its reassuring weight in his calloused palm, he couldn't help but marvel at the way it seemed to hum with an inner energy. Yordan carefully wrapped the exquisite sword in a soft woolen cloth, concealing its magnificence from prying eyes. He slung the precious bundle over his shoulder and stepped out into the bustling streets of Aralonis.

The city was just beginning to awaken, with shop owners setting out their wares and the smell of freshly baked bread wafting through the air. Yordan walked with purpose, his simple boots padding softly against the cobblestone streets. His unadorned linen tunic and breeches, the common attire of an Aralonic craftsman, allowed him to blend seamlessly into the growing crowds.

Skilled weavers hung intricately patterned tapestries, their vibrant colors telling stories of Aralonis' rich history. Potters arranged their wares - graceful vases, sturdy plates, and delicate cups - in neat rows, each piece a testament to their dedication to the craft. The metallic clang of blacksmiths at work mingled with the melodic calls of street vendors hawking their wares.

Yordan paused briefly at a stall selling fresh fruit, the sweet aroma of ripe melons and juicy berries tempting his senses. He exchanged a friendly nod with the vendor, a wizened old man with a twinkle in his eye, before continuing towards the palace.

As he crossed into the nobles' quarter, the streets grew wider and the buildings more ornate. Grand mansions lined the avenues, their facades adorned with intricate carvings and gleaming with polished marble. Well-dressed aristocrats strolled past, their finely tailored robes and glittering jewels a stark contrast to Yordan's simple attire. He paid little mind, focused solely on his mission to deliver the sword to the palace.

The closer Yordan got to the heart of the city, the more he could feel the energy of Aralonis thrumming through his veins. The towering spires of the Aralonic Sanctuary came into view, its white stone walls seeming to glow in the morning sun. Devoted Aralonites streamed in and out of the sacred building, their faces alight with reverence and purpose.

As he passed the Hall of Insight, Yordan couldn't help but overhear snippets of heated debates spilling out from its open windows. Scholars and philosophers engaged in lively discussions, their voices rising and falling as they grappled with questions of ethics, spirituality, and the nature of the divine.

Finally, the palace gates loomed before him, grand and imposing. The guards, resplendent in their purple and gold uniforms, eyed Yordan with a mix of curiosity and suspicion. He approached with confidence, his posture proud and his eyes clear.

Yordan stepped forward and addressed the guards with a respectful bow. "I am Yordan Arano, blacksmith and apprentice to the esteemed Ferran. I come bearing a sword commissioned by the prince himself."

The lead guard's demeanor shifted instantly, his eyes widening in recognition. "Ferran? We are well aware of your mentor's exceptional skill and his close relationship with the Prince. Please, follow me."

The guards stepped aside, allowing Yordan to pass through the grand palace gates. As he crossed the threshold, Yordan couldn't help but marvel at the opulence that surrounded him. The palace courtyard was a vision of grandeur, with meticulously manicured gardens, burbling fountains, and towering statues of Aralonis' revered leaders.

Servants scurried about, their crisp uniforms a stark contrast to Yordan's simple attire. He felt a twinge of self-consciousness, suddenly aware of his humble appearance amidst the splendor of the palace. Yet, as his hand brushed against the bundle containing the sword, Yordan felt a surge of pride. He had poured his heart and soul into crafting this masterpiece, and he knew that its quality would speak for itself.

Following the lead guard through the winding corridors of the palace, Yordan couldn't help but wonder if the Prince or his court knew that it was he, and not Ferran, who had crafted the sword. Would they recognize his skill and dedication? Or would they simply assume that the sword was the work of his esteemed mentor?

Yordan stepped into the grand throne room, his eyes immediately drawn upward to the magnificent chandeliers that hung from the soaring ceilings. The crystalline light danced and refracted, casting a dazzling array of colors across the polished marble floors. Each chandelier was a masterpiece, crafted from the finest gold and adorned with countless glittering gems. They seemed to float effortlessly in the air, as if suspended by some unseen magic.

As Yordan marveled at the opulent display, a lead servant approached him with a respectful bow. The servant was a tall, slender man with rich brown skin and a neatly trimmed beard. He wore a crisp white tunic, cinched at the waist with a golden sash that denoted his high rank within the palace hierarchy. His dark eyes sparkled with intelligence and a hint of curiosity as he regarded Yordan.

"Please, follow me," the servant said, his voice smooth and cultured. "The prince will see you in a private audience chamber."

Yordan nodded, his heart racing with anticipation as he followed the servant through a series of winding corridors. The walls were adorned with intricate tapestries depicting scenes from Aralonis' rich history - great battles, momentous discoveries, and the wisdom of the Aralonite sages. The air was heavy with the scent of incense, a subtle blend of spices and herbs that seemed to sharpen Yordan's senses and heighten his awareness.

Finally, they arrived at a small, unassuming door. The servant knocked twice, the sound echoing in the quiet hallway. "Please wait here," he instructed Yordan before slipping inside.

Yordan found himself alone in the corridor, his mind racing with thoughts of the impending meeting. He clutched the bundle containing the sword tightly to his chest, feeling the reassuring weight of the masterpiece, he had crafted. Would the Prince recognize the skill and dedication that had gone into its creation? Would he see beyond Yordan's humble status and appreciate the true value of the blade?

Lost in his thoughts, Yordan barely registered the sound of the door opening once more. He looked up, expecting to see the servant returning to usher him inside. Instead, he found himself face to face with Prince Joseph himself.

The prince cut an imposing figure, tall and regal with a slightly stooped posture that spoke of the weight of his many years. His white hair was neatly combed, framing a face lined with wisdom and experience. Piercing blue eyes seemed to bore into Yordan's very soul, assessing him with a keen intelligence that belied the prince's advanced age.

"You must be Yordan," Prince Joseph said, his piercing gaze sweeping over the young man. "Why didn't Ferran come himself?"

Yordan swallowed hard, his hands tightening around the bundle. "Your Highness, my mentor sends his deepest apologies. He has been rather busy as of late, and his age is slowly catching up with him. His movements are not as easy as they once were."

The prince nodded thoughtfully, a flicker of understanding in his eyes. "Ah, yes. Time spares none of us, not even the most skilled among us. But come, let us see this sword that has brought you to my palace."

With reverent hands, Yordan unwrapped the bundle, revealing the exquisite blade within. The sword seemed to catch the light, its polished steel gleaming like a mirror. The intricate swirling patterns and ancient Aralonic runes danced along the fuller, telling a story of courage and wisdom.

Prince Joseph's eyes widened as he took in the sight of the masterpiece. He reached out, his fingers hovering just above the blade, as if afraid to touch such perfection. "This is...extraordinary," he breathed, his voice filled with awe. "The craftsmanship, the attention to detail...I have never seen its equal."

Yordan's heart swelled with pride at the Prince's words of praise. With a respectful bow, he held out the sword, offering the hilt to the Prince. "With your permission, Your Highness, I would be honored to demonstrate."

Prince Joseph nodded, his eyes never leaving the gleaming sword. "Please, go ahead."

Yordan took a step back, giving himself room to maneuver. He held the sword aloft, the blade catching the light and casting a dazzling array of reflections across the chamber. With a fluid motion, he spun the sword in his hand, the blade singing through the air with a satisfying hum.

"As you can see, Your Highness, the sword is flawlessly balanced," Yordan explained, his voice filled with reverence for the craft. "The weight of the pommel counterbalances the blade perfectly, allowing for swift, precise strikes and effortless handling."

He continued to manipulate the sword, demonstrating a series of intricate flourishes and stances. The blade seemed to dance in his hands, an extension of his own body. Each movement was a testament to the countless hours he had spent honing his skills, perfecting his craft under Ferran's guidance.

"The fuller, as you may have noticed, is not merely decorative," Yordan continued, running a finger along the groove that ran down the center of the blade. "It serves to lighten the sword without compromising its strength, enhancing its overall balance and maneuverability."

Prince Joseph watched, enraptured, as Yordan showcased the sword's exceptional qualities. The young man's passion for his craft was evident in every word, every gesture.

"And the runes," Yordan said, his voice softening with reverence. "They are not merely symbols, but a testament to the values that define Aralonis - courage, justice, and the eternal wisdom of Toteko. Each one was painstakingly etched into the steel, a reminder of the principles that guide us."

The prince stepped closer, his eyes tracing the intricate patterns that adorned the blade. "Ferran has truly outdone himself," he murmured, his voice filled with admiration. "This sword is a work of art, a masterpiece of craftsmanship."

Yordan felt a twinge of pain at the prince's words. It was he, not Ferran, who had poured his heart and soul into the creation of this blade. But he knew that it was not his place to correct the prince's assumption.

"Your Highness, I shall pass on your compliments to my mentor," Yordan said, bowing his head. "He will be most pleased to hear of your satisfaction with the sword."

As Yordan and Prince Joseph admired the exquisite sword, a sudden commotion erupted just outside the chamber door. The sound of hurried footsteps and raised voices echoed through the thick wooden panels, growing louder with each passing moment.

Prince Joseph's brow furrowed; his attention torn away from the gleaming blade. Just then, the chamber door burst open, revealing a young man with sharp, aristocratic features and cold, piercing gray eyes. He was dressed in rich, dark-colored garments adorned with gold accents, his blond hair neatly styled in a manner that spoke of his noble status.

"Father!" the young man exclaimed; his voice filled with urgency. "I must speak with you at once. It's about the—" He stopped abruptly, his gaze falling upon Yordan and the sword in his hands.

Prince Joseph's expression hardened, his posture straightening as he turned to face the newcomer. "Lucien," he said, his tone a mix of exasperation and resignation. "I am in the middle of an important meeting. Can this not wait?"

Lucien's eyes narrowed, his lips twisting into a sneer as he regarded Yordan with barely concealed disdain. "And who is this...commoner?" he asked, his voice dripping with contempt. "Since when do you entertain the likes of him in your private chambers?"

Yordan felt his cheeks burn with a mix of embarrassment and anger. He knew his simple attire and humble bearing marked him as an outsider in this world of wealth and privilege, but to be dismissed so callously stung, nonetheless.

Prince Joseph sighed, his shoulders sagging slightly as he gestured towards Yordan. "This is Yordan Arano, apprentice to Ferran. He has come to deliver the sword that I commissioned."

Lucien's gaze flicked briefly to the sword, his expression one of bored indifference. "Ah, yes. The sword. How...quaint."

Yordan bit his tongue, fighting the urge to defend his work. He knew that engaging with Lucien would only cause more trouble for himself and his mentor. Instead, he bowed his head respectfully, his voice carefully neutral as he spoke. "Your Highness," he said, addressing Lucien with the proper title. "It is an honor to make your acquaintance. I apologize for any intrusion. I must take my leave."

Lucien waved his hand dismissively, clearly eager to be rid of Yordan's presence. "Yes, yes. Be on your way, then. My father and I have important matters to discuss."

Prince Joseph held up a hand, silencing his son's impatient words. "A moment, Lucien." He turned to Yordan, his expression softening. "Yordan, before you go, I want to express my deepest gratitude for your exceptional work. This sword is truly a masterpiece, a testament to Ferran's skill and dedication."

The prince nodded to his lead servant, who stepped forward with a small, ornate wooden chest. The servant opened the lid, revealing a glittering array of gold coins nestled within rich velvet folds. Yordan's eyes widened at the sight, his breath catching in his throat.

"Please, take this as a token of my appreciation," Prince Joseph said, gesturing to the chest. "I know that it is Ferran who will receive the payment for the commission, but I want you to have this, as a personal gift from me to you."

Yordan bowed deeply, his voice thick with emotion as he accepted the chest. "Your Highness, I am sure Ferran will be honored by your gift."

Prince Joseph smiled, a hint of warmth in his piercing blue eyes. "I have no doubt that you will, Yordan. May the Forge of Toteko temper your soul and give my regards to Ferran."

"And may it shape yours with wisdom and strength." Replied Yordan, bowing once more, clutching the chest to his chest as he backed out of the chamber. As the door closed behind him, he couldn't help but marvel at the turn of events. To have his work recognized and praised by the prince himself was a dream come true, a validation of all the long hours and hard work he had poured into his craft.

Lost in his thoughts, Yordan made his way through the winding corridors of the palace, retracing his steps to the grand entrance. As he stepped out into the bright sunlight, he was surprised to see a familiar figure waiting for him at the bottom of the palace steps.

"Sam!" Yordan exclaimed, a wide grin spreading across his face as he hurried to meet his friend. "What are you doing here?"

Sam stood tall and proud, though his eyes were clouded due to this blindness, there was no mistaking the warmth and intelligence in his expression. He leaned on a sturdy wooden staff, using it to navigate the bustling streets of Aralonis with uncanny precision.

"I had a feeling you might need a friendly face after your meeting with the prince," Sam said, his voice rich and melodious. "And from the look on your face, I'd say I was right."

Yordan laughed, "How can you tell what my face is expressing?" clapping his friend on the shoulder. "You know me too well, Sam. It was quite the experience, to say the least. The Prince himself praised my work! Can you believe it?"

Sam grinned, his sightless eyes crinkling at the corners. "Of course I can believe it. You're the most talented blacksmith in all of Aralonis, even if you're too humble to admit it. I've always said that one day, the nobles would recognize your skill."

Yordan felt a rush of affection for his friend. Sam had been by his side through thick and thin, offering unwavering support and encouragement even in the face of his own challenges. As they walked through the bustling streets, Yordan described the intricate details of the palace, painting a vivid picture for Sam's mind's eye.

"You should have seen the throne room, Sam," Yordan said, his voice filled with awe. "The chandeliers alone were a work of art, crafted from the finest gold and adorned with countless glittering gems. And the tapestries! They depicted the greatest moments in Aralonis' history, each one a masterpiece of color and detail."

Sam chuckled, his staff tapping a steady rhythm on the cobblestones. "It sounds like a sight to behold, my friend. Perhaps one day, I'll be able to see it for myself, in the Great Beyond."

Yordan's heart clenched at the thought. He knew that Sam's faith differed from his own, but he respected his friend's beliefs, nonetheless. As they walked, he found himself reaching into the pouch at his waist, his fingers brushing against the cool metal of the coins the prince had gifted him.

"Sam," Yordan said, his voice hesitant. "The prince gave Ferran a personal gift, a chest of gold coins. I was thinking...I'd like to donate some of it to the Luminar Citadel. I know you don't share my beliefs, but I want to honor Toteko and give thanks for the blessings he has bestowed upon us."

Sam paused, his expression thoughtful. "Yordan, you know I respect your faith, even if I don't share it. If donating to the Citadel brings you peace and fulfillment, then I support you wholeheartedly. Your beliefs are a part of who you are, and I would never ask you to compromise them."

Yordan felt a surge of gratitude for his friend's understanding. "Thank you, Sam. That means more to me than you know. And I want you to know that I respect your path as well. The way of the Ant, seeking truth through reason and empirical evidence...it takes a special kind of courage and dedication."

Sam laughed, the sound warm and infectious. "Ah, but the Ant's way is not for everyone, my friend. It can be a lonely path at times, always questioning, always wondering if you made the right choice."

As they walked, Yordan and Sam fell into a comfortable silence, each lost in their own thoughts. The bustling streets of Aralonis seemed to fade away, replaced by the quiet companionship of two friends who understood each other on a deep, fundamental level.

Finally, they reached the steps of the Luminar Citadel, its white stone walls gleaming in the afternoon sun. Yordan paused, his hand resting on the ornate bronze door handle. He turned to Sam, a question in his eyes.

"Will you come in with me?" he asked, his voice soft. "I know it's not your way, but I would be honored to have you by my side as I make my offering."

Sam smiled, his sightless eyes somehow seeming to meet Yordan's gaze. "Of course, my friend."

Together, they entered the Citadel, the cool air and hushed reverence of the sacred space enveloping them like a gentle embrace. Yordan approached the altar, his steps measured and purposeful. He reached into his pouch, withdrawing a handful of glittering gold coins.

As he placed the coins on the altar, Yordan bowed his head, his lips moving in a silent prayer of gratitude. He felt a sense of peace wash over him, a deep certainty that he was exactly where he was meant to be.

When he finished his prayer, Yordan turned to find Sam waiting patiently, a serene expression on his face. They exited the Citadel, blinking in the bright sunlight.

As they made their way back into the heart of the city, Yordan couldn't help but reflect on the extraordinary events of the day. From the Prince's praise to the quiet moment of reverence in the Citadel, he felt a sense of profound gratitude for the twists and turns of fate that had brought him to this moment.

Lost in thought, Yordan almost didn't notice the commotion up ahead. A crowd had gathered in the market square, their voices raised in a mix of excitement and consternation. Yordan and Sam exchanged a curious glance before quickening their pace to investigate.

As they drew closer, Yordan could make out the figure at the center of the crowd - a tall, imposing man with rich brown skin and a neatly trimmed beard. He wore the flowing white robes of a Zetian mystic, and there was an aura of otherworldly calm about him.

"People of Aralonis," the Zetian mystic began, his voice a melodic blend of authority and gentleness, resonating through the square like the whisper of the River Lumina itself. "In the pursuit of truth, we often tread paths obscured by doubt and shadow. Yet it is through these very shadows that we can discover the light that resides within us all."

Yordan felt a magnetic pull toward the mystic's words, as though they were strings binding him to an unseen truth. He noticed others in the crowd shared his rapt attention, their eyes reflecting the same mix of curiosity and yearning. Sam, sensing Yordan's captivation, followed closely as his friend moved closer to the speaker.

"Zetianism teaches us that divine wisdom is not confined to sacred texts or ancient rituals," continued the mystic, his gaze sweeping across those gathered around him. "It flows within each of us, waiting patiently to be awakened through introspection and meditation. We must learn to listen—not just with our ears, but with our hearts and souls."

The air seemed to thrum with an energy that was both unsettling and beautiful, as if the very fabric of reality was being woven anew before them. Yordan could feel the stirrings of something profound—a realization that went beyond mere understanding, touching upon a deeper connection with all things.

"In this moment," the mystic said softly, "we stand on the precipice of awakening. Let go of fear and allow yourselves to be guided by love and truth."

Yordan's heart swelled with emotion as he absorbed these words, feeling their power echoing within him like ripples on a pond. He glanced at Sam, whose face bore an expression of thoughtful contemplation.

But their shared moment was abruptly shattered by the distant clatter of armored boots and shouted orders echoing down the narrow street leading to the square. The crowd turned collectively at the sound—a wave of unease crashing over them.

"Soldiers," someone muttered under their breath, anxiety creeping into their voice.

Yordan felt a chill run down his spine as he looked toward Sam. They slipped away from the edge of the crowd, their footsteps quickening as they sought refuge in one of Aralonis' many winding alleyways.

From the shadows of the alleyway, Yordan watched with bated breath as Lucien emerged at the head of a phalanx of soldiers. His presence was an undeniable storm, a tempest of authoritative arrogance that swept through the square, leaving fear and confusion in its wake. The air itself seemed to shiver with tension as the soldiers encircled the Zetian mystic, their armor clinking ominously like an orchestra of malintent.

Lucien's expression was one of cold disdain; his piercing gray eyes seemed almost lifeless, devoid of any compassion or empathy. A command slipped from his lips, sharp and unyielding like a blade unsheathed. The soldiers moved in unison, a practiced brutality in their movements as they seized the mystic.

The crowd recoiled collectively as the mystic was dragged forward, his graceful composure marred by rough hands and hostile intent. There was a clarity to his serene face that spoke volumes, even as he was handled with such callousness. His eyes remained focused, not

30

on Lucien or the soldiers, but on something beyond their grasp—an inner sanctuary untouchable by physical force.

Yordan winced at the sound that followed—a sickening crunch that reverberated through the square like thunder. For a moment, it felt as though time itself had fractured around them, each heartbeat elongating into an eternity of disbelief and horror.

Sam turned away sharply, his sightless eyes casting downwards as if to shield themselves from witnessing what his other senses perceived so acutely. Yordan could feel Sam's silent grief beside him.

In that moment, Yordan found himself grappling with a turmoil that churned within him like a tempestuous sea. Why would Lucien act with such harshness? What purpose did this savagery serve? Was it meant to instill fear? To silence dissent? Or perhaps it was something more personal, a twisted need for validation that cloaked itself in authority.

Around them, the crowd had fallen into a hushed awe tinged with terror clearing away. Yordan clenched his fists tightly by his sides—not out of anger, but determination. The mystic's words still lingered within him, stronger than ever: love and truth over fear.

"People of Aralonis!" Lucien's words echoed with theatrical flair, each syllable delivered with an exaggerated grandeur. "This city is hallowed ground, dedicated to the teachings and revelations as bestowed upon us through the Aralonite Sanctuary and the Hall of Insight! We must not entertain false prophets whose messages originate from beyond these sacred walls, whose words are nothing but whispers in the wind or dreams brought on by fever."

Yordan exchanged a glance with Sam, whose expression remained calm yet resolute. They could feel an undercurrent forming in the crowd, a collective spirit that would not be easily snuffed out despite Lucien's attempts to enshroud it in darkness.

Lucien continued his tirade, Yordan turned to Sam. "We should go," he murmured softly. "There's nothing more to be gained here except more noise."

Sam nodded in agreement, his hand reaching out to find Yordan's shoulder—a gesture of solidarity as much as guidance. Together they began to weave their way through the throng of people, slipping past those who lingered in stunned silence or murmured amongst themselves.

The air outside the gathering felt alive, electric, as if charged by the very words that had passed between Lucien and the hopeful masses. Yordan and Sam walked side by side along the cobbled streets, their minds turning over the event like a stone made smooth by the River Lumina itself.

"Have you ever heard of messages coming from beyond?" Yordan broke the silence a question that had gnawed at him since Lucien's address. The idea of whispers carried on winds, dreams manifesting in feverish minds, was as foreign to him as it was intriguing.

Sam paused for a moment, his sightless eyes turned toward the sky as if searching for answers among the stars. "None that I can remember in my lifetime," he replied thoughtfully. "But then again, I rarely meet anyone who isn't Lumite, Aralonite, or an Ant. We tend to live within our own beliefs, unchallenged by external ideas."

His words settled between them like a gentle weight. It was true; their world was often defined by rigid lines drawn by faith and tradition. Yet here was a whisper of something different. Yordan kicked a loose pebble, watching as it skittered ahead down the path. "It makes me wonder," he said quietly. "Is this something new? Or something that's always been there, just waiting for us to pay attention?"

Sam smiled faintly, sensing the shift in Yordan's thoughts, the yearning for answers that lay somewhere beyond their current knowing. "Perhaps it's both," he said after a moment. "New to us because we're finally ready to listen."

"Whatever happens," Sam said firmly, placing his trust in Yordan's heart as well as his own understanding of truth-seeking, "we'll face it together."

Chapter Three

Yordan lay motionless, the quietude of night wrapping around him like a shroud. The flickering shadows cast by the moonlight danced across the walls of his modest chamber, weaving patterns that mirrored the turmoil within his soul. His room was a sanctuary of simplicity, adorned with little more than a single wooden shelf lined with scrolls detailing the teachings of Aralon and a small altar dedicated to Toteko, where an incense stick burned slowly, its smoke curling upwards like a prayer.

His eyes, wide open and unblinking, traced the ethereal path of the smoke. A gentle breeze from the open window rustled through his curly hair and sent a whispering sigh through the fabric of his sleeping robe, pulling him back to that fateful day when Lucien's cruelty had unfolded before him—a scene etched into his memory with painful clarity.

Two months had passed since that encounter, yet its echoes haunted Yordan's thoughts like ghostly murmurs in a cavern. He could still hear Lucien's derisive laughter mingling with the mystic's silent dignity and see his features framed by moonlight as he departed from their midst—unbowed but marked by sorrow.

The weight of it all settled heavily on Yordan's chest as he lay there, gazing into the abyss of his own uncertainty. He felt adrift upon the tides of his own convictions and doubts, drifting away from shore without sight of land. His mind churned with questions: How could one reconcile such brutal discord with beliefs rooted in compassion? And what role did he hold in this tangled web where righteousness often clashed against reality?

Outside, crickets sang their nocturnal hymns, interspersed with distant sounds carried on the cool night air a reminder that life continued onward despite inner tumult. Yordan knew he must find his way beyond this impasse if he were to honor both himself and those ideals he cherished.

Finally opening weary eyes once more to embrace moonlit serenity rather than shunning its illumination revealed no simple answers in its glow. Instead it filled Yordan instead with resolve borne from introspection rather than certainty itself; he resolved not only to seek understanding but also to forge pathways among discord.

As dawn broke over the valley where Aralonis lay cradled by the undulating hills, Yordan rose from his bed. The first light of morning painted the sky in hues of gentle pinks and golds, casting a warm glow upon the sleepy town. The air was sweet with the scent of dew-kissed earth and the promise of a new day.

Yordan stretched his limbs, feeling the ache of restlessness soften in the face of such beauty. His gaze swept across the room, lingering momentarily on a delicate scroll—an Aralonic verse he kept close to heart—before he turned to prepare for his morning ritual of reflection and meditation.

With renewed determination, Yordan stepped into the cool morning air. The path to Sam's bakery was lined with ivy-covered walls and fragrant blossoms that greeted him as old friends. This familiarity grounded him as he trod onward, each step bringing him closer to companionship and clarity.

The rich aroma of freshly baked bread welcomed him as he approached Sam's bakery, its wooden sign swaying gently in the breeze. Inside, a warm light flickered; it was a haven from the encroaching day's worries. Sam was there, bustling about with remarkable ease despite his blindness—a testament to years of skill honed through perseverance.

"Morning, Yordan," Sam greeted without turning, his hands moving through the dough with practiced ease. Yordan watched the effortless motions, the way Sam shaped and pressed as if the dough were an extension of him, molded by feel rather than sight. "I thought I heard your thoughtful steps approaching." "I thought I heard your thoughtful steps approaching."

"And here I hoped to surprise you!" Yordan replied with a chuckle, stepping into the cozy space where doughy warmth mingled with laughter.

Sam paused for a moment, listening intently as if hearing more than just Yordan's words. "Surprises come when you least expect them," he said sagely before gesturing toward a roasting pan. "I've got some special chicken cooking today. Or rather... burning."

Yordan feigned horror, eyebrows raised in mock disbelief. "Surely not again! How will Aralonis survive another atrocity?"

Sam laughed heartily, shaking his head as he continued kneading. "You jest now, but wait until you taste it," he retorted playfully. "Blindness teaches patience and precision—skills far more useful than sight sometimes."

There was truth in those words; Yordan marveled at Sam's ability to craft such wondrous meals through touch and intuition alone—a triumph against any presumed limitations.

"It's settled then," Yordan declared with feigned solemnity. "I shall save you from burning our breakfast."

"And I shall save you from your brooding thoughts," Sam countered lightly, fetching two steaming mugs from atop a shelf.

Together they shared warmth and camaraderie within those walls—their bond fortified by trust and seasoned with mirth—as outside the sun crept higher still over Aralonis' skyline promising hope anew amidst life's unending tapestry of challenges woven with tender ambition.

As they sat down to their modest breakfast, the aroma of spices and warm bread enveloping them, Sam's expression turned thoughtful. He took a slow sip from his mug, his unseeing eyes fixed somewhere beyond the room's confines, as if probing the unseen layers of Yordan's heart. The laughter subsided, replaced by a gentle seriousness.

"Yordan," Sam began, his voice steady and soothing like the gentle flow of the River Lumina at dusk. "We've spoken about many things over these years, but there's one matter I've watched you wrestle with silently."

Yordan met his gaze, though he knew Sam couldn't see him. He felt as if Sam could perceive more than anyone else ever could—beyond the simple veils that sight provided.

"It's Katherine," Sam continued, "You've never hidden your love for her. But I sense a shadow lingering whenever her name graces our conversations."

Yordan sighed deeply, setting his mug aside as he leaned back in his chair. "It's not my feelings for her that trouble me," he admitted. "It's... everything else."

37

Sam nodded knowingly. "Her father?"

"Yes," Yordan replied slowly. "There's no denying that Katherine and I share something profound. Yet she has made it clear she is not ready to marry—or perhaps she's not ready to face what marriage to someone like me would entail."

"And by 'someone like you,' you mean an orphan," Sam concluded softly.

Yordan felt a familiar pang at the word—a reminder of a past he could never change. "If I were to ask for her hand, I'm almost certain he'd refuse us the chance even to be together."

"The Aralites hold such traditions close," Sam said contemplatively. "But Katherine's heart belongs to you as much as yours does to her."

"That may be true," Yordan replied with a tinge of frustration, "Yet my status remains a barrier I cannot easily dismantle."

Silence enveloped the room then, broken only by the distant calls of merchants on the streets and children playing somewhere beyond Aralonis' bustling avenues.

Sam reached across the table, placing a reassuring hand on Yordan's arm. "You needn't face this alone," he said resolutely. "Have you told Katherine your fears?"

"I have," Yordan confessed, looking into his friend's earnest face. "She insists that time will change things—that patience is our ally—but I'm unsure how long I can endure being apart while carrying these uncertainties."

Sam pondered this quietly before speaking again. "Sometimes we must walk uncertain paths to find clarity," he mused gently. "The river does not always reveal its destination until we are nearly upon it."

"But what if the journey demands more than we're willing—or able—to sacrifice?" Yordan asked, his voice slightly trembling with unspoken fears.

"Then we must trust in what binds us together," Sam replied resolutely. "Faith in one another is sometimes all we truly have."

They sat in companionable stillness then—two souls adrift upon life's currents—joined not just by friendship but by shared moments that spoke of courage and perseverance against unseen tides.

Finally, Sam broke the silence with a gentle laugh. "You know," he began, his voice carrying the wisdom of years untethered by vision, "when I joined the Ants, one of the first things I learned was that they care not for titles or lineage. We are all just people—orphans or kings alike."

Yordan nodded, a smile tugging at the corners of his lips. "I remember," he said, his voice softening as memories of their youth came rushing back. "It was why we became friends." His mind wandered back to those early days when they met in the sun-dappled fields outside Aralonis. Young and eager, their hearts unfettered by societal constraints, it was Sam's acceptance and uncomplicated understanding that drew Yordan like a moth to flame.

"Yes," Sam said, shifting slightly in his seat as if sensing Yordan's reminiscence. "We found common ground despite our differences—a simple truth that transcends status."

A gust of wind whispered through the open window, rustling the curtains like the river's eternal song. Yet even this serenity seemed disturbed by an undercurrent of unease—a reminder of pressing matters that awaited beyond companionship's embrace.

"I've been hearing whispers about this Lumite, King Benjamin," Sam continued thoughtfully. "And not just from travelers passing through. Some Aralonites in the city have been talking—loudly—about how we aren't doing enough to support his vision."

Yordan leaned forward, intrigued yet uneasy. He had heard similar murmurs, but dismissed them as the usual grumbling of those unhappy with change. The thought that Benjamin's influence had spread beyond politics and doctrine, taking root among their own people, left a bitter taste in his mouth.

"What exactly are they saying?" Yordan asked, his voice low but firm.

Sam exhaled, his fingers absently tapping against his knee. "It's more than just loyalty to Benjamin—they're openly blaming Zetians for Aralonis' struggles. Calling them parasites, saying they drain resources while giving nothing back. They act like it's some great betrayal that the Aralonites don't stand with Benjamin against Zetopolis."

Yordan's jaw tightened. "That's dangerous talk."

"It's more than talk," Sam warned. "It's spreading. If someone with enough power fans these flames, we won't just be dealing with tensions—we'll be looking at open conflict."

Yordan ran a hand through his hair, his mind racing. He had felt unrest within their ranks, but he hadn't realized how deep the resentment ran.

"Perhaps it's time we stopped ignoring these whispers," Sam said, his blind eyes fixed on Yordan, seeing more clearly than most ever could. "Perhaps it's time we looked deeper—together."

Yordan nodded, the gravity of Sam's words settling over him like a cloak. As much as he cherished their moments of camaraderie, the world outside demanded attention and action. Rising from his seat, he cast a glance at the anvil near the forge, its shadow stretching across the ground like a silent sentinel.

"Perhaps tomorrow we can discuss it further," Yordan suggested with a reluctant sigh, feeling the weight of responsibility pull him back to his duties. With a knowing smile, Sam nodded, understanding the constraints that time and obligation placed upon them both.

The forge welcomed Yordan with its familiar symphony: the clink of tools against metal, the low hum of the furnace. Ferran was already there, sleeves rolled up past sinewy elbows as he shaped a glowing piece of iron with practiced precision. Sparks danced in the air around him like fiery fireflies.

"Yordan! Just in time," Ferran grunted without looking up from his work. His voice carried both welcome and urgency—a mixture of fellowship and demand that Yordan knew all too well.

He approached the anvil where Ferran was laboring over a set of swords commissioned for Prince Joseph's men. Each blade needed to be perfect, reflecting not just their craftsmanship but also the strength and resolve of Aralonis itself.

As Yordan picked up a hammer and began working alongside Ferran, he sensed a momentary peace—an unspoken rhythm that bound them to their shared purpose. Yet beneath this harmony lingered an undercurrent of frustration. The pile of unfinished swords was growing taller by the day.

"We're falling behind on Prince Joseph's order," Ferran lamented, pausing to wipe sweat from his brow with the back of his hand. "We've still got spear points to forge after this lot."

Yordan's hands paused mid-swing as he let out a heavy breath. Creating weapons had never been his calling—he found comfort in tools meant for creation rather than destruction—but these were uncertain times, and duty demanded adaptability.

"We'll manage," Yordan replied resolutely, more to reassure himself than anything else. "The people need this."

Ferran's eyes met Yordan's; they spoke volumes even in silence—stories woven with years of brotherhood forged in fire and smoke. There was no denying that unrest brewed beyond their walls—the whisperings that Sam had echoed still resonated within

Yordan's thoughts—and every sword they crafted served as both protection and potential peril.

Together they hammered out more blades under flickering lantern light until fatigue gnawed at their muscles—a reminder that no matter how fierce their resolve or skilled their hands may be, they were still bound by human limits.

Yordan found himself gazing absently at the forge's embers, their glow reminiscent of tales his grandfather used to tell him. Stories of his father—a man of wisdom and peace, revered for his teachings of Aralism. The image was incomplete, painted in fragments and hues Yordan couldn't fully grasp, much like his father's face—a ghostly presence that resided in the recesses of his memory.

The rhythmic clangs of hammer against steel provided a soundtrack to Yordan's musings. What would his father think of this place? Of this world he had never lived to see? The answer was hidden behind the indomitable silence that surrounded the manner of his father's death—an enigma that stirred an ache Yordan couldn't quite shake.

His father had been a teacher who inspired others with the tenets of Aralonic philosophy—an advocate for enlightenment through understanding rather than arms. Would he feel betrayed by the son who now fashioned weapons? Or would he understand that even tools of destruction can be wielded with integrity?

The forge's heat wrapped around Yordan like a cloak, laced with sweat and determination. He imagined his father standing beside him, an unseen mentor imbued with endless patience, whispering guidance only the heart could hear. Perhaps crafting these weapons was not so different from shaping ideas; both required precision and a deep respect for their potential impact.

As Yordan reshaped metal into blades, he pondered how they might one day serve more than conflict—perhaps as instruments to cut through darkness and reveal hope beneath. He remembered Aralon's teachings: Every action threaded into the tapestry of life bore consequences, both seen and unseen.

Though he would never know the sound of his father's voice or feel the warmth of his embrace, Yordan realized that he carried pieces of him in every choice made under starlit skies. There was solace in knowing that love endured beyond absence—a legacy forged in acts of love rather than words alone.

The chill night air crept into the forge as Ferran and Yordan set aside their work for the evening. As they wiped soot from weary hands, Yordan glanced out toward the horizon where dawn's promise lay slumbering under crescents of moonlight.

The forge was quiet, save for the occasional hiss of cooling metal and the rhythmic pounding of a hammer. The fires within had dwindled to a soft glow, casting long shadows across the anvil and creating a dance of light on Ferran's determined features.

Yordan watched as Ferran struggled with the final forge of a spearhead. Despite the man's formidable strength and expertise, fatigue was evident in the way his shoulders slumped ever so slightly with each strike. Yordan's heart stirred with empathy, remembering his own weariness during relentless days at the anvil.

"Let me help with that," Yordan offered, stepping forward. The words were as much a gesture of gratitude as they were of camaraderie, for Ferran had been there when Yordan needed him most.

Ferran grunted with relief, handing over the hammer without breaking rhythm. "You've got a keen eye for this, Yordan. And steady hands," he acknowledged. The weight of those words lingered between them—a testament to countless hours spent together crafting tools not just for survival but for something more transcendent.

As Yordan took over, he let himself be guided by the rhythm of metal upon metal, allowing each strike to align with purpose. Sparks flew in vibrant arcs, painting fleeting constellations that shimmered in the air before vanishing into memory.

"You know," Yordan said amidst their labor, "I often think back to how you were one of the few faces that seemed...familiar at my grandfather's funeral." The admission carried him back to that day: a sea of solemn strangers and overwhelming grief.

Ferran nodded. "Your grandfather was a good man—a rare blend of sternness and warmth," he replied wistfully. "It felt right to be there."

"When I approached you after, asking if you might take me on as an apprentice," Yordan continued, pausing briefly to shape the glowing spearhead with precision, "I was lost in many ways. No family left, no place where I truly belonged."

Ferran's hands found stillness as he listened. A poignant silence enveloped them before he spoke again. "And yet here we are, shaping the world one piece at a time."

Yordan smiled softly at that, recognizing how far they'd come both as craftsmen and companions—two souls bound by forge heat and shared purpose.

The rhythmic clang of metal on metal punctuated the air, each strike echoing their shared journey. Yordan glanced at Ferran, pondering the question that had lingered in his mind ever since he'd delved into the weighty history of his lineage.

"Ferran," he began, a hint of vulnerability lacing his voice, "did you ever know anything about my father? My grandfather was always reluctant to discuss him, except to say he was a teacher."

Ferran set down his hammer, the glow of the forge casting shadows across his weathered face. "Your father, you say?" He scratched his chin thoughtfully. "I remember whispers, fragments of stories about him being a teacher, yes. But there was always an air of mystery surrounding him."

Yordan's heart quickened, caught between hope and apprehension. The truth felt like a fog-shrouded path leading somewhere unknown. "Mystery?"

Ferran nodded slowly, his gaze distant as though peering into memories long buried. "It never quite made sense to me how he passed. There were rumors... talk of suspicious circumstances that didn't sit right with many folks." His voice dropped lower, almost lost to the crackling fire.

"Suspicious how?" Yordan pressed gently, feeling an old ache reawaken within him—the void left by questions unanswered.

Ferran sighed, his eyes meeting Yordan's with a mixture of reluctance and resolution. "Some said it was an accident... others whispered darker tales. That perhaps he knew something—or someone—he shouldn't have."

A chill ran down Yordan's spine despite the forge's warmth. It felt as if the world had momentarily stilled around them.

"But why would anyone target a teacher?" Yordan questioned aloud, grappling with the implications.

Ferran's brow furrowed in contemplation. "Teachers sometimes carry knowledge that can change minds and hearts—powerful enough to threaten those who hold sway over others." His words bore the weight of experience and understanding.

The silence that followed was heavy yet filled with unspoken possibilities—a testament to their shared journey towards uncovering truths long obscured.

Yordan resumed work on the spearhead, each strike imbued with newfound determination. The river of molten metal mirrored his thoughts: fluid yet resolute in its purpose to transform.

"Thank you for telling me, Ferran," he said quietly but firmly—a promise conveyed through gratitude.

Ferran clasped Yordan's shoulder briefly, conveying strength beyond words—a silent vow to stand by him on this path of discovery.

As they shifted their focus back to the work at hand, a question hovered unbidden in Ferran's mind—one that had lingered for years, quietly persistent in its absence of answers. He hesitated for a moment, his hammer poised above the anvil, before finally voicing it.

"Yordan, is it true what they say about your mother...?" Ferran let the question hang in the air, heavy with history and emotion. "About her passing while you tried to reach Lumina City?"

Yordan's hands stilled over the glowing metal, his breath caught somewhere between memory and reality. The forge's familiar warmth seemed to recede, leaving a chill seeping into his bones despite the fire.

"It was during our journey," Yordan began softly, as if picking through shards of a dream once vivid but now blurred by time. "We were only a few days' travel from Lumina City when she fell ill."

The memories rose unbidden: his mother's pale face under the unforgiving sun, each step forward more arduous than the last. They had halted their journey beside the River Lumina—a place both feared and revered for its whispered secrets.

"I remember she said she heard voices by the river," Yordan continued, his voice thick with recollection. "Voices telling her we needed to stay until she healed."

He could still picture her seated by the riverbank, eyes closed as if listening to something neither of them could see. The water murmured endlessly against the stones, carrying with it promises of healing and insight—promises that, in the end, went unfulfilled.

"But..." Yordan's voice faltered briefly as he confronted the truth that had haunted him for so long. "But she never did get better."

He had watched helplessly as life ebbed from her with each passing day beside those cryptic waters. The River Lumina offered no answers that he could decipher—only loss etched into his soul like scars on iron.

Meeting Ferran's gaze, Yordan nodded solemnly. "Yes," he admitted softly yet firmly—a simple affirmation burdened with complexity. It was a truth he carried like an amulet: painful yet integral to who he had become.

Ferran held Yordan's gaze for a moment longer—his eyes filled not with pity but understanding—all too aware of how shared stories bound them together across time and space in ways words alone never could.

For a long moment, silence stretched between them, punctuated only by the rhythmic pounding of Ferran's hammer and the gentle whisper of the forge. Yordan felt a swell of gratitude for his mentor's silent companionship bond forged over countless hours of labor and quiet conversations like this one.

He drew in a deep breath, steeling himself for the memories that threatened to overwhelm him. "I was only nine," Yordan began, his voice steady despite the tumult within. "Nine and lost—hungry, scared, and alone."

His mind drifted back to that time: to nights spent beneath an indifferent sky, where stars offered no warmth or solace; to days filled with an aching emptiness he believed would never end. Each memory was vivid, sharp as steel yet tinged with a misty veil of sorrow.

"I remember it like it was just moments ago," he continued. "Her frail body beside me as I prayed for some miracle from the river that never came. I thought... I thought if I just listened hard enough, I'd hear what she wanted me to hear."

Yordan paused again, allowing his eyes to wander over the glowing coals before him—a reminder of life's relentless march forward, even amidst despair. He swallowed back the lump rising in his throat.

"Then... one day," he murmured, almost as if recounting a dream he feared would vanish upon waking, "a family happened upon us while returning to Aralonis. They saw us there by the water's edge—saw her—and they stopped."

His gaze flickered upward to meet Ferran's once more. "For me," Yordan continued softly, "it was salvation wearing human form—a hand extended in kindness when hope had all but slipped through my fingers."

The silence swelled again between them as Yordan remembered how those strangers had lifted him gently from that desolate place where love turned into loss—and how they'd laid his mother to rest beside the ever-murmuring river.

"They took me back here—to Aralonis," Yordan went on. "It was my grandfather who welcomed me in after they returned with news of... well, what had happened."

His voice caught on the last words—words that seemed too solid for such weightless memories—but he pushed past them because he must; because everything led up until now remained woven into his very being like strands carefully interlaced within fabric by unseen hands.

As the memories unraveled in Yordan's mind, a gentle breeze rustled the leaves of the towering akeska trees that lined the path back to his modest home. The River Lumina's whispers accompanied him, a flowing symphony of secrets and wisdom that only those attuned could discern. His feet moved with practiced familiarity along the worn trail, his thoughts lingering on the family who had once pulled him from despair.

The sun dipped below the horizon, painting the sky with hues of amber and violet, casting ethereal shadows over Aralonis. Lanterns began to flicker to life along the streets, their soft glow reminiscent of fireflies dancing in the twilight. Yordan breathed deeply, savoring the mingling scents of earth and evening blossoms—a reminder that even amidst turmoil, beauty persisted.

Upon reaching his home, a quaint structure nestled within the Artisan's District, he paused at the threshold. The door creaked open with an old familiarity that welcomed him into the dim warmth of his dwelling. His eyes traced over the humble furnishings—a wooden table bearing scars of time, shelves cradling tomes and scrolls amassed in his pursuit of wisdom, and a hearth where embers still smoldered from earlier.

But tonight, it was his solitary bed that drew him most. Its simple frame stood against one wall, draped with a quilt that bore intricate patterns of Aralonic symbols—a token from Katherine during a rare moment when their worlds seemed aligned. The fabric still carried a faint trace of her essence, an intoxicating blend of honeyed jasmine and sandalwood.

As Yordan lay down upon it, he couldn't help but imagine her there beside him. Her presence would be a balm against the loneliness that sometimes curled around him like an unwelcome shadow. He yearned for her laughter to fill this space, for her voice to weave tales that would lull them both into dreams without boundaries.

But reality held its own weight; Katherine's place in society—a daughter bound by her father's machinations—was a barrier as formidable as any fortress wall. Still, in these moments before sleep claimed him, Yordan allowed himself the indulgence of envisioning what could be if not for such constraints.

His thoughts shifted toward troubling matters as weariness began to pull at his consciousness. Prince Joseph's recent actions loomed like storm clouds on a distant horizon—disquieting reports of commissioned weapons echoing through corridors both whispered and spoken aloud. The prince's motivations remained shrouded in layers Yordan hadn't yet pierced; yet he sensed undercurrents beneath this apparent preparation for conflict.

Why did Aralonis—which strove for harmony within and without—now arm itself so? It was a question that gnawed at him persistently, intertwining with fears about what these choices hinted might come.

Even as slumber finally overtook him, Yordan's mind danced with visions both wondrous and worrisome—the shimmering threads of destiny looping onward through dreams spun upon possibilities unconfined by waking understanding.

Chapter Four

Y ordan found himself standing at the edge of a misty glade, the air thick with the earthy scent of moss and dew-kissed leaves. Towering trees stretched their branches towards an ethereal sky, their leaves shimmering with an otherworldly iridescence. Amidst this dreamscape, the River Lumina flowed like a ribbon of molten silver, its surface alive with whispers and secrets waiting to be unraveled.

Yordan stepped closer to the water's edge, drawn by an inexplicable pull that resonated deep within his being. As he approached, a movement caught his eye—a figure emerging from the gossamer veil of mist that clung to the riverbank.

It was a stag, its form both regal and ethereal. Its coat gleamed with an inner luminescence, as if the very essence of starlight had been woven into each strand of fur. Antlers, intricate as the finest Aralonic scrollwork, crowned its head like a living testament to the mysteries of the natural world.

Transfixed, Yordan watched as the stag lowered its head to the river, its muzzle breaking the surface with a gentleness that belied its strength. As it drank, the water seemed to come alive, shimmering and dancing around the creature's form like a kaleidoscope of liquid light.

With each sip, the stag's body began to glow brighter, as if the river's essence were infusing it with an otherworldly radiance. Tendrils of luminous energy curled around its limbs, pulsing in rhythm with the gentle rise and fall of its chest. The air hummed with an almost imperceptible vibration, a song that resonated through Yordan's very bones.

As he stood there, mesmerized by the sight before him, the stag slowly lifted its head from the water. Droplets cascaded from its muzzle like falling stars, each one a tiny prism refracting the light into a spectrum of colors Yordan had never seen before.

Then, in a moment that seemed to stretch into eternity, the stag turned its gaze upon him. Eyes, ancient and knowing, met Yordan's own—twin pools of liquid amber that held the secrets of the universe within their depths.

In that instant, Yordan felt a profound connection, as if he were staring into a mirror that reflected not just his physical form, but the very essence of his soul. It was as if the stag could see through the layers of his being, perceiving the doubts, the fears, and the hopes that he carried within him like precious gems waiting to be unearthed.

The stag regarded him with a stillness that spoke of wisdom and understanding beyond mortal comprehension. Its gaze seemed to penetrate the very fabric of Yordan's being, weaving threads of light and shadow into the tapestry of his existence. In that moment, he felt a profound sense of connection, as if the stag were imparting to him a silent message that resonated within the depths of his soul.

The stag's eyes shimmered with an inner fire, flickering with the wisdom of ages past and the promise of revelations yet to come. Yordan found himself drawn into their depths, his own reflection merging with the luminous essence of the creature before him. In that ethereal space, where the boundaries between the physical and the metaphysical blurred, he felt a surge of energy coursing through his veins, igniting a spark of awareness that had lain dormant within him for far too long.

As he stood there, lost in the stag's unwavering gaze, the world around them seemed to fall away. The mist swirled and danced, forming intricate patterns that whispered of secrets long forgotten and truths waiting to be discovered. The River Lumina's gentle murmur became a symphony of whispers, each note carrying a fragment of knowledge that wove itself into the fabric of Yordan's consciousness.

In that timeless moment, Yordan felt a profound sense of purpose wash over him. It was as if the stag were guiding him towards a destiny that had always been written in the stars, a path that would lead him to the very heart of his own being. With each breath, he felt the weight of his doubts and fears dissipate, replaced by a newfound clarity and determination.

As the connection between them deepened, Yordan saw flashes of his own life reflected in the stag's eyes—moments of joy and sorrow, triumph and despair. He saw the faces of those he loved, their smiles etched into his memory like precious gems. And amidst those familiar images, he caught glimpses of a future yet to be written, a destiny that called to him from beyond the veil of the present.

The stag's presence seemed to fill the glade with an ethereal radiance, casting a warm glow upon the moss-covered ground and the iridescent leaves above. Yordan felt himself being drawn into that light, his spirit merging with the essence of the creature before him. In that moment of unity, he understood that the stag was not merely a physical being, but a manifestation of the very forces that shaped the world around them—a living embodiment of the mysteries that lay at the heart of existence itself.

As the connection between them reached its zenith, Yordan felt a sudden jolt, as if a bolt of lightning had struck him to his very core. His eyes flew open, and he found himself lying in his bed, sweat glistening on his brow and his heart racing with the intensity of the dream that had just consumed him.

Instinctively, he reached out beside him, seeking the comforting presence of Katherine, whose warmth and gentle breathing had been a balm to his restless soul. His hand met only the cool, rumpled sheets, their emptiness a stark reminder that she had slipped away during the night.

The room was bathed in the silver light of dawn, the first rays sneaking through the half-drawn curtains and casting elongated shadows across the walls. The air was thick with the lingering scent of lavender and honeysuckle, a sweet reminder of her presence that clung to the room long after she had departed. Yordan sat up, running a hand through his curls as he tried to shake off the remnants of his vivid dream—a vision that felt as if it belonged more to some otherworldly realm than to his own mind.

He rose from the bed, pulling on a simple linen shirt and stepping towards the open window. The distant sound of children laughing echoed from an alleyway, adding life to the quiet morning.

Yordan leaned against the windowsill, gazing out over the rooftops painted with hues of gold by the rising sun. His thoughts drifted back to Katherine—her captivating smile, her mischievous eyes filled with depth and understanding. She was always disappearing like this, leaving him with nothing but questions and an aching longing for her company.

The memories of last night surfaced in his mind; their laughter under a sky strewn with stars, whispered conversations about dreams and destinies woven together like threads in an intricate tapestry. Her words had been enigmatic yet comforting, hinting at secrets untold and mysteries uncovered only when one dared to leap into the unknown.

Yordan turned away from the window with a newfound determination—a resolve that mirrored his encounter with the stag in his dreamscape.

As he stepped out into the cobblestone streets, a gentle breeze carried whispers from River Lumina. Its voice entwined around him like an old friend. The river's murmurs were tantalizingly familiar, resonating deep within Yordan's soul as if guiding him with an invisible hand. He walked with purpose, the rhythm of his footsteps matching the gentle lapping of water against stone as he approached the river's edge. Sunlight danced on its surface, creating ripples of light that seemed to beckon him closer.

As he meandered through the bustling streets, his path took him away from the market stalls brimming with colorful fabrics and fragrant spices, away from the chatter of merchants hawking their wares. He ignored the pull of Ferran's shop pulled instead by an unseen force toward the river.

"Yordan," a voice called out, halting him in his tracks. He turned to find Sam standing nearby, his calm presence grounding amidst the chaos of the city.

Sam's sightless eyes were fixed ahead, yet Yordan knew they perceived more than physical vision ever could. "I don't believe this is the way to go to Ferran's shop," Sam said, his tone gentle but firm.

Yordan hesitated for a moment, caught between his friend's practical wisdom and the ethereal pull of River Lumina. "I know," he replied finally, his voice carrying a mixture of apology and determination.

"The river has a voice all its own today," Yordan mused, his gaze drifting back to the shimmering waters, so enticing in their mysteries.

Sam chuckled, the sound rich like a deep bell. "And you're all too eager to listen to voices not your own, my friend. If you start hearing it give fashion tips, let us know. We could both use some new inspiration."

Yordan laughed, the tension easing from his shoulders as the familiar banter wrapped around them like a warm cloak. "I don't know, Sam. Those Lumite priests with their gilded robes might have competition when I show up wearing river weeds and fish scales."

"Ah yes," Sam replied with feigned seriousness. "The avant-garde river ensemble—just in time for the next Festival of Light. You'll be the talk of Aralonis."

The two friends continued down the cobblestone path, their conversation weaving easily between jokes and shared memories. The air was alive with the scent of blooming jacarandas and the distant hum of a lute-playing bard entertaining a crowd nearby.

As they neared Ferran's forge, its forge casting an amber glow over the street, Yordan felt a flicker of nostalgia mixed with anticipation. This place held his past—even if his future beckoned elsewhere.

"Ah, Ferran's haven," Sam announced grandly as they paused outside the entrance. "A palace of industry and sweat-bound loyalty."

"Home sweet home," Yordan said softly, sensing that Ferran—a man as gruff as he was generous—would soon have a task for him that required both skill and heart.

As Yordan and Sam entered the blacksmith's shop, the familiar clang of metal against metal greeted them, echoing rhythmically like a symphony of toil. Ferran was already at the forge, his burly frame silhouetted against the roaring flames. Sparks danced in the air, a constellation of fiery stars that seemed to hold stories untold.

"Yordan!" Ferran's voice boomed over the clamor. "I've got a task for you that can't wait."

Yordan nodded, slipping off his linen shirt to reveal a sweat-stained undershirt—his uniform for the hours ahead. He approached the anvil with practiced familiarity, where stacks of raw metal awaited transformation into spearheads destined for the Prince's army.

The work was demanding but meditative. Each swing of the hammer sent vibrations through Yordan's arms, grounding him in the moment even as his mind wandered across distant thoughts. He envisioned the spearheads in their final form: sleek, sturdy, and precise—tools of war yet also symbols of protection for those they would defend.

Time slipped away as he fell into a rhythm, the shop's sounds becoming a backdrop to his internal musings. In these moments, he often found clarity, guided by an unseen hand much like the River Lumina whispered to its chosen.

But as he worked, a gentle voice pulled him back from his reverie.

"Katherine?" he asked without turning around, recognizing her presence instinctively before she even spoke.

"Yordan," Katherine's voice was both warm and urgent, like spring rain on parched soil. "I hoped I might find you here."

He turned to face her, taking in her familiar sight—the luster of her chestnut hair catching flecks of light from the forge. Her eyes held a deep intensity that always seemed to see straight into his soul.

Ferran grunted approvingly as he stepped aside, sensing that whatever Katherine had come for was important enough to pause their work. Saamael offered a knowing smile as he leaned against a work-bench, content to let his friend take center stage.

"What brings you to this palace of industry?" Yordan asked with a grin, wiping sweat from his brow with the back of his hand.

Katherine moved closer, her presence as soothing as a cool breeze through the shop. "There's something I must discuss with you—something concerning Aralism and...my latest journey."

Her frequent disappearances were part of who she was—a seeker driven by compassion and discovery—but each return carried new weight and meaning. Yordan felt a mixture of relief and curiosity; her words hinted at deeper truths he longed to uncover.

"Tell me everything," he said softly, setting down his tools as if signaling that this moment deserved undivided attention.

Katherine took a deep breath, allowing herself a moment to gather her thoughts, her eyes never leaving Yordan's. "In my travels, I found myself at the Tower of Scholars, nestled near the Aralist Temple," she began, her voice carrying the resonance of her discoveries. "There, among the musty tomes and scrolls, I uncovered the tale of a prophet named Tlenatl."

Yordan leaned forward, his interest piqued by the name. He recalled fragmentary mentions of Tlenatl from old stories but never in detail. He was intrigued by what Katherine might reveal—this woman who held pieces of the world's mysteries in her heart as if they were mere whispers.

"Who was he?" Yordan asked, his hazel eyes reflecting a curiosity that flared like sparks from his forge.

Katherine smiled knowingly. "Tlenatl was a Lumite back when they wandered before they settled in Anakuatl—a man gifted with inter-preting dreams and visions," she explained. Her green eyes twinkled with the thrill of her narrative. "His story begins with tragedy; he was sold into slavery as a young man, far from the lands he called home."

The forge's usual clamor quieted as if even the tools wished to listen. Saamael crossed his arms, nodding along as Katherine wove the tale.

"But it was during his captivity that Tlenatl's true gift became evident," she continued. "He served a king who was plagued by unsettling dreams that spoke of both doom and salvation. None could decipher them until Tlenatl came forth."

Yordan imagined Tlenatl standing before this king, his chains heavy but his spirit unyielding. There was something profoundly compelling about this tale—one of resilience amidst adversity.

Katherine's voice grew more animated. "Through his interpretations, Tlenatl not only saved himself but also became one of the king's most trusted advisors. His insights prevented a great famine—a testament to his wisdom and spiritual clarity."

"And how does this connect to Aralism?" Yordan queried thoughtfully, sensing Katherine's tale had deeper roots.

"The records I found indicated that Tlenatl was a precursor to what we know as Aralism today," Katherine explained. "His teachings on enlightenment and personal understanding influenced prophetic circles long before Aralon's revelations."

Yordan absorbed this revelation with deep contemplation. It was as though Tlenatl's story echoed through time, reaching across generations to touch him now—an unexpected link between Lumite traditions and Aralism's more recent path.

"Tlenatl spoke of dreams not just as messages from gods but reflections of one's inner truth," Katherine added softly.

"So he too sought deeper truths," Yordan murmured, understanding dawning like light over distant hills.

Yordan wiped the sweat from his brow, the familiar clang of the hammer against the hot iron ringing in his ears. His hands were still warm from work, but the moment he turned and saw Katherine, stood there, radiant under the late afternoon sun, her auburn hair catching the light just right.

"Thank you for sharing this revelation with me." Yordan said with a smile.

Yordan felt his pulse quicken. The moment seemed to stretch out between them, lingering like the warm breeze that passed through the open door of the smithery. Without thinking, he leaned down and pressed his lips to her cheek, his kiss soft but lingering just a fraction longer than necessary. Her skin was warm, and the scent of lavender clung to her, a contrast to the sharp scent of iron and coal that surrounded him.

As he pulled back, Yordan's lips hovered near her ear, his voice dropping to a whisper. "Can I see you later tonight?"

Katherine's lips curled into a coy smile. She tilted her head, her green eyes flashing with playful mischief. "Maybe," she replied, her tone light and teasing, before pulling away from him. The way she almost hopped off, the bounce in her step, left Yordan's heart beating a little faster.

He stood there for a moment, watching her as she disappeared down the street. The warmth of her cheek still seemed to linger on his lips, her playful "maybe" ringing in his ears. He smiled to himself, the world around him fading into a pleasant blur.

That is, until Sam's voice cut through the moment like a sharp blade. "It's an interesting story, that one," he said, his tone dismissive, clearly referencing Tlental's story.

Yordan blinked, snapping back to the present. He turned toward Sam, standing a few feet away near the entrance of Ferran's workshop.

Sam's expression was neutral, his arms crossed over his chest. He seemed unimpressed, and Yordan knew why—Sam had never quite understood the stories about divine revelations. But Yordan couldn't help but wonder how Sam could even hear him over the relentless clattering of Ferran's hammer against the anvil. The rhythmic clang of metal shaping metal usually drowned out everything, making conversations nearly impossible.

"How could you even hear me?" Yordan asked, his brows furrowed, genuinely curious. The noise of the blacksmith shop was constant, a symphony of hammers, fire, and iron.

Sam shrugged, a smirk pulling at the corner of his mouth. "I hear more than you think, Yordan. You're not the only one who's good at paying attention to details."

Yordan shook his head, a faint smile playing on his lips as he returned to the work at hand, but his thoughts remained elsewhere—on Katherine, on her soft laugh, on the way she had smiled at him just moments before. And as he worked, the clang of the blacksmith shop around him seemed quieter, more distant.

Yordan's sleep was far from peaceful. His mind plunged into a dream—one that felt more like a memory than a figment of his imagination. It wasn't his life he was seeing, though. No, this life belonged to Tlenatl.

Suddenly, he was no longer Yordan, but a young boy—Tlenatl—chained and sold to strangers. The rough, cold iron shackles bit into his wrists as he was pushed into a line of other slaves. The air was thick with the scent of sweat and despair, and Tlenatl's heart pounded with fear. His surroundings were foreign—a dusty market square where men traded lives for coins, the distant calls of traders echoing in his ears. But it all felt so real, so painfully vivid.

Tlenatl was no longer a boy but a young man, standing before a grand throne. The figure seated on it, an ancient king dressed in golden robes, looked down upon him with a mixture of curiosity and expectation. Tlenatl's mouth opened, and words poured out—words not his own, but words that came to him through dreams. He spoke of a famine yet to come, a great hunger that would sweep the land unless they prepared. He was terrified to speak, and yet, somehow, he knew what he said was true.

Another shift. Time seemed to leap forward, and now Tlenatl was no longer a slave but a trusted advisor at the King's side. He wore fine robes of his own, his hands free from chains, and the weight of responsibility on his shoulders felt almost crushing. The King's court was grand, filled with murmurs of those plotting and scheming, but the King himself trusted no one more than Tlenatl. The famine had come, just as Tlenatl had foreseen, but thanks to his warnings, the kingdom had prepared, storing grain and supplies to last through the harshest of seasons.

In flashes, Yordan—Tlenatl—watched as the years passed. Tlenatl's influence grew, and the King relied on him for more than just dreams. Tlenatl married, his wife a kind woman who stood by him as their family grew. He saw their children—bright, joyful faces—and felt the warmth of a life fulfilled, no longer the boy who had been sold but a man who had earned his place through loyalty, wisdom, and hard work.

And yet, as the dream progressed, the weight of those early chains still haunted him. In quiet moments, Tlenatl would sit by the fire, staring into the flames, the memories of slavery never truly leaving him. He had come far—he had built a life, raised a family—but the scars, both physical and emotional, were forever etched into his soul.

Yordan, as Tlenatl, felt those scars. He felt the weight of the chains, the hunger of those early days, the uncertainty. But he also felt the joy of freedom, the satisfaction of a life well lived, and the peace of having found his place in the world.

Then, in an instant, everything dissolved. The grand hall, the laughter of his children, the warmth of his wife's hands all disappeared. Yordan was jolted from the dream, gasping for air as if he had just surfaced from deep water.

He awoke in his bed, drenched in sweat. His heart hammered in his chest, and it took him a moment to realize where he was—his room in Aralonis, the familiar stone walls surrounding him, the cool air chilling his damp skin.

He felt disoriented, the dream clinging to him like a fog that refused to lift. He could still feel the echoes of Tlenatl's life, the sharp contrasts of slavery and power, hardship and fulfillment. It was more than a dream. It had been so real, too real.

He reached out, brushing his hand over the bed beside him, and found nothing but the lingering warmth of where Katherine had been. She was gone now, her side of the bed empty. The sheets were still slightly warm, a reminder of the intimate hours they had shared before sleep had claimed him. There was no doubt about what had happened between them, but now, in the quiet aftermath, it felt distant overshadowed by the vividness of the dream.

Yordan sat up slowly, his naked body slick with sweat, the night air cool against his skin. He ran a hand through his damp hair, trying to steady his breathing, but the dream—no, the vision—still swirled in his mind. He could feel the weight of Tlenatl's past as though it were his own. The chains, the King's trust, the life Tlenatl had built after years of hardship. It was like Yordan had lived it, felt every moment as Tlenatl had.

His mind raced. How could it have been so real? Was it just a dream conjured by his subconscious, or something more—a connection to Tlenatl but why Tlenatl?

He glanced toward the door, wondering when Katherine had slipped out, careful not to disturb him. The room was silent, save for his own heavy breathing. He swung his legs over the side of the bed, his feet meeting the cold stone floor, grounding him back in reality. Yet, the weight of the dream clung to him, making him question if reality was as solid as it seemed.

What did the dream mean? The vividness of Tlenatl's story, the way it intertwined with his own, made him wonder if it was a message or a warning. Or perhaps, a reminder of the sacrifices needed to achieve something greater.

But for now, all Yordan could do was sit in the darkened room, the remnants of the dream settling over him like the cool night air and try to make sense of a past that was not his own, but somehow felt as if it were.

Yordan stepped out into the cool morning air, still feeling the lingering weight of the vivid dream from the night before. The city of Aralonis was already coming to life, with merchants setting up their stalls and the distant sound of hammers ringing out from other blacksmiths hard at work. But Yordan's mind wasn't on his forge today.

He made his way through the winding streets, the scent of fresh bread growing stronger as he approached the bakery where Sam worked. The warm smell was a comfort, a reminder of simpler things amid his restless thoughts.

As he entered the bakery, he spotted Sam behind the counter, kneading dough with his strong hands, his expression focused. Despite his blindness, Sam's movements were practiced, fluid—each motion a testament to the skill he had developed over the years. His hands worked the dough with an ease that always amazed Yordan.

Yordan leaned against the doorway, smirking slightly. "I still can't believe you got so good at making bread with nothing but feel."

Sam didn't miss a beat, his hands still working the dough with practiced precision. He grinned and cocked his head in Yordan's direction. "There's a lot you can learn just by feel, my friend. Maybe you should give it a try—though I'm not sure you've got the patience for it."

Yordan chuckled, crossing his arms. "Patience? That's rich coming from the guy who once couldn't sit still for more than five minutes."

"Hey, people change," Sam shot back, rolling the dough out smoothly before setting it aside. "And besides, this bakery's better off for it. Imagine if I'd stuck with fighting or whatever you and I used to dream about when we were kids. No fresh bread for you."

"I'm sure I'd survive somehow." Yordan grinned, but the playfulness in his tone faded as the memory of his dream crept back into his thoughts. He ran a hand through his hair, hesitating before finally speaking again. "Actually, Sam, there's something I've been thinking about. After that dream I had last night, it's got me... restless."

Sam raised an eyebrow, though he didn't stop working. "You and your dreams. What was it this time? Dragons? Hidden treasures?"

"No, this one was different." Yordan frowned, his voice becoming serious. "It wasn't some random dream—it was about Tlenatl, the Lumite from all those old stories. It felt real, Sam. Like I was living through his life—being sold into slavery, serving the King, helping save the kingdom. I woke up covered in sweat, like I'd just lived his whole life in one night. I can't shake it."

Sam's expression shifted slightly, though his hands kept moving over the dough. "Yordan, don't dwell on dreams too much. They're dreams for a reason—just your mind trying to make sense of whatever's going on up there." He tapped his head, grinning slightly. "But since you're my best friend, if this dream means you want to go chasing some answers in Lumina City, I'm in. Even if I don't think this is going to solve whatever you're looking for."

Yordan smiled at that, feeling a little more at ease. Sam always had a way of grounding him, even when his mind was spinning with questions. "Thanks, Sam. I was thinking maybe you, me, and Katherine could head to Lumina City together. See if there's something there—anything that can explain what's been going on."

Sam raised an eyebrow, a smirk pulling at the corner of his lips. "Katherine, huh? Sounds like I'm about to be the third wheel on this little adventure."

Yordan laughed, shaking his head. "Come on, don't be like that. You'll be too busy to even notice with all the bread you'll be baking along the way."

"Right, right." Sam chuckled as he finished shaping the dough. "Well, as long as you promise not to make me carry the bags, I guess I'm in. But I still think you're reading too much into that dream."

Yordan leaned against the counter, watching his friend work with a newfound sense of calm. Maybe Sam was right. Maybe it was just a dream, and there wasn't anything more to it. But deep down, Yordan couldn't shake the feeling that there was something waiting for him, something important.

Yordan made his way back to Ferran's blacksmith shop, weaving through the familiar streets of Aralonis. The scent of coal and hot metal greeted him before he even reached the entrance, the warmth from the forge spilling out into the cool air. As he stepped inside, the rhythmic clang of hammers on iron filled the space, the comforting sound that had become a part of him over the years.

Ferran was already at work, his broad back bent over a glowing piece of metal. Sparks flew with each strike of his hammer, lighting up the dim workshop in bursts. Yordan joined him at his usual station without a word, the silent camaraderie of their shared craft settling over them like a well-worn cloak.

The forge was alive with activity. The flames roared, casting flickering shadows against the stone walls, while the smell of molten iron and burning coal permeated the air. The walls of the shop were lined with tools—hammers, tongs, and chisels—all meticulously organized. Weapons in various stages of completion lay scattered across the workbenches, from unfinished blades to nearly polished swords destined for Prince Joseph's army.

Yordan picked up a half-forged sword, its edge still rough, and placed it in the flames. The heat from the forge was intense, but it felt familiar. Calming. His hands moved almost on their own, working the metal into shape with practiced precision. The weight of the hammer felt right in his grip, each strike sending vibrations through his arms as he shaped the blade.

As they worked, neither spoke much, both absorbed in their tasks. The clang of metal, the hiss of steam, and the roar of the fire were all they needed to fill the silence.

Finally, when the sun reached its highest point in the sky, Ferran called for a break. He wiped the sweat from his brow, his grizzled face glowing with the heat of the forge. They sat on the stone bench outside the shop, sharing a simple meal of bread and cheese Ferran had brought out from the back.

Yordan hesitated for a moment, chewing thoughtfully before he spoke. "Ferran," he began, looking over at the old blacksmith, "I've been thinking about taking a mind retreat. Heading to Lumina City for a bit."

Ferran glanced at him, one eyebrow raised as he tore off a piece of bread. "You don't need to ask me, lad. You're a grown man now." He chuckled, shaking his head. "But since you did ask, I'll just say this: be safe. That's all I care about."

Yordan smiled, feeling a little lighter. He had expected a lecture about responsibilities or the importance of their work for Prince Joseph's army, but Ferran's easygoing nature won out once again. "Thanks. I just figured I should mention it, given how much we've got going on here."

Ferran waved a hand dismissively. "It'll all be here when you get back. It always is. Now, are you going to sit there and philosophize all day, or are you going to help me finish these swords?"

Yordan laughed and took another bite of bread before standing up, brushing the crumbs off his lap. "Alright, alright. Let's get back to it."

They returned to the forge, the heat enveloping them once more as they resumed their work. The sword Yordan had been shaping earlier glowed in the fire, and he pulled it out, its edges still jagged and unrefined. He placed it on the anvil, the metal sizzling as it met the cooler surface, and brought his hammer down, sparks flying with each strike.

The rhythmic clanging filled the workshop, each hammer stroke precise and deliberate. Beside him, Ferran worked on another blade, his movements slower but no less skilled. Together, they shaped the weapons meant for Prince Joseph's army, each blade forged with care and attention to detail.

Yordan could feel the weight of their purpose as they worked. These weren't just tools; they were instruments of war, weapons that would be held by men sent to fight in the name of the Lumite cause. The metal resisted under his hammer, but with every strike, it yielded a little more, becoming something stronger, sharper—ready for battle.

The afternoon wore on, the sun casting long shadows through the open doorway of the shop. The weapons took shape beneath their hands, each sword slowly transformed from raw material into a polished instrument of death. Despite the gravity of their work, Yordan found comfort in the familiar rhythm, in the feeling of the metal giving way beneath his hammer.

Finally, as the sun dipped lower in the sky, Ferran leaned back from his work and wiped his brow, his face streaked with soot and sweat. "Not bad, lad," he said, inspecting Yordan's finished blade. "These swords will serve Prince Joseph's army well."

Yordan held up the blade, its edge gleaming in the fading light. It was a fine piece of craftsmanship, sharp and well-balanced. He felt a sense of pride in their work, but also the weight of what these weapons represented. Tools of war, forged by his own hands.

"Thanks," Yordan replied, though his thoughts were still tangled with the dream, with the pull toward Lumina City. The weapons were important, but there was something else—something greater—that called to him.

But for now, the forge was his world. The heat, the hammer, the metal beneath his hands. And until he left for Lumina City, this was where he belonged.

Yordan stepped out of the forge, the sun dipping lower on the horizon, casting a warm, golden glow across Aralonis. The day had been long, and the weight of the hammer still lingered in his arms, but his mind was elsewhere—on Katherine. He hadn't been able to stop thinking about her since their morning encounter, and now, with the journey to Lumina City ahead of him, he felt the urge to find her, to see if she might come with him and Sam.

He made his way through the bustling streets, the familiar paths leading him toward the part of town where Katherine's family lived.

The streets were crowded with villagers finishing their daily tasks, merchants packing their wares, and children chasing each other in the fading light. But Yordan's focus was singular, his thoughts on her, and the strange mixture of nerves and excitement that always seemed to accompany seeing Katherine.

When he reached her family's home—a modest, well-kept house nestled among flowering trees—he spotted her in the small garden out front, tending to the plants with her usual grace. The sight of her immediately put a smile on his face. She stood up, brushing her hands on her apron, and when her eyes caught his, she smiled, her green eyes lighting up.

"Yordan," Katherine greeted him warmly, a hint of playfulness in her voice. She wiped her hands on a nearby towel, stepping toward him. "To what do I owe the pleasure?"

He couldn't help but let his gaze linger on her for a moment longer. The way the setting sun highlighted her auburn hair, the lightness in her step—it all tugged at something deep inside him. He smirked, leaning against the fence post casually. "What, I need a reason to come see you?"

Her smile widened, and she tilted her head slightly. "Maybe you do."

Yordan chuckled, stepping closer. "Well, maybe I'm here for a very good reason this time."

"Really?" Katherine's eyebrows raised in mock curiosity. "And what reason could that possibly be?"

"Sam and I are heading to Lumina City," Yordan said, his tone more serious now, though he still couldn't resist a touch of flirtation. "I was hoping you might want to join us. Could use the company of a pretty face on the road."

Katherine's laughter was soft, and she gave him a playful push on the chest. "Flatterer. You know I'd love to, but I've got responsibilities here. My family needs me right now. There's a lot to take care of, and I can't just leave them to handle it on their own."

Yordan frowned slightly, though he tried to mask his disappointment. "Really? You're telling me you'd rather stay here tending flowers than come explore Lumina City with me?"

Katherine crossed her arms, though her expression remained lighthearted. "As tempting as you make it sound, Yordan, I'm afraid my family comes first. Besides," she added, her tone teasing, "someone needs to keep you grounded. You get into enough trouble without me there to watch your back."

Yordan grinned, stepping even closer until there was barely a breath of space between them. "Maybe that's exactly why I need you with me. To keep me out of trouble."

She glanced up at him, her green eyes sparkling, but her smile softened into something more genuine. "I wish I could," she said quietly, reaching up to brush a strand of hair behind her ear. "But my father isn't doing well. I've got to help manage things while he's recovering. Maybe after things settle down, we'll have that adventure."

Yordan sighed, his gaze searching hers. He could see the truth in her words, the concern for her family, the duty she felt pulling her away. It was something he understood well. "I get it," he said, his voice softer now. "Your family needs you. But you know I'm going to miss having you around."

Katherine smiled again, this time more tenderly. "I'll miss you too, Yordan. But you'll be fine. You've got Sam, after all."

"Sam's a poor substitute for you," he quipped, though his heart wasn't in the teasing anymore. He leaned down, just close enough that his voice was a low murmur only she could hear. "But when I get back, we'll make up for lost time. Promise."

Her cheeks flushed just slightly, but she didn't shy away. "I'll hold you to that."

They stood there for a moment, the sounds of the village fading into the background as they looked at each other, the warmth of their unspoken connection hanging in the air between them. Yordan wanted to kiss her, to pull her close and forget about everything else. But he knew it wasn't the time.

Instead, he reached out, brushing a gentle hand against her cheek before stepping back, the moment lingering like a sweet memory already forming.

"You be safe, Katherine," he said quietly.

"I always am," she replied, giving him a soft smile before turning back to her garden.

Yordan watched her for a moment longer, his heart feeling both lighter and heavier at the same time. He turned to leave, the weight of her absence already settling in, but a renewed sense of purpose driving him forward. He had a journey ahead, and while Katherine wouldn't be there beside him, the thought of seeing her again once it was over gave him something to look forward to.

As he walked back through the streets of Aralonis, the setting sun casting long shadows behind him, Yordan couldn't help but smile to himself. Katherine may not be joining him on this journey, but the road ahead still held the promise of something greater.

Chapter Five

T he first rays of dawn spilled over the rooftops of Aralonis, casting long golden beams across the cobbled streets. Yordan adjusted the strap of his pack and glanced over at Sam, who stood beside him with his head tilted slightly, listening to the quiet hum of the waking city. The forge had been left behind, and so had the familiar comforts of home. They were setting out for Lumina City, and though excitement coursed through Yordan, he couldn't quite shake the wistful thought of Katherine staying behind.

"Ready to go?" Yordan asked, his voice light, though there was a subtle weight behind it.

Sam grinned, gripping his walking stick in one hand, his other hand resting against the edge of his pack. "Ready as I'll ever be. Just don't slow me down, Yordan. I know how you like to gawk at everything."

Yordan laughed and began walking, his boots crunching against the gravel path that led out of Aralonis. Sam followed with an ease that always surprised him. Though blind, Sam's steps were sure and confident, his stick tapping lightly in front of him. He didn't need guiding; he never did. Sam always seemed to sense the world in ways Yordan couldn't.

As they walked, the city faded behind them, replaced by open fields and the distant murmur of the River Lumina. Yordan's mood lifted as the road stretched out before them, the promise of adventure ahead. Still, as they talked and exchanged jokes, he couldn't stop his mind from drifting back to Katherine—her smile, her laugh, the way she had looked at him when he'd asked her to join them.

Sam must have picked up on it, as he always did. "You're awful quiet for someone who's supposedly thrilled to go on this journey," Sam said, his tone teasing. "What's got you so preoccupied? Wait," he paused dramatically, pretending to puzzle it out. "Don't tell me. It's Katherine, isn't it?"

Yordan shot him a mock glare, though he knew Sam couldn't see it. "Oh, come on. Can't a guy just enjoy the peace and quiet?"

Sam chuckled, shaking his head. "Peace and quiet, huh? You've mentioned her at least three times since we left, and we're barely an hour in. Face it, Yordan—you're smitten."

Yordan rubbed the back of his neck, a sheepish smile creeping onto his face. "Alright, maybe a little."

"A little?" Sam scoffed, his grin widening. "You've got it bad. I can practically feel the hearts floating around your head every time you talk about her."

"Alright, alright," Yordan said, laughing now. "I miss her, okay? But it's not like she's going anywhere. She'll still be in Aralonis when we get back."

"She better be," Sam quipped. "Otherwise, I'll have to deal with you moping around for the rest of your life, and I'm not sure I can survive that."

Yordan shook his head, grinning despite himself. "You're impossible, you know that?"

"Yeah, but you love me for it," Sam shot back, his tone light but with an undertone of genuine affection. Their banter was effortless, the kind that came from years of friendship. Sam always knew how to bring Yordan out of his own head, even when Yordan didn't realize he needed it.

As the hours passed and the sun climbed higher, their conversation shifted between lighthearted teasing and more serious topics, the road ahead, their hopes for what they might find in Lumina City, and the memories of their shared past in Aralonis. Yordan found himself appreciating Sam's presence more than ever. He might not believe in the significance of dreams or divine revelations, but he had still agreed to come along, no questions asked. That kind of loyalty was rare.

By the time they approached the Valley of Akeskauiya, known by many as the Valley of Reflection, the terrain had begun to change. The fields gave way to gentle hills, the air cooler and tinged with the scent of wildflowers. The River Lumina's distant glimmer was still visible, winding its way through the valley like a silver ribbon.

Sam slowed his steps, his head tilting slightly as if listening to something only he could hear. "Yordan," he said after a moment, his voice quieter now. "Can you see the Golden Deer?"

Yordan frowned, scanning the area. His eyes moved over the rolling hills and the clusters of trees, but he saw nothing unusual. "No," he said, his tone curious. "I don't see any deer. Why?"

Sam smiled faintly, his expression unreadable. "Nothing. Just wondering if they were still here."

Yordan looked at him, a question on his lips, but Sam didn't offer anything more. Instead, he adjusted his pack and started walking again, his stick tapping softly against the ground. Yordan followed, the question still lingering in his mind, but for now, he let it go.

The journey was just beginning, and Yordan couldn't shake the feeling that the road ahead would hold far more questions than answers.

As Yordan and Sam continued their steady trek into the Valley of Akeskauiya, the golden hues of the late afternoon sun began to blanket the rolling hills. The air here was cooler, carrying the earthy scent of wildflowers and fresh grass. The Valley always had a stillness about it, a peacefulness that made the rest of the world feel distant.

Yordan's steps slowed as memories crept into his mind. The last time he had come through this valley, the landscape had been alive with movement. He remembered golden deer grazing in the open meadows, their sleek coats shimmering in the sunlight like precious metal. He could see it so clearly in his mind: the quiet grace with which they moved, the way their antlers seemed to catch and hold the light. It had been years ago, and yet the image lingered, sharp and vivid.

But now, the valley felt... empty. His gaze swept over the landscape again, searching the hills and the trees for any sign of them, but the golden deer were nowhere to be seen. It unsettled him in a way he couldn't quite place, the absence of something that had once seemed so intrinsic to this place.

Sam's voice broke through his thoughts. "You've gone quiet again, Yordan," he said, his stick tapping lightly against the ground as he walked. "Thinking about Katherine, or is it something else this time?"

Yordan hesitated before answering, his tone quieter than usual. "Do you remember the golden deer?"

Sam raised an eyebrow, though he kept his pace even. "I've never seen them, obviously," he replied with a small smile. "But I know the stories. You told me about them once, didn't you? Said they were everywhere the last time you came through here."

"They were," Yordan said, his voice distant. "They were everywhere. Grazing, running—like the valley belonged to them. But now..." He gestured vaguely at the landscape, even though he knew Sam couldn't see it. "Now, it's like they're just... gone."

Sam tilted his head, his expression thoughtful. "That is strange. Even I know golden deer are supposed to be a staple of this place. Everyone in Aralonis talks about them like they're part of the valley's soul. If they're not here now... well, I'm sure someone in Lumina City will have an explanation. Or at least some grand story to spin."

Yordan glanced at him, his brows furrowed. "You think it means something?"

Sam let out a low chuckle, shaking his head. "You know me, Yordan. I don't put much stock in signs or omens. But I can tell you what the Aralonites believe." He tapped his stick on the ground for emphasis as he continued. "They say the golden deer are guardians of the valley. A sign of balance, prosperity, and divine favor. If they're here, it means Toteko's light is strong, that the land and its people are blessed."

"And if they're not here?" Yordan asked, though he wasn't sure he wanted the answer.

Sam hesitated, his usually teasing tone giving way to something more serious. "If they're not here, some say it's a warning. That something's out of balance—either in the valley or in the hearts of its people. It could mean trouble, hardship... or worse."

Yordan let Sam's words sink in as they walked, the quiet between them stretching long and heavy. He wanted to dismiss it, to tell himself that the golden deer were just animals, that their absence was nothing more than coincidence. But the valley felt different this time, and it wasn't just the deer. The air felt heavier, the silence too complete. It gnawed at the edge of his thoughts.

"You really don't believe in signs?" Yordan asked finally, breaking the silence.

Sam shrugged. "I believe in what I can see—or in my case, what I can feel, hear, touch. The rest? It's just stories people tell to make sense of things they don't understand. Doesn't mean they're not important to them, though."

Yordan nodded, though his thoughts were still tangled. The memory of the golden deer from years ago felt like it belonged to another life, one simpler and less burdened. Now, as he stared out at the empty hills, he couldn't help but feel a strange unease. What if Sam was wrong? What if their absence did mean something?

He glanced over at Sam, who walked beside him with the easy confidence of someone who had long since learned to navigate the world without sight. Yordan envied his steadiness, his ability to brush off uncertainty like it was nothing. But for Yordan, the questions wouldn't go away.

The valley stretched out before them, its beauty muted by the absence of the creatures that had once defined it. Yordan couldn't shake the feeling that the golden deer weren't just missing, they were absent for a reason. And that reason, whatever it was, felt far closer than he would have liked.

The sun dipped below the horizon, casting a deep amber glow over the Valley of Akeskauiya. Shadows stretched long and thin across the grass, and the distant murmuring of the River Lumina blended with the chirping of crickets. Yordan and Sam had decided to stop for the night, settling in a small hollow surrounded by gentle hills. The stillness of the valley wrapped around them, broken only by the crackling of the small fire Yordan was carefully tending.

Yordan crouched beside the fire pit, poking at the embers with a long stick, trying to coax the flames into burning hotter. Sweat beaded on his brow as he leaned closer, the heat from the fire stinging his face. His shirt sleeves were rolled up, and his hands were smudged with soot.

"Come on," he muttered under his breath, his eyes narrowing at the stubborn coals. He prodded at the fire again, shifting the wood to create a better draft. "You'd think after all the time I've spent around forges, I'd have mastered this by now."

"Careful, Yordan," Sam called from where he sat a few feet away, his hands deftly kneading dough on a makeshift board balanced across his knees. "You're starting to sound like the fire owes you something."

Yordan glanced over his shoulder, smirking despite himself. "Well, it owes you something. If this doesn't heat up, your bread's going to taste like soggy rocks."

Sam laughed, his fingers pressing into the dough with practiced ease. Though blind, his movements were confident, each fold and press of the dough precise. "Trust me, Yordan. The fire will come through. It's not the fire I'm worried about whether you can keep from burning your eyebrows off."

Yordan snorted and leaned back, wiping his hands on his trousers. "You're awfully cocky for someone who can't see the fire he's trusting me with."

"I don't need to see it," Sam replied, grinning. He ran his fingers over the dough, feeling its texture with a care that always impressed Yordan. "It's about listening. Feeling. You'd be surprised what you can pick up when you're not distracted by sight."

Yordan shook his head, the smirk still tugging at his lips. "You know, Sam, I'm not sure if I envy your perspective or if you're just trying to make me feel like an idiot."

"Why not both?" Sam quipped, his grin widening.

The fire finally began to roar, the coals glowing a bright orange that cast flickering light across their campsite. Yordan leaned back, satisfied with his work, and gestured toward the fire pit. "Alright, Baker Supreme, your stage is ready."

Sam chuckled and stood, carefully carrying the dough in a small pan he'd packed. "About time," he teased, moving toward the fire. He knelt down and set the pan just above the coals, his hands lingering near the heat as he judged the temperature. "This is perfect, actually. Good job, Fire Master."

"Thank you," Yordan said with a mock bow, settling onto a nearby rock. "Glad to know my efforts are appreciated."

The smell of baking bread soon wafted through the campsite, warm and inviting. Yordan leaned back, resting his elbows on his knees as he watched Sam tend to the pan, rotating it occasionally to ensure the bread was cooked evenly. Despite the lighthearted banter, there was a peaceful rhythm to their work—a sense of camaraderie that required no words.

"How long does this usually take?" Yordan asked after a while, tilting his head toward the pan.

"Not long," Sam replied, his voice calm and assured. "Breads like life, Yordan. You give it the right ingredients, the right conditions, and a little patience, and it'll turn out just fine."

Yordan raised an eyebrow, glancing at him with an amused expression. "That supposed to be some profound baker's wisdom?"

"Take it however you want," Sam said with a shrug, the corners of his mouth lifting in a knowing smile.

Yordan chuckled, shaking his head as he leaned back further, gazing up at the stars that had begun to scatter across the night sky. The valley seemed to glow under their light, the stillness of the night settling in around them like a soft blanket.

"You know," Yordan said after a moment, his voice quieter now, "this isn't so bad. We could almost forget we're out here chasing dreams and signs."

"Could've told you that," Sam replied, carefully lifting the pan from the fire. He set it aside to cool, sitting back on his heels. "Sometimes it's good to stop and enjoy the simple things. Like bread, for instance. Speaking of which—" He broke off a piece of the loaf and held it out toward Yordan. "Here. Fresh from the fire and made by yours truly."

Yordan took the offered piece, tearing off a bite. The crust was crisp, the inside soft and warm, with a flavor that was simple but comforting. He smiled, nodding in approval. "Not bad, Sam. You might just have a future in this."

"Glad to know you think so," Sam replied, grinning as he tore off a piece for himself. "Now let's just hope the rest of this trip turns out as well as the bread."

Yordan chuckled, but his gaze lingered on the fire, his thoughts drifting again. The golden deer, the absence of their grace in the valley—it nagged at him, even now. But as the warmth of the bread and the fire settled in his chest, he let the unease fade, at least for the moment.

For now, it was enough to sit by the fire, sharing bread and banter with his best friend under the stars. The road ahead would wait until tomorrow.

The fire had been extinguished, leaving the campsite in near-total darkness save for the faint shimmer of moonlight that filtered through the trees. The Valley of Akeskauiya was quiet now, its usual serenity amplified by the stillness of the night. Yordan lay on his back, his head resting against a rolled-up blanket, staring up at the canopy of stars scattered across the inky sky. Beside him, Sam's steady breathing indicated that his friend had already drifted off to sleep.

Yordan closed his eyes, the day's journey catching up with him. The scent of the smoldering embers lingered faintly, mingling with the earthy aroma of the valley. His muscles ached pleasantly from the day's walk, and sleep came to him easily.

But his dreams were anything but restful.

Yordan found himself standing on the edge of the River Lumina, though it looked different than he remembered. The water, which was usually a clear, gentle stream, seemed almost alive, its surface rippling unnaturally even in the absence of wind. The moonlight reflected off its surface, but the light was distorted, fractured like shards of broken glass.

He felt drawn to the river, his feet moving without conscious thought. As he stepped closer, the water began to hum, a low vibration that resonated deep in his chest. The hum grew louder, shaping itself into words—but they were words he couldn't understand, a language unfamiliar and strange. The river was speaking to him, its voice fluid and ethereal, but its meaning slipped through his grasp like water through his fingers.

"Wh-what are you saying?" Yordan whispered, his voice trembling, though no one was there to answer.

The river's voice grew louder, insistent, the sounds rising and falling like waves crashing against unseen rocks. It wasn't hostile, but neither was it comforting. It simply was a presence too vast and unknowable for Yordan to comprehend. His pulse quickened as the water seemed to shimmer and shift, revealing a figure at the edge of the riverbank.

A golden deer. Its sleek coat glistened under the moonlight, every movement elegant and deliberate. The deer lowered its head to drink from the river, its delicate frame outlined by the faint glow of the water. Yordan stared, mesmerized, the strange language of the river fading into the background as he took in the creature's beauty.

He stepped closer, his hand reaching out instinctively, though he wasn't sure why. He didn't want to startle it, didn't want to break the fragile stillness of the moment. But before his fingers could brush its golden fur, the deer stiffened.

Yordan froze. The deer's legs buckled suddenly, its body collapsing beside the river with a sickening thud. Its golden coat was marred by a gash that hadn't been there before, as though the wound had appeared out of nowhere. Blood poured from its side, the vivid red stark against the pale glow of the moonlight. The river, once shimmering and alive, began to change.

The blood from the deer seeped into the water, spreading like ink in glass. Yordan stepped back, his breath catching in his throat as the river transformed before his eyes. The shimmering current darkened, shifting into a deep crimson, its surface no longer gentle but churning violently, as if it were alive and enraged.

Then the screams began.

They came from the river itself, rising from the crimson depths—screams of agony, of despair, of countless voices crying out in pain. The sound pierced Yordan's mind, a cacophony of torment that shook him to his core. He clamped his hands over his ears, but it did nothing to drown out the horrific wails.

The river, now a stream of blood, surged toward him, its violent current clawing at the riverbank as though trying to reach him. Yordan stumbled back, his heart pounding as the screams grew louder, reverberating in his skull. The once-majestic deer lay lifeless at the edge of the water, its golden glow fading as the blood overtook everything.

"Stop!" Yordan cried, his voice lost in the chaos. "What is this?!"

But the river didn't answer. It only screamed.

Yordan jolted awake, his chest heaving as he gasped for air. His skin was slick with sweat, his blanket tangled around him as though he had been thrashing in his sleep. The dark stillness of the Valley greeted him, the quiet night a stark contrast to the vivid nightmare that still lingered in his mind.

He sat up, running a trembling hand through his damp hair, trying to piece together the fragments of the dream. The golden deer. The river speaking. The blood and the screams. It was all there, but disjointed, like scattered shards of glass that refused to form a complete picture.

"What was that?" he whispered to himself, his voice barely audible.

The dream felt too real, too vivid to be a simple trick of his mind. He could still hear the echo of the river's voice, though its words remained incomprehensible. And the sight of the blood-streaked deer haunted him, its lifeless body etched into his thoughts.

Yordan looked over at Sam, who was still sound asleep, his face peaceful. Yordan envied his friend's calm. Whatever that dream had been—vision, nightmare, or something else entirely, it had left him shaken.

He leaned back against the tree behind him, staring up at the stars as he tried to steady his breathing. The dream's meaning eluded him, but he couldn't shake the feeling that it was important, that it was connected to something far greater than himself. And that thought, more than anything, filled him with both unease and a strange, inexplicable determination.

The morning light cast a golden hue over the Valley of Akeskauiya as Yordan and Sam continued along the winding path toward Lumina City. The crisp air carried the faint scent of dew-soaked grass, and the tranquil chirping of birds provided a comforting backdrop. Yordan had found himself lost in thought more than once that morning, the fragmented images of his dream still lingering uneasily in his mind.

As they rounded a bend, Yordan noticed a group of people coming toward them. His steps slowed, his gaze narrowing. This was no ordinary group of travelers. They moved with a heavy weariness, many of them supporting one another or pulling makeshift carts laden with belongings—and, in some cases, injured companions. The sight immediately put Yordan on edge.

The diversity of the group was striking. Some had sun-darkened skin and hair adorned with beads or feathers, their clothing reflecting the earthy tones and patterns of Ojtlist traditions. Others were fairer, their sharp features framed by simple, practical garments. The mix of Ants and Ojtlists was apparent, their differences set aside in what Yordan could only assume was a shared hardship.

Yet, as the group drew closer, Yordan's skepticism flared. He recognized the guarded looks on their faces, the way many avoided eye contact or glanced warily at him and Sam. It didn't add up—not yet.

Yordan's gaze landed on an elderly woman walking near the edge of the group. Her silver hair was tied back in a simple braid, and she leaned heavily on a staff carved with intricate animal symbols, a clear mark of her Ojtlist beliefs. Something about her presence compelled him to step forward.

"Excuse me, ma'am," Yordan said, his tone careful. "What happened to all of you?"

The woman paused, her dark eyes narrowing as she studied him. Her grip tightened on her staff. "My name is Sira," she said, her voice steady but tinged with exhaustion. "We've come from the outskirts of Lumina City. Or rather, what was left of it after the Lumites drove us out."

Yordan blinked, the words hitting him harder than he expected. "The Lumites drove you out?" he repeated, his tone skeptical. "Why would they do that?"

Sira's gaze hardened. "Because we're not like them," she said sharply. "Because we don't follow their teachings. To them, that makes us heretics, unworthy of living near their precious city. They burned our homes, destroyed our crops, and killed those who resisted. This is what they do to anyone who doesn't kneel to their beliefs."

Yordan felt his jaw tighten. He glanced at the group behind her—injured men and women, frightened children clinging to their parents, carts laden with belongings that looked hastily packed. It was a pitiful sight, and yet... something about it didn't sit right with him.

"I've grown up around Lumites," Yordan said, his tone cautious but firm. "And I've heard the stories about their faith, about their zeal. But this?" He gestured at the group. "This doesn't sound like them. Why would they risk everything to push you out of your homes?"

Sira's lips pressed into a thin line, her expression darkening. "Because they think they're righteous," she said. "Because they think they speak for their god, and anyone who doesn't follow their way is a threat."

Yordan frowned, his skepticism deepening. He wanted to believe her, but it didn't fit with what he knew—or thought he knew—about Lumites. He couldn't reconcile the image of the devout, disciplined people he had heard about with the image of an army driving innocent families from their homes. It felt... wrong.

Sam, who had been silent through the exchange, seemed to sense the tension in Yordan's voice and posture. He stepped forward slightly, his hand brushing against Yordan's arm in a calming gesture. "I hope you have a safe journey," he said to Sira, his tone polite but measured.

Sira's sharp gaze flicked to Sam, her expression softening slightly. "Thank you," she said, her voice quieter now. "We'll need it."

With that, she turned and continued on her way, her staff tapping softly against the ground. The group followed, their movements slow and laborious as they made their way down the path.

Yordan watched them go, his arms crossed, the unease in his chest refusing to dissipate. The sight of the wounded and the weary tugged at something deep inside him, but his mind was clouded with doubt. Could the Lumites he thought he understood really be capable of this? Or was there more to the story than Sira had told him?

"You're quiet," Sam said after a moment, his voice breaking the stillness.

"I don't know," Yordan admitted, his voice low. "Something about this doesn't add up. If the Lumites are as righteous as they claim, why would they do something like this?"

Sam shrugged, his stick tapping lightly on the ground as they resumed their walk. "Sometimes, Yordan, righteousness blinds people to what's right. Or maybe Sira's got her own reasons for painting them in the worst light. Either way, it's not our fight—not yet."

Yordan nodded reluctantly, though the tension in his chest didn't ease. The road ahead seemed longer now, weighed down by the questions swirling in his mind. Whatever awaited them in Lumina City, Yordan couldn't shake the feeling that it was far more complicated than he had imagined.

As Yordan and Sam continued down the winding road through the Valley of Akeskauiya, the remnants of their earlier encounter with the refugees still played in Yordan's mind. The road had grown quieter since they left the main body of travelers behind, but as they neared the end of the seemingly endless stream of displaced people heading in the opposite direction, the sound of muffled conversation reached their ears.

The voices came from a small cluster of refugees—a few stragglers lagging behind the main group. They were seated on the side of the road, their belongings piled haphazardly nearby. A pot rested over a small fire, steam rising from what must have been a meager meal. The group looked just as weary as those who had gone before them, but their low conversation carried an intensity that drew Yordan's attention.

One of the speakers, a wiry man with dark, sun-worn skin, gestured animatedly as he spoke, his voice low but urgent. Yordan and Sam slowed their steps as they passed, their ears catching snippets of the exchange.

"I'm telling you," The man said, his tone insistent. "It was him—Ueuejtlakatl. Near Nahualis. He stood between the Ojtlists and the Lumites, like some guardian out of legend."

A younger man, seated with his knees drawn to his chest, shook his head skeptically. "And what? One man drove off an entire regiment. You expect me to believe that?"

The wiry man frowned but didn't back down. "Believe what you want, but I saw him. Tall, strong. His hair was gray, but he carried himself like a warrior. Skin dark as the riverbed. The Ojtlists say he's been protecting them for years. He's no ordinary man."

An older woman, sitting with her back against a weathered tree, spoke up next. Her voice was quieter but filled with conviction. "They say he has eyes that see through lies. That he knows your heart before you speak. He doesn't fight with weapons alone—he fights with wisdom, with something deeper."

Yordan slowed further, his curiosity piqued despite his skepticism. He stopped just off the path, turning slightly toward the group. "Who are you talking about?" he asked, his tone even, though his expression betrayed his curiosity.

The wiry man looked up at Yordan, sizing him up before answering. "Ueuejtlakatl," he said, the name heavy with reverence. "The Great Elder. Protector of the Ojtlists near Nahualis. Some say he's a myth, but I've seen him. He's real."

Sam tilted his head slightly, his stick resting lightly against the ground. "And he protected Ojtlists from Lumites?" he asked, his tone calm but with a thread of doubt.

The older woman nodded. "Not just once. Many times. They say the Lumites fear him, though they'd never admit it. He doesn't just fight them, shames them. Shows them for what they really are."

Yordan folded his arms, his skepticism growing. "You're saying one man—one old man—has done all this? And the Lumites, with their armies and their power, haven't stopped him?"

The wiry man's eyes narrowed slightly. "You doubt it because you haven't seen what the Lumites have done. You haven't seen what he's saved us from."

Yordan glanced at Sam, who shifted slightly but didn't speak. The tension in the air was palpable, and Yordan's own unease deepened. The idea of an old man standing against an entire army seemed absurd, like something out of a child's tale. Yet the conviction in their voices, the raw desperation—it was hard to ignore.

Sam, sensing the tension in Yordan's silence, stepped in. His voice was polite but firm. "I hope you all have a safe journey," he said, nodding slightly in the direction of the refugees.

The older woman's gaze softened, and she inclined her head. "And to you, travelers. May the road be kinder to you than it's been to us."

As they resumed their walk, the conversation lingered in Yordan's mind. The description of Ueuejtlakatl—strong, wise, able to protect those in need—stirred something in him. Was this man real? Was he just a story the refugees told themselves to hold onto hope in desperate times?

Yordan wasn't sure what to believe. The scars he'd seen on the refugees, their hollowed expressions, and the certainty in their voices painted a grim picture of Lumite actions. But it still didn't fit the image of the Lumites he thought he knew. Could the truth be somewhere in between?

As the road stretched on, Yordan found himself wondering: if this Ueuejtlakatl was real, could he be worth seeking out? And if he was, what answers—or questions—might he bring? The thought lingered, quiet but persistent, as the valley gave way to the open road once more.

Chapter Six

The midday sun hung high in the sky, its light glinting off the slow-moving waters of the River Lumina. The river's gentle murmur wove through the air, mingling with the occasional rustle of leaves and the distant calls of birds. Yordan and Sam walked along its edge, their footsteps crunching softly against the dirt path. The day was calm, serene even, but Yordan couldn't shake the unease that had lingered since their encounter with the refugees.

The water sparkled as it meandered lazily, reflecting the vivid blues of the sky. Yordan found himself watching it closely, his thoughts drifting. There was something hypnotic about the river's flow, something that seemed to pull at his attention in ways he couldn't quite explain.

And then he heard it.

The words were soft at first, so faint that he thought it might have been the wind playing tricks on him. But as they grew louder, more distinct, he realized it wasn't the wind at all. The voice was ethereal, echoing as though carried from some distant, unseen source.

"Head up the mountain."

Yordan froze mid-step, his gaze snapping to the river. The words had come from there—or at least, that's how it felt. The water rippled gently, the sunlight catching its surface, but there was no sign of anything unusual.

"Sam," Yordan said cautiously, his voice low. He turned to his friend, who was tapping his stick lightly against the ground as he walked. "Did you say something just now?"

Sam stopped, tilting his head toward Yordan with a raised eyebrow. "Say something? No. Why?"

"I thought I heard..." Yordan trailed off, glancing back at the river. The voice still echoed faintly in his mind, the words lingering like the remnants of a dream. He shook his head, rubbing the back of his neck. "Never mind. It's probably nothing."

But Sam didn't let it go. His grip tightened slightly on his stick, his tone turning serious. "Yordan, don't do that. If something's bothering you, just say it. What did you hear?"

Yordan hesitated, unsure how to explain. The words had felt so real, so tangible, and yet saying them aloud made him feel ridiculous. Finally, he sighed, meeting Sam's unseeing gaze. "I thought I heard someone say, 'Head up the mountain.' Like a voice, but... not a normal one. It felt—" He stopped, searching for the right word. "—otherworldly."

Sam was silent for a moment, his face unreadable. Then he let out a low chuckle, shaking his head. "Otherworldly voices telling you to climb a mountain? That's not exactly comforting, Yordan."

"I know how it sounds," Yordan said quickly, his frustration bubbling up. "But I'm not making this up. It was real. I heard it."

Sam sighed, leaning slightly on his stick. "Yordan, you've been on edge since we left Aralonis. And I get it—this whole trip has been strange, to say the least. But if you're starting to hear voices... well, I'm going to be honest. That worries me."

Yordan frowned, turning back to the river. The words had felt so clear, so undeniable. He couldn't dismiss them as a figment of his imagination, not with the weight they carried. But Sam's doubt, his casual dismissal, stung more than he wanted to admit.

"I'm not losing it," Yordan said firmly, though the uncertainty in his voice betrayed him. "Something's happening, Sam. I don't know what it is, but it's real."

Sam stepped closer, resting a hand on Yordan's shoulder. His touch was steady, grounding. "Look," he said, his voice softer now. "I'm not saying you're losing it. I'm saying maybe you're carrying more than you realize. This journey, everything we've seen so far—it's a lot. And sometimes, when your mind is stretched thin, it starts playing tricks on you."

Yordan didn't respond immediately, his eyes fixed on the river. The water continued to flow, its surface calm and undisturbed. Yet he couldn't shake the feeling that it was watching him, waiting.

"Maybe," he said finally, though he didn't believe it. The voice had been too vivid, too distinct. But for now, he let the matter drop, unwilling to argue with Sam.

They continued walking, the path winding along the river's edge, the sounds of nature filling the silence between them. But Yordan's mind was far from at ease. The words echoed in his thoughts, a quiet but persistent refrain: Head up the mountain. Whatever it meant, he couldn't ignore it.

As Yordan and Sam pressed onward, the serene beauty of the Valley of Akeskauiya began to give way to a subtle tension that Yordan couldn't quite place. The winding path drew them closer to Lumina City, but the familiar comfort of the land felt distant.

Yordan's attention caught on something fluttering in the breeze ahead. As they drew closer, he realized it was a banner, its crimson fabric emblazoned with the unmistakable image of a lion's head. The sight made him slow his steps. The lion's head—an emblem of the Lumites, a symbol he had always associated with their faith and authority—was something he expected to see in Lumina City itself, not out here in the wilderness.

"Sam," Yordan said, his voice cautious. "There's a Lumite banner ahead."

Sam turned his head slightly, his stick tapping the ground. "Hanging from a tree?" he asked, his tone neutral but curious. "That's... strange, isn't it?"

"Yeah," Yordan replied, frowning. As they continued, more banners came into view, hanging from branches like silent sentinels marking the path. Some of the lion emblems were freshly painted, their colors vibrant against the muted tones of the forest. Others looked older, their edges frayed and weathered. Yordan noticed, with a growing unease, that the symbol wasn't just on banners—he saw it carved into the trunks of trees, the etchings deep and deliberate.

"Why carve it into the trees?" he muttered, more to himself than to Sam. "This feels... wrong."

Sam's nose wrinkled slightly, and he slowed his steps. "Do you smell that?" he asked, his voice quieter now.

Yordan paused, sniffing the air. At first, he couldn't place it, but as they walked further, the odor became unmistakable—an acrid, metallic tang that turned his stomach. It was the smell of blood.

"Yeah," Yordan said, his hand instinctively reaching for the hilt of his belt knife. "I smell it."

Sam's grip on his stick tightened, his expression tense. "What is it?"

Yordan's eyes scanned the trees ahead, the unease in his chest blooming into full-blown dread. And then he saw it.

Hanging from one of the larger trees just off the path was a man. His skin was dark, as deep as the soil after a heavy rain, and his body bore the marks of violence. His hands were nailed to separate branches, his arms stretched wide in a grotesque imitation of an embrace. His feet were pinned to the trunk, a thick nail driven through each one. Blood streaked his arms and legs, dripping onto the ground below in slow, steady rivulets.

Yordan's breath caught in his throat. The man's head hung low, his chest rising and falling in shallow breaths. He was alive—but barely.

"Please," the man whispered, his voice raspy and weak. He lifted his head slightly, his dark eyes meeting Yordan's. "Help me."

Yordan froze, the sheer horror of the scene rooting him in place. He had seen pain and suffering before—scars from war, injuries at the forge—but nothing like this. This was deliberate. Cruel. It wasn't just an act of violence; it was a statement.

"Yordan," Sam said, his voice sharp, pulling him out of his shock. "What is it? What's wrong?"

Yordan swallowed hard, his voice shaking as he replied. "There's a man. Nailed to the tree."

Sam's face paled, and he tightened his grip on his stick. "What? Is he...?"

"He's alive," Yordan interrupted, his feet moving before he even realized it. He stepped closer to the tree, his heart pounding. "Hold on," he said to the man, his voice firm but gentle. "We're going to get you down."

The man coughed weakly, his body shuddering with the effort. "Please," he whispered again, his words barely audible. "They left me here... to die."

Yordan clenched his fists, anger bubbling up inside him. Whoever had done this had wanted it to be seen—a gruesome warning to anyone who might defy them. His mind raced as he tried to figure out how to free the man without causing him further harm.

"Sam," Yordan called over his shoulder, his voice steady despite the storm raging inside him. "I'm going to need your help."

Sam nodded, stepping closer despite his obvious discomfort. "Just tell me what to do," he said, his voice resolute.

Yordan's eyes flicked back to the banners fluttering in the breeze, the lion's head emblazoned on each one. The symbol stared back at him, its silent roar mocking him. This wasn't just cruelty—it was a message. And Yordan wasn't sure if he was ready to understand it.

Yordan took a deep breath, his eyes fixed on the gruesome scene before him. The man hung limply from the tree, his dark skin streaked with blood and his breaths shallow. Every instinct in Yordan screamed to act, but he knew he needed a plan.

"Sam," Yordan said, his voice steady despite the knot in his chest. "I need you to support his legs. I'm going to climb up and see if I can free his hands first."

Sam hesitated for only a moment before nodding. He planted his stick firmly into the ground and stepped forward, feeling for the man's legs. His hands found the bloodied limbs, and he braced himself beneath them. "I've got him," Sam said, his voice strained but determined. "Do what you have to."

Yordan scanned the ground quickly and spotted a smooth, heavy rock near the river bend. Grabbing it, he wiped it clean with his sleeve and approached the tree. He placed his hands on the rough bark, testing the hold, then began to climb. The tree was sturdy, its branches thick and unyielding, but the task felt monumental with the man's groans of pain echoing in his ears.

As he reached the man's first arm, Yordan examined the nail driven through the hand into the branch. It was long and rusted, but to his relief, it wasn't embedded deeply into the wood. He positioned the rock against the flat head of the nail, his heart pounding.

"Hold on," he said softly, glancing at the man's pained face. "I'm going to get you free."

The man groaned weakly in response, his head lolling to one side. Yordan gritted his teeth and began tapping the rock against the nail. The impact was awkward, but slowly, the nail began to loosen. Each strike sent vibrations through the branch, and he could feel the strain in his arm as he worked.

With a final, firm strike, the nail dislodged from the branch, and the man's arm fell free. Yordan grabbed it quickly, steadying the limb to prevent it from jerking too hard. "One down," he muttered, sweat dripping down his brow.

He shifted to the other arm, noticing the same situation: the nail was driven through the branch but not impossibly deep. He repositioned the rock, his muscles already aching from the effort, and began hammering again. The man groaned louder this time, the sound raw with pain.

"I'm sorry," Yordan murmured, his voice tight. He didn't stop, knowing hesitation would only prolong the agony. With another series of strikes, the second nail gave way, and the man's other arm dropped. Yordan caught it carefully, lowering it as gently as he could.

Breathing heavily, Yordan looked down at the man's feet, still pinned to the trunk. These nails were different, driven deep into the solid wood of the tree. There was no way to hammer them out without potentially harming the man further. He grimaced, his mind racing.

"Sam," Yordan called down, a sudden thought striking him. "Do you have a frying pan in your pack?"

Sam, still holding the man's legs, groaned slightly under the strain. "A frying pan? Yes, why? You planning to cook something while I'm holding a bleeding man?"

"Just hold him steady," Yordan replied, urgency cutting through his voice. He scrambled down the tree, quickly digging through Sam's gear until his fingers closed around the familiar handle of the pan. He held it up triumphantly. "Got it."

Climbing back up, Yordan wedged the lip of the pan beneath the first nail in the man's foot. The leverage was just enough to begin prying it loose. The man groaned in agony, his body jerking slightly, but Yordan pressed on.

"I'm sorry," Yordan said again, his voice almost pleading. "I know this hurts, but we'll get you down."

Using the pan as a lever, Yordan managed to loosen the nail enough to finish the job with the rock. With a series of firm strikes, the nail finally came free, and the man's first foot fell from the trunk. Yordan quickly shifted to the other foot, repeating the process. The man's groans grew quieter, his strength clearly waning, but Yordan worked as quickly as he could.

Finally, the second nail gave way, and Yordan caught the man's leg as it dropped. "Sam," he called, his voice strained. "We've got him. Lower him slowly."

Sam nodded, his face set with determination as he adjusted his grip on the man's legs. Together, they eased the man down, careful not to jostle him too much. When he was finally on the ground, Yordan knelt beside him, pulling a water flask from his own pack.

"Here," he said, holding it to the man's lips. "Drink."

The man's eyes fluttered open briefly, and he managed a small sip, his throat working weakly. Yordan supported his head, watching as some color returned to his face, though his breathing remained shallow.

"Who did this to you?" Yordan asked softly, though part of him dreaded the answer.

The man's eyes flickered, his voice barely a whisper. "The lion... the banners... Lumites."

Yordan felt his chest tighten, the familiar symbol from earlier flashing through his mind. He clenched his jaw, the weight of what he had seen settling heavily on his shoulders.

Sam, still catching his breath, leaned close. "What do we do now?"

Yordan didn't answer immediately. He stared at the man, his injuries, the cruelty of the act, and the symbol etched into the banners and trees. His mind swirled with doubt, anger, and a growing sense of urgency.

"We help him," he said finally, his voice steady despite the storm raging inside him. "And then we figure out what's really going on."

The sun hung low in the sky as Yordan and Sam trudged toward Lumina City, the wounded man slung between them. Each step was an effort, the man's weight pulling at their already tired muscles, but neither complained. The man's breathing was shallow, and Yordan could feel the heat of his fever radiating through his torn shirt. They needed help—and soon.

As they rounded a bend in the road, the city walls of Lumina came into view in the distance, their pale stone reflecting the golden light of the setting sun. But before they could reach the gates, a checkpoint emerged ahead: three armored guards standing beside a makeshift barricade. Their presence, though unexpected, brought a flicker of hope to Yordan's chest. Surely, they would help.

The guards were clad in polished steel plate armor, the sun glinting off its surfaces. Each breastplate bore the unmistakable emblem of the lion's head, a roaring symbol of Lumite authority, its eyes fierce and unyielding. The same symbol was etched into their shoulder pauldrons and engraved onto the crests of their helms. The rest of their armor was practical yet intimidating, with dark leather straps securing plates over chainmail. They were armed with swords sheathed at their sides and small round shields strapped to their backs, also emblazoned with the lion.

Yordan called out as they approached, his voice hoarse but hopeful. "Help! Please! We found this man nailed to a tree—he's badly hurt!"

The guards turned toward them, their postures stiffening as their eyes fell on the group. One of the guards, clearly the leader, stepped forward, his hand resting on the hilt of his sword. His face was obscured by his helm, but his voice carried a sharp, commanding tone. "What's this?"

"We found him in the valley," Yordan explained, panting slightly from the effort of carrying the man. "He's injured—someone nailed him to a tree. We need help!"

The second guard exchanged a glance with the leader, his expression darkening. The leader's hand tightened on his sword, and the tension in the air became palpable. Instead of moving to assist, the guard barked an order that froze Yordan in his tracks.

"Arrest them."

"What?" Yordan's voice cracked with disbelief. He stepped back instinctively, his grip tightening on the man's arm. "We're asking for help! He's dying!"

The third guard, who had been standing silently by his horse, mounted it swiftly at the leader's signal. "Ride back to the outpost," the leader ordered. "Bring a unit. Have them nail that heretic back where they found him."

The words struck Yordan like a blow to the chest. His mind reeled, struggling to process what he had just heard. "What are you talking about?" he shouted. "He's hurt—he needs care, not... not that!"

The leader ignored him, drawing his sword with a metallic scrape. The second guard advanced, his gauntleted hand grabbing Yordan's shoulder and shoving him to the ground with brutal force. Yordan landed face-first in the dirt, the impact jarring his ribs and sending a sharp pain shooting through his side.

"No!" Yordan yelled, twisting against the weight of the guard's knee pressing into his back. "This doesn't make any sense! We were trying to help!"

Sam, too, was forced to the ground, his stick knocked from his hand as the guards restrained him. Yordan's chest heaved as his cheek pressed into the dirt. His mind raced, a whirlwind of confusion and anger. Why were they being treated like criminals? The man they'd carried was barely alive—how could they look at him and decide to nail him back to a tree?

"You're making a mistake!" Yordan shouted, his voice muffled by the ground. He twisted his head, trying to catch a glimpse of the guards, but all he could see were their boots as they moved around him. "We're not the enemy here!"

"Quiet," the leader snapped, his voice cold and unyielding. "Troublemakers like you think you can defy Lumite law and get away with it. Not on my watch."

Yordan felt his wrists being wrenched behind his back, a rough rope biting into his skin as they bound him tightly. His body tensed with rage and helplessness, his mind screaming against the injustice of it all.

"Sam," Yordan called out, his voice quieter now, tinged with desperation. "I'm sorry."

Sam's voice came from nearby, strained but steady. "We're not dead yet, Yordan. Save your apologies for later. For now... try not to get yourself killed."

As the guards hauled Yordan and Sam to their feet, Yordan's eyes flicked toward the man they had tried to save. He was slumped on the ground, barely conscious, his dark skin pale from blood loss. The third guard was already galloping down the road, leaving dust in his wake.

Yordan's heart sank as he realized the full weight of their situation. This wasn't just a misunderstanding—it was something far worse. The lion's head emblems seemed to glare down at him, their silent roars a cruel mockery of his desperate pleas for justice.

For now, all he could do was grit his teeth and wait for a chance to act.

The sound of approaching hooves and clinking armor filled the air as the unit arrived. The rhythmic stomping of boots soon followed as a dozen soldiers, all bearing the lion's head emblem on their breastplates, dismounted or fell into formation. The leader of the checkpoint barked orders, splitting the soldiers into two groups.

"Take the heretic back to the tree," the leader commanded, pointing at the bloodied man Yordan and Sam had tried to save. "Make sure the punishment is carried out this time. The rest of you, with me. These two are heading to the Luminous Throne."

Yordan's stomach twisted as half the soldiers hefted the injured man like cargo, his limp form barely stirring as they carried him back toward the tree. Yordan opened his mouth to protest, but the sharp glare from one of the guards silenced him. His heart ached with helplessness as he watched them disappear down the road.

"Move," a guard barked, shoving Yordan roughly in the back.

The remaining soldiers surrounded Yordan and Sam, their weapons at the ready, as they began their march toward Lumina City. The sun was beginning to set, casting long shadows over the road as the group passed through the outskirts of the valley and into the more populated areas leading to the city gates.

As they entered Lumina City, Yordan couldn't help but take in the sights, though the circumstances made his observations bitter. The city was grander than he had imagined, its streets wide and meticulously paved with pale stone. Tall buildings of white limestone rose on either side, their facades adorned with intricate carvings of the lion's head and depictions of Lumite scripture. The streets bustled with life—merchants shouting their wares, children chasing each other, and robed priests reciting prayers at small shrines lining the roads.

Here and there, banners bearing the lion's emblem hung from windows and poles, their bright crimson fabric glowing in the light of the setting sun. Yordan's gaze lingered on a towering statue of a Lumite king, his stone likeness carved with precision and majesty, holding a scepter topped with the lion's head. It was a city steeped in pride and power, every detail a testament to the Lumites' belief in their divine right to rule.

Despite the grandeur, Yordan couldn't shake the anger simmering inside him. This wasn't how he wanted to see Lumina City—not as a prisoner, marched through the streets like a criminal. His wrists burned against the ropes that bound him, and every step felt like a mockery of the curiosity he'd once held about this place.

He glanced over his shoulder, catching sight of Sam. His friend's face was blank, unreadable, but Yordan could sense the tension in his posture, the quiet strength he used to hold himself together. Sam didn't speak, didn't complain. He simply walked, his stick gone but his steps still steady.

As they approached the heart of the city, the Luminous Throne came into view. It was a massive structure, its white stone walls gleaming in the fading light. The palace rose in tiers, each level adorned with ornate carvings and intricate reliefs depicting Lumite victories and divine blessings. At the center of the highest tier stood the throne itself, a grand seat carved from black obsidian, its base surrounded by a pool of shimmering water that reflected the fading light like molten gold.

The soldiers led Yordan and Sam past the public square and into the palace's lower levels, where the grandeur gave way to cold practicality. The air grew damp and stale as they descended into the dungeons beneath the throne. Iron-barred cells lined the stone walls, their interiors dimly lit by flickering torches.

Yordan and Sam were shoved into a cell, the heavy clang of the iron door slamming shut behind them echoing through the corridor. Yordan stumbled slightly, catching himself on the wall as he turned to face the guard standing on the other side of the bars.

The guard crossed his arms, looking them over with a mix of suspicion and disdain. "You two don't look like you're from around here," he said, his tone sharp. "Where are you from?"

Yordan hesitated for a moment before answering. "Aralonis."

The guard's eyes narrowed slightly, as if filing away the information, but he didn't say anything else. Instead, he turned and marched down the corridor, his boots echoing on the stone floor until they faded into silence.

Yordan let out a frustrated breath, sinking onto the small wooden bench in the corner of the cell. He leaned back against the cold stone wall, staring at the ceiling as he tried to process everything that had happened. "Sam," he said after a moment, his voice quiet. "You alright?"

"As alright as I can be," Sam replied, his tone light despite the situation. He sat cross-legged on the floor, his posture relaxed but his blank gaze fixed on nothing. "You know, for someone who can't see, getting arrested for trying to help someone is still a new experience."

Yordan let out a weak laugh, shaking his head. "Yeah, well, at least we're breaking new ground."

Despite the grim circumstances, Sam's calm presence steadied Yordan. But as he sat there, the weight of the lion's emblem loomed in his mind, its symbol etched into the stone walls of the palace above them. This wasn't just a misunderstanding—it was the beginning of something far more dangerous. And Yordan wasn't sure if he or Sam would get the chance to see the other side of it.

The sound of heavy boots echoed through the stone corridor, rousing Yordan from a restless sleep. He blinked, disoriented by the dim light and the stale air of the cell. Sam stirred beside him, lifting his head slightly as the creak of the iron door reached his ears.

The door opened fully, revealing three figures who stepped into the torchlight. The man in the center was the first to catch Yordan's attention. He was unassuming at first glance, dressed in finely tailored but simple clothing—a dark tunic and trousers, accented by subtle embroidery. His neatly combed dark hair was streaked with silver at the temples, and his face bore an air of calm composure. His presence, however, felt heavier than his appearance suggested, as if authority emanated from him effortlessly.

To his right stood a tall, broad-shouldered man clad in polished armor. The lion's head emblem gleamed prominently on his chest plate, and his sharp features were marked by a deep scar running from his cheekbone to his jaw. His piercing hazel eyes scanned the room with the precision of a man used to assessing danger.

To the left of the central figure was a lean, wiry man dressed in flowing crimson and gold robes. His olive-toned skin was deeply lined, and his dark eyes, though tired, carried an intense sharpness. A finely wrought chain of office hung from his neck, bearing the lion's head medallion—a symbol of his high rank.

The man in the center stepped forward, his demeanor surprisingly warm and almost apologetic. He spread his hands in a welcoming gesture.

"Please, rise up, fellow Aralonites," he said, his tone soft and inviting. "I apologize for the discomfort of your accommodations. Let me introduce myself and my companions." He gestured first to the armored man. "This is General Yoav, commander of my armies and a loyal servant of Lumina City."

The armored man, Yoav, gave a curt nod but said nothing, his gaze fixed on Yordan and Sam as if already calculating their potential threat.

"And this," the man continued, motioning to the robed figure, "is Chancellor Yusuf, my trusted advisor and counselor." Yusuf inclined his head slightly, his expression neutral but not unkind.

The man then rested his hand lightly on his chest. "As for me, my name is Benjamin."

Yordan's breath caught. He had heard stories of King Benjamin, the ruler of Lumina City, the man whose authority shaped Anakuatl. He hadn't expected the king to appear so... ordinary. Yet, there was no mistaking the weight of his presence.

Sam, still seated, tilted his head toward the voice, his expression unreadable. Yordan steadied himself and asked pointedly, "Do you have my friend's stick? You may not have been able to tell, but he's blind."

Benjamin's gaze shifted to Sam, his demeanor remaining calm and accommodating. "Of course," he replied smoothly. "All your gear is ready and waiting for you to take it when the time comes."

Sam reached for Yordan's arm, gripping it as he rose to his feet. Yordan helped steady him, the tension in the air thickening as he processed the situation.

"Why was that man nailed to the tree?" Yordan asked suddenly, his tone measured but firm.

The question hung in the air like a blade. All three men froze. Yoav's scarred face hardened, his hand instinctively brushing the hilt of his sword. Yusuf's expression flickered, a faint shadow of discomfort passing over his features before he returned to his practiced neutrality. Benjamin, however, did not react immediately. He stood still, his eyes meeting Yordan's directly.

When Benjamin spoke, his tone was calm but carried an edge of finality. "He was a troublemaker," he said evenly. "Someone who sought to turn Lumites away from Toteko and his divine message. Such actions cannot be tolerated."

Yordan felt Sam's grip on his arm tighten—a silent warning. Yordan's chest burned with unspoken anger, but he held his tongue, aware of the weight of their current situation.

"Please," Benjamin said, gesturing toward the open cell door. "Follow me."

With no other choice, Yordan and Sam stepped forward, guided by Benjamin's calm but commanding presence. Yoav and Yusuf fell into step behind them, the silence of their movements unnerving. As they walked through the dim corridors of the jail, Yordan couldn't shake the image of the man nailed to the tree—or the way Benjamin's serene demeanor seemed to mask something far darker.

As they ascended from the damp, shadowy corridors of the jail, the air grew lighter, though the tension hanging between the group remained oppressive. The faint smell of damp stone gave way to the faint aroma of incense wafting from somewhere above. King Benjamin led the way, his steps measured and deliberate, his demeanor seemingly unruffled. Yordan and Sam followed closely, with Yoav and Yusuf flanking them, the guards' boots echoing on the polished stone floors.

Benjamin glanced back at Yordan and Sam, his face composed, his voice as smooth as a diplomat's. "I must say," he began, "I understand your instinct—your compassion—to help someone you saw in pain. It is admirable in its own way." His tone was warm, almost paternal, yet it carried a weight that demanded attention.

Yordan, still clutching Sam's arm for guidance, felt a flicker of cautious hope. Perhaps this man wasn't as cold as he feared. Perhaps this was all a misunderstanding.

"However," Benjamin continued, his voice hardening slightly, "compassion must always be tempered with understanding of the law. You are not residents of Lumina City, so you could not have known our customs or the reasons for our actions. It is for that reason, and that reason alone, that I extend my forgiveness this time."

Yordan's heart sank slightly, the hope dimming. He didn't miss the emphasis on this time.

"If you were to intervene in such a matter again," Benjamin said, his gaze steady, "I would have no choice but to enforce our laws. And that would mean remaining in the jail—not for a night, but indefinitely. Do I make myself clear?"

"Yes," Yordan replied softly, his throat tightening.

Sam said nothing, his face impassive as he walked alongside Yordan. But Yordan could feel the tension in his friend's grip, a silent acknowledgment of the thin ice they were treading on.

As they reached the top of the staircase, the grand doors to the palace loomed ahead, their golden inlays shimmering in the torchlight. Intricate carvings of the Lumite lion and depictions of Toteko adorned the towering wooden panels, a testament to the craftsmanship and wealth of the kingdom. Benjamin paused before the doors and turned to face Yordan and Sam.

"You'll want these," he said, bending to retrieve a bundle of belongings laid neatly at the base of the stairs. He handed Yordan his gear, his expression unreadable, before passing Sam his stick and pack. "I trust you will find everything in order."

Yordan took the gear silently, slinging it over his shoulder. He handed Sam the stick, which his friend gripped tightly, his expression still unreadable.

Before they could move, Yoav stepped forward, his armored presence imposing as his sharp eyes bore into Yordan. "What is your purpose here, Aralonites?" he asked, his voice stern and edged with suspicion.

Yordan hesitated, his mind racing for an answer, but Sam spoke first, his tone calm and measured. "Travelers," he said simply. "We just wanted to see Lumina City and its many wonders."

Yoav's lips pressed into a thin line, his suspicion clearly unshaken, but before he could respond, Yusuf stepped forward with a soft smile that seemed almost out of place. "See, Yoav?" Yusuf said, his voice was gentle but confident. "No reason to fear. They are just two people from Aralonis, here to admire our beautiful culture."

Yordan's heart lifted slightly at Yusuf's words, though he couldn't fully let go of his unease. Yoav, however, didn't look convinced. He grunted, his hand resting on the hilt of his sword, before motioning for them to follow him.

The grand doors creaked open, revealing the sprawling entrance courtyard of the palace. Ornate columns lined the space, each one etched with symbols of Lumite faith and history. The moonlight bathed the marble floor, casting long shadows that danced with the flicker of torches.

Yoav walked ahead, his armored boots striking the ground with purpose. He led Yordan and Sam through the courtyard, the vastness of the palace's majesty pressing down on Yordan's chest. Despite his growing distrust, Yordan couldn't help but feel a flicker of awe at the craftsmanship and grandeur surrounding him.

As they reached the outer gate, Yoav pulled it open with a sharp, deliberate motion. He stood aside, gesturing curtly for Yordan and Sam to leave.

"Safe travels," Yoav said, though his tone carried no warmth.

Yordan and Sam stepped out into the cool night air, the gate slamming shut behind them with a resounding finality that echoed through the quiet streets.

For a moment, Yordan stood still, staring at the gate. His mind whirled with conflicting emotions, relief at being free, anger at the injustice they had witnessed, and a faint, naive hope that perhaps this had all been a misunderstanding.

Sam's voice broke the silence. "You alright?" he asked, his tone light but edged with concern.

Yordan nodded slowly, his gaze still fixed on the closed gate. "Yeah," he said, though he wasn't sure he believed it. As they began walking away from the palace, the weight of the evening pressed heavily on his shoulders, and the flicker of hope that had lingered within him felt fainter than ever.

Chapter Seven

The night air was cool and crisp as Yordan and Sam walked away from the palace, their steps echoing softly on the cobblestone streets of Lumina City. The towering silhouette of the Luminous Throne loomed behind them, its grand architecture bathed in pale moonlight. Yordan adjusted the strap of his pack, his thoughts swirling with unanswered questions.

After a few moments of silence, Yordan broke it with a question that had been gnawing at him. "What do you think that was all about?" he asked, his voice low but curious.

Sam tapped his stick lightly on the ground as he walked, his face tilted slightly upward as if listening to something Yordan couldn't hear. For a moment, he didn't respond, his brow furrowing in thought.

"I'm still trying to make sense of it," Sam said finally, his tone measured. "There's a lot to unpack, and I'm not sure I've got it all straight yet."

Yordan glanced at him, a flicker of concern crossing his face. He had always relied on Sam's ability to analyze situations, to see through the

111

surface of things even when he couldn't physically see. That his friend wasn't ready to share his thoughts yet made Yordan uneasy.

"Come on," Yordan pressed lightly, trying to coax something more out of him. "You must have some idea. They let us go, gave us our stuff back... Benjamin even seemed almost... reasonable."

Sam let out a quiet breath, his fingers tightening slightly on his stick. "Reasonable?" he echoed, a hint of incredulity in his voice. He didn't elaborate, letting the word hang in the air as they continued down the street.

The city was alive even at this hour, its streets bustling with Luminites going about their evening routines. Vendors with carts of glowing lanterns called out to passersby, and robed priests walked in clusters, their hushed conversations blending with the distant hum of activity. The Grand Temple of Toteko began to rise in the distance, its towering spires reaching toward the heavens like silent sentinels. Its golden dome gleamed faintly in the moonlight, the symbol of Toteko carved into its façade catching Yordan's eye.

"I don't know," Yordan admitted, his voice quieter now. "Benjamin didn't seem like what I expected. He didn't bark orders or throw his weight around. He even seemed to... understand, in a way."

Sam let out a low hum, his expression still unreadable. "Maybe," he said after a pause, "but we should be wary of him."

Yordan frowned, glancing at Sam again. "Wary? Why? He let us go, Sam. He could've kept us in that cell, or worse."

Sam stopped tapping his stick for a moment, his fingers gripping it tightly. "Exactly," he said, his voice firm. "He could have. But he didn't. That's not something I take lightly."

Yordan sighed, running a hand through his hair. "You're overthinking this," he said, his tone edging toward frustration. "Benjamin didn't seem cruel. And that man on the tree..." He hesitated, the image flashing in his mind. "Maybe he was... I don't know, a bad apple. Someone who was actually stirring up trouble."

Sam's face remained impassive, but he tilted his head slightly toward Yordan. "Is that what you think?" he asked, his tone carefully neutral.

"I'm just trying to see the best in all this," Yordan replied, his voice softening. "Not everything has to be sinister, Sam."

Sam didn't respond immediately. They continued walking, the sounds of the city filling the silence between them. The Grand Temple grew closer with each step, its sheer size and intricate design becoming more imposing as they approached. Golden statues of lion heads adorned its entrance, flanking the massive double doors, and lines of worshippers filtered in and out, their faces lit with reverence.

"I hope you're right," Sam said finally, his voice quiet but tinged with doubt. "I really do."

Yordan nodded, taking his friend's words as agreement rather than caution. He glanced at the temple ahead, its grandeur stirring a mix of awe and unease in him. But deep down, he held onto the belief that Benjamin's actions had been measured, even justified. It was easier that way, less complicated.

Yet, as they neared the temple's steps, Yordan couldn't shake the lingering shadow of doubt that clung to the edges of his thoughts—a shadow he was doing his best to ignore. For now, he chose to focus on the path ahead, the looming spires of the Grand Temple offering a distraction from the uncertainties that waited in the wings.

The vibrant hum of the city enveloped Yordan and Sam as they continued down the bustling streets. Lumina City at night was alive in ways Yordan hadn't anticipated—street vendors hawked their wares from stalls lit by soft-glowing lanterns, the warm light spilling over displays of fruits, roasted meats, and intricately spiced pastries. The air was rich with the mingling aromas of grilled skewers, sweet breads, and tangy sauces, and Yordan's stomach growled audibly, reminding him how long it had been since their last meal.

"Let's grab something to eat," Yordan suggested, nudging Sam lightly. "We've got some coin left from Aralonis. I'm sure one of these stalls will take it."

Sam tilted his head slightly, listening to the chatter of the marketplace. "I won't argue with that," he said. "Just make sure it's not something that'll leave us worse off than hungry."

Yordan chuckled, scanning the stalls until he spotted a vendor with a modest setup—a small cart laden with skewered meats sizzling over a charcoal grill. The vendor, a wiry man with a weathered face and a tightly tied crimson headscarf, flipped the skewers with practiced efficiency. His eyes flicked to Yordan and Sam as they approached, his expression unreadable.

"Two skewers," Yordan said, holding out a few coins. The vendor's gaze lingered on them for a moment too long, his hand hovering over the coins before he accepted them. He didn't speak, instead turning to retrieve two freshly grilled skewers, which he handed over with a curt nod.

"Thanks," Yordan said, though the man had already turned back to his work. Yordan exchanged a glance with Sam, who seemed to sense the same subtle tension in the interaction but chose not to comment.

As they walked away, Yordan bit into the skewer. The meat was tender, with a smoky char and a tangy glaze that hinted at unfamiliar spices. "Not bad," he said between bites, trying to brush off the odd feeling the vendor's demeanor had left him with. "What do you think?"

Sam, chewing thoughtfully, gave a small shrug. "Could use a bit more salt," he said lightly, though there was an undertone of detachment in his voice.

The streets seemed busier now, the flow of people thickening as they moved closer to the Grand Temple of Toteko. Yordan couldn't help but notice the looks they were getting—passing glances that lingered a second too long, subtle whispers exchanged between clusters of Lumites. Their gazes flicked between him and Sam, their expressions ranging from mild curiosity to faint disapproval.

"Are they staring at us?" Yordan muttered under his breath, leaning slightly toward Sam.

Sam tapped his stick lightly on the cobblestones, his lips quirking in a faint smile. "Hard to tell from my end," he replied dryly. "But I can feel the change in the air. Something's shifted."

Yordan tried to brush it off, telling himself it was nothing more than the natural reaction to strangers in a tightly knit city. But the weight of their gazes pressed on him, and he found himself gripping his skewer tighter, his appetite fading with each step.

The Grand Temple of Toteko loomed ahead, its golden spires gleaming faintly in the lantern light. The closer they got, the more Yordan felt its presence—imposing and awe-inspiring. The wide marble steps leading up to the entrance were flanked by massive statues of roaring lions, their expressions fierce and majestic. Worshippers moved in a steady flow, some bowing deeply as they entered, others emerging with serene expressions and folded hands.

Yordan and Sam paused at the base of the steps, finishing their skewers. Yordan tossed his into a nearby bin, watching the crowd as he wiped his hands on his trousers. The murmurs and sidelong glances didn't stop, and he couldn't shake the feeling that their presence was more than just a curiosity.

"Still think I'm being paranoid?" Sam asked softly, his tone laced with a mix of humor and seriousness.

Yordan hesitated, his eyes scanning the crowd. "They're just not used to seeing people like us," he said, though the words felt hollow even as he spoke them. "It's not a big deal."

Sam tilted his head slightly, as if listening to something only he could hear. "Maybe," he said after a moment, his voice noncommittal. "Let's hope you're right."

Yordan forced a smile, trying to shake off the unease creeping into his chest. They were here to see the wonders of Lumina City, to take in its culture and history—not to dwell on unfriendly stares. With a deep breath, he gestured toward the temple.

As Yordan and Sam approached the Grand Temple of Toteko, the scale of the structure became almost overwhelming. Its golden spires reached toward the heavens, the polished marble steps gleaming even under the dim light of the lanterns. The massive double doors, engraved with intricate depictions of Toteko and flanked by roaring lion statues, seemed to radiate authority and power.

At the base of the steps, three distinct lines had formed, each marked by a stone-carved sign atop a post. The first sign, adorned with a gilded lion's head, read Lumites. The line was bustling, filled with people dressed in the traditional crimson and gold robes of Lumina City, their heads high with confidence as they moved forward. Yordan noticed immediately how quickly the Lumite line flowed, with almost no delay as individuals entered and exited the temple in an uninterrupted rhythm.

The second sign, slightly smaller and etched with a simpler script, read Aralonites. The line consisted of individuals like Yordan and Sam—clad in neutral earth-toned clothes, many looking dusty and travel-worn. This line moved painfully slowly, advancing perhaps once after fifty Lumites entered or exited.

The third line read Zetians. This group stood with quiet patience, their expressions solemn but their eyes alert. Unlike the other two lines, the Zetian line didn't appear to move at all. Yordan scanned the group, noting the variety of their features, clothing, and the sense of quiet dignity in their demeanor. Yet, despite their calm, he couldn't ignore the frustration simmering beneath their stillness.

Yordan and Sam made their way to the line for Aralonites. Yordan sighed, adjusting the pack on his shoulder as he stood behind a man with a wide-brimmed hat, his face shadowed by the dim light. Sam tapped his stick lightly on the cobblestones, leaning slightly toward Yordan.

"Three lines," Sam said, his tone even but curious. "What's the deal?"

"Lumites, Aralonites, Zetians," Yordan replied quietly. He nodded toward the signs, though he knew Sam couldn't see them. "It's like they've got us all sorted out."

Sam hummed thoughtfully, tilting his head slightly. "And the flow of traffic?"

Yordan grimaced as he watched the Lumite line move smoothly forward. Another cluster of Lumites was ushered into the temple, their vibrant robes swishing as they ascended the marble steps. Meanwhile, his own line hadn't moved since they joined it. The Zetian line remained completely stationary, its people standing like statues, their eyes fixed forward as if daring someone to challenge them.

"It's... uneven," Yordan said, frustration creeping into his voice. "Lumites are pouring through like water in a stream. We've barely moved. And the Zetians? They haven't moved at all."

Sam turned his face slightly, his expression unreadable. "Seems fair," he said dryly.

Yordan let out a humorless chuckle, shaking his head. "Fair's not the word I'd use."

The line crept forward by a single step, and Yordan exhaled, trying to ignore the growing tension in the air. The disparity between the lines was impossible to ignore, and it gnawed at him. He wanted to believe this was just an efficient way to manage the flow of people, but the sharp divide felt deliberate, calculated.

"You noticing anything else?" Sam asked, his tone calm but edged with curiosity.

Yordan glanced around, his eyes scanning the area. He caught glimpses of Lumite guards stationed near the temple doors, their polished armor catching the light. Their hands rested casually on the hilts of their swords, their expressions bored but alert. The people in the Lumite line moved with ease, exchanging smiles and light conversation, while the Aralonites shuffled forward in near silence, their movements subdued. The Zetians, however, stood in resolute stillness, their presence a quiet defiance.

"It's not just the lines," Yordan said, lowering his voice. "It's everything. The way the Lumites move, the way the guards watch us—" He stopped himself, shaking his head. "Maybe I'm just tired."

Sam tilted his head, his lips quirking in a faint smile. "Maybe you're starting to see what I see."

Yordan frowned, his gaze drifting back to the Zetian line. One of the guards glanced their way, his eyes narrowing briefly before returning to his post. Yordan straightened, the weight of the moment pressing down on him. He wanted to dismiss Sam's words, to tell himself that this was just the way things worked in Lumina City, that it wasn't personal. But the unease in his chest wouldn't go away.

"We'll get in," Yordan said quietly, more to himself than to Sam. "We just have to wait."

Sam didn't respond immediately. His fingers drummed lightly against his stick as the line inched forward again—just once, while the Lumites surged ahead. "Patience," Sam said finally, his tone unreadable. "That's all we've got."

As they stood in the sluggish Aralonite line, the grandeur of the Grand Temple of Toteko loomed above them, its golden dome gleaming faintly in the moonlight. The disparity between the lines was impossible to ignore, and Yordan couldn't shake the feeling that this was more than just a temple visit. It was a reminder of something deeper, something that lingered in the shadows of this shining city.

The Aralonite line inched forward with excruciating slowness, the shuffle of weary feet and low murmurs of the crowd providing a monotonous backdrop. Yordan shifted his weight from one foot to the other, glancing occasionally at the Zetian line. It still hadn't moved, the same figures standing in place, their quiet patience unnerving in its intensity. Yordan's curiosity finally got the better of him.

Leaning slightly forward, he addressed the older man standing in front of him in the line. "Excuse me, sir," he said hesitantly. "Why doesn't the Zetian line move?"

The man turned to look at Yordan, his brow furrowed as if Yordan had just asked why the sky was blue. His expression was both puzzled and faintly exasperated. "Don't worry about it, son," he said curtly, his tone suggesting that the question was either naïve or dangerous—or both.

Yordan's cheeks flushed with embarrassment, and he immediately regretted asking. The older man's face softened slightly, but the message was clear: Drop it. The awkward silence that followed made Yordan wish he could fade into the crowd. He gave a sheepish nod and stepped back, deciding against any follow-up. The older man's gaze returned to the front of the line, his shoulders stiff with tension.

Time dragged on, slow progress making every moment feel like an eternity. Yordan stole occasional glances at the Lumite line, which continued to flow effortlessly into the temple, its members greeted warmly and ushered inside without pause. Meanwhile, the Aralonite line crept forward at a pace so slow it felt deliberate. By the time they reached the front, it felt as if two hours had passed.

Finally, a guard waved them forward, his expression neutral but his posture imposing. "Next," he called flatly, stepping aside to allow Yordan and Sam to pass.

As they stepped into the temple, the change in atmosphere was immediate. The noise of the bustling city faded into the background, replaced by the hushed reverence of the temple's interior. The ceiling soared high above them, its golden dome decorated with intricate mosaics depicting Toteko's divine radiance. Marble columns lined the hall, each one etched with prayers and adorned with golden lion motifs. Incense wafted through the air, filling the space with a heady, almost overwhelming aroma of frankincense and myrrh.

Sam tapped his stick lightly on the polished floor, turning his head toward Yordan. "Describe it to me," he said, his voice soft but insistent. "What do you see?"

Yordan took a moment to take it all in, his eyes moving across the sprawling temple. "It's... massive," he said, his voice tinged with awe. "The ceiling's covered in mosaics—gold and... I don't know, like these radiant patterns. There are columns everywhere, and they've got carvings of prayers, I think, and lions. A lot of lions."

Sam nodded slowly, his face calm but intent. "And the people?"

Yordan glanced around, noticing the crowd within the temple. Most of them were Lumites, dressed in crimson and gold, their movements fluid and unhurried. Some were kneeling in prayer, their hands clasped, and heads bowed, while others stood in small groups, chatting quietly as if in a marketplace rather than a sacred space.

"There are a lot of Lumites," Yordan said, his voice lowering as he observed more closely. "Some are praying, but... a lot of them are just talking. Like they're catching up with friends."

As he spoke, his attention was drawn to a group standing near one of the columns—a mix of men and women, their conversation punctuated with soft laughter. Their tones were lighthearted, but the words that reached Yordan's ears carried a cutting edge.

"Good thing the Zetians aren't getting in today," one of the women said, her voice lilting but cold. "Last time, they were like animals. No sense of how to act in a sacred space."

A man beside her chuckled, shaking his head. "You'd think they'd get the message by now. They don't belong here."

Another woman, younger than the first, leaned in. "It's embarrassing," she said, her voice dripping with disdain. "They don't even try to fit in. They're just... uncivilized."

The words hit Yordan harder than he expected. The casual cruelty, spoken with such ease amidst the splendor of the temple, clashed starkly with the supposed sanctity of the place. He tried to look away, focusing instead on guiding Sam further inside, but the comments lingered, an echo in his mind.

"Anything else?" Sam asked after a pause, his voice gentle but probing.

Yordan hesitated, swallowing against the unease rising in his chest. "Just... people talking. Lumites everywhere. Not many others."

Sam nodded again, his lips pressing into a thin line. "Figured as much."

They continued through the temple, weaving between clusters of worshippers and lingering conversations. The lion statues that adorned the space loomed large, their golden eyes gleaming in the low light. Despite the grandeur, Yordan couldn't help but feel the weight of the stares they'd received earlier—and the sharp divide between who was welcome and who wasn't.

The magnificence of the temple no longer felt awe-inspiring. Instead, it carried a silent message, one reinforced by the whispers and laughter of those who moved freely within its walls. Still, Yordan clung to a fragile hope that this disparity was a misunderstanding, something that could be explained or excused.

The air outside the Grand Temple of Toteko was a welcome change after the heavy incense and tense atmosphere inside. Yordan adjusted his pack, glancing over his shoulder at Sam, who tapped his stick lightly against the cobblestones as they descended the temple steps. The city seemed quieter now, though clusters of Lumites still moved about, their crimson and gold robes catching the soft glow of lanterns.

Yordan spotted a Lumite man leaning against a nearby column, his arms crossed as he observed the bustling Sacred Quarter. The man's polished attire and relaxed posture suggested he was a local, someone who might know the area well. Deciding to take a chance, Yordan approached him, keeping his tone polite.

"Excuse me," Yordan began, "do you know of a place where Aralonite visitors can stay?"

The man turned his head, his gaze flicking briefly over Yordan and Sam before a small smirk tugged at the corner of his mouth. "Yeah," he said casually, his tone laced with sarcasm. "Back in Aralonis."

The remark caught Yordan off guard. He blinked, unsure if he'd misheard. "Oh," he said, hesitating before stepping back. "That was... weird."

Sam's expression didn't change, but his grip on his stick tightened slightly. "Not so weird," he said evenly. "Seems like other Lumites don't really want non-Lumites here."

Yordan frowned, his steps slowing as he processed Sam's words. "You can't use the few interactions we've had to judge an entire people," he said, though his tone lacked its usual conviction. He wanted to believe what he was saying.

Sam tilted his head slightly, his lips pressing into a thin line. After a moment, he gave a reluctant shrug. "Maybe so," he admitted, though there was a hint of doubt in his voice.

They walked on, the Sacred Quarter sprawling around them in all its opulence. The towering structures, adorned with golden embellishments and intricate carvings, were a testament to Lumina City's wealth and pride. Yet, despite the grandeur, Yordan felt out of place, the earlier interactions gnawing at the edges of his mind.

"Let's find some other Aralonites," Yordan said, glancing around. "Someone's got to know where we can stay."

But finding their own people proved more challenging than Yordan expected. The streets of the Sacred Quarter were dominated by Lumites, their vibrant clothing and confident strides filling the spaces between the ornate buildings. Yordan scanned the crowds, his eyes searching for the more muted, practical attire of Aralonites, but they were few and far between. The few non-Lumites they did see moved quickly and quietly, their heads down, as if trying to draw as little attention as possible.

The Sacred Quarter's opulence began to feel stifling, and Yordan's frustration grew with each passing moment. Finally, after what felt like hours of wandering, they stopped near a vendor selling glowing lanterns. The vendor, a middle-aged woman with sharp eyes, seemed more focused on her wares than the pair standing before her.

"Excuse me," he began, keeping his voice polite. "We're looking for a place where Aralonites can stay. Do you know where we should go?"

The woman didn't respond immediately, her hands continuing to arrange the lanterns. After a moment, she glanced up, her gaze flicking briefly over Yordan and Sam. Her expression was neutral but carried an edge of impatience.

"You're in the wrong part of the city," she said curtly, her voice as brisk as her movements. She gestured southward, her hand pointing past the glowing lights of the Sacred Quarter. "Head to the Commoner's Quarter. That's where you'll find what you're looking for."

"Thank you," Yordan said, offering a small nod. He turned back to Sam, whose expression remained impassive, though his grip on his stick tightened slightly.

"Commoner's Quarter, huh?" Sam said as they began walking in the direction the vendor had indicated. His tone was dry, tinged with humor. "Guess that's where we're allowed."

Yordan sighed, glancing back at the glowing spires of the Sacred Quarter. "It's just how the city's organized," he said, though his voice lacked its usual conviction. "It's not like it's personal."

Sam raised an eyebrow, tilting his head slightly. "Isn't it?"

Yordan didn't answer, his steps quickening as they moved south. The grand architecture of the Sacred Quarter began to give way to simpler, less ornate structures. The streets widened slightly, the crowds thinning as they left behind the bustling heart of Lumina City's religious and noble districts. The lanterns lining the streets grew sparser, their glow dimmer, casting longer shadows that danced against the walls of modest homes and shops.

The silence between them stretched, but it wasn't uncomfortable. Sam tapped his stick lightly against the cobblestones, keeping pace with Yordan, who adjusted his pack and let out a low breath.

"At least we know where to go now," Yordan said, breaking the quiet. "And the Commoner's Quarter doesn't sound too far."

"Better than wandering around up here," Sam replied, his tone softening slightly. "Let's just hope it lives up to the name."

Yordan let out a quiet laugh, shaking his head. The tension from earlier lingered at the edges of his thoughts, but the familiarity of Sam's dry humor grounded him. Together, they pressed on, heading deeper into the southern part of the city, the glow of the Sacred Quarter fading behind them.

As Yordan and Sam stepped into the Commoner's Quarter, the contrast with the Sacred Quarter was stark. The grand marble façades and golden embellishments of Lumina City's northern districts gave way to modest stone buildings and tightly packed streets. Lanterns flickered in the cool evening breeze, casting a soft glow over the bustling thoroughfare. The air smelled of cooked meat, fresh bread, and faintly of damp stone, a mixture that was both comforting and grounding after the grandeur of the Sacred Quarter.

The streets were busy but lacked the confidence and flow of the Sacred Quarter. Vendors called out halfheartedly, their stalls lined with simpler wares, and children darted between the clusters of travelers and locals, their laughter adding a lively rhythm to the atmosphere. Yordan adjusted his pack as they moved through the maze of narrow streets, his eyes scanning the signs and storefronts for somewhere they could stay.

"There, the Restful Respite," Yordan said, nodding toward a modest building with a sign hanging above its entrance. The sign, slightly faded, read Restful Respite in a looping script. Beneath it, smaller text promised, Beds for travelers, meals for weary souls.

"Sounds promising," Sam said, his stick tapping lightly on the cobblestones as they approached.

Inside, the warm glow of a fireplace greeted them, the scent of roasted herbs and wood smoke filling the air. The main room was lively, with travelers gathered around mismatched tables, sharing meals and stories. The walls were adorned with tapestries of simple geometric patterns, and the wooden beams above were carved with intricate whorls and knots.

Behind the counter stood the innkeeper, a woman who immediately caught Yordan's attention. She had long, dark hair that fell in loose waves over her shoulders, her features sharp yet inviting. Her eyes were warm and curious as she greeted them with a smile that felt practiced but not insincere.

"Welcome to the Restful Respite," she said, her voice smooth and lilting. Her gaze lingered briefly on Sam before she added, "What can I do for you two?"

"A place to stay for the night," Yordan said, stepping forward. "We've been traveling all day and need somewhere to rest."

"Of course," she said, her smile broadening. "We've got bunks upstairs simple but comfortable. Dinners included if you're hungry."

"Sounds perfect," Yordan replied, reaching for the coin pouch at his belt. He handed over the payment, and the innkeeper slid two wooden tokens across the counter toward them.

As Yordan picked them up, she leaned slightly forward, her gaze shifting to Sam. "You've had a long journey, haven't you?" she asked, her tone softening. "You must be exhausted."

Sam tilted his head slightly, his expression calm. "We've managed," he said simply, his voice polite but neutral.

The woman, whose name tag read Jezzie, tilted her head, her smile becoming coy. "Well, if there's anything you need, don't hesitate to ask. Anything at all."

Yordan stifled a grin, glancing at Sam, who remained entirely composed. "We'll let you know," Sam said evenly, his tone giving nothing away.

Jezzie handed them a key with a small wooden tag and pointed toward the staircase. "Second floor, room five. Enjoy your stay, gentlemen."

"Thank you," Yordan said, nudging Sam slightly as they made their way to the stairs.

The upper floor was quieter, the hum of conversation from below fading as they climbed. The hall was narrow, lit by small oil lamps mounted on the walls, their soft glow casting gentle shadows. Room five was at the far end, and Yordan pushed open the door to reveal a modest but clean room with two bunk beds, each with neatly folded linens.

As they set down their packs, Yordan couldn't resist. He turned to Sam, his grin widening. "Seems like Jezzie wanted to get to know you better," he teased, leaning against the bedframe.

Sam, unfazed, began folding his walking stick, tucking it into his pack with practiced ease. "One thing about being blind," he said calmly, "is I can tell when someone's being more genuine based on their voice instead of just being attracted to my looks."

Yordan blinked, momentarily caught off guard by the reply. He let out a quiet laugh, shaking his head. "Fair enough," he said, sitting on the edge of the lower bunk. "Still, she seemed... interested."

Sam's lips quirked in the faintest hint of a smile. "She was polite," he said, shrugging slightly. "Nothing more."

Yordan chuckled, leaning back against the wall. The warmth of the room and the faint creak of the building's timbers were a welcome change from the cold streets outside. As he stretched his legs, he couldn't help but feel grateful for the companionship they'd found in each other's friendship.

The dining hall of the Restful Respite was as lively as the main room downstairs, filled with travelers from all corners of Anakuatl. The wooden tables, each slightly mismatched, were crowded with plates of steaming food and mugs of frothy drink. The scent of roasted meats, herbs, and freshly baked bread hung heavily in the air, and the hum of conversation added a warm, communal backdrop to the scene.

Yordan and Sam found an empty table near the edge of the room, close to a window that looked out onto the dimly lit street. Yordan adjusted his chair, leaning back slightly as he glanced toward the counter where the inn's staff busily delivered trays of food to the waiting guests.

"Smells good," Yordan said lightly, resting his forearms on the table. Sam nodded in agreement, his walking stick folded neatly beside him.

As they waited for their food, a voice from a nearby table caught Yordan's attention. It was sharp, cutting through the general murmur of the room.

"I can't believe we came all this way, only to stand in line all day and not even get into the temple," the voice said, carrying an edge of frustration. Yordan's eyes drifted toward the speaker—a young Zetian woman, likely in her mid-twenties. Her features were striking, her raven-black hair pulled back into a loose braid. She sat rigidly at the table, her arms crossed over her chest as she glared at the older man sitting across from her.

The older man, who Yordan assumed was her elder, had a kind but weary expression. His white hair was neatly combed back, and his sharp, intelligent eyes reflected both patience and understanding. His robes, though simple, carried an air of dignity, marked with subtle embroidery of Zetian symbols.

"Aisha," the elder said gently, his voice calm and measured, "I understand you are frustrated."

"Frustrated?" she snapped, her tone incredulous. "Uriah, this is worse than I expected. Standing in line for hours, only to be turned away without a second glance? And to top it off, we had to take hidden pathways to get here, like we're criminals just for walking through the city."

Uriah's lips pressed into a thin line, and he exhaled softly. "The paths were for your safety," he said, his tone soothing but firm. "You know how things are here. It's not ideal, but—"

"But nothing," Aisha interrupted, her voice rising slightly. A few heads turned in their direction, though she didn't seem to care. "This isn't just 'not ideal.' This is humiliating. And given the group they forced out a couple of days ago? I'm starting to wonder if we made a mistake coming here at all."

Uriah's face grew somber, and he leaned forward slightly, his voice dropping so only those closest could hear. "We cannot let fear stop us from seeking what we came for," he said quietly. "You knew this would not be easy."

Aisha shook her head, her jaw tightening. "Knowing it wouldn't be easy and seeing this... this mockery, this open contempt, are two very different things."

Yordan shifted in his seat, pretending not to eavesdrop, but he couldn't help but feel a pang of sympathy for the young woman. Her words echoed some of the unease he'd felt throughout the day, though he wasn't ready to admit it aloud. He glanced at Sam, who sat quietly, his expression neutral but his head tilted slightly, as if he, too, was listening.

Yordan couldn't stop himself. The frustration of the day, the slow-moving lines, and the tension simmering in the air got the better of him. He turned toward the Zetian woman, Aisha, his voice louder than he intended. "That group was removed for being troublemakers here in Lumina City."

The dining hall quieted slightly, a few heads turning toward the sudden outburst. Aisha, mid-sentence with her elder, stilled, her back rigid as she slowly turned to face him. Her dark eyes locked onto his, sharp and unyielding. The air between them crackled with something unspoken, something heated—not just anger, but scrutiny.

Boots clicking against the wooden floor, she closed the distance between them with deliberate steps, her braid swaying behind her. The low firelight caught the loose strands framing her face, giving her an almost haloed glow, though nothing about her expression was saintly.

She stopped just short of Yordan, tilting her head slightly, as if assessing whether he was worth her time. Yordan felt an unexpected tightness in his chest, though he wasn't sure if it was from embarrassment, defensiveness, or something else entirely.

"Ain't that the Lumite response every time?" Her voice was smooth but edged with steel, her lip curling ever so slightly in what might have been amusement—if not for the indignation burning behind her gaze. "Everything gets swep tunder 'troublemakers,' doesn't it? Makes it easy to pretend there's no real problem."

Yordan straightened, pulse quickening as her stare pinned him in place. "I'm not a Lumite." His voice came out steadier than he expected. "I'm an Aralonite."

Aisha arched a perfectly sculpted brow, a slow, almost mocking smirk spreading across her lips. "Oh, my mistake," she said, voice honeyed with sarcasm. "That must mean you got special treatment today. I saw you watching us in line while you strolled right in to see the 'beauty' of Toteko's followers."

Yordan opened his mouth to respond—to say what, he wasn't sure—but the words never came. The firelight flickered in her dark eyes, and for the briefest moment, something in her gaze wasn't just anger but challenge.

Then, as swiftly as she'd approached, she turned on her heel, breaking whatever strange pull had held him still.

"Uriah," she said, dismissing Yordan as though he were no longer worth her attention. "I've lost my appetite."

Uriah, who had remained seated throughout the exchange, let out a long sigh and rose slowly. His movements were deliberate, his face calm but weary. "Come, Aisha," he murmured.

Without another glance in Yordan's direction, she strode toward the stairs, her braid swaying once more, a final flick of defiance as she disappeared from view.

Yordan exhaled, realizing only then that he had been holding his breath.

Across the table, Sam, who had remained silent the entire time, leaned his elbows forward, his expression unreadable. After a pause, he finally spoke, voice low with knowing amusement. "Well. That went well."

Yordan dragged a hand through his hair, ignoring the warmth still lingering in his face. "I wasn't looking at her," he muttered.

Sam tilted his head, the corner of his mouth twitching. "Didn't say you were."

Yordan scowled, turning back to his food. The rest of the dining hall resumed its chatter, but in his mind, the echo of Aisha's voice—sharp, unshaken, utterly unimpressed with him—lingered longer than it should have.

"You may want to be careful," he said. "This isn't Aralonis. Clearly, things are different here."

Yordan frowned, running a hand through his hair. "How can that be true, though?" he asked, his voice tinged with disbelief. "Obviously, they didn't kick out all the Zetians. She's still here."

Sam tilted his head slightly, his lips pressing into a thin line. "She's still here," he agreed, "but does that mean she's welcomed here? Or that things are just a little more complicated than you think?"

Yordan hesitated, the weight of Sam's words settling over him. He glanced down at his untouched plate of food, the smell of roasted meat and herbs no longer as appetizing. The image of Aisha's fiery expression lingered in his mind, her passion and defiance leaving an impression he couldn't entirely shake. Something about Aisha's strength and conviction drew him in, leaving him unsettled in ways he didn't want to dwell on.

"Let's just eat our food and get some sleep," Sam said, his tone softer now but still edged with concern.

Yordan nodded slowly, picking up his fork. The tension in the dining hall eased as conversations resumed around them, but the echoes of the exchange lingered in Yordan's mind. As he ate in silence, he couldn't shake the feeling that he was missing something, some thread of understanding that could make sense of the uneasy dynamic in Lumina City. For now, he pushed the thought aside, focusing instead on finishing the meal and preparing for whatever the next day would bring.

Chapter Eight

Yordan stretched as he woke, the faint glow of dawn creeping through the small window of his shared room with Sam. The air in the Restful Respite was still, save for the occasional creak of the wooden beams. He threw on his boots, rubbed the sleep from his eyes, and made his way down the narrow staircase, the faint scent of embers and roasted herbs lingering from the night before.

As he stepped into the common area, he saw her: Aisha, seated in one of the chairs near the low-burning fire. The faint orange glow cast shadows across her face, highlighting the sharp lines of her cheekbones and the faint defiance in her gaze as she stared into the flames. She didn't look up, but her presence filled the room like a storm brewing on the horizon.

Yordan smirked, unable to help himself. He leaned against the doorway, crossing his arms. "Trying to unfreeze your cold heart?" he asked, his voice dripping with sarcasm.

Aisha's head tilted slightly, her eyes flicking up to meet his. Her expression was unreadable for a moment, but then her lips curved into a small, biting smile. "You ready to admit you were wrong about what happened?" she shot back, her tone sharp enough to cut.

Yordan pushed off the doorway and stepped closer, his smirk fading as his brow furrowed. "Wrong? About what, exactly? That the Lumites kicked out a group causing trouble? Or that maybe you're too eager to play the victim?"

Aisha stood, her movements swift and fluid. The distance between them shrank as she stepped forward, her gaze locked onto him. "You really think it's that simple, don't you?" she said, her voice rising slightly. "That the Lumites are just trying to keep order? Have you even looked at what they're doing to us? Or are you too busy convincing yourself they're the good guys?"

Yordan's jaw tightened, his own frustration bubbling to the surface. "I'm not saying everything they do is right," he said, his voice firm but measured. "But maybe—just maybe—it's not as black and white as you make it out to be."

Aisha let out a sharp laugh, her eyes flashing with anger. "Spoken like someone who's never had to hide who they are just to walk down the street," she snapped. "You think you understand because you had to wait in line for a few hours? Try having your whole existence questioned, your family ripped apart, and your people treated like animals."

Her words hit harder than Yordan expected, but he refused to back down. He stepped closer, his voice lowering but no less intense. "You think you're the only one who's suffered?" he asked, his tone was a mix of challenge and vulnerability. "You think the rest of us just have it easy? I came here to see the truth, not to have someone like you assume they know everything about me."

They were close now, the space between them charged with a tension that neither seemed to fully understand. Aisha's chest rose and fell with each sharp breath, her fiery gaze meeting Yordan's equally defiant one. The flickering firelight danced across their faces, casting shadows that seemed to blur the lines between anger and something unspoken.

"You're so sure of yourself," Aisha said, her voice quieter now but no less intense. "But you're blind to what's right in front of you."

Yordan leaned in slightly, his heart pounding as the heat of their argument gave way to an inexplicable pull. "And you're so wrapped up in your anger," he countered, his voice barely above a whisper, "that you push away anyone who tries to understand."

Their faces were inches apart, the tension crackling like the fire behind them. For a moment, it was as if the world outside the room ceased to exist, leaving only the two of them caught in the gravity of their clashing wills and shared pain. Neither moved, neither spoke, the unspoken words hanging heavy in the charged silence.

The fire popped, a sudden spark sending a shower of embers up the chimney, its crack echoing like a sharp punctuation in their silence. Aisha's eyes flashed, and in that split second, she lifted her hand and brought it down against Yordan's cheek with a resounding slap. The sting was immediate, hot against his skin, but it wasn't anger he saw in her eyes. It was something deeper, something raw and uncontained.

The world seemed to hold its breath, waiting for what would come next, as Yordan stood still, the air thick with unspoken emotions swirling around them like a tempest. He didn't flinch or step back. Instead, he let the moment wash over him, absorbing her reaction—the frustration, the passion, the truth behind her touch.

Then, as if drawn by an invisible thread that had finally pulled taut between them, Aisha surged forward. Her hands cupped his face with a gentleness that belied the force of the slap as she captured his lips in a kiss that ignited like fire catching dry tinder.

For an instant suspended in time, nothing else mattered. The world outside could have been swallowed by shadows and silence for all they cared. The only reality was the shared warmth of their breath and the certainty of Aisha's touch.

Yordan responded instinctively, arms wrapping around her slender form to draw her closer still. He felt her heart beating against his chest, each thud echoing his own tumultuous pulse until he pulled away slightly, panting against the sudden onslaught of emotions.

He looked into Aisha's eyes—dark pools now shimmering with a mix of challenge and yearning—and whispered hoarsely, "I am sorry."

In those words, lay more than an apology; they carried a plea for understanding and acceptance beneath their conflict-laden exchanges. Yet before he could say more or even fully comprehend what he sought forgiveness for beyond the surface disagreements between them, she drew him back into another fervent kiss.

This time there was no hesitation nor interruption from either side. The warmth from the hearth seemed to envelop them completely while outside night descended with velvet softness over Lumina City.

Yordan pulled back from the fervent kiss, his breath mingling with Aisha's in the charged space between them. He gazed into her eyes, seeing the smoldering desire that matched his own. With a gentle hand, he brushed a stray lock of hair from her face, his fingertips trailing along her cheek.

Aisha's lips parted slightly at his touch, her chest rising and falling with quickened breaths. The room seemed to narrow until it encompassed only the two of them, the crackling fire, and the unspoken connection that had ignited between them.

Slowly, deliberately, Yordan lowered Aisha to the floor. The thick rug cushioned her as he laid her down, never breaking eye contact. He hovered over her, drinking in the sight of her flushed cheeks and tousled hair fanned out beneath her.

Leaning in, Yordan placed a soft kiss on Aisha's forehead, then her nose, then captured her lips once more. She responded eagerly, hands sliding up his back to pull him closer. He took his time, savoring the taste and feel of her as his kisses traveled along her jaw and down the slender column of her neck.

Aisha let out a soft gasp as Yordan found a sensitive spot just above her collarbone. Encouraged, he lingered there, lips and tongue and gentle suction, determined to draw out more of those intoxicating sounds. Her fingers threaded into his hair, holding him close.

With reverent hands, Yordan pushed up the hem of Aisha's tunic, exposing the smooth skin of her stomach. He traced patterns there with his fingertips before following the same paths with his mouth - swirling, tasting, treasuring. Aisha arched into his touch, a breathy moan escaping her lips.

Emboldened, Yordan continued his sensual journey downward until he settled between her parted thighs. He looked up at her, silently seeking permission, and was met with a gaze dark with need. Maintaining eye contact, he slowly peeled away her remaining clothing, revealing her most intimate parts to his hungry eyes.

Yordan started with teasing kisses along her inner thighs, relishing how Aisha squirmed beneath him, her breath coming faster. He took his time, working his way inward until his mouth hovered right where she wanted him most. With a final glance up at her face, he closed the gap and put his lips and tongue to work.

Aisha cried out, hips lifting off the floor as Yordan began to devour her with single-minded focus. He explored every fold and crevice, driven by her responses, finding all the spots that made her gasp and moan. She was intoxicating - the taste of her, the sounds she made, the way she moved against his mouth.

Yordan lost himself in pleasuring her, pouring all his passion into the intimate act. His tongue swirled and delved, finding the sensitive nub at her center. He concentrated his efforts there, flicking and suckling until Aisha was a writhing, moaning mess beneath him.

Her fingers tightened in his hair almost painfully as her hips undulated against his face. Yordan could tell she was close by the way her thighs began to tremble and quake around him. Doubling his efforts, he pushed her closer and closer to the edge.

"Yordan, yes! Don't stop!" Aisha panted, her head thrashing from side to side. With a final press of his tongue, he sent her flying.

Aisha came with a keening cry, her back bowing off the floor as the pleasure crashed over her in intense waves. Yordan continued his ministrations, helping her ride out the high as long as possible. He felt her release coat his chin, the intimate essence of her passion.

Finally, Aisha collapsed back against the rug, boneless and sated. Her chest heaved as she tried to catch her breath, eyelids fluttering. When she managed to open them and meet Yordan's gaze, he saw they were glassy and unfocused, lost in a haze of bliss.

"That was... incredible," she panted, reaching for him weakly. Yordan crawled up her body, hovering over her once more. Aisha pulled him down into a languid kiss, tasting herself on his lips with a low moan.

As they kissed, Aisha's hands roamed over Yordan's shoulders and back before dipping lower. She palmed him through his trousers, feeling the thick ridge of his arousal straining against the fabric. Breaking the kiss with a gasp, she looked up at him with pleading eyes.

"Yordan, please. I need you inside me," she breathed, rolling her hips up to press against his hardness. "I want to feel you stretching me, filling me. Please..."

Yordan groaned at her wanton plea, desire spiking through him like lightning. Unable to deny her, he sat back on his knees to quickly shed his clothes. Aisha's eyes roamed hungrily over his bared skin, lingering on his impressive length as it sprang free.

Settling between her thighs once more, Yordan ran the tip of his cock through her slick folds, gathering the wetness. They both moaned at the contact, the delicious friction. He teased her entrance, circling and pressing gently but not breaching her yet.

"Is this what you want?" Yordan rasped, his voice rough with restraint. "You want my thick cock inside your perfect, tight little..."

"Yes!" Aisha cut him off with a desperate whine, trying to impale herself on him. Yordan groaned in unison with Aisha as he finally gave her what she craved, slowly sinking his thick length into her welcoming heat. Inch by delicious inch he filled her, stretching and claiming her most intimate depths. Aisha's back arched off the rug, her nails digging into his shoulders as she reveled in the exquisite sensation of being so thoroughly possessed.

"Oh gods," she gasped out, head lolling back in bliss. "You feel...m mm...so good."

He paused when he was fully seated inside her, giving them both a moment to adjust and savor the feeling of their bodies joined as one. Aisha's slick walls fluttered around him, gripping him like velvet vice. It took every ounce of Yordan's restraint not to immediately lose himself in her sweet embrace.

After a long, shuddering breath, he began to move - slow, deep strokes that dragged deliciously along her sensitive nerves. Aisha met each thrust with an upward roll of her hips, their bodies finding a primal rhythm as old as time itself.

The air around them grew thick and heavy, filled with the sounds of panting breaths, low moans, and the obscene slap of sweat-slicked skin against skin. The crackling fire cast a warm, sensual glow over their undulating forms as they lost themselves in carnal pleasure.

Yordan drank in the sight of Aisha beneath him - her tousled hair fanned out like a dark halo, kiss-swollen lips parted around needy sounds, dusky nipples peaked and begging for attention. He ducked his head to capture one between his lips, suckling and flicking with his tongue until she keened and arched into his touch.

Their pace gradually increased, bodies moving with more urgency as the pressure built low in their bellies. Aisha hooked her legs high around Yordan's waist, heels digging into his flexing backside to spur him on. The new angle allowed him to plunge even deeper, hitting that secret spot inside her that made sparks ignite behind her eyelids.

"There! Oh gods, right there!" she panted, nails scoring down his back. "Harder, please! I'm so close..."

Yordan pistoned his hips faster, plunging into Aisha's welcoming heat over and over. The wet sounds of their coupling echoed obscenely in the otherwise quiet room. Sweat beaded and ran down his spine as he chased their mutual completion, the rug burning deliciously against his knees.

Aisha could feel her peak fast approaching, that glorious precipice just out of reach. Every nerve ending sizzled with building electric heat, her inner muscles starting to quake and clench around Yordan's thick length. Desperate whimpers spilled from her lips between increasingly frantic movements of her hips.

Yordan could feel his own climax building, balls drawing up tight as Aisha's fluttering walls massaged his throbbing length. The exquisite friction was almost too much to bear, driving him closer and closer to the edge with each snap of his hips.

"I'm going to..." he panted in warning, instinctively starting to pull out. But Aisha had other ideas.

Aisha's legs tightened around his waist like a vice, locking him in place deep inside her. Yordan's eyes went wide with surprise, a strangled groan escaping him at the sudden shift. Aisha gazed up at him intently, eyes dark and pleading.

"No, don't pull away," she breathed, voice wrecked but resolute. "I want to feel you come inside me. I need it. Please..."

Her words ignited a primal surge of possession and need inside him. With a guttural growl, Yordan drove into her with renewed fervor, chasing the siren song of release that beckoned. Aisha cried out sharply, head tipping back as he pounded into her willing body.

"Yes! Just like that!" she keened, heels digging into his clenching backside. "Don't stop. Fill me up..."

Yordan could feel himself teetering right on the cusp, his movements growing erratic as the pressure peaked. Just as he was about to crest and empty himself deep inside Aisha's clutching heat, a sudden vision flashed before his eyes.

A majestic golden deer stood before him, its luminous coat shimmering in an otherworldly light. The creature's eyes met Yordan's, seeming to pierce straight through to his soul with ancient wisdom. As he stared transfixed, the deer's soothing voice echoed through his mind:

"Rise up, your true path awaits. Climb the sacred mountain and embrace your destiny."

Yordan jolted awake, his chest heaving as beads of sweat clung to his skin. The room was cloaked in shadow, the faint glow of dawn barely seeping through the edges of the shutters. His breathing was heavy, his mind spinning as the vivid fragments of the dream lingered in his consciousness.

He could still see it. Aisha, standing before him, her fiery gaze locked onto his as her dark hair cascaded over her shoulders. Her touch, the way her lips parted to speak, her presence had consumed him entirely in the dream. But then, as the moment reached its crescendo, the golden deer had appeared, its ethereal form glowing against the backdrop of his subconscious. Its voice echoed with impossible clarity, the words reverberating in his chest: "Rise up, your true path awaits. Climb the sacred mountain and embrace your destiny."

He ran a hand through his damp hair, groaning as the rush of emotions and sensations coursed through him. It had felt so real. Too real. His frustration mounted as he sat up, his bed creaking beneath him. He pressed his palms to his face, trying to will away the vividness of the dream and the heat still simmering under his skin.

"It was just a dream," he muttered under his breath, though the words felt hollow. His mind rebelled against the thought, replaying the details with stubborn clarity.

Then the guilt hit him, sharp and unrelenting. His hands dropped from his face as his gaze drifted toward the floor. He hadn't been thinking of Katherine. Not her laughter, her warmth, the way her presence steadied him. No, it was Aisha—someone he'd barely met, someone whose name he hadn't even known until their spat the night before. A woman whose fierce words and fiery temperament had annoyed and intrigued him in equal measure.

His fists clenched, his knuckles pressing into the mattress. "What's wrong with me?" he whispered to himself, his voice heavy with frustration and shame. Katherine was everything he wanted—steady, kind, loyal. She'd been there for him, someone he could trust without question. Aisha, on the other hand, was... what? A stranger. A source of tension and conflict. Someone he'd argued with in front of others like a fool.

But in the dream, she'd been something else entirely. Not just her sharp words or fiery gaze but the force of her presence, the way she challenged him, unsettled him. And that deer, that haunting voice—it had turned the dream into something more than just lust. It had made it feel... significant.

Yordan leaned forward, his elbows on his knees, his head hanging low. "Why her?" he muttered. "Why not Katherine?" He clenched his jaw, the weight of his confusion pressing down on him. He cared deeply for Katherine—he had no doubts about that—but the dream refused to let him go. It gnawed at him, planting seeds of doubt and questions he didn't want to face.

Was it guilt for how he had treated Aisha? Was it something deeper, something he couldn't yet name? Or was it simply his mind playing tricks on him, blending frustration and attraction into something that felt like more than it was?

He shook his head, forcing himself to push the thoughts aside. The room felt stifling, his sweat-dampened sheets clinging to his skin. He swung his legs over the side of the bed, planting his feet on the cool wooden floor. The faint sound of movement outside reminded him that the world was waking, but he still felt trapped in the dream's grasp.

With a deep breath, Yordan resolved to shake it off. It was just a dream, he told himself again. Nothing more. But as he stood and began to dress for the day, the lingering sensation of the deer's voice and Aisha's presence refused to leave him, hovering at the edges of his mind like a shadow he couldn't escape.

The soft creak of the wooden floorboards and the muted light filtering through the shutters signaled the beginning of another day at the Restful Respite. Yordan had already been awake for hours, unable to shake the strange mix of frustration and guilt that clung to him after the vivid dream. He sat on the edge of his bed, fiddling absently with the straps of his boots, when Sam stirred on the bunk above him.

Sam let out a groggy grunt as he swung his legs down, landing lightly on the floor. "Morning," he muttered, stretching his arms out wide before finding his stick and tapping it lightly on the ground.

"Morning," Yordan replied, his voice subdued. He straightened up, glancing at Sam as he grabbed his pack. "Let's head down. Breakfast should be ready by now."

Together, they made their way down the narrow staircase to the main hall, where the scent of fresh bread and roasted herbs wafted through the air. The room was already filling with travelers, the low hum of conversation creating a comfortable backdrop. Yordan scanned the crowd as they descended, his eyes flicking from table to table.

He didn't even realize he was searching for them until disappointment settled in his chest. Aisha and Uriah were nowhere to be seen.

"You go ahead and sit," Yordan said, "I'll grab something for us."

Sam nodded, his stick lightly tapping the floor as he found his way to the table and settled in. Yordan, however, made a beeline for the counter, where Jezzie was arranging plates with her usual mix of efficiency and charm. She looked up as he approached, her dark eyes bright with interest as a sly smile played at her lips.

"Good morning," Jezzie said smoothly. "What can I do for you, Yordan?"

He hesitated, shifting his weight slightly. "Hey, have—" He paused, feeling suddenly self-conscious. He rubbed the back of his neck before continuing, trying to keep his tone casual. "There were two people staying here, a woman with a long braid and a man with white hair, older. Did they—uh—leave?"

Jezzie's smile widened, a glint of amusement sparking in her eyes. She leaned slightly against the counter, her voice light but teasing. "Oh, you mean the fiery Zetian and her elder?"

Yordan's face flushed slightly, but he nodded. "Yeah. Them."

Jezzie shrugged, her tone almost playful. "They left very early this morning. Didn't say much about where they were headed. Just slipped out quietly before most people were awake."

"Right," Yordan said, a faint note of defeat creeping into his voice. "Thanks."

As Yordan turned back toward the table, he caught a flicker of amusement in Jezzie's eyes, though she didn't say anything. He clenched his jaw and forced himself to ignore whatever silent judgment she might have been holding. Something twisted in his chest—irritation, maybe, or something else he wasn't ready to name. He exhaled sharply through his nose and pushed forward, weaving through the tables until he reached Sam.

"You sound like you lost something," Sam said with a faint smirk as Yordan slid into the seat across from him.

Yordan shook his head, avoiding Sam's empathetic face. "Nothing. Just asked about a couple of travelers."

Sam leaned back slightly, his smirk widening. "Missing Katherine already, huh? You don't have to admit it to me—I get it. She's got that hold on you."

Yordan glanced up sharply, his mouth opening to shoot back a quick retort, but then he stopped. Sam's grin faltered slightly as he noticed the uncharacteristic silence from his friend.

"Hold on," Sam said, his voice dropping to a hushed tone. He leaned forward, lowering his stick to rest against the table. "You're not thinking about that girl from last night, are you? The Zetian?"

145

Yordan's face heated instantly, and he straightened in his chair, his movements stiff. "What? No," he said, his voice a little too loud, drawing a glance or two from nearby tables. He forced a laugh, waving a hand dismissively. "Why would I be thinking about her? She was... she was barely on my mind at all."

Sam raised an eyebrow, his expression calm but tinged with curiosity. "Uh-huh. And that's why that tone that screams overthinking something you don't want to admit."

Yordan scoffed, crossing his arms as he leaned back in his chair. "I don't know what you're talking about," he said, though his tone betrayed the slightest crack of defensiveness. "I was just curious if they were still here, that's all. It's not like I care or anything."

Sam's lips twitched in a faint smile, but he let the subject drop, leaning back in his chair with a knowing shake of his head. "Sure thing, Yordan," he said lightly. "Whatever you say."

Yordan stared down at the table, his fingers drumming against the wood as the room buzzed around them. Despite his best efforts to brush it off, Jezzie's words and Sam's teasing lingered, mixing with the vivid memory of his dream and the fiery presence of the woman who had somehow found her way into his thoughts.

Yordan tore into the crusty bread on his plate, his thoughts swirling as the morning light filtered through the inn's windows. Across the table, Sam was taking deliberate bites of his meal, his fingers brushing the edges of his plate every so often to orient himself. The low murmur of conversation in the dining hall provided a familiar backdrop, but Yordan's mind was elsewhere.

Between mouthfuls, he broke the silence. "I was thinking," he said casually, "how about I go climb the Sitlali Mountains just outside the city?"

Sam stopped mid-bite, his head tilting slightly as if trying to gauge whether Yordan was joking. He set his bread down and tapped the table lightly with his fingers, his version of a contemplative stare. "Climbing the Sitlali Mountains?" Sam repeated, his tone calm but with an edge of incredulity. "Are you out of your mind? You can't just decide to go scaling mountains on a whim."

Yordan shrugged, wiping crumbs from his hands. "Why not? I need some clarity, and there's nothing like a good climb to get your head straight."

Sam let out a short laugh, shaking his head. "And what? You're just going to leave me here while you go off chasing clarity? If you're going, I'm coming with you."

Yordan raised an eyebrow, leaning back in his chair. "Sam, I'll be faster on my own. Besides, do you even like climbing? Last I checked, you get nervous just standing on a hill, and you can't even see how high you are."

Sam's lips quirked in a faint smile, but his expression turned serious. "What's that supposed to mean? You think I'll slow you down just because I can't see? Sounds pretty ableist of you, Yordan."

Yordan chuckled, shaking his head. "Oh, come on, Sam. We both know it's not about that. You hate heights. Remember the time you panicked on that bridge near Aralonis? You clung to the railing like it was your long-lost mother."

Sam's cheeks flushed slightly, and he folded his arms. "I was being cautious."

"You were yelling at me to describe the cracks in the wood, so you'd know which ones to avoid," Yordan teased, grinning.

Sam let out a low sigh, his lips twitching into a reluctant smile. "Fine. Maybe heights aren't my favorite thing," he admitted. "But that doesn't mean I can't handle it."

Yordan leaned forward, resting his elbows on the table. "I know you can handle it, Sam. But I'm serious about going alone. It's not about leaving you behind, it's just something I need to do for myself. I don't know how to explain it, but... it feels important."

Sam was silent for a moment, his fingers tapping a rhythm against the edge of the table as he processed Yordan's words. Finally, he nodded, his expression softening. "All right," he said quietly. "If it's that important to you, I won't argue. But you'd better not go getting yourself killed up there."

"Don't worry about me," Yordan said with a smirk. He extended his hand across the table, palm up. "Come on. Shake on it."

Sam reached out, his fingers brushing Yordan's before clasping them firmly. The handshake lingered for a moment, less a gesture of agreement and more a shared understanding between brothers.

"Don't get into trouble while I'm gone, Sam," Yordan said, his tone light but carrying an undertone of genuine concern.

Sam leaned back with a small grin, folding his arms. "Same to you," he replied, his voice steady. "And don't think I won't know if you do. Just because I can't see doesn't mean I don't know when you're up to something."

Yordan laughed, standing and gathering his pack. "Fair enough. Try not to annoy Jezzie too much while I'm gone."

Sam chuckled, shaking his head. "Try not to annoy the mountain. I hear they don't like troublemakers."

As Yordan headed for the door, he cast one last glance over his shoulder. Sam was already reaching for another piece of bread, his movements unhurried and confident. The bond between them felt stronger than ever, and despite his teasing, Yordan knew he could count on Sam for anything.

The thought gave him a sense of grounding as he stepped outside, the crisp morning air filling his lungs. Ahead of him loomed the Sitlali Mountains, their peaks shrouded in mist, calling to him like a whisper in the wind. Whatever awaited him there, he knew it was something he had to face alone.

The morning air in Lumina City was crisp as Yordan stepped onto the cobbled streets, the towering spires of the Sacred Quarter gleaming faintly in the early sunlight. His boots echoed softly on the stones as he adjusted his pack, setting his gaze northward toward the looming Sitlali Mountains. Their jagged peaks pierced the sky, shrouded in a thin veil of mist that seemed almost ethereal. The golden deer's words reverberated in his mind: "Rise up, your true path awaits. Climb the sacred mountain and embrace your destiny."

He walked with purpose, weaving through the bustling streets. The Sacred Quarter was coming to life around him, filled with the hum of morning prayers and the rhythmic ringing of temple bells. As he moved farther from the inn, Yordan's eyes scanned the crowds out of habit, noting the familiar crimson-and-gold robes of Lumites and the more subdued earth tones of Aralonites.

Yet something felt off. The vibrant diversity he had grown accustomed to in Aralonis was conspicuously absent here. Where were the Zetians? Or the distinctive garb of the Ants and Ojtlists? Even travelers from other regions, with their unique clothing and symbols, seemed scarce. The streets were filled almost entirely with Lumites and a smattering of Aralonites.

Yordan's brows furrowed as the realization sank in. The city, grand and sprawling as it was, felt oddly uniform, as though it sought to erase the presence of those who didn't fit the dominant mold. His mind flickered back to the Zetian line outside the temple and the biting words Aisha had hurled at him. This is worse than I expected to see here. Her voice echoed in his thoughts, but Yordan shook his head, forcing himself to focus. He couldn't afford distractions.

The mountain, he reminded himself. The golden deer's voice had been clear, its words carrying an urgency that made his pulse quicken even now. Whatever answers he sought, whatever clarity he needed, they were up there hidden among the misty peaks of the Sitlali Mountains.

As he left the Sacred Quarter behind, the architecture shifted subtly. The gleaming marble and intricate carvings gave way to simpler stonework, the streets becoming narrower and less populated. The northern edge of Lumina City felt quieter, almost forgotten, as though the mountains themselves cast a shadow that kept the bustling energy of the city at bay.

The air grew cooler as he approached the city's edge, where the cobblestones gave way to a dirt path that wound its way toward the mountains. The towering peaks seemed larger now, their jagged silhouettes cutting into the clear blue sky. Yordan adjusted his pack again, feeling the weight of his gear but more so the weight of the task ahead.

Pausing at the base of the trail, he turned to take one last look at the city. From this vantage point, Lumina City seemed smaller, its spires no longer dominating the horizon but blending into the landscape. The golden glow of the Sacred Quarter was still visible, though distant, its grandeur muted by the sheer presence of the mountains that loomed above it.

Yordan exhaled deeply, his breath visible in the cool air. He couldn't explain it, but something about this path felt right. The golden deer's message, cryptic as it was, resonated deeply within him. It wasn't just a dream; it was a call to action, one he couldn't ignore.

He turned back toward the trail and began his ascent, the dirt path crunching underfoot as he climbed higher into the wilderness. The sounds of the city faded behind him, replaced by the rustle of leaves and the distant call of birds. The air grew thinner and colder, the scent of pine and damp earth filling his lungs.

With each step, Yordan felt a mixture of anticipation and unease. He didn't know what he would find at the top of the Sitlali Mountains, but the words of the golden deer spurred him onward. Rise up, your true path awaits.

Chapter Nine

The path up the Sitlali Mountains began as a gentle incline, winding its way through a dense forest of towering pines. The trees, their bark dark and weathered, reached skyward like ancient sentinels, their branches swaying gently in the cool breeze. The air was sharp with the scent of pine resin and damp earth, and Yordan felt his lungs fill deeply as he ascended. At first, the climb felt invigorating, his boots finding firm purchase on the soft, pine-needle-covered ground.

But the trail soon grew steeper, the terrain becoming rougher and more challenging. The dirt path gave way to loose stones and jagged rocks, forcing Yordan to carefully test each step. He gripped tree roots and protruding rocks to steady himself as the incline grew sharper. His breaths came faster now, the effort of the climb beginning to take its toll.

The mountain seemed alive around him, its presence both intimidating and awe-inspiring. The rustle of leaves in the wind, the distant call of birds, and the occasional snap of a twig beneath his boots created a symphony of wilderness that filled the silence. The mist that had shrouded the peaks earlier was closer now, tendrils of it curling around the trees like ghostly fingers.

Yordan paused to catch his breath, leaning against a boulder that jutted out from the hillside. His legs ached, and sweat trickled down his temples despite the cool air. As he stared out at the view below—a patchwork of forest and city shrinking into the distance—his mind drifted. He saw Katherine's face first, her soft smile and the warmth in her eyes when they were together. She grounded him, her steady presence a constant in his often-chaotic world. The thought of her brought a brief smile to his lips, a reminder of what waited for him back in Aralonis.

But then, unbidden, another image surfaced. Aisha. Her fierce gaze, her sharp tongue, the fire that seemed to radiate from her with every word she spoke. Yordan's smile faltered as a pang of guilt twisted in his chest. He didn't understand why she was so firmly lodged in his mind. He barely knew her, and yet... there she was, as vivid as if she were standing before him.

Shaking his head, Yordan pushed himself off the boulder and continued upward. His hands found purchase on a jagged rock, pulling him over a particularly steep section. The climb required more focus now, the loose rocks threatening to give way under his weight. He steadied himself with deliberate movements, his breathing heavy but controlled.

Why am I doing this? The question echoed in his mind as he paused again, his back pressed against the cool stone of a cliffside. Why climb these mountains because of a dream? Am I losing it? He exhaled sharply, wiping sweat from his brow. The golden deer's words replayed in his mind, their strange certainty pulling him onward.

"Rise up, your true path awaits. Climb the sacred mountain and embrace your destiny."

The words felt absurd now, almost laughable as he struggled to haul himself over another rocky ledge. But something deeper, something he couldn't name, compelled him forward. He wasn't just chasing a dream; he was chasing clarity, purpose, something that had been eluding him for far too long.

The forest began to thin as he climbed higher, the trees shrinking into sparse clusters, their gnarled roots clinging desperately to the rocky soil. The ground beneath him was uneven, a mix of loose gravel and large boulders that forced him to use his hands as much as his feet to keep moving upward. His fingers ached from gripping the rough stone, and his knees scraped against sharp edges as he pulled himself higher.

As the mist thickened, the temperature dropped, a biting chill seeping through Yordan's sweat-dampened clothes. He paused again, this time to take in the surreal beauty around him. The mist swirled like smoke, obscuring the view below and giving the world an otherworldly quality. The peaks above were hidden, their outlines faint and ghostly against the pale sky.

Yordan's thoughts drifted again, his mind a battlefield between Katherine's comforting presence and Aisha's fiery passion. He felt torn, conflicted, and utterly confused by the emotions swirling within him. Katherine was everything he'd ever wanted, but Aisha... Aisha was something he didn't understand, a force that unsettled and intrigued him in equal measure.

"Focus," he muttered to himself, his voice barely audible over the wind that had begun to whistle through the rocks. He gritted his teeth and pushed forward, his hands and feet moving with determination. The mountain seemed endless, its challenges unrelenting, but Yordan refused to stop. He didn't know what he was climbing toward, but he knew he couldn't turn back.

The path grew narrower, winding along a cliffside where one mis-step could send him plummeting into the misty abyss below. Yordan's heart pounded as he carefully navigated the treacherous terrain, his fingers gripping the cold stone for balance. The wind howled around him, carrying with it the faint scent of rain and the promise of even greater challenges ahead.

As he climbed higher, the weight of doubt pressed against him, but so did an inexplicable sense of purpose. Whatever awaited him at the summit, he knew he had to find it. With a final, determined breath, Yordan pulled himself over another ledge, the sound of his boots scraping against stone echoing in the stillness.

He paused, standing tall against the backdrop of the mist-shrouded mountains. His breath came in short gasps, his body trembling with exhaustion, but his gaze was fixed upward. The summit was still out of sight, hidden by the swirling mist, but Yordan felt its presence calling to him.

The climb had worn Yordan down to his core. His legs ached, his fingers throbbed, and his breath came in ragged bursts as he finally spotted the dark maw of a cave ahead. Relief washed over him like a wave. The opening was jagged and uninviting, but it promised shelter from the biting wind and the relentless incline. He trudged toward it, his boots crunching against loose stones until he stepped into the cool shadows.

The cave was shallow but sufficient, its floor uneven but dry. A faint trickle of water echoed somewhere deeper within, though the source was hidden by the darkness. Yordan dropped his pack onto the ground and sank against the rough wall, leaning his head back as he closed his eyes for a moment. The air inside was still, a stark contrast to the gusts that howled outside.

His stomach growled, a sharp reminder of the toll the climb had taken on him. He reached into his pack, pulling out a small bundle of food wrapped in cloth. Unwrapping it carefully, he revealed a simple meal: a few strips of dried meat, a chunk of hard cheese, and a piece of dense bread. It wasn't much, but it was enough to stave off the hunger gnawing at him.

Yordan paused before taking a bite. The habit was instinctual, ingrained in him since childhood. He closed his eyes and pressed his hands together, bowing his head slightly as he began an Aralonic prayer.

"Toteko," he murmured, his voice low but steady, "thank you for the strength to climb this far and for the sustenance that will renew me. May this meal give me the clarity and purpose I need to continue on this path you've laid before me."

He sat in silence for a moment after finishing, letting the prayer settle within him like a quiet echo. Then he picked up a piece of the bread, chewing slowly as he stared out at the faint light filtering into the cave's entrance. The food was plain, its texture coarse and unyielding, but it grounded him, giving him a sense of routine amidst the chaos of his journey.

As he ate, his thoughts began to drift again, despite his best efforts to keep them focused. First, there was Katherine. Her laugh, her touch, the way she seemed to bring out the best in him without even trying. She had been a constant in his life, a source of comfort and stability. Yordan had always envisioned her as part of his future, his companion, his partner, the person he would build a life with.

But then there was Aisha. He hadn't known her long, and yet she had left a mark on him. Her fiery passion, her unyielding defiance, the way her words cut through the air like a blade—all of it lingered in his mind, refusing to fade. She was so different from Katherine, like a storm compared to the calm of a gentle river. The intensity of her presence unsettled him, drawing his thoughts back to her again and again despite himself.

Yordan frowned, biting into a piece of the cheese as he wrestled with his own mind. Why do I keep thinking about her? he asked himself, his frustration mounting. Katherine was the one he wanted to spend his life with. She was the one who had stood by him, who knew him in ways no one else did. So why did Aisha, with her sharp words and piercing gaze, occupy so much space in his thoughts?

The answer eluded him, slipping through his fingers like the mist that shrouded the mountains outside. He leaned back against the cave wall, letting out a quiet sigh as he stared at the jagged ceiling above. His pulse quickened as the memory of Aisha's fiery confrontation at the inn replayed in his mind, her voice sharp and full of conviction. He didn't want to admit it, but something about her challenged him in a way he wasn't used to, a way that unsettled and intrigued him all at once.

"Katherine is who I love," he muttered under his breath, as if saying the words aloud would banish the confusion from his mind. But the cave remained silent, offering no clarity, only the faint echo of his own voice.

Yordan shook his head, finishing the last of his bread and wrapping the remaining food carefully before placing it back in his pack. The cave felt colder now, the shadows deeper, and the weight of his thoughts heavier than ever. He closed his eyes, leaning back against the wall as he let the exhaustion of the day wash over him.

Why am I here? he wondered. Why does my path feel so unclear, even as I climb higher? But no answers came, only the steady sound of his breathing and the faint trickle of water somewhere in the depths of the mountain.

Yordan froze mid-bite as a voice echoed faintly in the stillness. It wasn't a sharp call or a cry for help, but a smooth, resonant sound that sent a shiver down his spine. It carried an otherworldly quality, both familiar and distant, as if the voice was his own but layered with something ethereal.

"Yordan..."

His name floated through the air like a whisper on the wind. He turned sharply toward the cave's entrance, his heart pounding. The mist outside was still thick, curling lazily through the rocky outcroppings. He squinted into the gloom, scanning the landscape for movement.

"Hello?" he called, his voice cracking slightly. The sound echoed faintly, swallowed by the vastness outside.

Then the voice came again, clearer this time, reverberating like a gentle hum in his bones. "Yordan..."

He turned back toward the cave, the realization hitting him that the voice wasn't coming from outside—it was coming from within. His pulse quickened as he stepped hesitantly back into the shadows, his boots crunching softly on the uneven floor.

"Here I am," he said, his voice meek and unsteady as he peered into the darkness.

The cave was still, the trickling sound of water the only noise accompanying him. But as his eyes adjusted, Yordan noticed something—an almost imperceptible glow in the far corner of the cave. It pulsed faintly, like the ember of a dying flame, and then grew brighter before dimming again.

His breath caught in his throat, and he stepped closer, his movements slow and deliberate. The glow seemed to flicker in response, as though acknowledging his approach.

"Who are you?" Yordan asked, his voice trembling but laced with curiosity.

The glow grew stronger, illuminating the corner of the cave with a soft, golden light. It seemed to pulse in time with a heartbeat, radiating warmth that Yordan could feel on his skin despite the chill of the air. Then, the voice spoke again, layered and resonant, filling the cave like a chorus.

"I am that I am."

The words sent a shockwave through Yordan, a weight settling on his chest as if the air itself had grown heavier. The light pulsed brighter, casting shadows that danced wildly on the cave walls before dimming once more.

Yordan swallowed hard, his hands clenching into fists at his sides. The voice carried a weight he couldn't ignore, its simple yet profound statement echoing in his mind. He felt small and exposed, as though the very essence of his being was laid bare before whatever—or whoever—this was.

Yordan took a hesitant step closer, the golden light pulsing like a living thing. His breaths came shallow and fast as the weight of the voice's presence pressed down on him. The words it had spoken lingered in the air, resonating within him in ways he couldn't fully grasp.

"I... I don't understand," he said, his voice trembling.

The light pulsed brighter, filling the cave with a warmth that seemed to wrap around him like a shroud. The voice responded, its tone steady and commanding, yet not unkind.

"I am the god of your ancestors."

Yordan's eyes widened, his body frozen in place. He shook his head, his heart pounding so loudly it drowned out the faint trickle of water in the cave. His voice, barely above a whisper, escaped his dry lips. "Are you... Toteko?"

"I am known by that name," the voice replied, a ripple of authority flowing through its words, "but I have many names."

The light pulsed again, illuminating the jagged walls of the cave. Yordan staggered backward slightly, his legs giving way as he fell to his knees. His hands trembled as he raised them to cover his face, his head bowing low to the ground.

"I am not worthy to look upon you," he said, his voice cracking with a mix of fear and awe. "Please, do not ask me to."

There was a pause, the silence heavy and expectant. Then the voice came again, firm yet gentle, resonating with a clarity that left no room for argument.

"Look up and listen, Yordan."

His hands hesitated, then slowly lowered, revealing his pale face and wide eyes. He tilted his head upward, the golden light bathing his features as he forced himself to meet the radiance. His heart thundered in his chest, but he couldn't look away.

"I have heard the cries of all my people," Toteko continued, the voice reverberating through the cave. "Their pain, their anger, their despair. The divisions among them grow deeper, and I see the path ahead—one of destruction and ruin. I worry things will grow much worse if I do not act."

Yordan's throat tightened, his pulse racing as the voice's words filled him with both dread and awe. He felt the weight of Toteko's gaze, even though he could see no physical form. The light seemed to pulse in time with his heartbeat, surrounding him like an invisible force.

"So I have chosen to send you," Toteko said, the words final and undeniable.

"Me?" Yordan stammered, his voice weak. His mind reeled at the enormity of what he was hearing. He shook his head, his hands balling into fists on the cave floor. "Who am I to bring this message? I am merely a blacksmith."

The words escaped him in a rush, his disbelief and fear tumbling over each other. He thought of his forge, the steady rhythm of the hammer against iron, the simple, honest life he had led. He was no prophet, no leader. The weight of Toteko's declaration felt impossible to bear.

The light softened slightly, its glow steady and unwavering. "It is not your station, Yordan, that qualifies you," Toteko said, the voice gentle yet resolute. "It is your heart. I have seen your struggles, your doubts, your strength. You are not perfect, but perfection is not what I require. You have been forged, like iron in the fire, for this purpose."

Yordan clenched his fists as a wave of frustration overtook him. His heart pounded against his ribs, his breaths coming sharp and fast. The words Toteko had spoken still echoed in the cave, but instead of clarity, they filled him with turmoil. The gravity of the task set before him was crushing, and his doubts swelled until they could no longer be contained.

He stood suddenly, his legs trembling but holding firm as he faced the pulsing light. His voice cracked with the strain of his emotions, but it rose in defiance. "You... You've chosen the wrong messenger!" he shouted, his voice echoing in the cavernous space. "How can I speak to your people when I can't even tell you which woman I am truly in love with? How can someone as flawed as me carry your message?"

The cave seemed to shudder in response, the light swelling to fill every corner with a blinding radiance. Yordan staggered back, shielding his eyes with his arm, but the light pierced through even that meager protection. The voice that answered was no longer gentle or measured, it was a roar, a thunderclap that shook the very foundation of the earth.

"WHO MADE PEOPLE'S MOUTHS?" the voice boomed, shaking the air with its power. "WHO MADE THE DEAF, THE MUTE, THE SEEING, OR THE BLIND? DID NOT I? NOW GO!"

The force of the words knocked Yordan off his feet, sending him sprawling to the cave floor. His body trembled as he pressed his face to the cold stone, the weight of Toteko's presence bearing down on him like a storm. His ears rang with the voice's thunderous command, and for a moment, he couldn't move, couldn't breathe, consumed entirely by fear.

But then, as quickly as it had come, the overwhelming brightness began to soften. Yordan felt a warmth envelop him, not the searing intensity from before but something gentler, almost comforting. The light didn't recede—it grew closer, consuming him in its embrace. It wasn't just around him now; it was within him, coursing through his body like fire that burned without pain.

The voice came again, this time soft and soothing, like a whisper carried on the wind. "Yordan," it said, the name filled with a weight of care and purpose. "I shall send you to my people in Anakuatl, and through you, I shall reveal my wonders. You shall bring light to the darkness and smite those who kill the innocent in my name."

The words seeped into Yordan's very being, and he felt his fear begin to transform into something else—resolve, perhaps, or the faint stirrings of faith. His body trembled not from fear but from the sheer power of the light, which wrapped around him like a protective cocoon. He felt as though he were being lifted, carried into Toteko's embrace, his soul laid bare and reforged in the divine presence.

When the light began to recede, Yordan felt a strange sensation ripple through him, as if his entire body were aflame. Every nerve was

162

alive, every muscle taut with an energy he couldn't name. He gasped, clutching his chest as the burning sensation intensified but did not consume. It was as though he were being remade, his very essence reshaped by the encounter.

The cave, once so dim and cold, now seemed vast and endless, glowing faintly with the aftershocks of the divine presence. As the warmth began to ebb, Toteko's voice lingered, the final words resonating with a deep, quiet authority.

"I will be with you, Yordan."

The voice faded into the stillness, leaving behind a silence so profound it felt almost holy. Yordan slowly opened his eyes, his body still trembling from the encounter. The cave looked the same as before, its jagged walls and uneven floor unchanged, but Yordan knew with every fiber of his being that he was not the same.

The descent down the Sitlali Mountains was a blur to Yordan. The jagged rocks and loose gravel that had slowed his ascent were now navigated with reckless abandon. His legs burned, his lungs screamed for air, but he pushed onward, driven by the storm of emotions raging within him. His encounter with Toteko played over and over in his mind, vivid and overwhelming. But as he reached the base of the mountain and looked out at the land of Anakuatl, it all seemed... ordinary.

The mist still hung low over the trees, the distant spires of Lumina City gleaming faintly in the moonlight. Nothing had changed. No great signs, no divine transformation of the land. It all looked as it always had.

A deep sense of uncertainty clawed at Yordan. Did it really happen? he wondered. Was it just my mind playing tricks on me? The thought gnawed at him until he could bear it no longer. He took off at a sprint, his boots pounding against the dirt path as he rushed back toward Lumina City.

The journey was grueling. Every step felt heavier than the last, his body crying out for rest, but Yordan didn't stop. He couldn't. His mind was a whirlwind of doubt and fear, and the only thing grounding him was the thought of Sam—the one person who might help him make sense of it all.

By the time he reached the gates of Lumina City, the sky was a deep indigo, the stars faint pinpricks of light overhead. His chest heaved as he stumbled through the dimly lit streets, his legs threatening to give out with every step. The Restful Respite came into view at last, its warm light spilling out onto the cobblestones.

Yordan practically fell against the door, pushing it open with what little strength he had left. Inside, the common room was quiet, the hum of conversation subdued in the late hour. Jezzie was behind the counter, tidying up for the night. She looked up sharply at the sound of the door creaking open, her eyes narrowing as she took in Yordan's disheveled appearance. His clothes were filthy and damp with sweat, his hair matted, and his face pale with exhaustion.

"Hey!" Jezzie called out, her tone sharp. "We don't take beggars this late. You'd best move along—"

"Jezzie," Yordan rasped, his voice hoarse and weak. "Where... Where is Sam?"

The sound of his voice made her pause, recognition flickering in her eyes. "Yordan?" she said, her tone softening. "What in the world happened to you?"

From a corner of the room, Sam's head tilted toward the sound of Yordan's voice. He rose slowly, using his stick to navigate the space with ease. "I'm here," Sam said, his voice calm but curious. As Yordan staggered toward him, Sam added with a wry smile, "Did you run all the way back here?"

Yordan collapsed into a chair by the fire, his chest still heaving as he struggled to catch his breath. He rubbed his face with trembling hands, his mind racing. The warmth of the fire licked his skin, but it did little to calm the burning within him.

"I..." Yordan began, his voice barely audible. "Am I still alive?"

Sam froze, his brow furrowing. "What are you talking about?" he asked, his tone tinged with concern. He reached out, his hand finding Yordan's shoulder. "What happened to you on that mountain?"

Jezzie, who had been watching from the counter, grabbed a blanket and a cup of water. She hurried over, draping the blanket around Yordan's shoulders before placing the water in his trembling hands. "Here," she said gently. "You look like you're freezing."

Yordan didn't touch the water. His eyes stared blankly into the fire, his voice trembling as he spoke. "I must be dead," he whispered. "For I looked upon the lord Toteko, and it burned."

The room fell silent, the weight of his words hanging heavy in the air. Jezzie glanced at Sam, her expression a mix of confusion and concern. "What's he talking about?" she asked quietly.

Sam tightened his grip on Yordan's shoulder, his voice steady but firm. "Yordan," he said, his tone measured. "You need to get some rest. Whatever you think happened up there... the Lumites will think you've gone mad if you keep saying these things."

"But it was real," Yordan insisted, his voice rising slightly. "I felt it. The light, the voice—he spoke to me, Sam."

Sam exhaled slowly, his thumb brushing the edge of his stick. "I believe that you believe it," he said carefully, his tone almost soothing. "But you're exhausted. You've been climbing mountains and running through the city without stopping. You need sleep, Yordan. Let's figure this out when you've had time to rest."

Jezzie crouched beside Yordan, her voice soft. "He's right. You're no good to anyone like this. Just breathe, okay?"

Yordan's shoulders sagged, the fight draining out of him as his exhaustion overtook him. He nodded weakly, the blanket slipping from his shoulders as he leaned back in the chair. The firelight flickered across his pale face, and though his body was still, his mind churned with the memory of the light and the voice that had consumed him.

As sleep began to pull at the edges of his consciousness, Yordan whispered one final thought, almost to himself. "He said he'd be with me. But I don't know if I can do it."

Sam's hand remained on his shoulder, a steady anchor in the chaos. "You don't have to figure it all out tonight," Sam said quietly. "Just rest, Yordan. Just rest."

The dream consumed Yordan as if he were reliving the moment in perfect detail. The cave walls around him pulsed with golden light, their jagged edges softened by the radiance emanating from Toteko's presence. The warmth of the light wrapped around him like a cocoon, but it wasn't comforting, it was overwhelming. The voice reverberated in his chest, each word carrying an impossible weight.

"I have heard the cries of all my people."

The voice boomed, filling every corner of the cave, making the ground beneath him tremble. Yordan was on his knees again, his hands pressed against the cold stone floor as the light bore down on him. He felt the fire coursing through him, burning without consuming, the sensation both agonizing and purifying.

"You must rise and carry my message to all my people. You must show them the path away from destruction and toward unity."

The words echoed endlessly, like a drumbeat in his mind. Yordan looked up, his trembling hands lifting toward the light as if to beg for mercy. The radiance intensified, and Toteko's voice became all-encompassing, filling not just the cave but Yordan's very being.

"Trust in me, Yordan, as I trust in you."

The scene began to shift, the golden light receding into darkness, leaving Yordan alone in the cold, empty cave. The silence was deafening, pressing in on him as he tried to make sense of what he'd heard. But before he could gather his thoughts, the dream began to replay, the voice returning, the light flooding back, the words repeating over and over.

"You must rise and carry my message..."

Yordan woke with a gasp, his body drenched in sweat. His chest heaved as he sat up in the bunk, the blanket clinging to his damp skin. The room was dim, the faint glow of the dying fire in the common room below barely reaching his corner. Outside, the wind howled softly, the only sound in the stillness of the night.

"I can't do it," he whispered, his voice barely audible. He swung his legs over the side of the bunk, his feet touching the cool wooden floor. His hands trembled as he ran them through his hair, his thoughts a chaotic storm.

The dream had been so vivid, so unrelenting. He could still feel the fire within him, the pressure of Toteko's voice, the weight of the command he had been given. But now, in the quiet of the night, it all felt impossible.

"I've lost my mind," he muttered to himself, his voice growing louder. "I can't do it. How could I even try? I'm just... I'm just a blacksmith. What do I know about delivering messages or uniting people? I can't even figure out my own life—how am I supposed to lead anyone else?"

He buried his face in his hands, his elbows resting on his knees. Doubt clawed at him, its grip tightening with every passing moment. His encounter with Toteko felt both monumental and absurd, a responsibility too great for someone like him. The enormity of it was suffocating.

Yordan's mind raced, replaying every word of the dream, every moment of the encounter in the cave. He felt like a fraud, chosen for a task he was utterly unprepared for. The memory of the golden light, so vivid in his dream, now seemed like a distant, unreachable thing.

"What if I fail?" he whispered, his voice cracking. "What if I can't do it? What if I'm not enough?"

The fire in the common room crackled faintly, the sound grounding him for a moment. He looked around the dim room, the shadows dancing across the walls, and felt a profound loneliness. The weight of the mission pressed on him, suffocating in its intensity, and he had no idea where to even begin.

For a moment, he thought of Sam, the steady presence that had always been there to guide him when his own path felt uncertain. But even Sam couldn't help him now. This wasn't a problem that could be solved with logic or reassurance. This was something far beyond either of them.

Yordan stood, pacing the small space near his bunk. His thoughts churned, his heart racing as he tried to make sense of the impossible. Finally, he stopped, staring out the small window at the faint glimmer of moonlight over the rooftops of Lumina City.

"I'm not ready for this," he said softly, his voice heavy with despair. "I'll never be ready."

The wind outside seemed to whisper in response, its soft howling a quiet reminder of the mountain he had just descended. Yordan shivered, pulling the blanket tighter around his shoulders. Despite the warmth of the fire below and the lingering heat of the dream's memory, he felt cold—cold and utterly alone.

With a heavy sigh, he sat back on the bunk, his head in his hands. He didn't know how long he stayed like that, the weight of the mission pressing down on him until exhaustion finally claimed him once more. But even as he drifted back into a restless sleep, Toteko's voice lingered in his mind, a constant reminder of the path that lay before him.

Chapter Ten

The first rays of morning light crept through the shutters of Yordan's room, casting faint patterns on the wooden floor. He stirred, groaning softly as consciousness returned. His body ached, his limbs heavy as if he had been carrying the weight of the entire Sitlali Mountains. Slowly, he opened his eyes, blinking at the pale light. For a moment, he lay there, staring at the ceiling, his thoughts swirling.

Was it all a dream? he wondered, the vividness of the encounter with Toteko still fresh in his mind. The golden light, the thunderous voice, the searing fire that didn't burn—it all felt too real to be a figment of his imagination. Yet, as he looked around the modest room, everything seemed painfully ordinary. His pack sat slumped in the corner, his boots neatly placed by the door, and the faint sounds of the inn waking up drifted through the thin walls.

He sat up slowly, running a hand through his tangled hair. A deep sigh escaped him as he swung his legs over the side of the bed, his feet touching the cool floor. His body protested every movement, the soreness from his frantic climb and descent still fresh.

"Maybe it was just a bad dream," he muttered to himself, though the words felt hollow.

Pulling on his boots and throwing on a clean shirt, Yordan made his way downstairs. The familiar scent of fresh bread and roasted herbs greeted him, mingling with the soft hum of conversation from the early risers in the common room. Despite the warmth of the scene, a heaviness lingered in his chest, an invisible weight he couldn't shake.

As he stepped into the dining area, Jezzie was bustling behind the counter, her dark braid swaying as she moved. She looked up as Yordan entered, her eyes narrowing slightly as they met his. A faint smirk tugged at her lips, but there was concern behind it.

"Morning," she said, her voice light but probing. "You doing okay after last night?"

Yordan paused, her question catching him off guard. "What do you mean?" he asked, his brow furrowing as he approached the counter.

Jezzie leaned against the counter, crossing her arms as she studied him. "You don't remember?" she asked, her tone tinged with incredulity. "You came in here looking like you'd been chased by a ghost—or worse. Sweating, out of breath, like you'd run straight down from the Sitlali Mountains without stopping. You scared half the room the way you barged in."

She tilted her head, her expression softening slightly. "You looked like you saw something terrifying."

Yordan stared at her, his mind reeling as the fragments of the previous night resurfaced. The climb, the cave, Toteko's booming voice, the blinding light—it all rushed back with startling clarity. His hands clenched at his sides, and he felt his chest tighten as the weight of it settled over him again. But he forced a faint smile, shaking his head as if to dismiss her concern.

"I'm fine now," he said, his voice quiet but steady. Internally, though, his thoughts were anything but calm. Fine? he repeated in his mind. How can I be fine after... that?

Jezzie didn't look entirely convinced, but she nodded, stepping back to resume her work. "If you say so," she said lightly. "Just... try not to give us all another scare, yeah?"

Yordan nodded absently, making his way to a table by the fire. As he sat down, the warmth of the flames seeped into his weary body, but it did little to ease the chill that clung to his thoughts. He stared into the flickering light, his mind replaying Jezzie's words.

You looked like you saw something terrifying.

Terrifying didn't even begin to cover it. He had looked upon a god, felt his very soul laid bare, and been charged with a mission he couldn't comprehend, let alone accept. The memory of the light, the fire, the voice—it all felt as vivid now as it had in the moment. And yet, here he was, sitting in a quiet inn, surrounded by the mundane trappings of everyday life. It was almost enough to make him question his own sanity.

Yordan leaned back in his chair, letting out a slow breath. "I'm fine," he whispered to himself, as if saying it aloud would make it true. But deep down, he knew that nothing about him, nothing about his life—would ever be the same.

Yordan sat by the fire, his gaze locked on the flickering flames. The warmth danced over his skin, but it did little to thaw the icy tension coiled within him. His mind was a tempest, replaying every moment from the cave—Toteko's voice, the blinding light, the impossible weight of the mission placed upon him. He barely noticed the soft murmur of voices in the room or the clatter of plates from Jezzie's counter. It all faded into the background, dulled by the storm inside him.

A hand gently touched his shoulder, light and deliberate. Yordan blinked, startled from his thoughts, and turned to see Sam standing beside him, his familiar stick tapping the floor as he steadied himself. Sam's face bore its usual calm, though his lips curled faintly in a smile.

"Hey," Sam said softly. "I was worried you'd headed off somewhere on your own already. My stick found an empty bed this morning, and I thought you were gone."

Yordan managed a weak smile, leaning back slightly in his chair. "No, I'm here," he said, his voice low. "Just eating, trying not to feel like my legs are still on fire from last night."

Sam chuckled, pulling out the chair next to Yordan and easing himself into it with practiced precision. His stick rested across his lap as he leaned back, tapping the edge of the table lightly with his fingertips. "You know," he said with a playful lilt, "maybe that's a sign you should slow down. You're not some mountain goat, Yordan."

Yordan let out a short, humorless laugh, shaking his head. "Yeah, maybe."

The response was so flat, so uncharacteristic, that Sam tilted his head slightly, his brow furrowing. "What's with you? Did the mountain take more out of you than your legs? You're usually the one who can't stop talking."

Yordan didn't answer immediately, his gaze drifting back to the fire. His fingers tapped absently against the edge of his plate, his thoughts slipping back to the cave, Toteko's voice reverberating in his chest.

"I guess I'm just tired," he said finally, his tone distant. "A lot happened yesterday."

Sam leaned forward, his smile faltering as he tried to read Yordan's mood. "Tired, huh? That's all? You sure you didn't leave something important on the mountain? Your sense of humor, maybe?" He smirked, nudging Yordan's arm lightly.

But Yordan didn't react the way he normally would. There was no grin, no playful retort, just a faint shrug and a barely audible, "Maybe."

The air between them grew heavier, the warmth of their usual banter replaced by an unfamiliar silence. Sam's fingers tapped against the stick in his lap as he considered his next words.

"All right," Sam said carefully, his voice softer now. "Something's up. You don't have to tell me if you're not ready, but... this isn't like you. You're worrying me, Yordan."

Yordan's jaw tightened, his eyes never leaving the fire. He wanted to say something, to confide in Sam, but the words felt too big, too impossible to explain. How could he put into words the weight of what he'd experienced? How could he make Sam understand when he barely understood it himself?

"I'm fine," Yordan said quietly, his voice tinged with frustration—not at Sam, but at himself. "I just... need some time to think."

Sam nodded slowly, leaning back in his chair with a faint sigh. "Fair enough," he said. "But you know I'm here, right? Whatever's going on, you don't have to deal with it alone."

Yordan glanced at him, the corner of his mouth twitching in a faint attempt at a smile. "I know," he said. "Thanks."

Sam sat in silence for a moment, his hand resting on the table, his calm presence steadying the space between them. But even he could feel the shift in Yordan, the way his usual spark seemed dimmed. It wasn't just exhaustion, something deeper was weighing on him, something Sam couldn't quite reach.

As the fire crackled softly, Sam broke the silence with a gentle tease. "Just don't go running up any more mountains without telling me, okay? You might have strong legs, but I'd hate to have to come up there and drag you back down."

Yordan managed a faint chuckle, though it lacked the usual warmth. "Don't worry," he said, his tone half-hearted. "I've had enough mountains for a while."

Sam nodded, but the concern didn't leave his face. The two sat there, the silence stretching between them like an unspoken understanding. Yordan stared into the fire, its flickering light casting shadows that seemed to dance with the weight of his thoughts. Sam, though blind, could feel the tension in his friend, a quiet storm brewing just beneath the surface.

For now, Sam let it be, knowing Yordan needed time. But the bond between them felt heavier, the usual ease of their friendship replaced by something harder, more uncertain. Whatever Yordan had faced on the mountain, it had changed him—and Sam could only hope that when the time came, Yordan would let him in.

Yordan and Sam sat by the fire in the common room of the Restful Respite, the crackling flames casting dancing shadows on the walls. The early morning bustle of the hostel hadn't yet begun, leaving the two of them in a quiet pocket of time. Yordan stared into the fire, his hands loosely clasped in front of him, his thoughts still tangled from the events of the previous night.

Sam, sitting beside him with his stick resting across his lap, tilted his head slightly. The soft creak of the chair beneath him broke the silence. "You've been awfully quiet," he said, his tone light but tinged with curiosity. "For someone who came in like a storm last night, you're surprisingly calm now."

Yordan exhaled sharply, the memory of his frantic descent from the Sitlali Mountains and his wild entrance into the hostel still fresh in his mind. "I'm not sure 'calm' is the right word," he replied, rubbing the back of his neck. "I feel... unsettled. Like I need to clear my head."

Sam raised an eyebrow, his fingers brushing the edge of the stick. "And how do you plan to do that?"

"I was thinking," Yordan began hesitantly, "we could go to the Lumina River."

Sam leaned back slightly, his expression neutral but his silence speaking volumes. Yordan glanced at him, his brow furrowing. "What?" he asked. "What's that look for?"

"Nothing," Sam said after a moment, though his tone suggested otherwise. "I'm just wondering why the river is suddenly so important to you."

Yordan shifted in his seat, his gaze returning to the fire. "I don't know," he admitted. "I just... feel like it might help. After last night, I need to see something, figure something out."

Sam let the words hang in the air for a moment before leaning forward. "You're really not going to tell me what happened up there, are you?"

Yordan hesitated, then shook his head. "Not yet."

"Fair enough," Sam replied, though his tone carried a note of concern. He tapped his stick lightly against the floor. "All right let's go to the river. But don't expect me to stay quiet the whole way. I have questions, Yordan."

Yordan gave a faint smile, though it didn't reach his eyes. "You always do."

The sun was beginning to rise as they made their way out of the hostel and through the streets of Lumina City. The morning air was cool, and the faint scent of baked bread wafted through the alleys as vendors began setting up their stalls. Yordan led the way, his steps purposeful but his thoughts distant.

Sam followed close behind, his stick tapping against the cobblestones with practiced rhythm. For once, he was unusually quiet, and it began to wear on Yordan as they approached the outskirts of the city. The silence felt heavy, almost accusatory, and Yordan finally broke it.

"Are you mad at me or something?" he asked, glancing over his shoulder.

Sam snorted softly, his lips curving into a faint smirk. "Mad? No. Curious? Absolutely." He tilted his head, his stick brushing against a loose stone. "You've been acting strange ever since you came back last night, and now you're dragging me to a river like it's going to fix everything. That's enough to make anyone curious."

Yordan sighed, running a hand through his hair. "I'm not trying to be strange," he said. "I just... I need to see something for myself. After what happened, I need to know if—"

"If what?" Sam interrupted. "If your legs were actually on fire? Because let me tell you, they probably felt like it after you ran all the way from the Sitlali Mountains to the hostel without stopping."

Yordan groaned, shaking his head. "It's not about that, Sam."

"Then what's it about?" Sam pressed, his tone calm but insistent. "You're not exactly making this easy to follow, Yordan. You came in last night looking like you'd seen a ghost, muttering about fire and Toteko, and now you're taking me to a river without explaining why. Can you blame me for asking questions?"

Yordan stopped walking, his shoulders tense. "I don't have answers yet, all right?" he said, his voice quieter but strained. "I'm trying to figure it out myself."

Sam stood still for a moment, his expression softening. "Okay," he said, his voice gentler. "I'll give you time. But you've got to let me in eventually. Whatever this is, it's bigger than you, isn't it?"

Yordan didn't reply, instead turning back toward the road ahead. The faint sound of rushing water reached his ears, signaling that they were close to the river. He quickened his pace, eager to see if the Lumina River could provide the clarity he so desperately needed.

When they reached the riverbank, Yordan stopped and stared. The water flowed serenely, its surface glimmering in the sunlight. He crouched by the edge, dipping his hands into the cool current, the sensation grounding him in the present. But as he looked out at the river, there were no signs, no messages, nothing to confirm the extraordinary events of the previous night.

"Well?" Sam asked from a few steps behind him. "What do you see?"

Yordan crouched by the riverbank, the cool water lapping softly against the stones. He stared at the flowing current, his hands resting on his knees, and tried to quiet the noise in his mind. The river had spoken before—or at least he thought it had. The memory of that voice, ethereal and commanding, lingered in his thoughts like an echo he couldn't quite grasp.

Now, he strained to hear anything—a whisper, a hum, even the faintest sound that might confirm what he'd experienced. But the river was silent. Its steady flow was maddening in its ordinariness, each splash and ripple mocking the memory of his encounter. Yordan's jaw tightened as he leaned forward slightly, his pulse quickening.

Why won't you speak now? he thought, frustration bubbling within him. Was it all in my head? The silence pressed down on him, heavier than the weight of his exhaustion. The river's stillness felt deafening, each moment stretching into an eternity as he waited for something—anything—to happen.

Doubt crept in, sharp and insidious. What if it wasn't real? The thought struck him like a blow. What if I made it all up? What if I've gone mad? His hands clenched into fists, his nails digging into his palms as he fought to keep his thoughts from spiraling. The memory of the golden light, the searing heat, Toteko's voice—it had all felt so vivid, so undeniable. But now, in the face of this unyielding silence, it seemed distant, like a fading dream.

Yordan exhaled sharply, his breath shaky. And even if it was real, he thought bitterly, how am I supposed to do what Toteko asked? How do I even begin to bring his people together? They don't even see each other as equals. They fight, they hate, they kill—all in his name. How can I possibly change that?

The enormity of the task pressed down on him, threatening to crush him under its weight. He felt small, insignificant, a single man standing at the edge of an uncaring river, burdened with a mission he didn't understand and wasn't prepared for.

"Yordan?" Sam's voice cut through the fog of his thoughts, startling him. Yordan blinked, his head snapping up as he looked over his shoulder. Sam stood a few steps back, his stick resting lightly on the ground as he tilted his head toward Yordan.

"You still here?" Sam asked, his tone casual but with a hint of concern. "You've been awfully quiet for a guy who dragged me out here."

Yordan swallowed hard, his pulse still racing from the intensity of his internal struggle. He straightened up slightly, brushing his hands on his pants as if to shake off the weight of his thoughts. "Yeah," he said, his voice low. "I'm still here."

Sam frowned slightly, his fingers tapping against the stick in his hand. "You sure about that? You've got that faraway look again, like your head's up in the mountains instead of here by the river."

Yordan managed a faint smile, though it didn't reach his eyes. "I'm just... thinking," he said, turning his gaze back to the water.

Sam didn't press further, though Yordan could feel his friend's quiet scrutiny. The silence stretched between them again, but this time, it felt less oppressive. Yordan let out a slow breath, the sound of the river's flow grounding him, even if it didn't offer the answers he sought.

For now, the questions would remain unanswered, but Yordan couldn't shake the feeling that the silence itself was telling him something.

Yordan leaned back against a large stone by the riverbank, the cool breeze carrying the sound of flowing water and rustling leaves. Sam sat beside him, his stick resting across his lap, the blind man's face turned slightly toward the sun as though he could feel its warmth more keenly than most. The silence between them wasn't uncomfortable, but it was laden with unspoken thoughts. Yordan stared at the river, his mind swimming with doubts and questions that felt too big for him to carry alone.

Finally, he broke the silence, his voice quiet but direct. "Sam, can I ask you something?"

Sam tilted his head, a faint smile tugging at the corners of his lips. "You're asking if you can ask? That's a first. Go ahead."

Yordan hesitated, choosing his words carefully. "You've always been... clear about what you believe, about why you chose to be an Ant. But I don't think I've ever really asked you how you came to those decisions. How did you figure out what's right and wrong for you?"

Sam tapped his fingers lightly on the stick, his expression thoughtful. "That's a big question, Yordan," he said after a moment. "But I'll try to give you an answer that makes sense."

He shifted slightly, the sunlight catching the sharp angles of his face as he spoke. "For me, it's about what I can feel and sense. Not just with my hands or ears, but with my gut. I've always thought that if we're going to talk about what's right or wrong, it's not something handed down from a god or written in a book. It's about how our actions ripple out to the people around us. If what I do causes harm, I try to change it. If it helps, I lean into it."

Yordan listened intently, his eyes fixed on Sam. "So you don't think there's... like, a higher power guiding us?"

Sam smiled faintly, shaking his head. "Not in the way you mean. I think there's something to be said for the natural order of things, for balance. But the idea of a god controlling everything or having a specific plan for us? I can't get behind that. My life has been too full of chaos for me to believe that someone's been pulling the strings all along."

Yordan frowned slightly, his gaze drifting back to the river. "But how do you know what you're doing is enough? How do you keep yourself from doubting?"

Sam chuckled softly, the sound carrying an edge of weariness. "Oh, I doubt all the time, Yordan. Every day, I question if I'm doing the right thing. But that's part of it. I think doubt keeps us honest, makes us look harder at the choices we're making. I don't need divine approval or a perfect answer. I just need to know that I've done my best to be kind, to help where I can, and to stand against what I know is wrong."

Yordan absorbed Sam's words, turning them over in his mind. His friend's clarity, his unwavering sense of self, was both inspiring and unsettling. Yordan's own beliefs had always been tied to Toteko, to the faith he had grown up with, but now that foundation felt shaky. He had looked upon the god of his ancestors, heard Toteko's voice, and yet he felt more lost than ever.

"Sam," Yordan said after a pause, his voice softer, "how would you start? If you were trying to bring peace to all people in Anakuatl, how would you even begin?"

Sam let out a long breath, his hand resting lightly on the stick. "That's an even bigger question," he said with a wry smile. "And I'm

181

not sure I have an answer. But if I had to start somewhere, I'd say... listening. Really listening. Not just to what people say, but to what they need, what they're afraid of, what they're fighting for. Most people don't wake up in the morning wanting to hurt someone else. They're trying to protect something, even if it's in the wrong way."

Yordan nodded slowly, his gaze still on the river. "You think listening is enough?"

Sam tilted his head, his expression serious. "No. Listening is just the first step. After that, you have to act. You have to take what you've heard and use it to build something better. And that means compromise, sacrifice, and probably pissing a lot of people off. But if it's done with the right intentions, it's a start."

The two sat in silence again, the weight of their conversation settling between them. Yordan's thoughts churned, a mix of uncertainty and determination. Sam's words had given him something to hold onto, even if they didn't provide all the answers.

"Listening," Yordan murmured to himself, the word feeling both simple and monumental. He glanced at Sam, a faint smile tugging at his lips. "Thanks, Sam."

The walk back to the Restful Respite was quiet, the faint hum of Lumina City's daily life swirling around Yordan and Sam. The cobbled streets beneath their boots were uneven, their rhythms echoing softly with each step. Yordan's thoughts drifted as he walked, the weight of the morning still heavy on his shoulders. His eyes scanned the streets and alleyways, searching for something he couldn't name.

As they neared the heart of the city, Yordan noticed something strange: the absence of Zetians. He remembered the crowd at the temple and the separate lines, how the Zetian queue had barely moved—and Aisha's sharp words replayed in his mind. The streets seemed filled with Lumites and Aralonites, their distinct clothing marking their religious identities, but the Zetians were conspicuously missing.

Yordan frowned, his eyes narrowing as he scanned the alleys and side streets. "Have you noticed?" he said quietly, breaking the silence.

"Noticed what?" Sam asked, his head tilting slightly as he tapped his stick against the edge of the street.

"There's no one here," Yordan said, his voice tinged with unease. "No Zetians. Not since we left the river."

Sam's face was calm, but his lips pressed together in thought. "You think they're hiding?"

Yordan hesitated, his mind flashing back to Aisha's frustrated tone and her elder, Uriah, speaking in subdued resignation. "Maybe," he said. "Aisha said they had to take hidden paths to avoid trouble. I didn't believe her then, but now... I don't know."

Sam stopped mid-step, his stick pausing in the air as he tilted his head. "Horses," he said, his voice low. "I hear horses."

Yordan's body tensed, his ears straining to catch the distant rhythm of hooves on stone. Within moments, the sound grew louder, more distinct. A group of mounted soldiers appeared at the far end of the street, their figures cutting imposing silhouettes against the sunlight.

As they drew closer, Yordan could make out the lion-head emblem emblazoned on their tabards, a mark of the Lumite military. The soldiers were heavily armored, their pauldrons gleaming and their swords hanging at their sides. Their horses were large and well-trained, their hooves striking the cobblestones with precision.

The soldiers encircled Yordan and Sam in a smooth, practiced motion, their horses forming a tight perimeter around them. The commander, a stern-faced man with a scar running down his left cheek, raised a gauntleted hand to signal his men to halt.

"Identify yourselves," the commander barked, his voice sharp and authoritative. His steely gaze swept over Yordan and Sam, lingering on their travel-worn appearances.

Yordan swallowed hard, his mind racing. He straightened his posture, raising his chin slightly to meet the commander's gaze. "I'm Yordan Arano," he said clearly, though his voice wavered slightly. He gestured toward Sam, his hand trembling faintly. "And this is my friend, Sam. We're from Aralonis."

The commander's eyes narrowed, his expression unreadable as he considered Yordan's words. The silence stretched uncomfortably, broken only by the faint snorts of the horses and the creak of saddles.

Finally, the commander nodded, his stern demeanor softening slightly. "Carry on," he said curtly. "And stay out of trouble."

With that, he spurred his horse forward, the soldiers following his lead. The clatter of hooves echoed down the street as they rode away, leaving Yordan and Sam standing in their wake.

Yordan exhaled slowly, his hands unclenching as the tension eased from his body. "That was... something," he muttered, his voice low.

Sam, his expression as calm as ever, tapped his stick lightly against the ground. "You don't say."

Yordan shot him a faintly exasperated look but didn't respond. As they resumed their walk toward the hostel, his thoughts churned. The soldiers had barely spared them a glance after hearing they were from Aralonis, but the encounter left him uneasy. He couldn't shake the feeling that Lumina City was far more dangerous than it appeared on the surface—and not just for Zetians.

The Restful Respite came into view, its warm light spilling onto the cobblestone street as they approached. Yordan cast one last glance down the road where the soldiers had disappeared, a faint unease settling in his chest. Whatever was happening in Lumina City, he had a sinking feeling they had only scratched the surface.

The warm glow of the Restful Respite greeted Yordan and Sam as they stepped inside. The common room was busier now, with travelers gathered around tables, sharing food and conversation. Jezzie, ever the attentive innkeeper, was tending to a group near the counter when her eyes flicked toward the door. Upon seeing Sam, her face lit up with a playful grin.

"Back so soon, boys?" she called out, weaving through the room with practiced ease. Her dark braid swayed behind her as she approached, and her eyes locked onto Sam. "Sam, you didn't stay out too long, did you? Wouldn't want you catching a chill." Her tone carried a hint of teasing, her smile softening as she stopped in front of him.

Sam tilted his head slightly, his expression neutral as ever. "I appreciate the concern," he said, his tone polite but distant. "But I'm fine. Yordan made sure we didn't get into any trouble."

Jezzie's smile faltered for the briefest moment before she recovered, leaning in just a touch closer. "You know," she said lightly, her voice dropping a little, "if you ever need someone to help you unwind after all that wandering, you know where to find me."

Sam's brows lifted slightly, and he let out a soft, almost amused breath. "I'll keep that in mind," he said, though his tone remained neutral. He adjusted his grip on his stick and turned slightly toward Yordan, as if to shift the attention.

Yordan, however, didn't take the opportunity to tease as he usually would. He seemed distant, his gaze focused on the fire crackling in the hearth across the room. Jezzie followed Sam's glance, her smile faltering again as she noticed Yordan's faraway expression.

Sam frowned slightly, his head tilting as he turned fully toward his friend. "You all right, Yordan?" he asked, his tone laced with genuine concern. "Usually, you'd have some smart comment about me being uninterested."

Yordan blinked as if pulled from his thoughts, his hand absently brushing the edge of the counter. "Sorry," he said quietly, his voice barely above a murmur. "I'm just... still a little unsure of what to do."

Jezzie glanced between the two, sensing the shift in the mood. She straightened, the playful edge gone from her expression. "I'll get you both something to eat," she said softly before retreating toward the kitchen.

Yordan moved to sit by the fire, lowering himself into a chair with a heaviness that seemed to weigh down his entire frame. The flames flickered in his eyes as he stared into them, his thoughts churning. When Jezzie returned with their food, he murmured a quiet thanks before picking at the bread and stew, his appetite dulled by the storm in his mind.

Sam sat beside him, his stick resting across his knees as he began to eat. He didn't press Yordan, giving him the space to work through whatever was occupying his thoughts.

Yordan, meanwhile, found his mind circling back to the man they had found nailed to the tree. The image of his wounds, his pained voice asking for help—it all replayed in his mind, sharper now in the quiet of the common room. But as he tried to piece together the details, he realized with a pang of guilt that he couldn't remember anything that identified the man's beliefs or origins. His clothing had been simple, his appearance unremarkable beyond the horror of his injuries.

Was he a Zetian? Yordan wondered, his gaze still fixed on the fire. The thought gnawed at him. Or was he just another troublemaker, like Benjamin said? But what does that even mean here?

He rubbed his temples, the weight of the day pressing down on him. The idea that the man might have been a Zetian brought a new layer of complexity to his thoughts. If Aisha was right about the treatment of her people, then the man's punishment could have been less about his actions and more about who he was. But Yordan couldn't be sure, and the uncertainty ate at him.

"Yordan," Sam said quietly, breaking the silence. His friend's tone was gentle but firm, his hand resting lightly on the arm of Yordan's chair. "You're spiraling again. Eat something. You'll think clearer with food in your stomach."

Yordan nodded absently, taking a small bite of bread but barely tasting it. His thoughts remained on the tree, the man, the city, and the impossible task that Toteko had laid before him. The fire crackled softly, its warmth contrasting with the chill settling in his chest.

Sam leaned back, his expression unreadable as he listened to the faint hum of the common room around them. He didn't say anything else, but his presence was steady, an anchor against the current of Yordan's doubts.

For now, Yordan stayed quiet, unsure of what to say or where to even begin. But the questions lingered, their weight growing heavier with every passing moment.

Chapter Eleven

Yordan woke with a start, his body drenched in sweat despite the cool morning air that seeped through the cracks in the wooden walls of his small room at the Restful Respite. The faint sound of bustling city life began to stir outside, but he barely noticed it. He lay there for a moment, staring up at the ceiling, his mind spinning in circles.

Two weeks. Two weeks since he'd descended from the Sitlali Mountains, since he'd stood in the golden light of Toteko's presence, since the divine voice had thundered through his soul with a mission that felt as impossible now as it had then.

In the quiet of the mornings and the stillness of the nights, Yordan had hoped—prayed—for something more. A whisper, a dream, another sign that what he'd experienced wasn't a cruel twist of his imagination. Yet, night after night, his dreams were nothing but mundane, disjointed flashes of meaningless faces and places. The silence felt louder than anything he had ever known, pressing against his chest like an unseen weight.

He sat up, his legs swinging over the side of the bed, his elbows resting on his knees as he buried his face in his hands. What am I supposed to do now? The question haunted him every day since his encounter. He had clung to the hope that Toteko would guide him further, but now that hope felt like it was slipping through his fingers.

And then there was the matter of the Zetians. Aisha's words had planted a seed of doubt in his mind, a seed that had grown as he wandered Lumina City. The divide between the religious groups was stark, and nowhere was it more apparent than in the treatment of the Zetians. They moved through the city like shadows, avoiding attention, speaking in hushed tones, their gazes cast downward. It was as if they didn't exist at all to the Lumites and Aralonites who filled the streets with their loud voices and vibrant clothing.

He had tried, in his way, to bridge the gap. He had approached Zetians in the market, in the alleys, near the Grand Temple, but every attempt ended the same.

"I don't want any trouble," they would say, their voices tight with fear or frustration. "Leave me alone."

No matter how carefully he approached or how kindly he spoke, the result was always the same. He would watch them hurry away, their backs stiff, their heads low, leaving him standing there with unanswered questions and a growing sense of helplessness.

He rubbed his temples, the frustration boiling inside him. What good is this mission if I can't even talk to the people I'm supposed to help? He had come closer to the truth about the Zetians' treatment in Lumina City, yes, but what good was truth without action? Without understanding?

The last two weeks played over in his mind like a cruel joke. Days of wandering, of watching, of hearing nothing but silence in the moments he needed guidance most. Even Sam, for all his steady support, had begun to look at him with a quiet concern, his teasing fewer and his questions more pointed. Yordan couldn't blame him. He felt like he was floundering, his steps faltering even before his journey had truly begun.

He pushed himself to his feet, the creak of the floorboards breaking the silence of the room. He dressed quickly, his movements sharp and jerky as if he could shake off his frustration through sheer force of will. As he laced up his boots, his thoughts circled back to the mountain, to the fire that had burned without consuming him, to the booming voice that had called him by name.

"I will be with you," Toteko had said. But where was he now?

Yordan exhaled sharply, running a hand through his disheveled hair. He stepped to the small window, pushing it open to let in the morning air. The sights and sounds of Lumina City spilled in, a mix of life and routine that felt achingly normal compared to the storm raging inside him.

Somewhere out there, among the tangled streets and towering spires, the answers he sought lay hidden. But with each passing day, they felt further away, the weight of his doubts growing heavier with every silent night.

"How do I even begin to bring peace to all people in Keleret?" he whispered to himself, the words a plea to the wind. The city offered no reply, its life continuing unabated as if unaware of the young man standing at the window, burdened by a mission that felt as vast and unyielding as the mountains he had climbed.

Yordan woke with a groggy start, sunlight streaming through the cracks in the shutters. Rubbing his eyes, he turned toward the other bed in the small room he shared with Sam, only to find it empty. The blanket was neatly folded at the foot of the bed, and Sam's stick, which usually leaned against the wall beside it, was nowhere to be seen.

Frowning, Yordan swung his legs over the side of his bed and stood. "Where'd you sneak off to?" he muttered to himself, running a hand through his messy hair. He quickly dressed, his curiosity piqued and made his way downstairs to the common room of the Restful Respite.

The warmth of the fire hit him first, the comforting crackle filling the room. Yordan paused at the foot of the stairs, his eyes scanning the bustling space. It didn't take long to find Sam—he was seated in one of the well-worn chairs by the hearth, his posture relaxed, his stick resting across his lap.

Jezzie was there too, her presence unmistakable as she leaned over to set a plate of food on the small table in front of Sam. She murmured something Yordan couldn't hear, her voice low and playful, before letting her hand linger on Sam's shoulder, her fingers trailing down his arm in a way that was anything but subtle. With a faint smirk, she turned and sauntered back toward the counter, her braid swinging behind her.

Yordan's brows shot up, a mischievous grin spread across his face. So that's where he was, he thought, his amusement already growing as he carefully approached, trying to move as silently as possible across the creaking floorboards. Just as he was about to pounce with a sly remark, Sam's voice cut through his thoughts.

"Morning, Yordan," Sam said evenly, his head tilting slightly toward him. "How are you?"

Yordan stopped mid-step, his grin faltering. "How did you—"

"Your boots," Sam interrupted with a faint smile. "You're light on your feet, but those boots of yours aren't exactly quiet. Nice try, though."

Yordan shook his head, chuckling as he dropped into the chair across from Sam. "You're impossible, you know that?"

Sam's smile widened slightly as he reached for the plate in front of him, his fingers deftly navigating the edge of the table. "I try."

Yordan leaned back, crossing his arms as he studied his friend. "So," he said, his tone casual but his grin returning, "how's your morning been?"

"Fine," Sam replied simply, taking a bite of bread.

"Just fine?" Yordan pressed, his tone light and teasing. "Nothing interesting to report? No late-night adventures? Maybe something—or someone—worth mentioning?"

Sam paused, his head tilting slightly as he considered Yordan's words. "Not particularly," he said after a moment, his tone neutral.

Yordan narrowed his eyes, leaning forward slightly. "Come on, Sam. I saw Jezzie just now. She seemed pretty... friendly. Are you seriously going to sit there and tell me nothing happened?"

Sam shrugged, his expression giving nothing away. "Jezzie's always friendly. She's the innkeeper. It's kind of her job."

Yordan groaned, dragging a hand down his face. "You're killing me here, Sam. Just admit it. You spent the night with her, didn't you?"

Sam took another bite of bread, chewing thoughtfully before replying. "You seem awfully interested in my personal life this morning."

"That's not a no," Yordan shot back, pointing a finger at him. "You're dodging."

Sam's lips quirked into a faint smirk. "I'm not dodging. I'm eating breakfast. There's a difference."

Yordan leaned forward, resting his elbows on the table as he stared at Sam. "You're the most frustrating person I've ever met, you know that?"

Sam chuckled softly, the sound low and amused. "I've been told."

For a moment, the two sat in silence, the fire crackling between them. Yordan sighed, shaking his head. "All right, fine. I'll drop it. For now."

Sam raised an eyebrow, his smirk still in place. "Generous of you."

Yordan leaned back in his chair, still watching his friend with a mix of amusement and exasperation. Sam, as always, was impossible to crack, and Yordan couldn't help but admire—and be annoyed by—his ability to stay calm under pressure.

"Just so you know," Yordan said finally, his tone light but teasing, "if you ever do decide to admit anything, I'm all ears."

Sam's smile widened slightly, his fingers brushing the edge of his stick. "I'll keep that in mind," he said, his tone dry.

Yordan laughed, shaking his head as he reached for a piece of bread from his own plate. Despite Sam's evasiveness, the exchange felt like a brief return to normalcy, a moment of lightness amidst the growing tension that lingered in the back of Yordan's mind. But even as he smiled, part of him wondered if Sam's calm exterior was hiding more than he let on—just as Yordan's own thoughts were far more tangled than he cared to admit.

As the fire crackled between them, Yordan finished his bread and leaned back in his chair. He glanced at Sam, who was sitting comfortably, his stick resting across his lap. The morning sunlight filtered through the windows of the Restful Respite, casting warm, golden light over the common room.

Yordan hesitated for a moment before speaking, his voice measured. "Hey, Sam. What do you think about going to the Lumina Library with me today?"

Sam tilted his head slightly, the motion deliberate, as though weighing the question. "The library? What are you looking for there?"

"Not sure yet," Yordan admitted, rubbing the back of his neck. "But it feels like something worth doing before we get our gear together for the trip back to Aralonis tomorrow. Who knows, maybe I'll find something useful. What do you say?"

Sam let out a soft chuckle, tapping his stick lightly against the floor. "I guess I can't say no to a trip with my overly curious best friend. Sure, let's go."

With a faint grin, Yordan stood and stretched, the tension of the past few weeks still lingering in his shoulders. He grabbed his pack, slinging it over one shoulder, and waited as Sam rose, his movements sure and practiced.

The streets of Lumina City were alive with their usual morning energy as the two stepped outside. Merchants called out from stalls, their voices mingling with the clatter of carts and the hum of conversation. Yordan led the way, his eyes scanning the bustling streets as they made their way toward the library.

But as they walked, something gnawed at him. He saw Lumites in their distinct garb, their faces animated as they haggled, chatted, and moved through their daily routines. Aralonites, too, dotted the streets, their clothing and mannerisms familiar to Yordan. But there were no Zetians. Not a single one.

He hadn't seen any at the Restful Respite, nor along the roads to the temple or the river. Now, even in the more public parts of the city, they were absent. The streets bustled with life, but it was as if the Zetians had been erased from the tapestry entirely.

Yordan's thoughts turned inward as he walked, his expression tightening. Aisha said they had to take hidden paths, he thought, his jaw clenching slightly. She said they weren't allowed the same freedom here. But how could that be true? How could they live like ghosts in their own land?

His mind wandered further, circling back to his encounter with the man nailed to the tree. He had tried to piece together the man's identity, but no details stood out—no clothing, no symbols, nothing that would definitively mark him as a Lumite, an Aralonite, or a Zetian. Yet, in the back of his mind, a small voice whispered that Aisha's warnings might hold more truth than he'd wanted to admit.

Yordan's pace slowed briefly as the thought took hold. Was he a Zetian? The idea twisted in his gut, filling him with a mix of guilt and frustration. If the man had been punished simply for being Zetian, what did that mean for Lumina City and the people who claimed to follow Toteko's will? The question burned in his mind, but he kept it to himself, unwilling to voice his growing doubts to Sam—not yet.

"Yordan," Sam said, breaking the silence as he tapped his stick lightly against the ground. "You still with me, or are you lost in one of those big thoughts of yours?"

Yordan blinked, startled from his reverie. "Yeah," he said quickly. "I'm here. Just thinking."

"Figured as much," Sam replied, a faint smirk playing at his lips. "You've been quiet since we left. Something on your mind?"

"Not really," Yordan lied, his voice casual. "Just thinking about what we might find at the library."

Sam hummed softly, clearly unconvinced, but he didn't press further. They continued walking, the spires of the Lumina Library coming into view as they rounded a corner. Its grand facade loomed above the surrounding buildings, its intricate stonework gleaming in the sunlight.

As they approached, Yordan cast another glance around the street. Still no Zetians. The absence weighed heavily on him, but he kept his thoughts to himself, focusing instead on the imposing structure before them. If the library held any answers, Yordan was determined to find them. But even as he climbed the steps beside Sam, the questions swirling in his mind refused to be silenced.

The Lumina Library stood just a short walk south of the Grand Temple of Toteko, its towering spires visible from much of the Sacred Quarter. Its architecture was no less impressive than the temple itself, though it lacked the same overtly spiritual iconography. The outer walls were constructed of pale stone that gleamed faintly in the sunlight, intricate carvings of vines and scrolls winding their way across its surface. Tall, arched windows glinted with golden light, and the grand entrance, flanked by two statues of lion-headed figures holding open books, seemed to invite visitors to enter a sanctuary of knowledge.

As Yordan and Sam stepped inside, the world outside seemed to fade away. The interior was vast, the ceilings impossibly high and adorned with painted frescoes depicting scenes of Lumite scholars studying under golden rays of divine light. Massive oak shelves lined the walls, stretching up toward the ceiling and filled with leather-bound tomes, scrolls, and loose manuscripts. A soft, golden glow emanated from lanterns suspended in mid-air, their flames flickering gently but casting no smoke.

The smell hit Yordan immediately—a mix of aged parchment, the faint metallic tang of ink, and an unexpected undertone of lilac. It was an odd combination, but not unpleasant. Sam inhaled deeply, tilting his head slightly. "Smells... refined," he said quietly, his voice carrying a hint of curiosity.

Yordan glanced at him, his lips twitching into a faint smile. "Refined is one word for it."

The quiet murmur of voices echoed through the space, punctuated by the soft shuffling of feet and the occasional creak of a chair. Scholars and seekers of knowledge moved between the shelves, their expressions a mix of focus and awe.

Yordan approached the central desk, where a Lumite librarian sat, her sharp features framed by neatly braided hair. She glanced up as they approached, her deep green robes marking her as an attendant of the library.

"Can I help you?" she asked, her tone polite but brisk.

Yordan hesitated briefly, then spoke. "I'm looking for texts about Tonalcoatl."

The librarian arched a brow, her expression unreadable. "Tonalcoatl?" she repeated, as if to confirm. When Yordan nodded, she stood without another word, motioning for them to follow her.

She led them through a maze of shelves and alcoves, the faint rustle of her robes the only sound. Finally, she stopped before a section marked with a golden plaque that read Founders and Prophets. She gestured toward the shelves with a faint smile. "Good luck," she said simply. "There have been many readers of these texts. I hope you find what you're looking for."

With that, she turned and walked away, her robes swishing as she disappeared around a corner.

Sam tilted his head toward Yordan, his lips quirking into a dry smile. "Well, that was helpful," he said, his tone laced with sarcasm.

Yordan smirked faintly, running a hand over the spines of the books on the shelf. "Better than nothing," he said, though he couldn't help but agree with Sam's assessment.

Sam tapped his stick lightly against the floor, his expression thoughtful. "Too bad there aren't any texts for me to read," he said, his tone neutral but carrying an undertone of frustration. "You'd think a place this grand would have something for the blind."

Yordan paused, glancing at his friend. "Maybe they do," he said, though the words felt hollow. He doubted the Lumina Library catered to anyone outside their ideal image of a scholar.

Pushing the thought aside, Yordan turned back to the shelves and began pulling books. The bindings were varied—some ornate and gilded, others plain and worn with age. He carried an armful to a nearby table, the wood polished to a gleaming finish, and sat down, spreading the books out before him.

One of the first texts he opened was an account of Tonalcoatl's visions. The pages were filled with detailed descriptions of the prophet's ascent into the Sitlali Mountains and his divine revelation of the Grand Temple's completion. The words painted a vivid picture of golden light, a serpent coiled in the heavens, and Toteko's voice guiding the Lumites to their destiny.

As Yordan read, an old memory surfaced—his mother's voice, warm and patient, as she told him a story before bed, a story about the Grand Temple before it became what it was today. She had spoken of Tonalcoatl, not as a figure of distant legend, but as a man who had fought for something beyond himself. "He did not seek power," she had said, brushing his hair back as she often did. "He saw a vision, a place where all could gather under Toteko's light, a temple not for a single people, but for all who carried faith in their hearts."

He had been too young to question it then, but now, flipping through the brittle pages before him, the memory carried a weight he could not ignore. He thought of Tlenatl—his dream had felt real, lived, as if he had been the man himself. Sold into slavery as a boy, bound in chains before he could even understand what freedom meant. Yet, even in captivity, Tlenatl had dreamt of Toteko, had listened to the whispers of prophecy. Those visions had led him to save a kingdom from famine, to earn the favor of a king, to rise above the status he had been forced into.

But Tlenatl had never been free. Not truly. His fate had been tied to the rulers he served, his purpose given shape by the trust he earned but could never entirely own. Even as a revered prophet, he had still been a servant of men before he was a servant of Toteko.

Yordan's fingers tightened around the pages. That was why he needed to understand Tonalcoatl more than Tlenatl. Because Tlenatl's story, for all its triumphs, had been born of survival, of a boy clawing his way to safety in a world that had never meant for him to rise. Tonalcoatl, however, had shaped his own path. He had seen something greater—not survival, but creation.

If there was still hope for the Grand Temple to be more than what it had become, then it was buried somewhere in the foundations of what Tonalcoatl had originally envisioned.

Yordan's brow furrowed as he read, his finger tracing the faded script. The text spoke of Tonalcoatl as a man of unwavering faith, chosen by Toteko to bring the Lumites together during a time of division. But it also hinted at challenges he faced from within—dissent among his followers, doubts about his visions, and conflicts with neighboring groups.

Another text caught his eye, this one detailing the construction of the Grand Temple. It mentioned Lumel, a figure described as the architect of the temple's intricate design. According to the text, Lumel had been inspired by Tonalcoatl's visions, his plans mirroring the divine patterns seen by the prophet in the light of Toteko. The text was technical and dense, but it hinted at a deep reverence for both the temple and the unity it symbolized—at least in the early days.

As Yordan read, the silence of the library seemed to press in on him. The words blurred slightly as his mind drifted. Unity, he thought. That's what they claimed this temple was built for. But look at it now. The Grand Temple was a place of division, its walls symbolizing barriers rather than bridges. The Lumites controlled it, the Aralonites tolerated it, and the Zetians were barely allowed near it.

He glanced at Sam, who was sitting quietly, his stick resting across his lap as his head tilted slightly toward the ambient sounds of the library. Yordan's thoughts churned as he returned to the text, determined to find something—anything—that might help him understand how to move forward.

As Yordan flipped through the worn pages of the Luminescence, the holy text for the Lumites, he felt the weight of its age and significance. The parchment was delicate under his fingertips, its golden edges faded but still faintly gleaming. The elegant script that filled its pages was meticulous, the ink a deep black that seemed to defy time. He scanned passage after passage, the language poetic and dense, its layered meanings difficult to parse for someone outside the Lumite faith.

One section caught his eye. A passage near the center of the book was marked with faint underlines and annotations in the margins. The handwriting of whoever had made the notes was sharp and purposeful, the ink a slightly different shade, as if it had been added long after the original text was written.

The passage read:

"And so, Toteko declared: Let the chosen rise as stewards of the light, for it is only through the pure flame that the path may be revealed. The faithful shall guard the flame, and through them, my light shall guide the world."

In the margin beside the passage, a note had been scrawled:

"The flame must be protected, even from those who claim to seek it. Purity requires vigilance."

Yordan frowned, tilting his head as he traced the words with his eyes. The handwriting reappeared several pages later, next to another passage:

"Beware the false bearers of light, for they shall bring only shadow to the world. The faithful must cleanse the shadow to preserve the truth."

Again, the same margin note appeared: "Purity requires vigilance."

Yordan felt a strange unease settle over him as he continued flipping through the book. The phrase was written multiple times in the margins, each occurrence near a passage that spoke of stewardship, vigilance, or the duty of the faithful to protect Toteko's will.

To Yordan, the words seemed innocuous enough—a reminder of devotion, perhaps. But their repetition, combined with the annotations' sharp tone, gnawed at the edge of his thoughts. The writer's insistence on purity and vigilance carried an unsettling weight, a fervor that felt more rigid than reverent.

Then, as he turned another page, his eyes caught something else—a name scratched into the margin, just barely legible under the faint light. The first name was obscured by a series of dark, jagged lines, as though someone had deliberately tried to erase it. But the last name was still visible: Taron.

Yordan's brow furrowed as he stared at the scratched-out name. He ran his finger lightly over the text, feeling the faint grooves where the ink had been etched into the page before being so violently scratched away. Taron, he repeated silently. The name tugged at something in his memory, but he couldn't place it. It was familiar, yet distant, like an echo of something he'd heard in passing.

"Find something interesting?" Sam's voice broke the silence, pulling Yordan out of his thoughts.

Yordan glanced up, blinking. "Maybe," he said slowly, his voice uncertain. "There's this section someone marked up. It keeps repeating this phrase about purity and vigilance. And I found a name... Taron. The first name's scratched out."

Sam tilted his head slightly, his expression curious but unreadable. "You think it means something?"

Yordan shrugged, closing the book carefully. "I don't know. Maybe nothing. But the way it's written... it feels deliberate. Like whoever wrote it wanted it to stand out."

Sam nodded, his fingers tapping lightly against the edge of the table. "Well, it's something to keep in mind. Maybe it'll make more sense later."

Yordan nodded absently, his thoughts still lingering on the annotations and the scratched-out name. He slipped the Luminescence back onto the shelf. As Yordan closed the last book he had been leafing through, his mind still turning over the strange annotations and the scratched-out name, he stood to return it to the shelf. A nearby stack of books caught the edge of his elbow as he turned, toppling with a loud thud that echoed through the hushed sanctity of the library.

Several heads snapped toward him, their expressions a mix of disdain and annoyance. Yordan froze, his face flushing crimson as he mouthed, "Sorry," in as quiet and apologetic a tone as he could manage.

Sam, seated nearby with his stick resting across his lap, pressed his lips together tightly, his shoulders shaking faintly. "I can hear the death stares," he murmured under his breath, barely containing his amusement. Yordan shot him a brief glare but said nothing, crouching quickly to gather the fallen books.

As he scooped up the last one, a few loose pages slipped out and fluttered to the ground. He frowned, setting the books back onto the table as he reached for the papers. The first thing he noticed was the heading at the top of one of the pages: General Jareth Taron.

Yordan's hand froze mid-motion, his heart skipping a beat. The name—Taron—was the same as the one scratched into the margins of the Luminescence. He quickly scanned the rest of the page, his brow furrowing as he tried to make sense of the text. It appeared to be a detailed report or correspondence, though the language was dense and military in tone, referencing campaigns and decisions made by the general.

His eyes darted toward the book he thought the pages might have fallen from, but when he opened it, the contents didn't match. He tried the next book in the stack, then another, but none of them seemed to belong to the loose pages.

A strange feeling prickled at the back of his neck—a mix of curiosity and unease. He glanced around the library, the other readers now engrossed in their work once more, their earlier annoyance forgotten. Sam tilted his head slightly, his brow raised in silent question.

On a whim, Yordan folded the pages carefully and slipped them into the inner pocket of his tunic. His movements were quick and deliberate, his pulse quickening as he rose to his feet. "Come on," he said quietly to Sam. "Let's get out of here."

Sam stood, gripping his stick as he moved to Yordan's side. "You sure you didn't do any permanent damage to the library?" he teased, his tone light but his ears tuned to the subtle tension in Yordan's voice.

"Not yet," Yordan muttered, brushing past him and heading toward the exit. Sam followed, his stick tapping lightly against the floor as they made their way through the labyrinth of shelves and back toward the grand entrance.

As they stepped outside, the bright sunlight momentarily blinded Yordan, making him squint. He kept a steady pace, his mind racing with questions about the pages now tucked safely inside his clothes. General Jareth Taron. The name seemed to loom over his thoughts like a shadow, its significance unknown but impossible to ignore.

"All right," Sam said as they walked down the steps of the library, his tone casual but curious. "Are you going to tell me what's got you all tense, or do I have to guess?"

Yordan hesitated, his hand brushing against the hidden pocket. "Later," he said, his voice low. "I need to think about it first."

Sam nodded, his expression unreadable. "Fair enough," he replied, though his tone suggested he'd press for answers sooner rather than later.

As they walked away from the library, Yordan couldn't shake the feeling that he had stumbled onto something significant that could explain more about the city, the temple, and the mysterious tensions that seemed to thread through everything in Lumina City. But for now, he kept the pages close, the questions burning in his mind as they headed back toward the Restful Respite.

The room at the Restful Respite was quiet save for the sounds of Yordan and Sam packing their gear. Yordan carefully rolled up his blanket, tying it securely before slipping it into his pack. Sam worked with practiced efficiency, his hands deftly feeling the edges of his belongings to ensure everything was in its proper place. The warm glow of the late afternoon sun streamed through the window, casting long shadows on the wooden floor.

For a while, neither of them spoke. The silence wasn't uncomfortable, but it carried the weight of unspoken thoughts. Finally, Sam broke it, his voice calm but tinged with curiosity.

"Yordan," he said, his fingers brushing the edge of his pack. "Do you still believe you saw Toteko up in the mountains?"

Yordan froze for a moment, his hand hovering over a leather strap. He let out a slow breath, his shoulders sagging slightly as he sat back on his heels. "I know what I saw," he said softly, his gaze drifting toward the window. "Or at least, I think I do. It felt real, Sam. More real than anything I've ever experienced. But..." He hesitated, running a hand through his hair. "But sometimes I wonder if I just pushed myself too hard. If I passed out from the climb and dreamed it all."

Sam tilted his head, his stick resting across his lap. "That's what I've been trying to figure out," he said, his tone thoughtful. "You're not the type to make things up, Yordan. But a part of me wonders—why you? Why would Toteko choose you, of all people, to see him? I don't mean that to doubt you," he added quickly. "It's just... strange."

Yordan nodded slowly, his hands resting on his knees. "I've asked myself the same question," he admitted. "I'm just a blacksmith from Aralonis. I'm not a priest or a scholar or... anyone important. But if it was real, if Toteko really did speak to me, then why hasn't he said anything since? It's been silence, Sam. Nothing but silence."

Sam tapped his stick lightly against the floor, the sound rhythmic and deliberate. "Maybe he's waiting for you to figure it out," he said quietly. "Or maybe silence is part of the message."

Yordan frowned, his brow furrowing deeply. "What kind of message is silence?"

Sam shrugged, his expression calm. "I don't know. But you've been carrying this weight ever since you came back down from the mountains. Maybe the answer isn't in waiting for him to speak again. Maybe it's in what you do next."

Yordan considered Sam's words, the weight of them settling over him like a heavy blanket. He wanted to believe in what he'd seen, to trust that the vision was real and that Toteko had chosen him for a reason. But the doubt lingered, gnawing at the edges of his mind.

The room fell into silence again as Yordan returned to his packing, his movements slower now, more deliberate. He glanced over at Sam, who was neatly tying up his pack, his expression unreadable.

After a moment, Yordan cleared his throat, a faint smirk tugging at his lips. "So," he began, his tone lighter, "are you planning to sleep in your own bed tonight, or will Jezzie be lucky enough to entertain you again?"

Sam paused mid-motion, his stick resting against the bedframe. A faint flush crept up his cheeks, though his expression remained calm. "You really don't know when to let something go, do you?" he replied, his voice dry.

Yordan chuckled softly, the sound easing some of the tension in the room. "Just trying to keep things interesting," he said, slinging his pack over his shoulder.

Sam shook his head, a faint smile tugging at his lips. "For your information, I'll be in my own bed tonight," he said. "But if you're so curious about Jezzie, maybe you should be the one to talk to her."

Yordan laughed, the sound genuine despite the heaviness that still lingered in his chest. "Not a chance," he said, heading toward the door. "She's all yours, Sam."

Sam rolled his eyes, grabbing his stick and following Yordan out of the room. As they walked down the hallway, the conversation faded into a comfortable silence, each of them lost in their own thoughts as they prepared for the journey ahead.

Chapter Twelve

The Lumina River wound its way lazily through the Valley of Akeskauiya, its surface shimmering in the mid-morning sun. The water's soft murmur was the only sound accompanying Yordan and Sam as they walked along its banks. The lush greenery of the valley surrounded them, its vibrancy a stark contrast to the turmoil that churned within Yordan. His boots crunched against the dirt path, his eyes scanning the horizon with a mixture of hope and frustration.

"Do you see any golden deer?" Sam asked suddenly, his voice breaking the quiet. He tapped his stick lightly against the ground, his head tilting slightly toward Yordan.

Yordan exhaled sharply, shaking his head even though Sam couldn't see the gesture. "No," he said, his tone edged with irritation. "It's been three days since we left Lumina City, and still nothing. No deer, no signs, no anything."

Sam hummed softly, his expression calm despite the tension radiating off Yordan. "Maybe they've decided to take a vacation," he said lightly, though his attempt at humor didn't seem to land.

Yordan didn't reply. His mind was elsewhere, caught on a memory that refused to let go. Two days ago, as they'd made their way through a grove of trees near the river, they had stumbled upon the man nailed back to the tree. The once-vivid image of pain and desperation had been replaced by decay, the man's rotting corpse, a haunting reminder of what he had witnessed in Lumina City.

The sight had stayed with him, gnawing at his thoughts. At the time, he had wanted to believe Benjamin's explanation, that the man was a troublemaker deserving of punishment. But now, as the days stretched on and the silence from Toteko grew louder, doubt began to creep in. What if he wasn't a troublemaker? Yordan thought, his chest tightening. What if he was innocent? What if he was killed for something as simple as speaking out?

The questions burned in his mind, each one a spark feeding a growing fire of frustration. He couldn't shake the image of the man's lifeless body, the nails pinning him to the tree like some grotesque offering. None of it made sense—none of it fit with the teachings of Toteko that Yordan had grown up with. The god of his ancestors was just, merciful, a beacon of light for all people. How could such brutality be done in his name?

"Yordan?" Sam's voice pulled him from his thoughts. Yordan blinked, realizing he had stopped walking. He glanced at his friend, who was standing patiently, his stick resting lightly against the ground.

"Yeah," Yordan said quickly, shaking his head as if to clear it. "I'm here."

"You sure?" Sam asked, his tone gentle but probing. "You've been quiet. Quieter than usual, I mean."

Yordan hesitated, his gaze drifting back to the river. "I'm just... trying to make sense of everything," he admitted, his voice low. "Toteko told me to bring his people together, but I don't even know where to start. And now, with everything we've seen... it just doesn't make sense."

Sam tilted his head, his expression thoughtful. "What doesn't make sense?"

"All of it," Yordan said, the words spilling out before he could stop them. He gestured vaguely toward the valley, the river, the distant mountains. "Toteko's silence, the man on the tree, the way the Zetians are treated, the tension between the Lumites and everyone else. None of it adds up. How am I supposed to bring people together when I don't even understand what's happening?"

Sam nodded slowly, his grip tightening slightly on his stick. "Maybe you're not supposed to have it all figured out yet. Maybe the point is to keep going, even when it doesn't make sense."

Yordan let out a bitter laugh, shaking his head. "That's easy for you to say. You didn't have a god tell you to fix this mess."

"No," Sam agreed, his tone steady. "But I do know this—you're not going to find answers by standing still."

Yordan sighed, his shoulders slumping as he ran a hand through his hair. He looked back at the river, its surface glinting in the sunlight. It offered no answers, no guidance, just the steady, unchanging rhythm of its flow.

Please, he thought, his mind reaching out in desperation. Say something, anything. Show me you're there. But the silence pressed down on him, heavier than ever, leaving him feeling small and alone in the vastness of the valley.

"Come on," Sam said after a moment, his voice light but encouraging. "The golden deer aren't going to find themselves."

Yordan managed to faint a smile, though it didn't reach his eyes. He started walking again, his footsteps heavy, his thoughts a storm of doubt and frustration. The path ahead seemed as uncertain as ever, but for now, it was the only thing he could hold onto.

The night was quiet, save for the occasional rustle of leaves and the soft crackle of the fire. Yordan sat cross-legged a short distance from the flames, his arms resting on his knees as he gazed into the glowing embers. The warmth of the fire was comforting, but his thoughts were anything but.

Sam lay a few feet away, his steady, rhythmic breathing indicating he was already deep in sleep. His stick was nestled beside him, its familiar presence a constant in their travels. Yordan glanced at him briefly, a flicker of gratitude crossing his mind for the steadfast friendship Sam had always offered. But tonight, even Sam's grounding presence couldn't ease the unease in Yordan's chest.

He turned his attention back to the fire, his eyes drawn to the dance of the flames. The shapes they formed seemed almost alive, flickering and shifting as if carrying whispers, he couldn't quite hear. As he stared deeper, the fire seemed to take on a new form—a face, familiar yet unexpected, emerging from the glowing embers.

Katherine, he thought, his breath catching. Her soft features were unmistakable, her expression serene yet tinged with concern. The sight of her in the fire brought a brief wave of comfort, a reminder of the life he had left behind. But as quickly as the image formed, it began to change.

The delicate lines of Katherine's face sharpened, her features transforming her into someone else. Yordan's stomach tightened as he recognized the new face staring back at him: Aisha. Her eyes were fierce, burning with a mix of defiance and passion that seemed to mirror the fire itself. Her expression was unreadable, a challenge and an enigma all at once.

He found himself back in the Restless Respite, the air thick with swirling tendrils of smoke from the fire. Aisha emerged from the haze like a goddess, her bronze skin glistening with beads of moisture. Rivulets of sweat cascaded down the graceful curve of her neck, tracing sinuous paths along her collarbone before disappearing into the soft swell of her breasts.

Yordan's pulse quickened, his skin flushing with heat that had nothing to do with the fire. In the dream, he reached for her, his fingers aching to caress the smooth expanse of her thigh, to tangle in the damp curls at the nape of her neck. She responded with a smile that was pure lust, her full lips parting as she pressed herself against him.

He could almost feel the weight of her in his arms, could almost taste the honeyed sweetness of her mouth as she kissed him with a hunger that bordered on desperation. Her hands roamed his body with bold exploration, igniting sparks of pleasure that threatened to consume him. He groaned as she nipped at his lower lip, her fingers digging into the firm muscles of his back.

But even as he drowned in the flood of desire, a small voice whispered in the back of his mind, reminding him that this wasn't real. The Aisha in his arms was a figment, a shadow of longing that could never be fulfilled. The realization was like a bucket of cold water, shocking him back to the present.

Yordan blinked, shaking his head as if to dispel the vision. The fire was just a fire again, its flames crackling and casting flickering shadows on the surrounding trees. He exhaled sharply, rubbing a hand over his face as he tried to steady his thoughts.

What's wrong with me? he wondered, his heart racing. Why am I thinking about her? The memory of Aisha's intensity, her unwavering gaze and sharp words, clashed with the warmth and familiarity he felt for Katherine. The contrast left him unsettled, his emotions a tangled mess he couldn't unravel.

He glanced over at Sam, still sound asleep, oblivious to Yordan's inner turmoil. For a moment, Yordan envied his friend's ability to find rest so easily. He sighed, leaning back against a nearby rock and letting his head fall back as he stared up at the stars.

The fire crackled softly, the only witness to his silent struggle. Despite the stillness of the night, Yordan felt anything but calm. The faces in the flames lingered in his mind, their meanings as elusive as the answers he sought. And as he closed his eyes, hoping for sleep, he couldn't help but wonder if the images were a sign—or just another trick of his restless imagination.

One week later at midday the sun hung high in the sky, casting its golden light over the horizon as Yordan and Sam trudged along the well-worn path. The sight of Aralonis in the distance, its walls rising proudly against the rolling hills, brought a wave of relief that washed over Yordan like a cool breeze. His steps quickened, his boots kicking up small clouds of dust as he glanced at Sam, whose pace remained steady despite the miles behind them.

"There it is," Yordan said, his voice carrying a hint of fatigue and anticipation. "Home."

Sam nodded, his head tilting slightly as if sensing the shift in the air. "Smells like the city," he said, a faint smile tugging at his lips. "Always a mix of iron, bread, and... people."

Yordan chuckled softly, the tension of the past weeks easing slightly as they approached the gates. The walls of Aralonis loomed closer, their sturdy stone a testament to the city's resilience. The banners bearing the sigil of Aralonis—crossed hammers over an anvil—fluttered gently in the noon breeze. The guards stationed at the gates gave them a cursory glance before waving them through, their familiarity with Yordan evident in their disinterest.

Once inside the bustling streets, the sounds and smells of Aralonis enveloped them. Merchants called out their wares, the clang of black-smiths' hammers echoed from the forges, and the chatter of townsfolk filled the air. Yordan's chest swelled with a mix of pride and comfort as he took it all in.

He turned to Sam, reaching out to clasp his friend's shoulder in a brief but firm handshake hug. "Thanks for sticking with me," Yordan said, his voice earnest. "I'll see you tomorrow, yeah?"

Sam grinned, tapping his stick lightly against the ground. "You can count on it. Try not to get into trouble before then."

"I'll do my best," Yordan replied with a faint smile, releasing his grip and stepping back.

As Sam headed toward his usual haunts, Yordan adjusted his pack and set off toward Ferran's forge. The streets of Aralonis were familiar, each turn and corner etched into his memory. The forge wasn't far, its location marked by the plume of black smoke rising above the rooftops. The rhythmic clang of hammer on anvil grew louder as he approached, a sound as familiar to Yordan as his own heartbeat.

The forge came into view, its stone structure sturdy and unassuming. The heat of the fires was palpable even from the entrance, and the smell of molten metal and ash filled the air. Yordan stepped inside, the heat wrapping around him like an old, familiar blanket.

Ferran stood at the anvil, his broad shoulders hunched as he hammered a glowing blade with precision. His movements were deliberate, each strike of the hammer sending sparks flying into the air. His silver-streaked hair was tied back, and his weathered face was set in deep concentration.

"Ferran!" Yordan called out, his voice cutting through the din.

The older man paused, straightening as he turned toward the entrance. His sharp blue eyes softened as they landed on Yordan, and a rare smile spread across his face. "Well, I'll be," Ferran said, setting the hammer aside and wiping his hands on a rag. "Look who finally decided to come back."

Yordan grinned, stepping forward to clasp Ferran's hand firmly. "Good to see you, old man," he said, his voice carrying a mix of affection and respect. "I missed this place."

"Missed the forge or the work?" Ferran asked, his tone teasing as he pulled Yordan into a brief but hearty embrace.

"Both," Yordan admitted, glancing around the familiar workshop. The tools were neatly arranged on the walls, the forge fire burned brightly, and the smell of hot iron lingered in the air. It felt like home—solid, unchanging, and dependable.

Ferran stepped back, his sharp gaze scanning Yordan as if assessing him. "You've got that look," he said knowingly. "Like you've seen more than you bargained for."

Yordan hesitated, the weight of the past weeks pressing down on him again. "It's... been a lot," he said finally, his voice quieter. "But it's good to be back."

Ferran nodded, clapping Yordan on the shoulder. "Well, you're here now. We've got work to do, and I'm sure you'll be itching to get your hands dirty soon enough."

Yordan managed a small smile, the familiar warmth of Ferran's presence easing some of the turmoil in his chest. For the first time in what felt like weeks, he felt a flicker of peace. Here, in the forge, surrounded by the steady rhythm of work and the unwavering support of the man who had raised him after his grandfather's passing, Yordan felt like he could breathe again.

The day had finally cooled, the sun dipping low on the horizon and casting a warm, golden hue over the forge. Yordan and Ferran sat outside on a sturdy wooden bench, their backs resting against the cool stone wall of the forge. Each held a wooden cup of water, condensation dripping down the sides, and a damp cloth rested on their heads, offering a semblance of relief from the relentless heat of the forge's fires.

Ferran leaned back, his cup balanced on his knee, a sly smile creeping across his face. "So," he began, his voice teasing, "I assume the first thing you did when you got back was go see Katherine, right?"

Yordan shifted slightly, glancing down at his cup as if it held an answer. "Actually," he said, his tone a bit sheepish, "I haven't gone to see her yet."

Ferran turned his head, his brows lifting in genuine surprise. "You haven't?" he asked, his voice carrying a mix of disbelief and humor. "Yordan, it's been what—over a month since you and Sam left Aralonis? And you're telling me you didn't rush over there the second you got back?"

Yordan rubbed the back of his neck, his cheeks flushing slightly. "I just... haven't gotten around to it yet," he mumbled, his words awkward and evasive.

Ferran studied him for a moment, the sharpness in his gaze tempered by the familiar affection of a mentor who had raised Yordan as his own. Then his expression shifted, a glint of curiosity in his eyes. "Hold on," Ferran said, sitting up a little straighter. "You've got that look."

Yordan frowned, confused. "What look?"

"The look of a man trying to avoid something," Ferran said with a grin. He leaned forward slightly, his elbows resting on his knees. "So, who was it? Did you meet someone in Lumina City?"

Yordan froze for a moment, his grip tightening slightly on his cup. "What? No," he said quickly, though the hesitation in his voice betrayed him.

Ferran's grin widened, his eyes twinkling with amusement. "Ah, I see," he said, nodding as if he had unraveled some grand mystery. "You did meet someone. Come on, spill it. What's her name?"

Yordan let out a long sigh, leaning back against the wall and staring up at the darkening sky. "I didn't meet anyone," he said finally, his voice quieter. "Not really."

"Not really?" Ferran pressed, his tone still light but with a hint of genuine interest.

Yordan hesitated, his gaze fixed on the horizon. "There was this girl," he admitted after a moment. "But we didn't... I don't know. We didn't exactly meet. It was more like... we crossed paths."

Ferran tilted his head, his curiosity growing. "And now you wish you had met her?"

Yordan shrugged, his expression a mix of uncertainty and frustration. "Maybe," he said softly. "I can't stop thinking about her, but it doesn't make any sense. I don't even know her. And then there's Katherine..."

Ferran leaned back, his expression softening as he watched Yordan wrestle with his thoughts. "Sounds like you've got a lot on your mind," he said after a moment, his tone more serious. "But let me give you some advice. Don't let what-ifs and maybes keep you from moving forward. If there's something you need to figure out, do it. Just don't let it stop you from living your life."

Yordan nodded slowly, the weight of Ferran's words settling over him. He glanced over at the older man, a faint smile tugging at his lips. "Thanks, Ferran," he said quietly.

Ferran clapped him on the shoulder, the familiar gesture carrying more comfort than words. "Anytime," he said, his voice warm. "Now finish your water and get some rest. You've got a lot of work ahead of you, whatever it is you decide to do."

As the night deepened, the two sat in comfortable silence, the glow of the forge behind them casting long shadows on the ground. Yordan's thoughts churned, but for the first time in days, he felt a faint glimmer of clarity—just enough to take the next step, wherever it might lead.

The moonlight bathed the quiet streets of Aralonis in a gentle glow, the air crisp with the promise of autumn. Yordan walked briskly, his boots scuffing against the cobblestones, as he made his way to Katherine's parents' home. The familiar path felt charged with anticipation, his heart racing with every step.

When he reached the house, he stopped beneath her window. The upstairs room, faintly lit by the glow of a lamp, was unmistakably hers. Yordan bent down, picked up a small pebble, and gently tossed it against the glass. The light clink barely disturbed the stillness of the night, and there was no response.

He tried again, the second pebble hitting with a slightly louder tap. Still nothing. Yordan sighed, running a hand through his hair, and picked up another pebble. This time, he threw it with just a bit more force. It clinked sharply against the window, and the curtain twitched before the window creaked open.

"Who's throwing—" Katherine's voice began, the irritation evident. But as her deep green eyes landed on Yordan, her expression softened instantly. "Yordan!" she exclaimed, her voice brimming with excitement. "Stay there, I'm coming down!"

She disappeared from the window, leaving Yordan grinning faintly as he stepped back onto the cobbled street. Moments later, the front door opened, and Katherine came rushing out, her auburn hair cascading down her back in loose waves that shimmered under the moonlight. Her steps were light and quick, and she practically flew into his arms.

"You're back!" she said breathlessly, wrapping her arms tightly around his neck. She pulled back just enough to look into his face, her eyes searching his before she leaned in, pressing a warm, lingering kiss to his lips. Yordan felt the tension of the past weeks melt away, if only for a moment.

When they broke apart, Katherine's hands stayed on his shoulders, her face glowing with happiness. "When did you get back?" she asked softly, her voice filled with warmth and curiosity.

"Just today," Yordan replied, his voice low and steady. He brushed a loose strand of her hair away from her face, his fingers lingering for a moment. "I had to see you."

Katherine's expression softened further, her lips curving into a radiant smile. "I'm so glad you did," she said sincerely, her voice barely above a whisper. "I've missed you."

Yordan hesitated, his hand dropping to his side as a flicker of uncertainty crossed his face. "Katherine," he said, his tone tinged with an uncharacteristic seriousness, "I need to talk to you."

Her smile faded slightly, replaced by a look of concern. "Of course," she said immediately, squeezing his hand. "Is everything all right?"

Yordan nodded, though the weight in his chest told a different story. "Let's head to my place," he suggested. "It's not far."

"All right," Katherine said, taking his hand in hers and intertwining their fingers.

They walked in silence through the quiet streets, the gentle hum of the night surrounding them. The faint rustle of leaves and the distant sounds of the city seemed muted compared to the steady rhythm of their footsteps. Yordan found himself glancing at Katherine, her hair catching the moonlight like strands of polished copper, her presence grounding him in a way he hadn't fully realized he needed.

As they approached his home, the weight of what he wanted to say pressed down on him, but he pushed it aside for now. For the first time in weeks, the chaos inside his mind felt quieter, tempered by the warmth of Katherine at his side. Whatever was to come, at least he wasn't facing it alone.

Inside Yordan's home, the warm glow of the hearth cast flickering shadows across the modest room. Katherine sat in a simple wooden chair near the fire, her hands resting lightly in her lap, her auburn hair cascading over one shoulder. Yordan paced back and forth, his movements restless as though he was trying to work through the weight of his own thoughts. The faint crackle of the fire was the only sound for a moment, filling the space between them.

Katherine watched him intently, her green eyes tracking his every step. "Yordan," she said softly, breaking the silence. "You said you needed to talk to me. So talk to me. What happened out there?"

Yordan stopped mid-step, turning to face her. His expression was a mix of uncertainty and determination, his brow furrowed as he struggled to find the right words. "I... I don't know where to start," he admitted, his voice low. He ran a hand through his hair, letting out a sharp exhale. "I climbed the Sitlali Mountains because I thought... I don't know. I thought I needed clarity. I thought maybe the golden deer, or the river would give me some sort of sign."

Katherine tilted her head slightly, her expression patient. "And did they?"

Yordan hesitated, his gaze dropping to the floor. "Not the way I expected," he said finally. He looked back at her, his eyes filled with a quiet intensity. "I found a cave near the summit. I went inside to rest, and then... it happened."

Katherine leaned forward slightly, her fingers tightening in her lap. "What happened?" she asked, her voice steady but tinged with curiosity and concern.

Yordan swallowed hard, his hands clenching at his sides. "I heard a voice," he said, his words slow and deliberate. "It wasn't like anything I've ever heard before. It was... ethereal, almost like it was coming from inside me and around me at the same time. It called my name, Katherine. And when I answered, there was this light... it was overwhelming. I—" He stopped, his breath hitching as the memory surged forward. "I saw Toteko."

Katherine's eyes widened slightly, her composure faltering for a moment. "You saw Toteko?" she repeated, her voice barely above a whisper.

Yordan nodded, his gaze distant as if he were reliving the moment. "I don't know how else to explain it. Toteko told me they were the god of my ancestors, the one known by many names. And they said they heard the cries of all his people in Anakuatl—the Lumites, the Aralonites, the Zetians, and beyond. They said things are getting worse, that this path will lead to destruction if no one steps in."

Katherine's lips parted slightly, but no words followed. Her expression shifted—eyes flickering with something he couldn't quite place.

Yordan stepped closer to her, his voice growing more impassioned. "They said they chose me to deliver his message. To bring their people together, to save them from this chaos. But, Katherine, I don't even know where to start. I'm just a blacksmith. How am I supposed to bring peace to all of Anakuatl?"

Katherine sat back in her chair, her gaze shifting to the fire as she tried to absorb his words. Katherine's expression remained unreadable, her lips pressing into a thin line as she absorbed his words. Yordan watched the flicker of something in her eyes—hesitation, doubt, or perhaps something else entirely.

"Yordan," she said slowly, turning her gaze back to him. "If you believe, if you truly believe Toteko chose you—then I believe you." Her voice was steady, her words deliberate, but there was a flicker of uncertainty in her eyes.

Yordan let out a shaky breath, his shoulders relaxing slightly. "Thank you," he said softly, his voice laced with gratitude.

Katherine hesitated, brushing her fingers on the edge of her chair. "But," she began, her voice faltering slightly, "what does this mean for you? For us? You're talking about something... massive. Something dangerous."

"I don't know," Yordan admitted, his voice heavy. He sat down on the edge of the table across from her, his hands resting on his knees. "I don't have all the answers, Katherine. I'm still trying to make sense of it myself."

Katherine nodded slowly, her gaze dropping to her lap. Katherine's expression remained unreadable, her gaze steady, but Yordan caught the subtle shift in her posture—the way her fingers curled slightly in her lap, the way her breath hitched just before she spoke. A quiet tension lingered between them, something unspoken pressing against the space they shared. He wasn't sure what she was thinking, but he could feel the weight of it in the silence, in the way her eyes held his as if searching for something—an answer, a certainty he couldn't yet give.

She looked up at him, her expression softening. "Yordan," she said, her voice gentle but firm. "I'll support you. Whatever this means, whatever you decide to do, I'm here. Just... don't shut me out, okay?"

Yordan's eyes met hers, and for the first time that night, a faint smile broke through the tension on his face. "I won't," he promised. "I don't think I could do this without you."

The fire crackled softly between them, its light casting flickering shadows on the walls. The air was thick with unspoken fears and questions, but for now, they sat together in the stillness, their bond unshaken even in the face of the unknown.Yordan looked at her, truly looked at her, the soft curve of her lips, the way her auburn hair framed her face like threads of fire catching the light. Her expression was one of quiet strength, even as her hands trembled slightly in her lap. Yordan felt something stir within him, a mixture of gratitude, love, and the desperate need for connection in the face of all his uncertainty.

"Katherine," he said softly, her name a whisper on his lips.

She looked up at him, her eyes searching his. Before either of them could say another word, Yordan leaned forward, closing the distance between them. Their lips met in a kiss that started tender but quickly deepened, the weight of everything unsaid pouring into the embrace. His hand reached up to cup her face, his fingers brushing against the warmth of her skin, as if anchoring himself to her in this moment.

Katherine rose from her chair, her movements fluid as she stepped into Yordan's arms. Their kiss deepened, a dance of lips and tongues that spoke of desire and desperation. Yordan's hands roamed her back, pulling her flush against him until he could feel the beat of her heart against his chest.

Slowly, deliberately, Katherine turned in his arms until her back was pressed against him. Yordan's breath hitched as his fingers found the laces of her dress. He began to undo them with careful reverence, exposing inch after inch of smooth, creamy skin. As the fabric slipped from her shoulders, he leaned down, his lips finding the juncture where her neck met her shoulder.

Katherine shivered under his touch, a soft gasp escaping her lips as Yordan trailed a line of hot, open-mouthed kisses along her skin. His hands slid the dress down further, his fingertips grazing the sides of her breasts before the garment pooled at her feet. She stepped out of it, turning to face him, and Yordan's heart nearly stopped.

It wasn't Katherine standing before him, but Aisha. Her bronze skin seemed to glow in the firelight, her raven hair cascading over her shoulders and brushing against the swell of her breasts. Her eyes, dark and intense, were filled with a hunger that made Yordan's blood run hot.

"Aisha," he breathed, his voice a mix of confusion and awe.

She didn't respond, at least not with words. Instead, she closed the distance between them, her naked body pressing against his still clothed one. Her hands fisted in his shirt, yanking him down into a searing kiss that stole the breath from his lungs.

Yordan's mind went blank, he pulled back slightly, his breath coming in short gasps as he tried to make sense of what was happening. Aisha stood before him, her dark eyes smoldering with desire, her full lips parted and glistening from their heated kiss.

As if sensing his confusion, Aisha reached up and cupped his face, her thumbs brushing lightly over his cheekbones. "Yordan," she whispered, her voice low and sultry. "Don't think. Just feel."

Her words washed over him like a spell, and suddenly the questions didn't matter anymore. All that mattered was the feel of her skin against his, the intoxicating scent of her hair, the way her body molded perfectly to his. With a low growl, Yordan wrapped his arms around her waist and lifted her up. Aisha's legs instantly locked around his hips as he carried her to the bed, their lips meeting in another searing kiss.

He laid her down gently on the soft furs, his eyes roaming over her naked form with undisguised hunger. Aisha's skin seemed to glow in the firelight, the shadows accentuating the curves of her breasts and hips. Yordan's hands followed the path of his gaze, his calloused fingers gliding over her smooth flesh, mapping every dip and swell.

Aisha arched into his touch, a soft moan escaping her lips as Yordan's mouth found her neck. He trailed hot, open-mouthed kisses down her throat, his tongue darting out to taste her skin. When he reached her breasts, he paused, his breath ghosting over the dusky peaks of her nipples.

"Please," Aisha whispered, her fingers threading through his hair. "Touch me."

Yordan obliged, his lips closing around one hardened bud while his hand cupped the other breast. Aisha cried out, her back bowing off the bed as he suckled and licked, his teeth grazing the sensitive flesh. Her hands scrabbled at his shoulders, nails digging into his skin as she tried to pull him closer.

While his mouth lavished attention on her breasts, Aisha's hands slid down Yordan's back, her fingers dipping beneath the waistband of his trousers. She could feel his hardness pressing against her thigh, the evidence of his desire straining against the fabric. With deft movements, she untied the laces and pushed the garment down, freeing his thick, heavy cock.

Yordan groaned against her skin as Aisha's hand wrapped around his length, her fingers stroking him from base to tip. He was so hard it was almost painful. Yordan blinked, and suddenly Katherine was beneath him again, her auburn hair fanned out on the pillow, her green eyes dark with desire. The vision of Aisha had been so vivid, so real, that for a moment he couldn't distinguish between fantasy and reality.

A wave of guilt washed over him, mixing with the aching need that still pulsed through his veins.

"Yordan?" Katherine whispered, her hand coming up to cup his cheek. "Is everything alright?"

He swallowed hard, trying to push away the lingering image of Aisha's bronze skin and smoldering gaze. "I'm sorry," he murmured, his voice rough with emotion. "I just... I got lost in my head for a moment."

Katherine's brow furrowed slightly, concern etched in the lines of her face. "Do you want to stop?" she asked softly, her thumb brushing over his cheekbone.

Yordan shook his head, leaning down to capture her lips in a tender kiss. "No," he breathed against her mouth. "I need you, Katherine. I need to feel you."

She melted into his embrace, her arms winding around his neck as she deepened the kiss. Yordan lost himself in the taste of her, in the softness of her skin and the gentle curves of her body. He pushed away the thoughts of Aisha, the confusion and guilt, focusing only on the woman in his arms.

Their lovemaking was slow and reverent, a reaffirmation of their bond in the face of all the uncertainty that lay ahead. Yordan worshipped Katherine's body with his hands and mouth, pouring all of his love and devotion into every touch. When he finally slid inside her, their bodies joining as one, it felt like coming home.

Afterwards, they lay tangled together on the bed, sweat cooling on their skin as their heartbeats gradually slowed. Katherine's head rested on Yordan's chest, her fingers tracing idle patterns on his stomach. Yordan held her close, his eyes fixed on the ceiling as his mind churned with conflicting thoughts and emotions.

"Yordan," Katherine murmured, her voice soft in the stillness of the room. "Whatever happens, whatever path you choose... I'm with you, always."

Yordan tightened his arm around her, pressing a kiss to the top of her head. "I know," he whispered, his voice thick with emotion.

The morning sun filtered through the small window of Yordan's home, casting warm, golden light across the room. Yordan stirred awake, the weight of sleep slowly lifting as his mind came into focus. He blinked a few times, sitting up and running a hand through his hair. The bed beside him was empty, just as he had expected it to be. Katherine must have slipped out early, likely to avoid her parents' questions about where she had been all night.

Despite knowing this, Yordan couldn't shake a pang of guilt that gnawed at him. As he rubbed his face, the memories of the previous night came rushing back—not just the passion he shared with Katherine but the intrusive, unbidden thoughts that lingered during their embrace. Why was I thinking about Aisha? he wondered, his chest tightening. What is wrong with me? Katherine deserves better than this.

Shaking his head as if to rid himself of the thoughts, Yordan dressed quickly, his movements brisk and almost mechanical. He didn't have time to dwell on his guilt. There was work to be done, and Ferran's forge awaited. Grabbing his pack and tools, he stepped out into the bustling streets of Aralonis.

The morning air was crisp, the sounds of merchants setting up stalls and townsfolk beginning their day filling the streets. Yordan's boots clicked against the cobblestones as he made his way toward the forge, his mind still clouded with thoughts of Katherine, Aisha, and Toteko's impossible mission.

As he turned a corner, the sight ahead made him stop dead in his tracks.

In the middle of the street, an older man was surrounded by a group of Aralonite soldiers. His clothes, though worn, bore the intricate patterns and muted colors often associated with Zetian craftsmanship. His face, weathered and lined with age, carried an air of quiet dignity despite the tension in his expression. He stood with his hands raised, palms outward, as the soldiers barked orders and closed in on him.

"You're under arrest," one of the soldiers growled, his hand resting on the hilt of his sword. "You have no right to be here. Prince Joseph's orders are clear."

"I've done nothing wrong," the man said calmly, though there was a faint tremor in his voice. "I'm just passing through on my way to Zetopolis."

"You think we care about your excuses?" another soldier snapped, stepping closer with his sword drawn. "You're a Zetian. That's reason enough."

The older man's gaze briefly flicked toward Yordan, his eyes meeting his for just a moment. There was no plea for help, no desperation, just a quiet resignation that made Yordan's chest tighten even further.

Yordan froze for a moment, his eyes locked on the scene unfolding in the street. The older man, clearly Zetian from his attire and the intricate patterns embroidered on his worn robe, stood surrounded by a small unit of Aralonite soldiers. Their stances were tense, hands on the hilts of their swords, as if ready to strike at the slightest provocation. The older man's hands were raised in a gesture of surrender, but his calm demeanor only seemed to irritate the soldiers further.

Yordan clenched his jaw, his boots crunching against the cobblestones as he approached. His heart pounded in his chest, but his steps were deliberate and steady, his blacksmith's build lending him an air of quiet authority.

"Commander," Yordan called out, his voice firm but respectful as he addressed the soldier leading the group. The man turned to face him, his sharp features marked by a permanent scowl. His armor bore the emblem of Aralonis—a crossed hammer and anvil—etched into the polished metal.

"What's going on here?" Yordan asked, his tone carefully measured. "What's this man done to deserve being surrounded like this?"

The commander narrowed his eyes, clearly annoyed at the interruption. "Who are you to ask questions of the city guard?" he snapped.

"I'm Yordan," he said, keeping his voice calm. "A blacksmith of this city. And I'm asking because this doesn't look right. What's his crime?"

The commander snorted, his grip tightening on the hilt of his sword. "His crime," he said, his voice dripping with disdain, "is being a Zetian spy."

Yordan blinked, his brow furrowing in confusion. "A spy?" he repeated, glancing at the older man. The Zetian didn't look like a spy—he looked like a weary traveler, his robes dusty and his face lined with age and exhaustion. "What proof do you have of that?"

The commander's scowl deepened. "Proof?" he spat. "He's a Zetian, wandering near Aralonis without cause or explanation. That's all the proof we need."

Yordan's stomach churned at the blatant prejudice in the man's words. "So, you're saying he's guilty just because he's Zetian?" he pressed, his tone edging toward anger.

The commander stepped closer, his eyes narrowing dangerously. "Watch yourself, blacksmith," he warned. "This is official business, and you're sticking your nose where it doesn't belong. This man is being detained, and that's the end of it."

Yordan glanced at the older man, who remained silent but met his gaze with calm, steady eyes. There was no fear there, only a quiet resolve that made Yordan's heart ache. He turned back to the commander, his hands clenched into fists at his sides.

"This doesn't feel right," Yordan said, his voice low but steady. "If he's innocent, you're punishing a man for no reason. If he's guilty, then he deserves a fair trial, not whatever this is."

The commander sneered, his hand tightening on his sword. "You're awfully bold for a blacksmith," he said coldly. "But boldness won't protect you if you keep questioning the guard. Leave now, or you'll be joining this spy in chains."

Yordan's blood boiled at the man's arrogance, but he forced himself to take a step back. He wasn't in a position to fight the city guard, at least not yet. For now, all he could do was bear witness and hope to learn more.

He turned his gaze to the older Zetian man, giving him a faint, almost apologetic nod. The man returned it with a small, understanding smile, as if to say he didn't blame Yordan for stepping away.

The soldiers began binding the man's wrists, their rough handling making Yordan's stomach twist. As the small unit started to lead the man away, Yordan stood frozen, his mind racing with questions and doubts. A spy? he thought bitterly. Or just another victim of fear and hatred?

His hands tightened into fists at his sides as he watched them disappear down the street. He didn't have the power to stop this—not now—but the seeds of anger and determination were already taking root in his heart.

Yordan's boots scuffed against the cobblestones as he walked away, his head hanging low, the weight of the earlier encounter pressing down on him like an iron anvil. The image of the older Zetian man being led away by the soldiers was burned into his mind, his calm yet resigned expression haunting. I should have done something, Yordan thought bitterly. But what could I have done?

"Hey," a voice said quietly but firmly, pulling Yordan from his thoughts.

He looked up, startled, to see a young man standing a few paces away. He appeared to be about Yordan's age, his features unmistakably Zetian—sharp cheekbones, deep-set eyes, and skin a warm bronze hue. His hair was tied back in a simple knot, and his clothes, though modest, carried the intricate patterns typical of Zetian craftsmanship.

"Come with me," the man said, his tone low and clipped.

Yordan blinked, confusion flickering across his face. "What?" he asked, his voice cautious.

"Come with me," the man repeated, his gaze darting around the street as if ensuring no one was watching. "Now."

Yordan hesitated for a moment, his instincts telling him to be wary. But something in the man's tone—a mixture of urgency and defiance—compelled him to follow. Without another word, he fell into step behind the Zetian, the two weaving through the winding streets of Aralonis in silence.

After several minutes, they arrived at a modest home tucked away in a quieter part of the city. The exterior was unassuming, its weathered stone walls blending seamlessly with the surrounding buildings. The Zetian man pushed open the door, gesturing for Yordan to enter.

Inside, the home was small but filled with life. A woman who Yordan assumed was the man's mother knelt by a loom in the corner, her hands deftly working the threads. An older woman, likely his grandmother, sat by the fire, her fingers busy with a piece of embroidery.

"Who's this?" the older woman asked sharply, her eyes narrowing as she glanced up from her work.

"A stranger," the man said, his voice guarded. He motioned for Yordan to sit at the small wooden table in the center of the room. Yordan complied, his hands resting uneasily on his knees.

The Zetian man sat across from him, his posture tense, his gaze piercing. "Who are you?" he demanded, his tone laced with suspicion. "And why did you step in back there?"

Yordan took a deep breath, steadying himself. "My name is Yordan," he said simply. "I'm a blacksmith here in Aralonis."

The man frowned, his expression skeptical. "And yet you care about an old Zetian man being arrested? Why?"

"Because it wasn't right," Yordan said firmly, meeting the man's gaze. "He didn't do anything. The soldiers couldn't even give me a real reason for arresting him. They called him a spy, but I didn't see any evidence of that."

The man leaned back slightly, crossing his arms over his chest. "You think you're the first Aralonite to claim they care about injustice? Forgive me if I don't trust your words."

Yordan's jaw tightened, but he kept his tone measured. "I understand your doubt," he said. "I haven't done much to prove myself. Honestly, I feel like I've done nothing. I watched those soldiers take him away, and I didn't stop them. But I care. I care enough that it's been eating at me ever since it happened."

The man studied him for a long moment, his dark eyes searching Yordan's face for any sign of deceit. The tension in the room was thick, the quiet hum of the loom and the crackle of the fire the only sounds.

"You stepped in," the Zetian man said finally, his voice quieter. "That's more than most would do."

Yordan nodded, his shoulders relaxing slightly. "I couldn't just stand by," he said. "But it doesn't feel like enough. I want to help, but I don't know how."

The man's posture softened, though the suspicion didn't entirely leave his expression. "Help, you say," he murmured, almost to himself. He glanced toward the older woman by the fire, who was watching them intently. She gave a small, almost imperceptible nod.

"My name is Ayome," the man said, extending a hand across the table. His grip was firm, his eyes still wary. "If you truly want to help, we'll see if your actions match your words."

Yordan returned the handshake, his grip steady. "I meant what I said," he replied. "I just need to know where to start."

Ayome nodded slowly, his expression thoughtful. "Then we'll start by talking," he said. "There's much you don't know about what's happening to my people, and if you're serious about helping, you need to understand the truth."

Yordan nodded, a faint glimmer of determination sparking in his chest. For the first time in weeks, he felt like he was taking a step forward—even if he didn't yet know where the path would lead.

As Yordan stepped out of Ayome's modest home, Ayome followed him to the door, his expression still cautious but no longer cold. Before Yordan stepped into the street, Ayome spoke, his voice low and steady.

"May the Echoes of Toteko keep you steady," Ayome said, his dark eyes watching Yordan carefully.

Yordan paused, the weight of the words resonating with him in a way he couldn't quite place. He nodded respectfully. "Thank you, Ayome," he replied, his voice earnest.

With that, Yordan turned and began his walk toward the Luminar Citadel, the seat of Prince Joseph's rule in Aralonis. The streets of the city bustled with activity, the midday sun casting long shadows as merchants hawked their wares and townsfolk hurried about their errands. The familiar clink of hammers from nearby forges mingled with the murmur of voices, but Yordan's focus was fixed on the towering structure ahead.

The Luminar Citadel rose like a fortress at the northern edge of Aralonis, its stone walls gleaming faintly in the sunlight. Unlike the modest homes and workshops that filled the city, the citadel was a testament to the craftsmanship of generations past. Its intricate carvings of flames adorned the arched entryway, while its turrets pierced the sky, their banners bearing the blue and gold sigil of Aralonis fluttering in the breeze.

As Yordan approached, the guards at the main gate stood at attention, their armor polished and emblazoned with the same sigil. One of them, a burly man with a weathered face, stepped forward, his hand resting on the hilt of his sword.

"I'm here to request an audience with Prince Joseph," Yordan said, his voice steady despite the flutter of nerves in his chest.

The guard eyed him for a moment before nodding. "Very well," he said curtly. "Head straight ahead. There's a line forming in the audience chamber. Wait your turn."

"Thank you," Yordan replied, inclining his head before stepping through the gates.

Inside the citadel, the air was cooler, the high ceilings and polished stone floors lending an air of solemnity to the space. The halls were adorned with tapestries depicting Aralonis's rich history—scenes of legendary blacksmiths, heroic warriors, and the founding of the city. Yordan's steps echoed faintly as he walked toward the audience chamber, his eyes briefly flicking to the intricate murals before focusing on the task at hand.

When he entered the audience chamber, he found himself in a large, circular room with a high, vaulted ceiling supported by carved stone pillars. At the far end of the chamber sat Prince Joseph, his throne-like chair made of iron and oak, as solid and commanding as the man himself. Above him, the sigil of Aralonis was prominently displayed, flanked by purple and gold banners.

A line of petitioners stretched through the room, each waiting their turn to speak. Yordan took his place at the back, his arms crossed loosely as he waited. The minutes dragged on, the line moving slowly as people presented their cases, each vying for the prince's attention.

Finally, it was Yordan's turn. As he stepped forward, Prince Joseph looked up, his piercing blue eyes lighting with recognition. A faint smile curved his lips as he gestured for Yordan to approach.

"I recognize you," the prince said warmly, his tone tinged with curiosity. "But remind me what your name is again?"

Yordan bowed slightly, his voice steady as he replied, "I am Yordan, my lord. A blacksmith, an apprentice to Ferran. You commissioned a sword from him some time ago, which I had the honor of delivering to you."

Prince Joseph's smile widened, his eyes glinting with approval. "Ah, yes, I remember now," he said, his tone amiable. "That sword was a fine piece of craftsmanship. Ferran continues to impress with his craft, it seems."

Yordan inclined his head again, a faint sense of pride swelling in his chest. "Thank you, my lord," he said. "It means a great deal to hear that from you."

The prince leaned forward slightly, his expression curious. "So, Yordan, what brings you here today? Surely not another delivery from Ferran?"

Yordan took a deep breath, his mind racing as he prepared to speak. This was his moment, and he couldn't afford to waste it.

Yordan took a deep breath, steadying his nerves before speaking. "My lord," he began, his voice clear but respectful, "I've come to ask for the release of the older Zetian man your soldiers arrested earlier today."

The murmurs among the courtiers and other petitioners began immediately, a ripple of quiet conversations moving through the chamber. Prince Joseph leaned back in his iron-and-oak chair, his expression softening into something almost paternal. His sharp blue eyes regarded Yordan with a mixture of amusement and patience, as though a grandfather explaining a simple truth to an inquisitive child.

"My boy," the prince said, his tone warm yet condescending, "you must understand that the man in question was not arrested without reason. He is a spy, working against the interests of Aralonis. His release would jeopardize our safety and stability."

Yordan frowned but stood his ground. "With all due respect, my lord," he replied, "your own commander told me they found nothing on him when they searched him. No documents, no weapons, nothing to suggest he was anything other than a traveler."

The murmurs grew louder, courtiers whispering behind hands as Yordan's words echoed through the chamber. Prince Joseph's smile faltered slightly, but he quickly masked it with an air of calm authority.

"Spies often carry their secrets in their minds, not their pockets," the prince said gently, as though it were an obvious truth. "That man's presence here is enough to raise suspicion."

Before Yordan could respond, another voice rang out, smooth and calculated. "If I may, Father."

Lucien, Prince Joseph's son, stepped forward from the crowd of courtiers. His sharp features and predatory grin made Yordan's stomach twist. Lucien walked a slow circle around Yordan, his boots clicking against the polished stone floor, his eyes studying the blacksmith like a hawk sizing up its prey.

"Shall we clarify what this so-called traveler's intentions were?" Lucien said, his tone dripping with mock courtesy. He produced a small scroll, unrolling it dramatically. "This Zetian man, whose name is conveniently absent from your petition, was reportedly sent to gather information on several prominent individuals within Aralonis."

He began reading aloud, his voice ringing through the chamber: "Lord Tarik of the Eastern Watch. Lady Miren of the Merchant's Guild. General Orin of the City Guard. And let's not forget... Ferran, master blacksmith, and his apprentice, Yordan."

The last name hung in the air, and Yordan felt a chill run down his spine as the murmurs among the courtiers turned into an audible buzz.

Lucien's grin widened as he folded the scroll and tucked it away. "Doesn't sound like a harmless traveler to me," he said, his tone razor-sharp.

Yordan clenched his fists, forcing himself to remain calm. He looked up at Prince Joseph, his voice steady but firm. "My lord," he said, his words deliberate, "if this man truly has ill intentions, I will take responsibility for him. On my life, I vouch for him. Please, release him."

The murmurs stilled, all eyes turning to Prince Joseph. The prince's gaze lingered on Yordan, his expression thoughtful and conflicted. Finally, he nodded, though hesitation was evident in the set of his jaw. "So be it," he said, his voice carrying the weight of his authority. "Lucien, ensure this man is released."

Lucien's grin disappeared for a moment, his jaw tightening. He muttered under his breath, just loud enough for Yordan to hear, "Purity requires vigilance." Then, with a feigned smile, he said, "We appreciate your petition, Yordan the blacksmith. Rest assured, we will honor it."

Yordan inclined his head, keeping his tone neutral. "Thank you, my lord," he said, addressing Prince Joseph directly. Without waiting for further commentary, he turned and walked out of the chamber, his steps steady but his mind racing.

As he made his way back through the streets of Aralonis, the weight of what had just transpired settled heavily on his shoulders. By the time he reached Ferran's forge, the familiar clang of metal on metal was a welcome comfort. He stepped inside, the heat of the forge and the smell of iron grounding him as he prepared to face whatever came next.

The rhythmic clang of hammer on metal filled the forge, its steady beat usually soothing to Yordan. But today, the sound grated against his nerves, his thoughts spiraling as he worked. The tools laid out before him—chisels, tongs, and files—gleamed under the firelight, their edges precise, their purpose clear. Nearby, swords in varying stages of completion lined the wall, their blades catching the glow of the forge's fire. Each one was a testament to clarity and craftsmanship, things Yordan felt he sorely lacked.

His hands moved mechanically, shaping the glowing steel in front of him, but his mind wandered. Would it be easier just to end this all now? The thought was sudden, sharp, and terrifying. His grip on the hammer faltered for a moment, and he set it down, leaning heavily against the workbench.

Toteko hasn't told me what to do, he thought bitterly. I don't even know if I did the right thing today. What if I just made everything worse?

He stared at the tools again, their sharp edges taking on a sinister cast in his mind. The fire crackled loudly behind him, the heat wrapping around him like an oppressive weight.

"Yordan!" Ferran's voice cut through his spiraling thoughts, loud and commanding.

Yordan straightened abruptly, turning to face Ferran, who was striding toward him with a look of deep concern etched on his face. The older man's silver-streaked hair clung to his damp forehead, and his sharp blue eyes bore into Yordan with the intensity of a master smith scrutinizing a flawed blade.

"Did you vouch for a Zetian?" Ferran asked bluntly, his tone leaving no room for evasion. "A Zetian who supposedly had our names on a list to be spied upon while he was here in Aralonis?"

Yordan swallowed hard, his heart pounding. He met Ferran's gaze, knowing there was no point in lying. "I did," he said, his voice steady but quiet. "I saw him being arrested earlier today. The guards said they found nothing when they searched him—no weapons, no documents. Lucien only produced 'evidence' after I petitioned Prince Joseph."

Ferran's brow furrowed deeply, his jaw tightening as he processed Yordan's words. "Yordan," he said, his voice softer but still laced with concern, "what's brought this on? What are you doing getting involved in something like this?"

Yordan hesitated, his thoughts churning. Should I tell him? he wondered. The weight of Toteko's message loomed over him, but he still wasn't sure if Ferran would understand—or believe him.

Before he could answer, the forge door swung open, and Sam burst in, his stick tapping against the floor as he moved with uncharacteristic urgency. His usually calm demeanor was replaced by a tension that Yordan rarely saw in him.

"Yordan," Sam said, his tone sharp, "what did you do? The whole city is ablaze with the news of who you vouched for."

Yordan froze, the air in the forge suddenly feeling too thick to breathe. "What do you mean?" he asked, though he already knew the answer.

"I mean," Sam said, stepping closer, his voice lowering but no less intense, "everyone's talking about the blacksmith's apprentice who convinced Prince Joseph to release a Zetian spy. People are saying you've put the city in danger."

Ferran's concerned gaze shifted between the two younger men, his frown deepening. "Yordan," he said again, this time more firmly, "what exactly have you gotten yourself into?"

Yordan's mind raced as the weight of his actions began to settle on him fully. He looked at Ferran, then at Sam, his friends and mentors now drawn into the storm he had inadvertently created. I wanted to help, he thought desperately. But what if I've only made things worse?

The forge, once his sanctuary, now felt like a crucible, the fire and tools surrounding him a reflection of the pressure building inside. He knew he needed to answer Ferran's question—and soon—but the truth felt heavier than any blade he had ever forged.

Yordan glanced between Ferran and Sam, feeling the weight of their expectant gazes. Ferran's sharp, calculating eyes bore into him, while Sam's expression, though neutral, carried a quiet patience. Yordan hesitated, his hands tightening into fists at his sides. They need to know, he thought, though doubt gnawed at him.

Taking a steady breath, he looked at Ferran. "There's something I need to tell you," he said slowly, his voice wavering slightly. "Back in the Sitlali Mountains, I... I think I saw Toteko."

The forge grew uncomfortably silent. The only sounds were the distant crackling of the fire and the rhythmic clang of metal from a nearby workshop. Ferran's face remained unreadable, his piercing gaze fixed on Yordan. Sam, standing a little to the side, tilted his head slightly. Though Yordan had already told him this, he said nothing, letting the moment unfold as though he was hearing it anew.

"You believe you saw Toteko," Ferran said evenly, his tone giving away nothing.

Yordan nodded. "Yes. In a cave near the summit. I heard a voice calling my name—and there was this light. Overwhelming, like it filled every part of the cave. I couldn't look away. The voice... it said it was Toteko."

Ferran glanced at Sam, his brow furrowing slightly. "And you didn't mention this before?"

Sam shrugged, leaning lightly on his stick. "I already know," he said, his tone calm but with a faint edge of skepticism. "He told me after he came running back to the hostel like his life depended on it. I figured he believed what he saw, even if I don't believe in Toteko—or any god, for that matter."

Ferran shifted his gaze back to Yordan, studying him closely. "And since then," he asked, his voice steady but probing, "has Toteko spoken to you? In any way? A vision, a dream, a sign?"

Yordan hesitated, his shoulders slumping slightly. "No," he admitted quietly. "Nothing. Just silence."

Ferran leaned back slightly, crossing his arms. His expression remained impassive, but there was a hint of concern in his eyes. "And yet," he said slowly, "you vouched for a Zetian spy today, risking not just your reputation but possibly your life. What's driving you, Yordan? Why are you taking these risks?"

Yordan glanced at Sam, who remained quiet, his expression unreadable. Turning back to Ferran, he swallowed hard, debating whether to share more. The name he'd seen scribbled on the library page surfaced in his mind again, the unanswered questions gnawing at him.

Yordan's voice steady but laced with curiosity asked, "Do you know the name Jareth Taron?"

Chapter Thirteen

T he mention of the name had an immediate effect on Ferran. His
jaw tightened, his grip on his folded arms shifting as though
the question unsettled him. The faint flicker of something darker—pain, anger, or perhaps regret—flashed across his face, but he
quickly masked it.

Ferran's silence hung heavily in the air, his expression unreadable
as he seemed to weigh his words carefully before responding. Ferran's gaze darkened, his jaw tightening as he leaned heavily against the
workbench. He let out a long, weary sigh, running a hand through his
silver-streaked hair. "I know the name," he said finally, his voice low
and measured. "Jareth Taron wasn't just a name in a book, Yordan.
He was a man I met—served under, even—when he led a military
campaign against Zetopolis. I made weapons for him and his men
while serving as a soldier myself."

Yordan straightened slightly, his curiosity sharpening. "You knew
him?" he asked. "What was he like?"

Ferran nodded, his expression growing distant as he pulled memories from the depths of his mind. "He was a great warrior," Ferran said,

his voice tinged with a mix of admiration and bitterness. "A brilliant strategist. He had this way of seeing the battlefield like a chessboard, always thinking three moves ahead. He commanded loyalty, not because he demanded it, but because he earned it. When Jareth spoke, you believed in what he was fighting for, even if the cause wasn't your own."

Yordan frowned, his brow furrowing as he considered Ferran's words. "Then what happened to him?" he asked. "His name was scratched out in a library book I found in Lumina City, but I saw it again in another text. Why would someone try to erase his name?"

Ferran's face darkened further, his fingers curling into a fist on the workbench. "That's the question, isn't it?" he said, his voice dropping to a near growl. "One day, while we laid siege to Zetopolis, Jareth vanished. No warning, no explanation—he was just gone."

Yordan's eyes widened slightly. "Vanished? In the middle of a siege?"

"Yes," Ferran said grimly. "It caused chaos. His second-in-command, Yoav, took over, but Yoav was no Jareth. He called Jareth a coward, and claimed he'd fled the battle. But I never believed that. Cowardice didn't suit Jareth. He was too... deliberate for that. Whatever the reason, his absence was felt immediately. Without him, our siege was broken in less than a week. The Zetians drove us back, and the army dissolved like smoke in the wind."

Ferran's voice grew quieter, the bitterness in his tone replaced by a note of regret. "We lost everything we'd gained in that campaign. And the men—many of them blamed Yoav, but just as many cursed Jareth for leaving us. Some said he'd been killed. Others whispered darker things, that he'd defected to the Zetians. To this day, no one knows the truth."

Yordan leaned forward slightly, his pulse quickening. "Do you think he's still alive?" he asked, the question slipping out before he could stop himself.

Ferran gave him a long, measured look. "If he is," he said slowly, "he's been keeping to the shadows for a long time. But if you've seen his name scratched out in a book, it means someone wants him forgotten. And in my experience, Yordan, people only try to erase names when those names still have power."

The words hung heavy in the air, the forge's crackling fire the only sound as Yordan processed what he'd just heard. Ferran's revelation painted a picture far more complex than Yordan had anticipated, and the weight of it settled heavily on his shoulders. Jareth Taron wasn't just a name, he was a mystery, one that seemed to intertwine with the tangled threads of Yordan's journey.

The forge was alive with the heat of the flames, the rhythmic clang of Ferran's hammer echoing through the space. Yordan focused intently on shaping the blade before him, his thoughts still churning from the conversation with Ferran earlier. The weight of Jareth Taron's story, the unanswered questions about Toteko, and the events at the palace all pressed heavily on his mind. He barely noticed the sound of the forge door opening until Katherine's voice cut through the noise like a blade.

"Yordan!" she called, her tone sharp and brimming with frustration.

Yordan flinched, setting the blade down on the anvil as he turned to see her striding into the forge. Her auburn hair was pulled back hastily, a few strands falling loose around her flushed face. Her green eyes were blazing, the intensity of her expression catching even Ferran's attention as he paused mid-swing.

"Katherine," Yordan began, wiping his hands on a rag, "what's wrong?"

"What's wrong?" she repeated, her voice rising slightly. "I just heard about what you did before Prince Joseph! You vouched for a Zetian spy?"

Yordan winced at the way she said it, her words carrying more accusation than question. He opened his mouth to respond, but Katherine kept going, her anger spilling out in rapid-fire sentences.

"Do you realize what people are saying about you? That you're reckless? That you've endangered Aralonis? Yordan, what were you thinking?"

Ferran shifted uncomfortably, stepping back slightly as if to give them space, though his watchful gaze lingered.

Yordan exhaled, his hands gripping the edge of the workbench as he steadied himself. "I couldn't let them hold him without proof, Katherine," he said, his voice firm but not defensive.

"They called him a spy, but there was nothing on him. The guards admitted it. The only so-called 'evidence' came out of Lucien's mouth after I pressed them on it."

"And you think that's reason enough?" Katherine shot back, crossing her arms. "You went against Prince Joseph's judgment. Do you know how dangerous that is?"

"I do," Yordan said, his jaw tightening. "But what was I supposed to do? Stand there and let them take an innocent man? He didn't deserve that, Katherine. I couldn't just ignore it."

Katherine shook her head, her frustration evident. "You're risking everything on this, Yordan. Everything. And for what? Some man you don't even know?"

Yordan felt the sting of her words but pushed back, his voice rising slightly. "Because it was the right thing to do! Toteko" He stopped himself, clenching his fists as he tried to find the words. "I don't even know if this is what Toteko wanted, but I couldn't let that man be punished without reason. What kind of person would I be if I turned a blind eye?"

Katherine's expression shifted, the anger in her eyes dimming slightly but giving way to something more conflicted. "And what if you're wrong, Yordan?" she asked, her voice softer but still heavy with emotion. "What if he really is a spy, and your decision puts everyone in danger? What if this vision of yours is leading you down the wrong path?"

Yordan's heart sank at her words, doubt creeping in like a shadow. What if she's right? he thought. What if I've made a terrible mistake? He met her gaze, searching for something—understanding, reassurance—but found only uncertainty.

"I don't know," he admitted quietly, his voice barely above a whisper. "Maybe I did screw up. But I couldn't stand there and do nothing, Katherine. I couldn't."

Katherine looked at him for a long moment, her lips pressing into a thin line as if she were holding back a flood of emotions. Finally, she stepped back, her arms still crossed tightly.

"I need to go," she said abruptly, her tone clipped. "I can't do this right now."

"Katherine" Yordan started, but she turned on her heel and walked out of the forge, the door slamming shut behind her.

The silence that followed was deafening. Yordan stood frozen, his chest tight as he stared at the door, the weight of their unresolved fight settling heavily on his shoulders. Ferran finally broke the silence, his hammer resting on the anvil.

"That didn't look like it went the way you hoped," Ferran said cautiously, his voice carrying a note of sympathy.

Yordan shook his head, running a hand through his hair. "No," he said softly, his gaze dropping to the floor. "It didn't."

The forge's fire crackled in the background, but for Yordan, the warmth of the flames did little to ease the cold knot of doubt and guilt forming in his chest.

The day had stretched longer than Yordan could bear, and as he trudged home through the dimly lit streets of Aralonis, his body ached with exhaustion. The distant sounds of the city settling for the night barely registered in his ears. His mind was still replaying his heated argument with Katherine, Ferran's questions, and the whispers of doubt that refused to leave him.

When Yordan rounded the corner to his modest home, his steps faltered. His breath hitched, his pulse hammering against his ribs as his eyes locked onto the front wall. Streaks of red paint—thick, erratic, violent—slashed across the wood and stone, the color too raw, too deliberate, like fresh blood smeared in rage. Symbols curled and twisted in jagged lines, their meaning just out of reach, but the intent behind them was unmistakable.

"Purity Requires Vigilance."

The phrase leapt out from the chaos, stark and purposeful. Yordan's fingers twitched at his sides, his chest tightening as the words dragged him back—to the Lumina Library, to the margins of a worn, time-stained book, where that same phrase had been scrawled beside warnings of false faith and corrupted hands. His breath came shallow, the weight of the moment pressing down like a hammer poised over an anvil.

Yordan let out a heavy sigh, his shoulders slumping. I must have made a mistake, he thought bitterly. His hand brushed against the wooden frame of his door as he pushed it open and stepped inside. The interior of his home, usually a sanctuary, felt suffocating now. He could still feel the day's events clawing at the edges of his mind, refusing to let him rest.

He set down his pack, not even bothering to inspect the damage further. His steps were slow and heavy as he moved to his small bed in the corner of the room. Crawling beneath the worn blanket, Yordan let his head fall into his hands. His thoughts swirled in a torrent of doubt and despair.

I can't do this. I can't be the one Toteko chose. What did I think I could accomplish? The questions lashed at him, relentless and cruel. It would've been better if I never went up to that cave. Better if I never heard Toteko's voice.

The weight of his emotions pressed against him, thick and unrelenting. He lay back, staring up at the dark ceiling. The shadows seemed alive, twisting and shifting like the doubts in his mind. He could feel the overwhelming pull of despair, threatening to drag him under.

You're not strong enough for this, a cruel voice whispered in his head. You're no prophet, no savior. You're just a blacksmith who's out of his depth.

Yordan clenched his jaw, willing himself not to let the tide of emotions consume him. But his resolve was slipping. The enormity of the task before him, the growing hostility around him, and his own festering doubts were too much to bear. He closed his eyes, hoping for sleep to take him, but all he found was the echo of his own fears.

For the first time since descending from the Sitlali Mountains, Yordan felt the weight of his mission might crush him entirely.

The morning sunlight streamed into Ferran's forge, casting long streaks of light across the tools and unfinished blades scattered about. Yordan stepped inside, expecting the usual rhythm of the day—working the fires, hammering metal, and exchanging the occasional banter with his mentor. But today, Ferran was waiting for him at the workbench, his expression serious and his hands clasping a folded piece of parchment.

"Yordan," Ferran said, his tone leaving no room for argument, "I need you to take this note and head to the Sitlali Mountains immediately."

Yordan blinked, caught off guard by the abruptness of the request. "The Sitlali Mountains? What's going on?"

Ferran held up a hand to silence him, his gaze steady. "It's not a request. It's an order. You need to leave as soon as possible."

Yordan frowned but nodded, stepping forward to take the note. As he moved to unfold it, Ferran's hand shot out, stopping him. "Not here," he said firmly. "Not until you're clear of Aralonis. Do you understand me?"

Something in Ferran's voice made Yordan pause, his instincts telling him not to press the matter further. He folded the note carefully and tucked it into his pack, nodding again. "I understand."

Ferran's gaze softened slightly, though the tension in his posture remained. "Good," he said. Then, with a tone both formal and heartfelt, he added, "May the forge of Toteko temper your soul."

Yordan straightened, meeting his mentor's eyes as he replied, "And may it shape yours with wisdom and strength."

The exchange lingered in the air between them, heavy with meaning. Yordan knew better than to ask questions Ferran wasn't ready to answer, so he simply adjusted his pack and stepped toward the door. Ferran didn't say anything else, his eyes following Yordan until he was out of sight.

As Yordan made his way through the bustling streets of Aralonis, he wrestled with a mix of curiosity and unease. Ferran's urgency had left him unsettled, but his trust in his mentor outweighed his questions. Deciding not to delay, he headed straight for Sam's place.

Sam's modest home was quiet when Yordan arrived, the faint sounds of the city barely reaching this corner. Yordan hesitated for a moment before pulling out a piece of parchment and quickly scrawling a note:

"Sam, Ferran has sent me on a mission away from the city. I'll explain when I return. Be well, my friend."

He left the note on the small table by the door, ensuring it was in a spot where Sam would easily find it. With a final glance around, Yordan adjusted his pack again and set off toward the city gates.

The journey ahead was unknown, but the trust he placed in Ferran and the solemnity of the task spurred him forward. As the gates of Aralonis faded behind him, the words of their exchange echoed in his mind, grounding him as he began his trek toward the Sitlali Mountains.

The soft rustling of leaves and the gentle murmur of the Lumina River filled the cool night air as Yordan slept, his campfire reduced to faint embers. The rhythmic flow of the water seemed to seep into his dreams, pulling him into a vivid and unsettling vision.

He stood on the edge of a dense forest by the riverbank, the surroundings impossibly vivid. The air felt charged, crackling with an unexplainable energy that made his breath hitch. Across the river, a figure emerged from the shadowy tree line—a woman. Her presence was immediate and commanding, her striking features catching the moonlight as she stepped forward with deliberate intensity.

She stood at 5'6", her slender yet athletic build exuding both grace and undeniable strength. Her heart-shaped face was framed by vibrant red hair that tumbled down her back in loose waves, glowing like embers in the pale light. But it was her eyes—striking, icy blue—that rooted Yordan in place. They were fierce, piercing, and filled with an intelligence that felt as though they could see straight through him.

Her stance was defensive, her arms crossed tightly over her chest as she glared at him with open suspicion. "Who are you?" she demanded, her voice sharp and cutting, carrying no warmth.

Yordan opened his mouth, but no words came out. He didn't know how to explain what he himself didn't understand. Instead, he raised his hands in a gesture of peace, taking a tentative step closer to the water.

"I... I don't know why I'm here," he stammered, his voice barely above a whisper. "I just... I feel like I need to meet you."

Her glare deepened, her blue eyes narrowing as she tilted her head slightly, studying him. "That's your excuse?" she asked, her tone dripping with disbelief. "You feel like you need to meet me? Do you realize how ridiculous that sounds?"

Yordan winced, his shoulders sagging slightly. "I know it sounds strange," he said, his voice firmer now, though still uncertain. "But I'm not here to harm you. I just"

"—Don't know my name," she finished for him, cutting him off with a scoff. "Good. Let's keep it that way."

Her words stung, but Yordan found himself unable to look away. She was like fire—blazing, untouchable, and captivating in a way that left him off balance. Despite her distrust, there was something about her presence that struck a chord deep within him, though he couldn't explain why.

"Listen," he tried again, his voice softening, almost pleading. "I don't know why, but something tells me this is important. You're important. Please, just"

"Important?" she interrupted, her tone sharp as a blade. She tilted her head further, her eyes narrowing. "You don't even know me. You're either the bravest fool I've ever met or the dumbest. Maybe both."

Yordan exhaled sharply, a nervous laugh slipping out despite himself. "Probably both," he admitted.

For a fleeting moment, he thought he saw the faintest hint of a smirk tug at the corners of her mouth, but it disappeared as quickly as it had come. She stepped closer, the river the only thing separating them now, and the intensity in her eyes didn't waver.

"Whatever this is," she said, her tone cold but slightly softer, "don't think it means I trust you. I don't. And I'm not sure I ever will."

Before Yordan could respond, the world around him began to shift. The vibrant forest blurred, the sound of the river growing louder and more chaotic until it roared in his ears. The woman's fiery hair and icy gaze began to fade, her presence lingering even as the vision dissolved entirely.

Yordan jolted awake, his breath ragged and his heart pounding in his chest. The embers of his campfire glowed faintly, casting dim shadows against the night. He sat up, rubbing his face as the dream replayed in his mind in vivid detail. Her sharp words, her piercing blue eyes, her fiery hair, they felt so real, as though she had been standing right in front of him.

He stared at the river, its gentle flow now starkly ordinary compared to the roaring waters of his dream. The questions churned in his mind, each one louder than the last. Who is she? Why did I see her? And why do I feel like I need to find her?

The dream left him with no answers, only an overwhelming sense of urgency and confusion. One thing was clear: whoever she was, her presence had ignited something deep within him. Whether it was curiosity, determination, or something else entirely, Yordan couldn't shake the feeling that his journey had just become far more complicated.

The Valley of Akeskauiya stretched out before Yordan, a serene expanse of gold and green hues, caught in the gentle grip of late fall. The air was cool, carrying with it the faint tang of soil dampened by recent rains. As he walked, his boots pressed into the fertile earth, his eyes scanned the landscape. Even in the decline of the season, the valley's beauty lingered, vibrant and alive in its quiet way.

Something caught his eye—a single bloom standing defiantly among the fading grasses. Its petals were a deep, crimson red, their edges kissed with gold, as if they were painted by the last rays of the setting sun. It stood alone, slender and unwavering, a vivid spark of life amidst the muted backdrop. Yordan crouched, his fingers brushing the soft petals with reverence.

"Tzikaru," he murmured, the name coming unbidden to his lips. He remembered his grandfather pointing out this flower when he was a child, explaining how it thrived in the fertile valleys. Its name had stayed with him, as bright in his memory as the flower itself was now. Carefully, he plucked it, cradling the delicate bloom in his calloused hands.

Rising to his feet, Yordan resumed his path. The fresh scent of the valley air began to sour as he neared his destination. The stench of death hit him like a wall—thick, sickly-sweet, and inescapable. He instinctively pulled his scarf up over his nose, but it did little to shield him. His stomach churned, and he slowed his steps, bracing himself.

There it was—the tree. And still nailed to it, the rotting remains of the man Yordan had failed to save. His body hung limp, the flesh darkened and sagging, grotesquely twisted by the grip of decay. Flies swarmed in a chaotic cloud, their droning filling the air like a sinister dirge. The nails that bound him to the tree were rusted, the bark beneath them streaked with dried blood and other unspeakable stains.

Yordan stopped a few paces away, his chest tightening as he stared at the grim sight. Guilt pressed down on him, heavy and suffocating. He clenched the tzikaru in his hand, its soft petals a fragile comfort against his rough palm. Slowly, he dropped to one knee, bowing his head as he held the flower in front of him.

"Toteko," he whispered, his voice raw and trembling, "if you can hear me... forgive me. I wasn't strong enough to save him. I failed."

He reached forward and placed the tzikaru at the base of the tree. Its vivid crimson and gold stood in stark contrast to the dark, stained bark, a fleeting symbol of life and beauty amid so much death. His fingers lingered on the ground, pressing into the damp earth as if grounding himself there.

"I'm sorry," he said, his voice barely audible. His eyes lifted to the ruined figure nailed to the tree, his heart twisting in his chest. "I wasn't strong enough. I should've been better, but I wasn't. I... I failed you."

The valley seemed to hold its breath, the silence heavy and oppressive. Yordan knelt there, the stench of decay and the sight of the man's ruined body burning into his mind. He closed his eyes, trying to block it out, but the image remained. When he finally rose, the world around him felt heavier, as if the burden of his guilt was something the valley itself now shared.

The Restless Respite stood in its familiar corner of Lumina City, a modest yet welcoming hostel with warm lanterns casting a golden glow against its stone facade. As Yordan pushed open the wooden door, the comforting hum of murmured conversations and the occasional clink of dishes greeted him. Jezzie was at her usual spot behind the counter, her eyes lighting up the moment she saw him.

"Yordan!" she exclaimed, her tone warm and filled with genuine surprise. She stepped around the counter, her vibrant energy as infectious as ever. "You're back! But..." Her smile faltered slightly as her gaze darted past him, looking for someone else. "Where's Sam? He's not with you?"

Yordan hesitated, adjusting the pack slung over his shoulder. "Sam's back in Aralonis," he said evenly. "I'm here for work, and I didn't want to ask him to make the trip again so soon."

Jezzie's expression softened, though her curiosity lingered. "I see," she said, her voice laced with a hint of disappointment. "Well, it's good to see you, even if it's just you this time." She gestured toward the counter. "Same arrangement as before?"

"Yes," Yordan replied, nodding. "I'll need a room."

Jezzie quickly handed him a key, her hand brushing his slightly as she did. "Welcome back, Yordan," she said with a bright smile. "If you need anything, just let me know."

He nodded again, giving her a polite but reserved smile before heading up the stairs to his assigned room. The familiar creak of the wooden floorboards beneath his boots felt almost comforting as he made his way down the narrow hallway. Once inside, he set his pack down by the bed and locked the door behind him.

The room was small but clean, with a single bed tucked against the wall and a modest desk by the window. The faint scent of lavender lingered in the air, a touch Jezzie must have added since his last visit. Yordan pulled the chair out from the desk and sat down, his hand reaching into his pack to retrieve the folded note Ferran had given him before he left Aralonis.

He unfolded it carefully, the faint crinkle of the parchment loud in the otherwise silent room. His eyes scanned the neatly written words, and his brow furrowed as he read the instructions:

"Head to the Sitlali Mountains. Gather as much of the sacred ore as you can fit into your pack. You will also need to bring back a Sitlali quartz stone. These materials are vital. Do not delay."

Yordan leaned back in the chair, the weight of Ferran's words settling over him. He could almost hear Ferran's voice in his head, steady and commanding, as if the old blacksmith were standing right beside him. His fingers traced the lines of the note as he reread it, his mind turning over the significance of the request.

The sacred ore of the Sitlali Mountains was rare, revered for its unique properties in forging steel. It was said to be indestructible, a gift from Toteko's forge itself. The Sitlali quartz stone, on the other hand, was used for honing blades to an edge so fine it was almost mythical. These were no ordinary materials Ferran had tasked him to retrieve—they were sacred, powerful, and essential for something Yordan couldn't yet understand.

His gaze drifted to the window, where the faint glow of Lumina City's streets flickered against the darkening sky. The weight of the task ahead loomed large, but there was something else—an almost magnetic pull toward the mountains, as though the Sitlali Peaks were calling to him once again.

Yordan folded the note carefully and slipped it back into his pack. He sat there for a moment longer, his hands resting on the desk, before rising to his feet. Tomorrow, he would set out. But tonight, he needed to rest. The journey ahead promised to test him, not just in body but in spirit. As he lay down on the small bed, his mind lingered on the instructions and the significance of what lay ahead. The Sitlali Mountains awaited, their secrets still shrouded in mystery.

The dawn broke over Lumina City with a pale light, the sky painted in soft hues of lavender and gold. Yordan rose early, his thoughts heavy with the task ahead. After a quick bite of bread and dried fruit Jezzie had left for him in the common area of the Restless Respite, he thanked her in passing and stepped into the cool morning air, his pack slung over his shoulder and his boots echoing softly against the cobblestones.

The city was waking up, with shopkeepers opening their stalls and Lumite guards patrolling the streets. Yordan's gaze wandered as he made his way toward the northern edge of the city, where the Sitlali Mountains loomed. The streets were bustling, but as he looked closer, a familiar absence gnawed at him. There were no Zetians, not even one. Despite knowing they lived within the city's walls, their absence was conspicuous. The thought weighed on him, though he pushed it aside for now. He had more pressing matters to attend to.

As the grand spires and ornate stone buildings of Lumina City gave way to the rougher outskirts, Yordan tightened his pack straps and faced the imposing silhouette of the Sitlali Mountains. The peaks jutted into the sky, their rugged forms bathed in the golden light of morning. The air grew cooler as he approached, a crispness that carried the faint scent of pine and stone.

The path began gently, winding through a forest at the mountain's base. Yordan's boots crunched against the dirt and scattered leaves, the sound punctuating the quiet stillness of the morning. As he climbed higher, the terrain shifted. The forest thinned, giving way to rocky outcroppings and jagged cliffs. The trail became steeper, forcing Yordan to steady himself with his hands as he climbed.

The climb was arduous, and the sharp incline left his legs burning. Sweat trickled down his brow despite the cool mountain air. He paused for a moment on a narrow ledge, catching his breath as he gazed out over the valley below. The view was breathtaking—rolling hills and dense forests stretched as far as the eye could see, the sun casting long shadows over the land. Yet, Yordan's thoughts were not on the beauty before him but on the task that lay ahead.

The sacred ore. The Aralonic Codex spoke of it in reverent tones, describing it as a material unlike any other. It was said to react differently when it met Toteko's flame, bonding in ways that ordinary metals could not. This ore, paired with Sitlali quartz, was believed to create weapons of unparalleled strength, imbued with a spiritual energy that only Toteko's blessings could forge.

"Toteko's flame," Yordan murmured to himself, the words feeling heavy on his tongue. His fingers brushed against the hilt of the small blade at his side, a simple tool compared to what the sacred ore could create. He couldn't help but wonder what Ferran intended to do with these rare materials. Was it simply for a commission? Or was there something deeper, something Ferran hadn't yet shared?

The path grew narrower as he climbed higher, the rocky terrain becoming more treacherous. He focused on each step, his hands occasionally gripping the jagged rocks for balance. His mind drifted again to the words of the Codex, the reverence with which it described the ore and its connection to Toteko. Was it true? Could a material hold divine energy? Or was it just a legend woven into the faith?

As Yordan ascended, the air grew thinner, each breath sharper and more deliberate. The morning sun climbed higher, casting long shadows across the rocky landscape. His thoughts flickered between the sacred task at hand and the doubts that still lingered in his heart. Toteko's silence since the cave still gnawed at him, leaving him questioning not just his mission but his worthiness to undertake it.

Pushing those doubts aside, Yordan pressed on, his eyes fixed on the peak above. The Sitlali Mountains held their secrets tightly, but he was determined to uncover them. He couldn't shake the feeling that this journey was more than just about the sacred ore. Something deeper called to him, something he couldn't yet name.

The enclave Yordan found was modest—a shallow cave carved into the rock of the Sitlali Mountains, barely deep enough to shield him from the biting wind that had picked up as he ascended. The stone walls carried the faint scent of earth and minerals, and the ground was uneven but dry, a small mercy for his aching body. He sat down heavily, pulling out a small waterskin to quench his thirst, his breath still labored from the climb. The vast silence of the mountains pressed in on him, broken only by the occasional gust of wind or the faint rustle of loose pebbles.

As he leaned back against the cool rock, Yordan allowed his eyes to close, his thoughts racing. The task Ferran had given him, the visions, Toteko's voice in the cave—it all swirled together in his mind, an unrelenting storm of doubt and confusion. He muttered a prayer under his breath, though even that felt hollow.

What am I even doing here? he thought bitterly.

Suddenly, the stillness of the enclave was shattered by a brilliant flash of light. It burst forth without warning, illuminating the cave in a radiant glow that banished all shadows. Yordan's eyes snapped open, his heart leaping into his throat. Before him stood a being of impossible beauty and terrifying presence, their form radiant and otherworldly.

The being was tall, with a body that shimmered as though woven from sunlight and flame. Their eyes burned with an intense golden light, their features almost too perfect to look at directly. Feathery, glowing wings unfurled behind them, their edges flickering like the embers of a fire. A soft hum filled the air, resonating deep in Yordan's chest like a hymn from some unseen choir.

Instinctively, Yordan scrambled back, his hand reaching for the hilt of his blade, though he knew it would be useless against such a presence. "Who—" His voice broke, and he tried again, forcing the words out. "Who are you?"

The being tilted their head slightly, their voice calm but echoing with an authority that filled the air like thunder. "I am Tlanextli," they said, their name carrying a weight that seemed to reverberate through the very stone of the cave. "I was sent by Toteko."

At the mention of Toteko, Yordan froze, his hand dropping from his blade. The emotions that had been simmering within him—doubt, anger, confusion boiled over at once. He surged to his feet, his voice rising as he stepped forward, trembling with frustration.

"Sent by Toteko?" he repeated, his tone incredulous and bitter. "Do you know what's happened to me since I spoke to Toteko? I've felt like I've been losing my mind! I've had visions I don't understand, dreams that haunt me, and a silence that's louder than anything I've ever known! If Toteko wanted me to do something, why wouldn't they just tell me?"

Tlanextli regarded him calmly, their fiery gaze unwavering. They didn't flinch at his outburst, nor did they reprimand him. Instead, they stepped closer, their light softening slightly, as if to ease the weight of their presence.

"You have struggled," Tlanextli said, their voice quieter now, almost gentle. "I see the burden you carry, Yordan. I see the doubts that weigh upon you, the anger that burns within you. Toteko's path is not always clear, and the silence you feel is not abandonment. It is the forging of your soul, like metal in the fire."

Yordan's fists clenched at his sides, his breath uneven. "You say that, but I don't feel forged. I feel... broken. Lost."

Tlanextli's wings folded slightly, their radiant form bending as they knelt to meet Yordan's eyes. "Even the strongest blade begins as a shapeless piece of iron, hammered and tempered until it becomes what it was meant to be. You are still being shaped, Yordan. Toteko has not forgotten you."

The words struck something deep within Yordan, though his anger still smoldered. He looked away, his jaw tight. "If Toteko hasn't forgotten me, then why send you now? Why not come themselves?"

Tlanextli stood again, their gaze steady. "Because even the most faithful need reminders. Toteko's will is vast, and their love for all their people extends beyond what you can yet see. But know this, Yordan: you were chosen not because you are perfect, but because you are willing. And that willingness is enough."

Yordan swallowed hard, the heat of his anger cooling slightly as Tlanextli's words settled over him. The being's presence was overwhelming, but there was something in their voice—a quiet understanding—that chipped away at his frustration. He nodded slowly, though his heart was still heavy with doubt.

"What now?" he asked, his voice low. "What am I supposed to do?"

As Tlanextli's light softened, their form still radiant but less overwhelming, they extended a hand toward Yordan. The gesture was not threatening, but it carried the weight of purpose. Yordan hesitated, his emotions still tangled in doubt and frustration, but something in Tlanextli's steady gaze compelled him to step closer.

"Yordan," Tlanextli began, their voice resonant yet calm, "I was sent not only to remind you of your purpose but to entrust you with a message for Toteko's people. This is the Kamanali, the truth that must be spoken to unify all who walk this land. You must carry it with you, speak it with conviction, and live it with your actions."

Yordan blinked, his hand instinctively reaching for the small notebook and charcoal stick he carried in his pack. His voice was quieter now, a shadow of the defiance he'd shown earlier. "I... I'll write it down," he said, pulling out the items and settling onto one knee. "Please, go on."

Tlanextli folded their glowing wings slightly, their form towering yet intimate in the small enclave. Their words came measured, deliberate, as though each syllable carried divine weight.

"First," Tlanextli intoned, "all people are one, bound together by the light of Toteko. Let them remember that no tribe, no faith, no nation exists apart from this truth. Unity must be sought above all else, for division will destroy what the light has created."

Yordan wrote quickly, his charcoal stick scratching against the parchment. The words felt heavy in his hand, their simplicity belying their profound depth.

"Second," Tlanextli continued, their golden eyes fixed on Yordan, "leaders must serve with compassion and wisdom, not through fear or manipulation. Power is a gift, not a weapon, and it must be wielded for the good of all, especially the most vulnerable."

Yordan paused for a moment, his heart tightening. Compassion and wisdom, he thought. He could feel the truth of the words, though they seemed impossibly far from the reality of Amapano's leaders.

"Third," Tlanextli said, their tone shifting slightly, as though addressing something deeply personal, "harmony must be restored between humanity and the land. The mountains, the rivers, the forests—they are not yours to own but to care for. Those who forget this will find the land turning against them."

Yordan's hand faltered for a moment as he processed the gravity of those words. He glanced briefly toward the entrance of the enclave, where the vastness of the Sitlali Mountains stretched beyond his view.

"Fourth," Tlanextli said, their voice softening, "each soul must seek inner balance. Transformation begins within, and only by understanding oneself can one hope to bring peace to others."

Yordan swallowed hard, the memory of his own struggles—his doubts, his guilt—surfacing sharply. He nodded slightly, though his hand trembled as he wrote.

"And finally," Tlanextli concluded, their voice growing firm again, "justice must prevail. Innocence must be protected, and oppression must be broken. Those who exploit others, who twist Toteko's name to justify harm, will face the light's reckoning."

Yordan set down the charcoal stick, his hand aching from writing so quickly. He stared at the parchment, reading and rereading the words he had just transcribed. Each sentence seemed to pulse with its own life, as though the message itself carried the weight of divine truth.

He looked up at Tlanextli, his voice shaky but resolute. "I... I don't know how I'll deliver this. I'm just one person. What if I fail?"

Tlanextli stepped closer, their light enveloping Yordan like a warm embrace. "Toteko's light will be with you, even when you feel it least. Do not think you are alone, Yordan. You carry the strength of those who came before you and the hope of those who will come after."

Yordan nodded slowly, his doubt still present but tempered by a flicker of purpose. He folded the parchment carefully and placed it into his pack, tucking it away as though it were the most precious thing he owned.

"Carry this message, Yordan," Tlanextli said, their voice softer now. "Speak it, live it, and it will guide not just you, but all who hear it."

Before Yordan could respond, the radiant being began to fade, their light dissolving into the shadows of the enclave. The hum of their presence softened until only the sound of Yordan's own breathing remained.

He sat there for a moment, staring at the space where Tlanextli had stood. The message of the Kamanali weighed heavily in his pack—and in his heart. Rising to his feet, he adjusted his belongings and stepped out of the enclave, the words still echoing in his mind. He didn't know where this path would lead, but for the first time in weeks, he felt a spark of clarity amidst the chaos.

The air grew thinner as Yordan climbed higher into the Sitlali Mountains, the rocky terrain biting into his boots with each step. The path wound upward, jagged outcroppings of stone offering glimpses of the vast expanse of Anakuatl below—a land he had always known, now burdened with a message he wasn't sure how to deliver. His pack pressed heavily against his shoulders, a constant reminder of Ferran's task, but the weight of the Kamanali felt heavier still in his mind.

He stopped at a small plateau, the early afternoon sun casting sharp shadows across the uneven ground. Yordan scanned the area, his eyes narrowing as he spotted a dark vein running along the surface of a nearby cliffside. It was faint, partially obscured by weathered rock and patches of lichen, but it had the telltale shimmer of something precious. His heart quickened as he approached, hoping this could be the sacred ore Ferran had tasked him to find.

Pulling out a small hammer from his pack, Yordan crouched by the vein, tapping at the rock with practiced precision. The sound echoed in the stillness, sharp and rhythmic. Small shards broke away, revealing more of the vein's metallic luster. But as he struck harder, his hopes dimmed. The metal, though striking, didn't carry the weight or texture described in the Aralonic Codex. It was ordinary ore—useful, perhaps, but not what he needed.

Yordan exhaled sharply, frustration tightening in his chest. He sat back on his heels, staring at the dull fragments scattered around him. I'm wasting time, he thought bitterly. Ferran sent me here for a reason, and I can't even find what I'm supposed to.

He turned to gather his tools, his eyes catching a faint glint in the sunlight. Just a few paces away, nestled in the crook of a boulder, was a cluster of quartz crystals. The Sitlali quartz. Their translucent surfaces refracted the light, creating tiny rainbows that danced across the surrounding rocks. Yordan's frustration gave way to a faint flicker of hope as he approached the crystals.

He knelt down, brushing away the loose dirt and debris that clung to their bases. Each piece was smooth yet jagged, their edges sharp enough to catch his fingers if he wasn't careful. He selected a few of the larger ones, wrapping them carefully in cloth before placing them in his pack. The weight shifted slightly, a small reminder of the task half-complete.

Sitting back against the boulder, Yordan let his gaze drift out toward the horizon. The view was breathtaking—the vast expanse of Anakuatl stretching endlessly, the valleys and rivers weaving a tapestry of life. Yet the beauty felt distant, his thoughts clouded by the enormity of the Kamanali.

How am I supposed to do this? he wondered, his brow furrowing. How do I bring this message to people who barely see each other as the same? To people who hate each other? How do I even start?

The silence around him offered no answers, only the steady whisper of the mountain wind. Yordan leaned forward, resting his elbows on his knees, his hands hanging loosely. He had felt the truth of the Kamanali as Tlanextli spoke it—its simplicity, its power. Yet the practicalities of delivering it seemed impossible. He was a blacksmith, not a prophet. Who would listen to him? And even if they did, what could he possibly say to unite people who had been divided for so long?

The memory of the man nailed to the tree surged forward, unbidden. The stench of death, the sickening sight of his decay—it clung to Yordan like a shadow. He had failed that man, just as he feared he might fail everyone else. The weight of his doubt threatened to crush him.

But then his fingers brushed against the strap of his pack, and he felt the folded parchment within. The words of the Kamanali, carefully written in his own hand, were there. Waiting. A reminder of the message he carried, even if he didn't yet fully believe in his ability to deliver it.

Yordan stood, slinging the pack over his shoulder. The quartz was a start, but the sacred ore still eluded him. He glanced back at the vein of ordinary metal, then turned his gaze upward toward the higher peaks. The path was still steep, and his doubts lingered, but he couldn't stop now.

Adjusting his pack, he began to climb again, the sun dipping lower in the sky. Each step felt heavier, not just from the physical strain but from the questions that refused to leave his mind. The Kamanali was a truth he couldn't deny, but how to share it with a fractured world was a mystery he feared he might never solve.

Yordan pressed forward, the jagged cliffs of the Sitlali Mountains looming above him as the afternoon sun beat down. His hands were raw from wielding his tools, and his muscles ached from climbing and hammering at vein after vein of rock. Each time he chipped away at the stone, his heart carried a flicker of hope, only for it to falter when the metal beneath proved ordinary. The sacred ore still eluded him, its legendary properties nothing more than a whisper in the pages of the Aralonic Codex.

He paused on a narrow ledge, wiping the sweat from his brow with the back of his hand. His breathing was heavy, his body weary, but the stubborn resolve that had carried him this far urged him to continue. Looking up at the steep path ahead, he decided to try one more time. His eyes scanned the cliffside for any glimmer or marking that might suggest the presence of the ore.

Another vein caught his attention—faint, dark, and embedded in the rock above him. Yordan climbed up carefully, his boots slipping slightly on the loose gravel. The sharp incline made his legs burn, but he grit his teeth and pushed through, his hand gripping the cool stone for balance. When he reached the vein, he steadied himself, pulling out his hammer and chisel.

The first strike rang out sharply, echoing through the mountain air. Small fragments of rock fell away, revealing more of the vein beneath. Yordan's strikes grew more focused, his frustration manifesting in the force of each blow. But as he exposed more of the metal, his heart sank—it was nothing special. Just more of the same.

He let out a heavy sigh, sitting back against the rock. The disappointment weighed on him as much as his pack, and for the first time, he felt the temptation to give up. The sacred ore, the Kamanali, the climbing all felt impossible. Looking out over the valley below, its golden hues now deepening with the setting sun, he decided.

It's time to head back, he thought, slinging his pack over his shoulder. The trek back to the Restless Respite would be long, and the fading light warned him not to linger. With a heavy heart, Yordan began his descent.

The path down was treacherous, the loose gravel shifting beneath his boots with every step. As he navigated a particularly steep section, his foot slipped. He lost his balance, his arms flailing as he tried to grab hold of something to stop his fall. But the momentum was too much. He slid down the rocky slope, the rough surface scraping his hands and arms as he tumbled downward.

When he finally came to a stop, Yordan lay still for a moment, his body aching and covered in dust. He coughed, spitting out grit, and slowly pushed himself up. His palms stung, the raw scrapes a sharp reminder of his carelessness. Dusting himself off, he muttered a curse under his breath.

As he looked around, something caught his eye. Just a few feet away, partially hidden beneath a layer of dirt and stone, was another vein. It was darker than the others he'd seen, with a faint, almost otherworldly sheen that seemed to pulse faintly in the waning light.

Yordan's heart quickened, a mix of hope and desperation driving him forward. Kneeling before the vein, he pulled out his tools with shaking hands. He struck the rock carefully, his hammer falling with precision as he chipped away at the surrounding stone. With each blow, the vein grew clearer, its shimmering surface unlike anything he had ever seen.

His breath caught in his throat as he realized what he had found. This wasn't ordinary ore. It was the sacred metal Ferran had described—the one whispered about in the Codex. The way it gleamed in the fading light, catching every color of the sunset, was unmistakable.

Yordan worked quickly, breaking off pieces of the ore and carefully wrapping them in cloth before placing them in his pack. The weight grew heavier with each piece, but he didn't care. This was what he had come for, what he had struggled for. His exhaustion faded into the background, replaced by a surge of determination.

When his pack could hold no more, Yordan sat back on his heels, his hands trembling as he stared at the vein. He had enough, but the task had taken everything from him—his strength, his resolve, his doubts. Slinging the pack over his shoulder, he stood, his body sore but his heart lighter.

As he began his descent once more, the mountains seemed quieter, as if they, too, acknowledged the significance of what he carried. The sacred ore pressed against his back, its weight a constant reminder of the journey still ahead. With the Sitlali Mountains fading behind him, Yordan felt a small flicker of hope that perhaps, just perhaps, he was on the right path after all.

Yordan trudged through the streets of Lumina City, his body aching with every step. The weight of his pack, filled with the sacred ore and Sitlali quartz, bore down on him like a physical manifestation of his exhaustion. The familiar sight of the Restless Respite finally came into view, its warm glow spilling out into the night. Relief flooded through him as he pushed open the door and stepped inside.

Jezzie was at the counter, her sharp eyes immediately locked onto him. Her cheerful demeanor faltered as she noticed the state he was in—dust-covered, scraped, and visibly drained. She hurried over, hands on her hips.

"Yordan, by Toteko's forge, you look like you've been dragged through the entire Sitlali range!" she exclaimed, her tone half-scolding, half-concerned. "Go put that pack in your room and get back down here. You're sitting by the fire, and I'm getting you bandaged up."

Yordan glanced down at himself, noticing the bloodied scrapes on his hands and arms, along with the faint bruises already forming. "Yeah," he muttered, giving her a sheepish smile, "I guess you're right."

He shuffled up the stairs, his legs feeling heavier with each step. Once in his room, he placed his pack carefully on the floor, ensuring the sacred materials were secure. The sight of the bed was tempting, but he knew Jezzie wouldn't let him rest until she'd seen to his injuries. With a sigh, he made his way back downstairs.

Jezzie was waiting for him by the fire, a small basket of bandages and ointments in her hands. She motioned to a chair with a firm nod. "Sit."

Yordan complied, lowering himself into the chair with a groan. The warmth of the fire washed over him, easing the chill that had settled into his bones during the descent. He leaned back, closing his eyes briefly, but Jezzie's voice snapped him back.

"Actually," she said, setting the basket down on a nearby table, "you're taking a bath first. No way am I bandaging you up when you're covered in dirt and who knows what else."

Yordan opened his mouth to protest but thought better of it. She had a point. With a resigned nod, he got up and headed to the small washroom in the hostel. The hot water stung against his scrapes and bruises, but it was a welcome relief. By the time he emerged, clean and refreshed, he felt marginally better—though still utterly drained.

He dressed in fresh clothes and returned to the fire, where Jezzie was waiting with the basket. She gestured for him to sit again and then got to work, dabbing at the worst of his scrapes with a cloth soaked in antiseptic.

"You're lucky nothing's too deep," she muttered, her focus intense as she cleaned a gash on his forearm. "What were you even doing up there, fighting the mountains?"

"Something like that," Yordan said with a tired grin.

As Jezzie wrapped a bandage around his hand, Yordan glanced at her, a mischievous glint in his eye. "I won't tell Sam you were flirting with me while patching me up."

Jezzie froze for a moment, then rolled her eyes dramatically. Without warning, she smacked the bandage against a scrape on his shoulder. Yordan let out a surprised grunt, flinching slightly.

"If I wanted you," Jezzie said with a smirk, her tone playful but firm, "it wouldn't be that hard to get you."

Yordan laughed softly despite the sting, shaking his head. "Fair enough," he said, leaning back as she finished bandaging his shoulder.

"There," Jezzie said, stepping back and surveying her work with satisfaction. "You're all set. Try not to throw yourself off a mountain again anytime soon, okay?"

"I'll do my best," Yordan replied, the warmth of the fire and Jezzie's care easing some of the weight he'd been carrying. As she packed up the bandages, Yordan let his gaze linger on the flames, his thoughts already turning to the next steps in his journey.

Chapter Fourteen

T he morning came gently, the golden light of dawn spilling through the windows of the Restless Respite. Yordan stood by the counter, his pack slung over his shoulder, now lighter without the burden of uncertainty but heavier with the sacred ore and quartz. Jezzie stood opposite him, her usual mischievous glint tempered with genuine concern.

"You sure you're ready to head out already?" she asked, her arms crossed. "You're still looking like you could use another day's rest."

Yordan smiled faintly, the corners of his lips lifting in appreciation. "I've rested enough. Besides, Ferran's expecting me back in Aralonis, and I'd rather not disappoint him."

Jezzie sighed, shaking her head. "Well, take care of yourself, Yordan. And don't go running up any mountains this time."

"I'll try to behave," Yordan replied with a chuckle. He hesitated for a moment before adding, "Thank you, Jezzie. For everything."

"Just come back in one piece next time," she said, waving him off as he stepped out into the crisp morning air.

The city was just beginning to stir as Yordan made his way to the northern gates. The streets, now familiar to him, held a strange weight. The absence of Zetians still gnawed at the back of his mind, a silent reminder of the divisions in Anakuatl. But he pressed on, crossing the gates and stepping onto the path that would lead him back through the Valley of Akeskauiya.

The valley stretched before him like a carpet, the grasses swaying gently in the autumn breeze. The air was cool, carrying the faint scent of earth and wildflowers. Yordan's boots crunched softly against the ground as he walked, his pack a steady weight against his back. The journey was peaceful but slow, the solitude giving him time to think—perhaps too much time.

By the time he reached the Lumina River, the sun was dipping low in the sky, casting long shadows across the valley. The water sparkled in the fading light, its gentle flow a soothing backdrop to the quiet of the evening. Yordan found a spot near to the bank and set down his pack, pulling out a small bundle of rations. After eating, he leaned back against a smooth rock, the warmth of a small fire crackling nearby.

As he gazed at the river, a movement caught his eye. There, on the opposite bank, stood a golden buck. Its coat shimmered like molten sunlight, its antlers rising majestically toward the heavens. The creature bent its head, sipping from the river with a grace that seemed otherworldly. Yordan's breath caught in his throat, his heart pounding as he watched.

A shadow passed overhead, and Yordan looked up to see a falcon soaring high above. Its wings spread wide against the twilight sky, its cry piercing the stillness. The moment felt charged, as though the valley itself held its breath.

Then, faintly, Yordan thought he heard a voice. It was soft, like the murmur of the river itself, but the words were unmistakable: "Be ready and be not afraid for what is to come."

Yordan froze, his pulse racing. He scanned the river, his eyes darting from the buck to the water, but there was no sign of another presence. The buck raised its head, meeting Yordan's gaze for a fleeting moment before turning and disappearing into the tall grasses. The falcon circled once more before vanishing into the horizon.

His hand trembled as he reached for his pack, his mind a whirlwind of thoughts. Was that Toteko? Or another messenger? Or... was it just the river playing tricks on me?

The uncertainty gnawed at him, but something about the moment felt undeniably sacred. Yordan closed his eyes briefly, offering a silent prayer for guidance, then set about securing his camp for the night.

As the fire crackled softly beside him, Yordan lay down, his head resting on his pack. The words he had heard echoed in his mind, mingling with the images of the buck and the falcon. Sleep came slowly, the weight of his mission pressing heavily on him. But despite his doubts and fears, a small flicker of hope burned within, a fragile but steady flame against the darkness of the unknown.

The night was silent, save for the soft crackle of Yordan's fire and the gentle murmur of the Lumina River flowing nearby. The stars overhead cast a pale light on the valley, but Yordan's mind was restless, his thoughts a tangle of questions and doubts. As exhaustion finally overtook him, he drifted into an uneasy sleep, his dreams quickly pulling him into their grasp.

He found himself standing by the river, its waters shimmering unnaturally under a silver sky. The air felt thick, heavy with unplaceable tension. Across the river stood a woman—a striking figure with vibrant red hair cascading down her back in loose waves. Her blue eyes, piercing and unyielding, locked onto his with a mixture of curiosity and disdain. Her slender yet athletic build seemed almost ethereal, her presence commanding the space around her.

Yordan took a hesitant step forward, his voice breaking the stillness. "Who are you? Where can I find you?"

The woman tilted her head, a faint smirk playing on her lips, but her eyes betrayed no warmth. "You only want me for your lustful dreams," she said, her tone cutting like a blade. Her words hit Yordan like a physical blow, his heart sinking as he tried to respond.

"No, that's not—" he began, but before he could finish, the scene shifted.

The woman's features melted away, transforming seamlessly into another familiar face. Aisha now stood before him, her dark hair framing her striking features with an allure that felt almost dangerous. Her presence was magnetic, her confidence intoxicating. She stepped forward, her movements slow and deliberate, her lips curling into a mischievous smile.

"You don't have to deny it," Aisha said, her voice smooth as silk, dripping with temptation. "I know what you want."

Yordan felt his breath hitch as she moved closer, the river parting around her as she stepped into its shallows. Her hands brushed the water's surface, trailing ripples that seemed to shimmer like liquid gold. With each step she took, she shed an article of clothing, the fabric floating away in the current. Her bare shoulders gleamed in the moonlight, her form remaining hidden just beneath the waterline.

He wanted to look away, to deny what he was feeling, but his body betrayed him. His feet remained rooted to the ground as she approached, her gaze locked onto his with a confidence that unnerved him. The water reached her waist, her form tantalizingly obscured by the shimmering current.

"Come to me," she whispered, her voice beckoning him like a siren's call. She reached out a hand, her fingers brushing the air between them. Just as she began to rise from the water, the world around him seemed to explode into light.

Yordan's eyes snapped open, his chest heaving as he sat upright. His body was slick with sweat, his heart racing as if he had just run a great distance. The fire beside him had burned low, its embers glowing faintly in the predawn darkness. The gentle murmur of the Lumina River filled the silence, a stark contrast to the vivid intensity of his dream.

He ran a hand through his hair, his fingers trembling slightly as he tried to steady his breathing. The images of the red-haired woman and Aisha lingered in his mind, their presence haunting and vivid.

What is happening to me? he thought, his mind was a storm of confusion and guilt. He couldn't understand why these dreams plagued him, or why they felt so real. The vision of the red-haired woman had been sharp, almost tangible, yet her words had stung. And Aisha—her presence had been so alluring, so overpowering—it left him feeling hollow and ashamed.

Yordan pulled his knees to his chest, resting his forehead against them as he tried to make sense of it all. Was this a message? A warning? Or were these dreams simply the product of a restless mind, burdened by doubts and unspoken desires?

The sky began to lighten, the faintest hint of dawn creeping over the horizon. Yordan exhaled slowly, forcing himself to push the thoughts aside. Whatever these dreams meant, he couldn't afford to dwell on them now. The journey ahead demanded his focus, even as the shadows of his dreams threatened to consume him.

The towering gates of Aralonis stood before Yordan, their familiar archways bathed in the soft glow of the afternoon sun. His steps quickened as he entered the bustling streets, the sounds of merchants, cartwheels, and distant laughter filling the air. Despite the life teeming around him, his thoughts were heavy, weighed down by the sacred ore and quartz in his pack—and by the message he carried in his heart.

Ferran's forge came into view, smoke curling from the chimney and the rhythmic clang of hammer against metal ringing out into the street. Yordan approached, his boots crunching on the dirt as he stepped inside. The heat hit him instantly, the fire roaring in the hearth casting flickering shadows across the walls. Ferran stood at the anvil, his broad back to the door, muscles straining as he brought the hammer down on a glowing piece of steel.

"Ferran," Yordan called, his voice hoarse from days of travel.

The older man froze, turning sharply. His face lit up as he dropped the hammer onto the anvil and crossed the room in quick strides. Without hesitation, Ferran pulled Yordan into a rough embrace, his laughter booming over the sounds of the forge.

"Yordan! You're back!" Ferran exclaimed, stepping back and gripping Yordan's shoulders. His sharp eyes scanned him briefly before darting to the pack on his back. "Did you find them?"

Yordan unslung the pack and set it on the nearest workbench. With careful hands, he unwrapped the cloth, revealing the shimmering sacred ore and the translucent Sitlali quartz stones. The firelight danced on their surfaces, their otherworldly glow unmistakable. Ferran's expression softened, awe and pride mingling in his gaze.

"You actually found them," Ferran said quietly, his voice thick with emotion. He reached out, his calloused fingers brushing against the ore. "By Toteko's forge, you've done it."

As Ferran examined the materials, his eyes caught on a folded piece of parchment tucked into the side of the pack. His brow furrowed as he picked it up, unfolding it with care. The words of the Kamanali stared back at him, scrawled in Yordan's precise handwriting. Ferran's lips pressed into a thin line as he read, his eyes narrowing slightly.

"What's this?" he asked, holding up the parchment. "Where did this come from?"

Yordan hesitated, his throat tightening. He glanced down at his hands, still raw from the climb. "It's something I wrote," he said carefully, his voice low. "But the words... they're not mine. In the cave, I saw someone—something. They called themselves Tlanextli, a messenger of Toteko. They gave me this message, said it was for all the people of Anakuatl. The Kamanali."

Ferran's gaze lingered on Yordan for a moment, his face unreadable. He folded the parchment slowly, setting it down beside the ore. "And since then?" he asked, his tone gentler now. "Have you heard anything else?"

Yordan shook his head, his shoulders sagging slightly. "Nothing. Just silence. Every day, I've questioned if it was real or if I'm just losing my mind. But these words... they feel like they're burning inside me, Ferran. I have to do something with them. I just don't know what."

Ferran let out a long sigh, his hands bracing against the workbench as he looked down at the materials. "You've taken on a lot, Yordan," he said finally. "More than most men ever will. And I can't tell you what to do with this message. But what I can do is make sure you're prepared for whatever comes next."

Yordan frowned, confused. "What do you mean?"

Ferran straightened, his gaze sharp and resolute. "The ore you've brought back is special, Yordan. It's rare, powerful, and it reacts uniquely to Toteko's flame. We're going to forge something from it—something to protect you. A weapon—something you can carry with you, not just to defend yourself, but to remind you of what you're fighting for."

The weight of Ferran's words settled on Yordan, their gravity pressing against the doubts swirling in his mind. He thought of the struggles he'd already faced, the dangers he'd narrowly avoided. The idea of having something tangible, something forged with purpose, filled him with a sense of determination he hadn't felt in weeks.

"Then let's do it," Yordan said, his voice steady. "Whatever it takes."

Ferran nodded, a faint smile tugging at the corners of his mouth. "Good. Get your tools. We've got work to do."

As Yordan moved to unpack his belongings, he felt a flicker of clarity amidst the chaos. The sacred ore, the Kamanali, the journey ahead—it was all beginning to take shape. And for the first time, he felt ready to face whatever lay ahead.

The forge roared with life, the flames licking hungrily at the sacred ore resting within the crucible. Yordan stood beside Ferran, his brow slick with sweat despite the chill that crept in through the open doorway. The air was thick with the acrid scent of burning coal, mingling with the metallic tang of hot steel. His hands gripped the tongs tightly, his arms aching from holding the crucible steady as the heat grew.

"How much longer, Ferran?" Yordan asked, glancing at the older man, who was meticulously tending to the flames. His voice carried a note of frustration, his eyes flicking to the faint glow emanating from the ore. "It feels like it should be ready by now. This is the same heat we use for regular swords."

Ferran didn't look up, his focus trained on the forge. With practiced precision, he shoveled more coal into the hearth, stoking the fire to an even greater intensity. The flames leaped higher, their heat washing over the room in waves.

"This isn't like forging regular steel, Yordan," Ferran said, his tone steady but firm. He straightened, brushing soot from his hands. "Tzilkarit steel requires heat far beyond what we'd use for ordinary weapons. It has to be hot enough to separate the impurities from the ore. If we try to work it too soon, it'll shatter under the hammer, and all this effort will be for nothing."

Yordan frowned, his grip tightening on the tongs. "But why does it need to be this hot? Steel is steel, isn't it?"

Ferran finally turned to face him, his expression a mixture of patience and authority. "This isn't just steel," he said, gesturing toward the crucible. "The ore you brought back from the Sitlali Mountains is infused with properties that make it unique—stronger, lighter, more durable. But to unlock that potential, it has to go through a process unlike any other. My master called it the 'Cleansing Flame.' Without it, the metal is just raw ore, no different from what you'd find in any mountain."

Yordan's brow furrowed as he absorbed the explanation. "Your master taught you this?" he asked, his voice quieter now.

Ferran nodded, his gaze distant for a moment as if recalling a memory long buried. "Aye," he said, his tone tinged with something Yordan couldn't quite place—pride, perhaps, or sorrow. "I learned it while serving under Jareth Taron. He demanded weapons that could withstand anything—sieges, duels, the worst conditions imaginable. My master was one of the few who knew how to work this ore, and he passed that knowledge down to me."

Ferran's eyes sharpened as they met Yordan's. "We were forging weapons for a war, Yordan. Back then, I didn't think much about what they'd be used for—just that they needed to be perfect. And now, here we are again, working with the same ore. Only this time, I hope it's for something better."

Yordan swallowed hard, the weight of Ferran's words settling over him. He looked back at the forge, the glow from the crucible intensifying as Ferran adjusted the bellows. The heat was nearly unbearable now, the flames burning white-hot.

"Keep an eye on the color of the metal," Ferran instructed, pointing to the crucible. "When it's the color of the sunrise—bright and golden, with no shadows—that's when it's ready. Until then, we wait and keep the heat steady. No rushing it."

Yordan nodded, his frustration giving way to a sense of awe. This wasn't just forging—it was something more, something sacred. As he worked beside Ferran, his focus sharpened, his movements precise. The room seemed to hum with energy, the firelight casting flickering shadows on the walls.

The minutes stretched into hours, the heat pressing against them like a living thing. Yordan wiped sweat from his brow, his muscles straining as he adjusted the crucible under Ferran's guidance. Slowly, imperceptibly, the ore began to shift. Its dull sheen brightened, taking on a golden hue that seemed to pulse with its own inner light.

"There," Ferran said, his voice cutting through the haze of heat and exhaustion. "It's ready."

Yordan stared at the crucible, his breath catching in his throat. The metal within glowed like molten sunlight, its surface flawless and alive. Ferran reached for his tongs, his movements deliberate as he lifted the crucible and poured the molten ore into a prepared mold.

As the metal hissed and cooled, Yordan felt a strange sense of reverence settle over him. This wasn't just a weapon they were forging—it was something far greater, something that felt like it carried the weight of Toteko's will. For the first time in weeks, he felt a flicker of hope that perhaps, just perhaps, he was on the right path.

The forge blazed relentlessly, its glow casting flickering shadows across Ferran's workshop as the night deepened. Yordan and Ferran worked in near silence, their focus unyielding as they took turns at the anvil, the rhythmic sound of hammer meeting steel echoing through the space. Sweat dripped from their brows, their hands blackened with soot, but neither wavered in their task.

The sacred ore, now tempered by the Cleansing Flame, was cooled and reheated with precision. Each fold of the metal added to its strength, creating a blade that shimmered with an otherworldly iridescence, the patterns of the damascene rippling like liquid silver under the firelight.

Ferran stepped aside to rest briefly, his eyes heavy with exhaustion. "You've got an hour," he muttered to Yordan, patting his shoulder as he slumped onto a nearby bench. Yordan nodded, gripping the hammer tightly as he took over the work.

The blade, still in its raw form, began to take shape under Yordan's steady hand. The curve of the edge was delicate yet purposeful, designed for precision and power. He hammered with deliberate strikes, folding the metal over and over to achieve the strength and beauty described in the Aralonic Codex. Each blow felt like a step closer to something greater, something sacred.

When Ferran returned, refreshed from his brief rest, he inspected the blade with a critical eye. "Good work," he said, nodding with approval. "But the etchings come next."

They worked together to create intricate designs along the fuller of the blade. Using fine tools, Ferran etched protective symbols and flowing geometric patterns that spoke of both the strength and divine purpose of the sword. The symbols seemed to shimmer in the firelight, their meaning steeped in the traditions of Anakuatl's people.

As Yordan rested, Ferran turned his attention to the guard and hilt. The crossguard, shaped like the wings of a falcon, took form under his skilled hands. Its edges were sharp and clean, a testament to the speed and precision it represented. The hilt was wrapped in rich brown leather, its surface embossed with delicate motifs of the desert flowers, a quiet homage to life in harsh terrains.

The pommel was the final touch, an orb of polished obsidian. Ferran worked carefully, engraving it with a glyph for "protection" and an inscription for "shield." The obsidian gleamed darkly, its surface reflecting the firelight like a shard of night sky.

As the first rays of dawn broke through the workshop windows, Yordan and Ferran stood side by side, their exhaustion momentarily forgotten as they gazed at the completed sword. It was a beautiful blade that carried the weight of its origins and the hope of its purpose.

Ferran turned to Yordan, his voice thick with pride. "It's finished," he said. "Now, what do you wish to name it?"

Yordan stared at the blade for a long moment, his mind racing through the possibilities. The blade felt alive in his hands, its balance perfect, its weight a testament to their labor and devotion. Finally, he spoke, his voice quiet but firm.

"Tlamashta," Yordan said, the word rolling off his tongue with a reverence that felt right.

Ferran repeated the name softly, nodding as if testing its weight. "Tlamashta," he said again, a faint smile tugging at his lips. "A fitting name for a blade forged for more than just battle."

Yordan held the sword up, the pattern catching the morning light, its etchings glowing faintly as if imbued with their own energy. He felt a sense of awe and responsibility settle over him, the Kamanali burning in his mind as he gripped the hilt. This was more than a weapon—it was a symbol of the journey he had undertaken and the path he still had to walk.

"Let's hope it serves its purpose," Yordan said, lowering the blade and meeting Ferran's gaze.

"It will," Ferran replied confidently, his hand resting on Yordan's shoulder. "And so will you."

Yordan placed Tlamashta carefully on Ferran's workbench, the blade gleaming faintly in the forge's light. He ran his hand along the hilt one last time, a sense of pride and awe swelling in his chest before he stepped back.

"I'm going to head home, get some rest," he said to Ferran, his voice heavy with exhaustion. "Keep it safe for me, will you?"

Ferran nodded, crossing his arms as he leaned against the bench. "Don't worry. It'll be here when you're ready. Go rest—you've earned it."

Yordan gave him a faint smile and turned toward the door. The cool night air hit him as he stepped outside, a stark contrast to the forge's relentless heat. The streets were quiet, the usual bustle of Aralonis dulled by the late hour. When he reached his home, relief washed over him as he saw no new graffiti marring the walls. For the first time in what felt like weeks, he allowed himself to feel a small measure of peace.

The warm sunlight filtering through the window was the first thing Yordan registered as he stirred from his slumber. The next was the ice-cold shock of water splashing over his face and chest, jerking him upright with a sputtered shout. He flailed for a moment, his mind racing in confusion.

"What in Toteko's name—?" Yordan gasped, wiping water from his face, his heart pounding.

As his vision cleared, he scanned the room, his breaths heavy. Standing at the foot of his bed was Sam, his stick in one hand and an empty bucket in the other. A smug grin stretched across Sam's face as he tilted his head toward Yordan.

"Good afternoon, Yordan," Sam said with mock politeness. "I see my efforts weren't wasted."

"You!" Yordan barked, pointing an accusatory finger at him. "You did this?"

"Who else would it be?" Sam replied, tapping his stick lightly on the ground. "I went to Ferran's and you weren't there. When he said you were home, I thought I'd come and check on you. Turns out you sleep like the dead, so I improvised."

Yordan groaned, grabbing the nearest towel to dry himself off. "Sam, you could've just knocked!"

"I did," Sam said smugly. "Twice, in fact. Then I tried yelling. You're lucky I didn't use something worse than water."

Still grumbling under his breath, Yordan rubbed the towel over his arms, wincing when it brushed against a partially healed cut from his tumble down the Sitlali Mountains. The sting made him hiss softly, shaking his hand as if to ward off the pain.

Sam's head tilted slightly, his ears catching the subtle change in Yordan's demeanor. "You hurt yourself yesterday at the forge?"

Yordan, ever quick with a retort, smirked and replied, "No, I fell down the Sitlali Mountains and then got a royal healing session from Jezzie."

The sarcasm in his tone was enough to make Sam chuckle softly, but his response was swift and calculated. He swung his stick lightly, connecting with the back of Yordan's head with a dull thunk.

"Ow!" Yordan exclaimed, rubbing the spot where the stick had landed. "What was that for?"

"For being a smartass," Sam said evenly, though there was amusement in his voice. "And for making me trek all the way here to wake you up. Do you know how much effort that took?"

Yordan rolled his eyes, tossing the damp towel onto the floor. "Fine, fine. I'm awake now. Happy?"

"Not until I hear what you and Ferran were up to yesterday," Sam said, leaning casually against his stick. "He seemed... different when I spoke to him. And I know you well enough to guess there's a story there."

Yordan hesitated for a moment before letting out a resigned sigh. "Alright, alright. Give me a minute to clean up and then we can talk. But no more water, or I swear—"

"No promises," Sam interrupted with a grin, tapping his stick on the floor. "But I'll wait outside."

As Sam left the room, Yordan shook his head, a faint smile tugging at his lips despite his lingering irritation. With a sigh, he set about getting himself ready, preparing for yet another long day ahead.

The late morning sun beat down mercilessly as Yordan and Sam walked along the bustling streets of Aralonis. The city was alive with its usual sounds of trade and chatter, but Yordan's mind was elsewhere, preoccupied with his mission and the weight of his recent vision. As they turned a corner near a wide market square, Yordan's eyes caught sight of a group of soldiers, their polished armor glinting in the sunlight. At the center of the commotion stood Lucien, his imposing figure astride a powerful Valley Horse, its sleek coat shimmering with sweat.

Surrounded by the soldiers was a group of Zetians, their distinct features and muted clothing making them stand out against the otherwise lively crowd. Yordan's steps faltered as he realized who they were—Ayome, his calm demeanor unshaken despite the tense situation, stood protectively in front of his family. Beside him was his grandmother, frail but resolute, and his mother, clutching the hand of Ayome's younger brother, who looked no older than ten. A younger Zetian woman with fiery eyes stood off to the side, her jaw set in defiance. The sight struck Yordan like a blow, his heart pounding in his chest.

"Sam, wait here," Yordan said firmly, his voice low but urgent. Sam's head tilted slightly, his expression tightening with concern, but he nodded, gripping his stick as Yordan stepped forward.

Yordan approached cautiously, his eyes fixed on Lucien, who sat tall on his horse, his gaze cold and calculating. "Lucien!" Yordan called, his voice steady despite the anger bubbling beneath the surface. "What is this? Why are you surrounding them?"

Lucien turned his head sharply, his sharp features twisting into a sneer. "Ah, the blacksmith," he said, his voice dripping with condescension. "Have you come to petition for more Zetian spies, Yordan?"

"They're not spies," Yordan said firmly, stepping closer. "Ayome welcomed me into his home, shared what little they had. These are innocent people—"

Before he could finish, Lucien yanked the reins of his Valley Horse, spurring it forward. The massive animal closed the distance in a heartbeat, its powerful hooves striking the ground mere inches from Yordan. Lucien's boot lashed out, catching Yordan square in the chest and sending him sprawling to the ground.

Yordan gasped, the air knocked from his lungs as he hit the dirt. He struggled to push himself up, his vision swimming. Ayome's voice rang out, calm but commanding, as he addressed his family. "Stay calm. Don't move."

The soldiers' spears remained trained on Ayome and his family, their points gleaming menacingly in the sunlight. Lucien dismounted his horse with practiced ease, his boots crunching against the dirt as he approached Yordan. His sneer deepened as he loomed over him.

"So you admit to conspiring with the enemy," Lucien said coldly, his words sharp as a blade. He stomped down just above Yordan's left eye, the heel of his boot cutting into the flesh. Blood trickled down Yordan's face, warm and sticky, but he refused to cry out, glaring up at Lucien through the pain.

Lucien crouched slightly, his voice dropping to a venomous whisper. "Purity requires vigilance," he said, his tone almost ritualistic. Straightening, he barked an order to one of the guards. "Stand him up. He marches with them."

A soldier grabbed Yordan roughly by the arm, hauling him to his feet. The blood from the cut above his eye blurred his vision, but he caught Ayome's gaze. The man's expression remained calm, though a flicker of concern crossed his face as their eyes met.

Lucien mounted his horse again, casting a disdainful glance at Yordan before addressing the group of soldiers. "We march to the Luminar Citadel. Let Prince Joseph decide their fate."

The group began to move, the soldiers forcing Ayome and his family forward with sharp jabs of their spears. Yordan stumbled slightly, the ache in his chest and the sting above his eye making every step a challenge. As they passed the market square, the bustling crowd fell silent, their eyes avoiding the scene unfolding before them. Yordan's mind raced, his anger and frustration mingling with a gnawing sense of helplessness.

Toteko, he thought desperately, if you truly sent me, then give me strength. Because right now, I have none.

The gates of the Luminar Citadel loomed ahead, their massive iron bars casting long shadows across the ground. Yordan clenched his fists, his resolve hardening despite the pain. Whatever came next, he would face it. For Ayome, for his family, and for the people of Anakuatl.

Chapter Fifteen

The soldiers herded the group through the back entrance of the Luminar Citadel, their heavy boots echoing against the stone floors. The cool, dimly lit corridors were a stark contrast to the chaos outside. Yordan's breath came in shallow bursts, his chest still aching from Lucien's kick, but his vision was slowly beginning to clear. Blood from the gash above his left eye had dried in a sticky trail down his cheek, and he wiped at it absently as they descended the narrow stone steps.

Ahead of them, Ayome walked steadily, his calm demeanor unchanged even as his younger brother clung to his side, eyes wide with fear. The women, including Ayome's grandmother and mother, had been led away in a different direction, their protests met with the cold indifference of the guards. Yordan's heart sank as he watched them disappear around a corner, but he forced himself to stay focused on the present.

The steps curved downward, the air growing cooler and heavier with each step. The walls around them were bare stone, save for a bold, hastily scrawled inscription that caught Yordan's eye: Purity requires vigilance. The words seemed to taunt him, their harsh lines etched with a fervor that made his stomach churn.

He took a deep breath, trying to center himself, and turned his attention to the young boy walking just behind Ayome. The boy's steps were hesitant, his small hands clutching the fabric of his brother's tunic for reassurance.

"What's your name?" Yordan asked softly, his voice gentle despite his weariness.

The boy looked up at him, his dark eyes wide and searching. "Tequih," he said quietly, his voice barely audible over the sound of their footsteps.

Yordan managed a small, reassuring smile, though his heart ached at the boy's obvious fear. "Tequih," he repeated, the name rolling off his tongue with a certain reverence. "That's a strong name."

The boy didn't respond, but he seemed to relax slightly, his grip on Ayome's tunic loosening just a little. Yordan glanced at Ayome, who met his gaze with a calm but watchful expression.

"We're going to make it," Yordan said, his voice firm and steady as he addressed both brothers. "My friend Sam—he'll get help. He's resourceful, and he won't leave me here."

Ayome's lips pressed into a thin line, his calm demeanor showing the faintest crack of doubt, but he nodded nonetheless. "Let's hope your friend is as dependable as you believe," he said quietly, his tone betraying no emotion.

Yordan looked back at Tequih, who was now watching him with cautious hope. He felt a surge of determination swell within him, his earlier doubts and exhaustion momentarily forgotten. "We'll get through this," he said, his gaze shifting between the brothers. "Together."

The descent into the depths of the Luminar Citadel felt like stepping into the underworld itself. The stone walls, slick with dampness, exhaled the musty scent of mildew and old suffering. Torches flickered in their iron sconces, their flames swaying with the unseen drafts that slithered through the corridors like restless spirits. Every footstep echoed, swallowed by the cavernous gloom below.

At the base of the winding staircase, the corridor opened into a vast chamber, its ceiling vanishing into darkness. The oppressive air was thick with a metallic tang—iron and sweat, the scent of confinement. Before them, five guards stood in rigid formation, their polished lamellar armor gleaming dully in the torchlight. The iron-barred cell behind them was large enough to house many prisoners at once, a fact that sent a cold shiver through Yordan's aching body.

The guards watched their approach with thinly veiled amusement, their smirks like the jackals that prowled the edges of battlefields, waiting for the wounded to fall. Yordan's stomach coiled in anticipation, instinct warning him an instant before the violence erupted.

The first guard lunged, seizing Yordan by the arm with a vice-like grip. A second joined him, wrenching his other arm behind his back. He gritted his teeth, twisting to break free, but they were stronger, their brute force overwhelming. Before he could brace himself, they hurled him into the cell. His body crashed onto the unforgiving stone, the impact rattling through his ribs. The back of his skull struck the ground, sending a blinding explosion of pain through his vision.

The world blurred, his breath coming in ragged gasps as he fought to steady himself. Shouts rang through the chamber—Tequih's frightened cries, Ayome's snarl of defiance, the guards' laughter, sharp as broken steel. The beating came swift and merciless. Boots slammed into Yordan's ribs, driving the air from his lungs in a ragged wheeze. A fist collided with his temple, snapping his head to the side. He barely had time to register the pain before another blow struck his gut, sending bile up his throat.

Through the agony, he caught a glimpse of Tequih, curled on the floor, a guard's boot driving into his ribs. The boy's scream tore through Yordan like a blade, but before he could force himself upright, another impact sent him sprawling.

Ayome fought with all the desperation of a man who had nothing left to lose. His fist cracked against a guard's jaw, sending the man stumbling, but it wasn't enough. Two others descended on him, striking him with cudgels until he crumpled to his knees. Blood dripped from his split brow, tracing a dark path down his cheek. He tried to rise, but a mailed fist caught him across the face, and he collapsed with a grunt of pain.

Yordan's thoughts swam through a haze of pain and the iron taste of blood on his tongue. His body refused to obey, curling inward as he instinctively shielded his ribs from the relentless kicks. Each impact sent fresh agony, lancing through his limbs, his breath coming in wheezing gasps. Somewhere in the fog of suffering, Tequih sobbed, a sound so raw with terror that it sent another spike of fury through him.

Then, a voice like thunder split the air.

"Enough!"

The word crashed through the chamber, ringing against the stone walls with authority that could not be ignored. The guards froze mid-strike, their fists and boots poised in the air. They turned as one toward the figure standing in the archway, their breath heavy with exertion, their smirks vanishing into expressions of uneasy restraint.

Through the haze of pain, Yordan forced himself to focus. A man strode into the chamber, his steel-plated boots clicking sharply against the floor. His cloak, black as the abyss, was trimmed with gold embroidery, marking him as an officer of high rank. The torchlight caught the polished gleam of the sigil on his breastplate—the crest of the prince. His presence alone sapped the air from the room.

"I said enough," the officer repeated, his voice edged with quiet menace. "You were given orders. The prisoners are to be kept alive for questioning."

The guards shifted, their eyes flickering between each other. Yordan could see the hesitation in their movements—resentment buried under forced obedience. One of them, a man with a jagged scar across his cheek, clenched his jaw before muttering, "Yes, commander."

The pressure in the room eased—until a sudden weight crushed into Yordan's back. Pain flared as a guard—that scarred bastard—dropped his full weight onto him, pressing his chest against the stone floor. His ribs screamed in protest, white-hot agony stealing his breath. His cheek scraped against the damp rock, his vision flashing with sparks as the weight pinned him down.

"Please, stop!" Tequih's voice cracked, the sheer terror in his tone piercing through Yordan's pain. "You're hurting him!"

The guard laughed, a sound as cruel as it was gleeful. His boot shifted, pressing down harder, grinding Yordan's chest into the floor. Every shallow breath burned, his ribs straining against the unrelenting force. Stars flickered at the edges of his vision.

"Well, well," the guard sneered, glancing toward Tequih. "Looks like we've got a little hero on our hands."

Yordan twisted his head just enough to see—the moment the second guard grabbed the boy by the arm. Tequih let out a sharp cry, his small body yanked upward, feet barely touching the ground. The boy thrashed, his legs kicking in desperate defiance, but the guard's grip was like iron.

"You want me to stop?" the first guard hissed, his voice slithering toward Tequih. "You want me to let your precious brother go?"

Tequih's wide eyes shimmered with fear, his throat bobbing as he swallowed down a sob. "Y-yes," he whispered, his voice barely audible.

The guard's smile widened. "Then learn to keep your mouth shut."

With a vicious shove, he released Tequih. The boy crumpled to the floor, his head cracking against the stone with a dull thud. He lay still, stunned, his small hands trembling.

Yordan willed his body to move—to push himself up, to grab the bastard by the throat and tear him away from Tequih—but his limbs refused. His strength had bled out onto the cold floor along with his resolve.

Then the lead officer stepped forward, his eyes locking onto the guard still pressing Yordan into the ground.

"I said stop." His tone was lethal.

The pressure lifted abruptly, Yordan gasping in a deep, burning breath as the weight was finally removed from his back. His ribs screamed in protest, his lungs seizing, but he didn't collapse. He refused.

The commander's cold gaze flicked between the guards, his disappointment evident in the way his mouth curled into a tight line. "Prince Joseph has ordered Yordan be brought to the throne room. Clean him up."

Yordan barely had time to process those words before two guards seized him, dragging him upright. His vision blurred, pain searing through his battered limbs. But through the haze, a thought anchored him.

Tequih was still breathing. Ayome was still alive.

And if the prince wanted to question him, that meant his fate had not yet been sealed.

The commander's eyes narrowed, his hand tightening around his still-dripping member. "The Prince himself ordered this?" he growled, his voice laced with suspicion.

"Yes, sir," the soldier confirmed, his gaze darting nervously between the commander and Yordan's battered form. "His orders were explicit. The prisoner is to be cleaned up and brought before him without delay."

The commander's jaw clenched, a muscle twitching in his cheek as he glared down at Yordan. For a long, tense moment, he seemed poised to defy the order, his boot still pressing cruelly against Yordan's heaving chest. But then, with a disgusted snort, he stepped back, tucking himself away and zipping up his trousers.

"Get him up," the commander snapped, jerking his chin towards Yordan. "And make sure he's presentable. We can't have him dripping piss all over the prince's throne room."

Two guards hauled Yordan roughly to his feet, their hands digging into his bruised and bleeding flesh. He swayed unsteadily, his head spinning from the sudden change in position. They half-dragged, half-carried him out of the cell, his bare feet scraping against the rough stone.

In a small, dimly lit chamber, they stripped him of his remaining tattered clothing and doused him with icy water from a bucket. Yordan gasped and shuddered as the frigid liquid sluiced over his battered body, washing away the blood, sweat, and urine that caked his skin. The guards scrubbed at him roughly with coarse rags, their callused hands reopening half-healed wounds and sending fresh rivulets of blood trickling down his sides.

Once they deemed him sufficiently clean, they tossed a rough-spun tunic and trousers at his feet. Yordan struggled into the clothing, his fingers clumsy and uncooperative. The fabric chafed against his raw, abraded skin, but he welcomed the small measure of dignity it provided.

Flanked by the guards, Yordan limped through the winding corridors of the citadel, each step sending shards of agony lancing through his battered frame. His mind raced as he tried to comprehend the reason behind the prince's summons.

As they approached the massive, ornately carved doors of the throne room, Yordan's heart hammered against his bruised ribs. The guards shoved him forward, and he stumbled across the threshold, blinking in the sudden brightness.

The throne room of the Luminar Citadel loomed before Yordan as he was marched inside, his shoulders squared despite the weight of the chains that bound his wrists. The grandeur of the space was undeniable—tall, arched windows filtered the midday sun, casting intricate patterns of light across the polished stone floor. Ornate banners bearing the crest of Aralonis draped from the high ceiling, their vibrant colors contrast sharply with the somber atmosphere. The murmurs of courtiers and petitioners filled the air, a hum of intrigue and speculation.

Yordan's gaze swept across the room, and his heart twisted as he saw Ferran. The older man, his shoulders heavy with exhaustion and worry, stood near the center of the room. His weathered face looked pale against the heat of the forge that usually colored his cheeks. As Yordan was led closer, Ferran dropped to his knees, the sound of his movement cutting through the low buzz of the room.

"Please, Prince Joseph," Ferran said, his voice loud and trembling with emotion. His rough hands pressed against the cold stone floor. "Please release Yordan to me. Whatever his offense, I swear to you, I will ensure he never commits it again. There is no way he conspired with Zetian spies."

The room grew quieter, the courtiers leaning in to catch every word. Prince Joseph, seated upon his gilded throne, regarded Ferran with an unreadable expression. His robes of deep crimson and gold were immaculate, his presence commanding and yet calm. At his side stood Lucien, the faintest smirk curling at the edge of his lips. As Joseph turned his gaze to him, Lucien gave a subtle shake of his head, his message clear.

Before the prince could speak, Ferran bent forward, pressing his forehead to the ground. His voice cracked as he pleaded further. "Yordan is like my adopted son. I've raised him since he lost his grandfather as a boy. Please, your grace, let me take him home. I beg you."

The court murmured again, whispers of pity and skepticism rippling through the gathered crowd. Prince Joseph's expression softened so slightly as he looked down at Yordan, who stood silently, his chains clinking faintly as he shifted his weight.

After a pause that felt like an eternity, Joseph spoke, his voice firm but tempered. "Release him to Ferran."

A sigh of relief escaped Ferran as he lifted his head, his face lined with gratitude and worry. Yordan was unshackled, and as he stepped forward toward Ferran, he felt the weight of the court's gaze bearing down on him. He reached Ferran's side, but something within him stirred—a defiance, a resolve he couldn't suppress.

Yordan turned back toward Prince Joseph, his voice steady but laced with fire. "My lord Joseph," he began, and the room fell silent. "Please also release Tequih, the boy among those captured. He is no older than fourteen. Surely, he is no threat to you. Or has it become law to torture children?"

The court erupted into murmurs, sharp and accusatory whispers filling the air. A few gasps broke through, and more than one noble shifted uncomfortably where they stood. Lucien's smirk disappeared, replaced with a cold glare as his eyes fixed on Yordan. Prince Joseph's lips pressed into a thin line, his eyes narrowing slightly as he considered Yordan's words.

Ferran's hand gripped Yordan's arm tightly, as though to pull him back, but Yordan held his ground, meeting Joseph's gaze directly. The weight of his words hung in the air like an anvil, each murmur from the court adding to the tension.

Lucien finally stepped forward, his voice cutting through the noise. "Father, this boy," he said, his tone sharp, "was found in the company of those who seek to undermine your rule. Purity requires vigilance."

Joseph raised a hand, silencing Lucien. He leaned forward slightly on his throne, his piercing gaze meeting Yordan's. "You make bold accusations, Yordan of Aralonis," he said, his voice low but carrying through the chamber. "Do you take responsibility for this child's actions, as you did for the man?"

Yordan didn't flinch, his chin lifting slightly. "Yes, my lord," he said, his voice unwavering. "I take full responsibility. On my life, I swear he is no spy."

The court grew silent again, the weight of Yordan's declaration reverberating through the room. Prince Joseph leaned back in his throne, his expression unreadable as he contemplated the young blacksmith's words.

Ferran's grip tightened on Yordan's arm, but he said nothing, his eyes flicking between the prince and his defiant apprentice. Lucien, meanwhile, bristled with irritation, his jaw tightening as his father's silence stretched on.

Finally, Joseph's lips parted, and the court held its breath, waiting for his verdict.

Prince Joseph leaned forward slightly on his gilded throne, his expression calculated, the tension in the air palpable. He fixed Yordan with an appraising look before finally speaking, his voice steady but laden with authority.

"If you don't mind waiting," he said, his tone almost casual, "the boy will be brought to you."

The court murmured softly at the prince's decision, the noise quickly silenced by a raised hand. Yordan bowed his head in deference, his heart pounding as he stepped back to stand beside Ferran. He exchanged a glance with his mentor, who gave him a subtle nod, though his eyes betrayed the same apprehension Yordan felt.

The moments stretched into what felt like an eternity. The throne room remained oppressively quiet, save for the faint rustle of courtiers shifting in their places. Yordan's thoughts raced, his stomach twisting with uncertainty. He had taken a gamble, and now he could only hope that the prince's word would hold true.

Finally, the heavy doors to the throne room creaked open. Tequih entered, led by a guard. The boy's face was pale, his eyes wide with a mix of fear and relief. When he spotted Yordan, his expression shifted, his steps quickening into a run. Yordan dropped to one knee, catching the boy as he barreled into him, wrapping his arms around Tequih in a firm, reassuring embrace.

"You're safe now," Yordan murmured, his voice steady despite the storm of emotions within him.

Ferran stepped forward, bowing low before the prince. Without another word, he gently guided Yordan and Tequih to follow him, their exit from the throne room deliberate and silent. As they passed Lucien, the nobleman's glare burned into Yordan, his lips curling into a sneer. The weight of Lucien's disdain followed them all the way to the doors of the Citadel.

The sunlight outside was blinding after the dim confines of the throne room, and the fresh air carried a sense of liberation that Tequih seemed to feel immediately. The boy looked up at Yordan, his voice trembling as he asked, "Why did you help me?"

Yordan paused, kneeling again to meet Tequih's gaze. His words were simple, but they carried the weight of his conviction. "Because saving you from that horrible existence inside of there," Yordan said softly, "is enough for now."

Tequih's lip quivered, his small body trembling as he fought back tears. Before he could speak again, Ferran's calm, steady voice broke the moment. "Don't cry yet, Tequih," he said, his hand resting gently on the boy's shoulder. "Wait until we're back at my forge to let it out. You'll feel safer there."

Yordan straightened, his gaze shifting to Ferran. "Did Sam come and get you?" he asked, his tone tinged with gratitude and curiosity.

Ferran nodded, his expression softening as he replied, "Yes. And thankfully he did too. Otherwise..." His voice trailed off, but the unspoken words hung heavy in the air. Who knows if you would have made it out of there.

As they made their way through the streets of Aralonis, the tension in their small group began to ease. Tequih stayed close to Yordan's side, his small hand clutching the fabric of his tunic. Ferran walked slightly ahead, his presence a steady force. The bustling city around them faded into the background as they moved toward the forge, a sense of quiet determination uniting them.

When they finally reached Ferran's forge, the familiar heat and scent of metal welcomed them. Tequih's eyes darted around, taking in the tools and machinery with a mix of wonder and trepidation. Ferran gestured toward a small bench in the corner, his voice kind but firm. "Sit there, Tequih. Rest a bit. You're safe now."

Yordan exhaled deeply, his shoulders relaxing as he looked around the forge. Despite the chaos of the day, he felt a small measure of relief.

For now, they had won this battle. But he knew all too well that the war was far from over.

The air in Ferran's forge felt heavy with tension as Yordan stepped inside, the familiar scent of metal and heat wrapping around him. The comforting crackle of the forge fire was accompanied by a voice that cut through the quiet.

"You're lucky to have made it out of there," Sam said, his tone calm but firm. He stood near the anvil, his stick lightly tapping the ground as he oriented himself. Though blind, his words carried a weight of understanding that made Yordan pause.

"I know," Yordan replied, his voice low. His gaze shifted toward Tequih, who sat quietly on a small bench in the corner. The boy's small frame was hunched, his shoulders trembling as he wiped at his cheeks with the back of his hand. His tears were silent, but they spoke volumes.

Sam tilted his head slightly, his brow furrowing. "Who's the boy?" he asked, his tone more curious than probing.

"He's Ayome's brother," Yordan answered simply, his eyes still fixed on Tequih. The boy's fear and exhaustion were palpable, and Yordan felt a protective pang in his chest.

Yordan rummaged through a storage chest near the forge, finding a set of clean, modest clothes that looked like they might fit Tequih. He walked over, kneeling to meet the boy's gaze. "Here," he said gently, handing the clothes to him. "These should be more comfortable than what you have now."

Tequih nodded, his small hands clutching the fabric tightly. As the boy moved to a quieter corner to change, Yordan turned his attention to his own state. His clothes, torn and stained from his time in the Citadel prison, were a stark reminder of what he had endured. He stripped them off and replaced them with a fresh tunic and trousers, the simple act wanting to shed a layer of the weight he carried.

As Yordan adjusted the fit of his tunic, Ferran approached from the back of the forge. In his hands was the sword they had forged together, its shimmering damascene blade catching the light of the forge fire. Ferran held it out to Yordan, his expression solemn.

"Keep it close," Ferran said, his voice quiet but firm. "You may need it soon."

Yordan took the sword, its weight familiar and grounding in his hands. He studied the blade for a moment, the intricate patterns etched along its surface a testament to the bond he and Ferran had forged, both in steel and in life. He nodded his thanks, strapping the weapon securely to his side.

"I can't leave yet," Yordan said, breaking the silence.

Ferran frowned, his eyes narrowing slightly. "Why not?"

Yordan leaned against the workbench, his expression troubled. "If I leave now, they'll think I'm running to Zetopolis. Lucien's men will use that as an excuse to hunt me down, or worse, target Tequih and Ayome's family again." He glanced toward the boy, who was now sitting quietly in his new clothes, his small hands folded in his lap. "I need to make it seem like I'm still here, in Aralonis. At least for a while."

Sam, who had been quietly listening, tilted his head in Yordan's direction. "And what about the boy?" he asked, his voice measured. "You know they'll come for him."

Yordan's jaw tightened, his gaze shifting back to Ferran. "That's why I need to get him out of here. The fanatics won't stop until they've silenced every Zetian they see as a threat. If Tequih stays here, they'll kill him."

Ferran let out a heavy sigh, his hand running through his graying hair. "It's a dangerous plan, Yordan. For both of you."

"I know," Yordan said, his voice steady. "But I can't do nothing. I won't."

The forge fell silent, the crackle of the fire the only sound as the weight of Yordan's words settled over them. Tequih's wide eyes looked toward Yordan, a mix of fear and fragile hope shining in them. Yordan met the boy's gaze and offered a small, reassuring smile.

"We'll figure this out," Yordan said softly, his hand briefly resting on the hilt of his sword. "We have to."

Sam tilted his head toward Yordan, his expression serious despite the faint smile tugging at the corner of his lips. "Use me," he said simply. "I'll dress like you and lie in your bed at your home. It'll make it seem like you're staying. If anyone comes to check, they'll think you're still in Aralonis."

Yordan blinked, surprised by the suggestion. He glanced at Ferran, who raised an eyebrow but said nothing. Turning back to Sam, Yordan gave a small nod, reaching for a scabbard to hold Tlamashta. The sword slid into its sheath smoothly, its weight familiar at his side. "Sounds like a plan," he said. "But we'll need to wait until nightfall to get out of Aralonis. It's too risky during the day."

Ferran, leaning against the forge's workbench, crossed his arms. "Don't worry," he said calmly. "Take the boy west, to Nahualis. No one will think you'll head west. If they figure out you're gone, they'll head south, straight toward Zetopolis. It'll buy you time."

Yordan turned to Tequih, who sat quietly on the corner bench, his wide eyes filled with uncertainty. Kneeling to meet his gaze, Yordan asked softly, "Are you okay coming with me to Nahualis? It's for your safety."

Tequih nodded hesitantly, his lips pressed into a thin line. He didn't say much, but the slight inclination of his head was enough for Yordan to understand. The boy was scared, but he trusted him.

As Yordan stood, Sam approached, his stick tapping lightly against the ground until he stopped in front of him. "Yordan," Sam began, his voice quieter now, "what happened to you in that prison?"

Yordan hesitated, his hand brushing the hilt of his sword as he searched for the right words. His memories of the Citadel, of Lucien's cruelty and the suffocating weight of being accused, flickered through his mind like ghosts. "It's hard to explain," he said finally. "But I saw things there... things I don't ever want to see again. I couldn't save everyone, Sam. I tried, but I wasn't strong enough."

Sam's hand found Yordan's shoulder, his grip firm but reassuring. "You're stronger than you think," he said quietly. Then, with a more practical tone, he added, "But you need to run. Staying here, trying to fight this in plain sight—it's suicide."

Yordan sighed, nodding reluctantly. "You're right," he admitted.

Sam stepped back and tilted his head toward Ferran. "I'll need some clothing to look like him. Something that'll pass in the dark."

Ferran chuckled softly, moving toward a storage chest. "I think I can manage that," he said, pulling out a set of clothes similar to what Yordan often wore. Handing them to Sam, he added, "You'd better hope no one looks too closely."

Sam smirked, taking the clothes and holding them up. "I don't need them to look closely. I just need to lie still and breathe. That should be enough to fool them."

Yordan glanced between his best friend, his mentor, and Tequih. The weight of their plan settled over him, but he pushed the doubt aside. They had a chance—a slim one, but a chance nonetheless. With nightfall as their shield, they would act, and with any luck, they would find safety beyond the borders of Aralonis.

Chapter Sixteen

The moon hung low in the sky, casting pale light across the cobbled streets of Aralonis as Yordan and Tequih slipped out of the city under the cover of night. The gates loomed behind them, their shadowy figures barely visible as the pair moved silently toward the western horizon. The cool night air carried the faint scent of smoke and metal from the forges, mingling with the earthy aroma of the surrounding countryside.

Yordan walked ahead, his hand instinctively resting on the hilt of Tlamashta. The leather wrapping on the hilt was deep brown, dyed with crimson undertones, and it felt warm and familiar under his grip. Each step he took echoed softly in the stillness, his boots pressing against the dirt path that stretched toward the distant Teoyojtika Forest. His eyes scanned the horizon, every sound sharpening his senses. He didn't trust the quiet—not after what he'd endured.

Behind him, Tequih's smaller steps faltered. The boy's soft, uneven breathing reached Yordan's ears, causing him to slow and glance back. Tequih had stopped, his gaze fixed intently on Yordan's sword. The young Zetian's hazel eyes reflected a mix of curiosity and unease, the faint moonlight highlighting his furrowed brow.

"Is something wrong?" Yordan asked, his voice low but steady as he turned fully to face the boy.

Tequih blinked, his lips pressing into a thin line before he hesitantly shook his head. He looked as though he wanted to say something but stopped himself, his eyes darting back to the sword. Yordan followed his gaze, realization dawning on him.

He let out a soft sigh, loosening his grip on the hilt and letting his hand fall to his side. "Sorry," he said gently, his tone carrying a hint of apology. "I've just never traveled this way before. It's all new to me, and I guess it's making me a little nervous."

Tequih didn't respond at first, his expression guarded. But after a moment, he gave a slight nod, his gaze lingering briefly on Yordan's face before returning to the ground. He shifted his small pack and continued walking without a word, his steps quieter now, as if he wanted to disappear into the shadows.

Yordan exhaled deeply, feeling the weight of the boy's silence. He turned back toward the path ahead, his eyes scanning the darkened trail as they drew closer to the Teoyojtika Forest. The towering trees stood like sentinels in the distance, their silhouettes jagged against the starlit sky. The forest's reputation preceded it—a sacred and mysterious place, home to both legend and danger. Nahualis was said to lie within, a hidden sanctuary amidst the dense wilderness.

The path beneath their feet grew softer as they left the worn roads of Aralonis behind. The air began to change, growing cooler and carrying the faint scent of pine and moss. The faint chirping of crickets was the only sound, a rhythmic accompaniment to their quiet journey.

Tequih's pace slowed again, but this time Yordan didn't stop. He could hear the boy's footsteps trailing behind him, uneven and hesitant, and it tugged at something inside him. Tequih was no soldier, no traveler—just a boy ripped from his home, thrown into chaos. And yet, here he was, following Yordan into the unknown.

Yordan glanced over his shoulder, catching a glimpse of Tequih's tired face. He slowed his steps slightly, allowing the boy to close the distance. The gesture was small, but it felt necessary—a silent reassurance that they were in this together.

The edge of the Teoyojtika Forest came into view, its dense canopy shrouded in darkness. The trees stretched impossibly high, their thick trunks cloaked in shadows that seemed to breathe with the night. As they stepped closer, the earthy scent of the forest enveloped them, rich and intoxicating. Yordan paused, taking in the sight before glancing back at Tequih, who stood close now, his hazel eyes wide as he stared at the ancient woods.

"We'll rest once we're deeper inside," Yordan said quietly. "The trees will hide us."

Tequih nodded again, his silence unchanged but his steps more resolute as he followed Yordan into the forest. The night swallowed them whole, the faint starlight disappearing beneath the dense canopy of leaves. Every step forward felt like stepping into a new world, one full of secrets and unseen challenges.

Yordan's hand instinctively brushed against the hilt of his sword again, but this time, he let it rest lightly there, a reminder of the strength he carried—not just for himself, but for the boy who now depended on him. As the shadows deepened around them, he whispered a silent prayer, hoping Toteko's guidance would see them through the journey ahead.

The dream began as a swirl of indistinct images, colors blending into shadows, and shadows forming into shapes. Yordan felt weightless, detached, as though he were both a part of the scene and an observer outside of it. Slowly, the haze sharpened, and he found himself looking down upon Ferran's forge.

The forge was alive with its familiar glow, the flames licking the air as Ferran worked tirelessly. Sweat glistened on his brow, his hammer striking metal with rhythmic precision. But something felt wrong—there was a coldness that seeped into the warm glow of the fire, a creeping dread that made Yordan's heart race even as he floated above the scene.

The door to the forge creaked open, and Ferran paused, wiping his brow with a cloth. "Who's there?" he called, his voice steady but edged with suspicion.

Men emerged from the shadows, their faces obscured but their intent unmistakable. Ferran straightened, his hammer gripped tightly in his hand as he took a cautious step forward. "If you've come to steal," he began, his voice firm, "you'll find nothing worth your lives."

The men didn't respond. Instead, the first lunged forward, a glint of steel catching the forge's light as a blade plunged into Ferran's side. Yordan felt his stomach drop, a scream caught in his throat that he couldn't release. Ferran staggered but didn't fall, swinging his hammer with desperate strength, striking one of his attackers across the jaw.

But there were too many. Another knife sank into his back, and then another into his chest. Blood splattered against the glowing embers of the forge, sizzling as it met the fire. Ferran's knees buckled, his body collapsing onto the stone floor. His breathing was ragged, his eyes staring upward—toward Yordan.

"Yordan..." Ferran whispered, his voice barely audible as the light left his eyes.

The scene shifted violently, the forge disappearing into darkness. Yordan's heart pounded as he felt himself pulled through the void, a cold wind rushing past him. When the darkness parted, he found himself staring into his own home. The small, familiar room was dimly lit by the soft glow of a fire in the hearth.

Sam lay on Yordan's bed, his stick propped against the wall beside him. His chest rose and fell steadily with the rhythm of sleep, his face calm and untroubled. But then the shadows shifted again. The door creaked open, and the same bloody men who had killed Ferran slipped inside, their blades glinting in the firelight.

"Sam!" Yordan tried to scream, but no sound came out. He watched helplessly as the men crept closer, their movements slow and deliberate. Sam stirred slightly, his hand moving toward his stick, but it was too late. The first man raised his blade high, the firelight dancing on the steel as it began its deadly descent.

Yordan jolted awake, his body drenched in sweat. His chest heaved as he gasped for air, his heart hammering against his ribs. The faint glow of the dying campfire cast flickering shadows across the trees, and for a moment, he wasn't sure if he was still dreaming.

Tequih lay nearby, curled beneath a thin blanket, his small body rising and falling with the steady rhythm of sleep. The sight of the boy brought a fragile sense of grounding to Yordan, pulling him back to the present. He sat up, running a trembling hand through his damp hair, his fingers tangling in the mess of curls.

He scanned the forest around them, every crackle of the firewood and rustle of the leaves sending a spike of fear through him. The dream had felt so real—too real. His mind raced with the images of

311

Ferran's bloodied body and Sam's impending doom, the helplessness of watching it all unfold.

It's just a dream, he told himself, trying to steady his breathing. It's not real.

But doubt gnawed at him. The visions of Toteko, the golden deer, and now this—they all felt interconnected, each pulling him deeper into a web he couldn't untangle. What if the dream wasn't just a dream? What if it was a warning?

Yordan closed his eyes, pressing the heels of his palms against them as though to erase the images that lingered in his mind. "Ferran," he whispered softly, his voice cracking. "Sam..."

He glanced at Tequih again, the boy's peaceful sleep a stark contrast to the storm raging within Yordan. He couldn't afford to break down now, not with so much at stake. Taking a deep breath, he forced himself to lie back down, staring up at the canopy of trees above. The flickering shadows of the fire danced across the leaves, and Yordan whispered a prayer to Toteko, his voice barely audible.

"Please," he murmured, "let them be safe."

Yordan awoke to the sound of distant hoofbeats. At first, the rhythmic pounding made his heart race, fear gripping him as his mind leapt to the worst possibility—soldiers. His hand instinctively moved toward the hilt of Tlamashta as he pushed himself upright, his eyes scanning the early dawn haze for movement.

But instead of armored riders, he saw a band of Valley horses moving gracefully across a field near the edge of the Teoyojtika Forest. Their manes rippled in the soft morning breeze, and their coats gleamed in the slanted rays of the rising sun. Yordan relaxed slightly, lowering his hand as he watched them graze, their powerful forms exuding both beauty and raw strength.

The herd was a kaleidoscope of colors—deep chestnuts, dappled grays, a few golden palominos, and sleek black coats. Their movements were fluid, each step deliberate, their heads dipping to graze before rising again, ears flicking toward every sound. They were wild, untamed, and utterly mesmerizing.

Yordan eyes were drawn among the herd was a blood bay stallion, its coat a rich, deep red that seemed almost luminous against the morning light. Its black mane and tail flowed like silken shadows, and its muscular frame made it stand out among its peers. A single white sock marked its left front leg, and a bold, straight stripe ran down the center of its face, splitting the symmetry of its features in a way that made it even more striking.

The stallion moved with an air of dominance, its head held high as it grazed, the other horses keeping a respectful distance. Yordan couldn't tear his eyes away. This was no ordinary Valley horse. There was a majesty to it, a presence that demanded attention. Yordan felt an inexplicable pull, a sense that this horse was meant for him.

He reached into his pack, pulling out a length of sturdy rope. The sound of him rifling through his belongings stirred Tequih, who blinked groggily before sitting up. The boy's hazel eyes widened when he saw Yordan holding the rope, his expression immediately shifting to apprehension.

"Wh-what are you doing?" Tequih stammered, his voice still thick with sleep.

Yordan crouched next to the boy, his face calm but resolute. "Take this," he said, handing Tlamashta to Tequih, its weight unfamiliar in the boy's hands. Then, he pulled a folded piece of paper from his tunic—the message of the Kamanali—and pressed it into Tequih's free hand.

"If I get killed trying to wrangle that horse," Yordan said, his voice low and steady, "you make your way to Nahualis. Share this message with them and keep the sword safe. Do you understand?"

Tequih's eyes darted between the sword and the paper, his mouth opening and closing as if searching for words. "But... why?" he finally managed, his voice barely above a whisper.

Yordan's gaze shifted to the blood bay stallion, its proud form grazing at the edge of the herd. "Because I need that horse," he said simply. "And if this goes wrong, someone has to carry the message forward. That's you, Tequih."

The boy stared at Yordan, his confusion and fear evident. But Yordan didn't wait for further protests. He stood, gripping the rope tightly as he began walking toward the herd. Each step was deliberate, his movements slow and non-threatening. The horses nearest to him lifted their heads, their dark eyes watching him with wary curiosity.

Yordan's focus remained locked on the blood bay. The stallion flicked its ears toward him but didn't move, its strong neck bending as it tore another mouthful of grass. As Yordan drew closer, the other horses shifted uneasily, some trotting a few paces away. The stallion, however, remained still, its gaze sharp and assessing.

The morning air was cool, but Yordan felt sweat bead on his brow as he closed the distance. His heart pounded in his chest, his grip tightening on the rope. The stallion's muscles tensed, its nostrils flaring as it finally lifted its head to regard him fully. For a moment, they locked eyes—man and beast, both unyielding.

"Easy," Yordan murmured, his voice soft and even. "I'm not here to hurt you."

The stallion snorted, pawing the ground with one powerful hoof. Yordan stopped a few paces away, holding his ground but not advancing further. He let the rope dangle loosely in his hand, his body language calm and unthreatening.

Tequih watched from a distance, clutching the sword and paper tightly to his chest. His breath caught as the stallion took a cautious step forward, its ears flicking back and forth. Yordan remained still, his gaze steady, his heart pounding like a war drum in his chest.

"Come on," Yordan whispered, his voice barely audible over the rustling grass. "You and me—we'll be something greater together."

The stallion tossed its head, letting out a sharp exhale. Then, slowly, it took another step closer. Yordan's fingers tightened around the rope, his pulse quickening. He knew this was only the beginning, but the connection was there—a fragile thread of understanding that might just hold.

The quiet of the field was shattered by the sharp snap of a twig beneath Yordan's boot. The blood bay stallion's head shot up, its ears pinning back as its muscles coiled like a spring. In a flash, it reared up, its front hooves pawing the air with a sharp, powerful motion. Yordan barely had time to react before the sudden movement knocked him off balance, sending him sprawling backward onto the grass.

Pain jolted through his back as he hit the ground, the wind knocked out of him. The stallion snorted loudly, its nostrils flaring as it turned to bolt. Yordan, acting on pure instinct, scrambled to his feet and flung the loop of his rope toward the horse's neck. The lasso caught, cinching just enough to stop the stallion in its tracks.

For a moment, the horse froze, its muscles taut as it processed what had just happened. Then it exploded into motion, dragging Yordan across the rough field. Grass and dirt flew into the air as Yordan clung desperately to the rope, his hands burning from the friction. He gritted his teeth, his body bouncing and sliding across the uneven terrain.

The stallion's strength was overwhelming, but Yordan refused to let go.

The horse suddenly stopped, twisting its body and turning its powerful neck to assess its captor. Without warning, it charged, intending to trample Yordan and break free of the restraint. Yordan barely managed to roll out of the way, the stallion's hooves thundering past him. Heart pounding, he anticipated the horse's next move, quickly pulling himself to his feet as the stallion turned for another attempt.

This time, as the stallion barreled toward him, Yordan darted to the side and gripped the rope with both hands. Using its momentum, he swung himself toward the horse's flank, his body slamming against its side. His hands found purchase on the stallion's thick mane, and he gritted his teeth as the horse bolted again, the rope taut between them.

The stallion's powerful strides jostled Yordan violently as he struggled to throw his leg over its back. His arms burned from the strain, his fingers digging into the coarse hair as he finally managed to swing his leg up. With a desperate heave, he pulled himself over the horse's back, clinging tightly as it bucked wildly in protest.

The stallion reared again, twisting and leaping in an attempt to throw Yordan off. Each motion sent jolts of pain through Yordan's legs and arms as he clung to the horse, his fingers white-knuckled around the rope and mane. The world around him became a blur of movement, his vision bouncing with each violent motion. Sweat poured down his face, mingling with the dirt and grass stains on his skin.

"Easy!" Yordan shouted, his voice hoarse and desperate. "I'm not letting go!"

The stallion let out a high-pitched squeal, its nostrils flaring as it twisted and bucked again. Yordan's legs burned with effort, his thighs gripping the horse's sides as tightly as he could manage. His body felt like it was being torn apart, every muscle screaming in protest. He wasn't sure how much longer he could hold on.

And then, suddenly, the stallion slowed. Its breaths came in deep, heavy bursts as its wild motions lessened. Yordan felt the shift beneath him, the raw energy and fury gradually giving way to exhaustion. The horse came to a stop, its sides heaving with exertion as it stood still for the first time.

Yordan's own breaths were ragged, his body trembling as he stayed seated, afraid to make any sudden movements. The stallion turned its head slightly, one sharp, dark eye locking onto him. It took a deep, shuddering breath, the tension in its body finally beginning to ease.

"You're not going anywhere," Yordan murmured, his voice barely above a whisper as he patted the horse's damp neck. The stallion flicked its ears, seeming to process his words before it let out a resigned snort.

For a moment, the field was silent except for the sound of their labored breathing. Yordan, still gripping the mane, felt his legs relax slightly, though every muscle in his body screamed in protest. He couldn't believe it—the horse had stopped fighting.

The stallion shifted its weight, standing tall and proud despite its exhaustion. Yordan could feel its power beneath him, its raw strength tempered by a reluctant understanding. It wasn't submission—it was acceptance.

As the first light of dawn crept over the horizon, Yordan allowed himself a small smile. "Taurtepetl," he said softly, the name rolling off his tongue like a quiet promise. "That's who you are."

Yordan sat astride Taurtepetl for a few moments longer, letting the horse adjust to his weight. The stallion's breathing was still heavy, its nostrils flaring, but its wild energy had tempered into a wary calm.

Yordan leaned forward slightly, patting the horse's damp neck with a steady hand.

"Let's go," Yordan murmured gently, guiding Taurtepetl with a soft tug of the rope. The stallion shifted under him, hesitating at first, but then began to walk forward, each step deliberate and measured. Yordan kept his movements slow and non-threatening, cooing quietly as the horse responded, its ears flicking toward his voice.

As they approached the resting site, Tequih sat up from where he had been crouched near the fire. His hazel eyes widened as he saw Yordan approaching with the blood bay stallion, its powerful frame illuminated by the soft glow of the embers. Taurtepetl's coat shimmered in the faint light, and the proud tilt of its head made it seem almost otherworldly.

"You did it," Tequih said, his voice barely above a whisper. But then, confusion clouded his expression, and he stood, his gaze darting between Yordan and the stallion. "Why would you do something this crazy? You could've been killed!"

Yordan slid off Taurtepetl's back, landing on the ground with a soft thud. He kept a firm grip on the rope as he turned to face Tequih. "This way," he said, his voice calm but resolute, "if we get surrounded, you can escape."

Tequih blinked, his brow furrowing as he tried to process Yordan's words. Before he could respond, Yordan gently handed him the lasso still looped around Taurtepetl's neck. "Hold this," Yordan said, his tone firm but encouraging. "Keep it steady."

Tequih hesitated, his hands hovering uncertainly before finally taking the rope. The boy's grip was tentative, his eyes flicking nervously to the massive stallion. Taurtepetl's ears twitched, and he shifted slightly, his muscles tensing as he felt the change in the rope's hold.

"It's okay," Yordan said softly, pulling another length of rope from his pack. He began fashioning a makeshift halter, his hands moving deftly as he worked. All the while, he spoke in low, soothing tones, both to the horse and to Tequih. "He'll be skittish for a while—it's in his nature. But if we show him we're not here to hurt him, he'll come around."

Tequih's hands trembled slightly as the stallion snorted, tossing its head. Yordan glanced at him and offered a small smile. "You're doing fine," he said. "Just keep the rope steady."

When the halter was finished, Yordan stepped forward, carefully slipping it over Taurtepetl's head. The stallion flinched at first, tossing his head again, but Yordan held firm, his movements slow and deliberate. "Easy, boy," he murmured, cooing softly as he secured the halter. "We're not your enemy."

Once the halter was in place, Yordan stepped back and gestured for Tequih to come closer. "Now," he said, his voice steady, "come over here and pet him. Let him get used to you."

Tequih hesitated, his wide eyes fixed on the towering stallion. "What if he—?"

"He won't," Yordan interrupted gently. "Just move slowly and let him see you mean no harm."

Tequih took a cautious step forward, his hand outstretched. Taurtepetl's ears flicked, and his dark eyes watched the boy intently. For a moment, it seemed as though the stallion might back away, but then Tequih's hand brushed against his neck, and the horse stilled.

"There you go," Yordan said with a nod. "See? He's not so bad."

Tequih's hand lingered on Taurtepetl's coat, his touch growing more confident as the stallion remained calm. "He's... strong," Tequih said, awe creeping into his voice.

Yordan chuckled softly. "That he is. His name is Taurtepetl—it means 'Bull of the Mountain.' Fitting, don't you think?"

Tequih nodded, his fingers running gently through the horse's mane. "Taurtepetl," he repeated, the name rolling awkwardly off his tongue at first but growing steadier with each attempt. "He's incredible."

Yordan smiled, his gaze shifting between the boy and the stallion. For the first time in what felt like days, he allowed himself a moment of quiet pride. This was a start—a small step, but a step nonetheless. Together, they had gained a powerful ally, one who would help carry them forward on the uncertain road ahead.

As the first light of dawn filtered through the dense canopy of the Teoyojtika Forest, Yordan and Tequih worked together to dismantle their camp. The morning air was cool and damp, heavy with the scent of moss and earth. Yordan moved methodically, packing away their gear while glancing occasionally at Taurtepetl, who grazed lazily a few paces away.

Once the camp was cleared, Yordan approached the blood bay stallion and gave its flank a reassuring pat. He turned to Tequih, who stood nearby, clutching his pack with a nervous expression.

"Come on," Yordan said, motioning toward the horse. "Let's get you up there."

Tequih blinked, his brow furrowing. "Me? Why?"

"Because if something happens," Yordan explained, threading his fingers to give the boy a boost, "you'll need to escape. Taurtepetl will get you out of here faster than you could ever run."

Tequih hesitated, his gaze shifting between Yordan and the horse. Finally, with a reluctant nod, he stepped forward and allowed Yordan to hoist him up. The boy settled awkwardly into position, clutching the makeshift halter as if it were a lifeline. Taurtepetl snorted, shifting slightly under the unfamiliar weight, but a few soothing words from Yordan kept him steady.

"Do you think the Aralonites will find us?" Tequih asked, his voice tense as they began their journey deeper into the forest.

Yordan walked beside the horse, his hand on the hilt of Tlamashta. His eyes scanned the shadowed trails ahead, alert for any signs of movement. "I don't know," he admitted. "But having a horse gives us an advantage. We'll move faster, cover more ground."

The forest was alive with the rustling of leaves, the distant calls of birds, the occasional crack of twigs underfoot. The path ahead was uneven, with roots twisting like veins through the earth, but Yordan kept a steady pace, guiding Taurtepetl carefully. The morning light filtered through the trees in fragmented beams, casting a golden glow over their path.

After a long stretch of silence, Tequih finally spoke. "What's on that folded piece of paper you keep?"

Yordan glanced back at the boy, his jaw tightening slightly. "Why do you ask?"

"Because you're risking your life for it," Tequih said, his tone blunt. "You're dragging me through forests and valleys, and you haven't even told me why it's so important."

Yordan sighed, running a hand through his hair as he walked. "It's a message," he said finally. "A message from Toteko."

Tequih's eyebrows shot up. "Toteko?" he repeated, skepticism heavy in his voice. "You're saying Toteko gave it to you?"

"I saw them," Yordan said, his voice quieter now. "In the cave on the Sitlali Mountains. Toteko spoke to me, told me I had to deliver a message to the people of Anakuatl."

Tequih's expression darkened. "So you only care because Toteko told you to care," he said bitterly.

Yordan stopped walking and turned to face him. Taurtepetl snorted softly, shifting his weight as Yordan placed a steadying hand on the halter. "No," Yordan said firmly. Then, after a pause, he added, "Okay, maybe a little at first. But someone opened my eyes while I was in Lumina City. Seeing how the Zetians are treated there—how they're barred from the Temple of Toteko—changed something in me."

Tequih's gaze didn't soften. "You could've seen that a long time ago. Why now?"

Yordan sighed again, his shoulders slumping slightly. "I don't have a good answer for that," he admitted. "I should've seen it sooner. But I see it now, and I'm trying to do something about it."

The boy was quiet for a moment, his fingers tightening around the rope as Taurtepetl shifted beneath him. Finally, Tequih asked, "So, what's on the paper? That message from Toteko?"

Yordan hesitated, his hand brushing against the folded paper tucked safely inside his tunic. "They're... guidelines," he said slowly. "What Toteko wants for their people. How we're supposed to live, to treat each other."

Tequih frowned. "Guidelines?"

Yordan nodded, his gaze distant. "It's not a list of rules. It's more than that. It's about understanding each other, helping each other. Building something better."

The boy didn't respond, his expression was unreadable. Yordan turned back to the path, his grip tightening on Taurtepetl's halter as they continued deeper into the forest. The weight of the Kamanali felt heavier now, pressing against his chest with every step. But for the first time, he felt a flicker of hope that maybe, just maybe, he could find a way to deliver it.

The Teoyojtika Forest stretched endlessly around Yordan and Tequih as they ventured deeper into its heart, the canopy above growing denser with each passing day. The towering trees swayed gently in the breeze, their leaves rustling like whispered secrets. The air was cool and damp, heavy with the earthy scent of moss and decayed wood.

By the second night, their journey had left them both weary. They made camp in a small clearing surrounded by ancient oaks, their gnarled roots twisting like sleeping serpents across the forest floor. Taurtepetl stood nearby, his imposing frame blending into the shadows as he grazed quietly, his ears twitching at every distant sound.

Tequih lay wrapped in his blanket, his soft breaths barely audible over the crackling of the fire. Yordan sat nearby, his back against a tree, one hand resting on Tlamashta's hilt. The fire cast flickering shadows on his face, highlighting the dark circles under his eyes. He had tried to stay vigilant, scanning the forest for any sign of Nahualis, but the truth gnawed at him—they were hopelessly lost.

He closed his eyes briefly, his mind replaying the fragment of a map he had seen back in Aralonis. It had been vague at best, a rough sketch showing Nahualis somewhere in the vast forest, but no roads or clear markers. It could be anywhere, and they had no guide, no clue. Frustration coiled in his chest like a snake, its fangs sinking into his resolve.

As the fire burned lower, exhaustion began to weigh heavily on Yordan. He shifted his position, trying to shake off the creeping fatigue. His head dipped slightly, then jerked up again. But the third time, he couldn't fight it. His eyes closed, and he drifted into a restless sleep.

The forest was gone. Yordan found himself standing in an otherworldly clearing bathed in soft, golden light. The air shimmered with warmth, and the ground beneath him was covered in lush, emerald grass that seemed to glow faintly. At the center of the clearing stood a massive tree unlike anything he had ever seen.

Its bark was the color of polished gold, shimmering and radiant, and its leaves were a vivid green, each one tipped with golden edges that caught the light like tiny flames. The tree pulsed gently, as though it were alive in a way that went beyond mere plants. Its branches stretched upward, touching the sky, and its roots dug deep into the ground, anchoring it firmly to the earth.

Yordan felt a strange pull toward the tree, an invisible thread drawing him closer. As he approached, a voice resonated through the clearing, deep and melodic, yet undeniably commanding.

"Yordan," the voice called, reverberating through his very bones. "You seek answers, yet you do not know where to find them."

He stopped, his breath catching in his throat. "Who are you?" he asked, his voice trembling.

"I am the keeper of knowledge, the memory of those who have walked before you," the voice replied. "I am rooted in the truths of this world and the next. You must find me, Yordan, for I have much to show you."

Yordan's eyes widened as he looked at the tree. "Find you? How? Where?"

The tree pulsed again, its golden bark glowing brighter. "I am hidden where the forest breathes its deepest, where the whispers of the past linger. Seek me, and I shall pass my knowledge to you."

Before he could respond, the scene began to shift. The golden light dimmed, and the tree's vibrant leaves began to fall, dissolving into golden dust as they touched the ground. The clearing faded, and darkness crept in, swallowing the vision whole.

Yordan jolted awake, his heart racing. The fire had burned low, its embers glowing faintly in the predawn gloom. Tequih was still asleep, his small frame curled beneath his blanket. Taurtepetl snorted softly nearby, pawing at the ground.

Frustration bubbled up in Yordan's chest as he realized he had fallen asleep on his watch. He pressed the heels of his hands to his eyes, trying to steady his breathing. But the dream lingered, vivid and unsettling. The golden tree, the commanding voice—it felt so real, as though he had truly been there.

"Dammit," he muttered under his breath, running a hand through his hair. "I'm losing it."

He looked around the clearing, his eyes scanning the shadows for any signs of danger. Everything was as it had been, unchanged, yet he couldn't shake the feeling that the dream meant something important. But how could he find a tree that might not even exist?

Yordan sighed, leaning back against the tree he had been resting against. His thoughts churned, torn between the urgency of the dream and the reality of their situation. The forest was vast, uncharted, and unforgiving. But deep down, he couldn't ignore the pull of the tree's message.

He stared into the dying embers of the fire, the words echoing in his mind: "Seek me, and I shall pass my knowledge to you."

The Teoyojtika Forest loomed around them, its dense foliage muting the light and sound, creating an almost otherworldly atmosphere. Yordan walked ahead, his hand resting on the hilt of Tlamashta, the faint clinking of his scabbard breaking the stillness. Behind him, Tequih sat astride Taurtepetl, the stallion's muscles taut and ears flicking at every rustle of the undergrowth. The forest seemed alive, its towering trees and tangled vines pulsing with an unseen energy.

"Stay close," Yordan said softly, his voice barely louder than a whisper. Tequih nodded, clutching the rope halter tightly as Taurtepetl snorted, the stallion's breath visible in the cool forest air.

The silence shattered without warning. Shadows moved among the trees, and figures emerged as if the forest itself had come to life. Men

325

and women stepped from behind the thick trunks and low-hanging branches, their movements fluid and deliberate. They were clad in armor unlike anything Yordan had seen before—leather reinforced with carved bone and dark wood, adorned with intricate patterns that seemed to mimic the flowing lines of nature. Their faces were partially obscured by masks painted with vibrant designs, some resembling animals, others bearing abstract geometric patterns.

Each figure held a composite bow, its polished wood gleaming faintly in the dappled light. The arrows were already nocked, their tips aimed with precision at Yordan and Tequih. The sharp tension of the bowstrings hummed in the air, a silent warning that any sudden movement would be met with swift retaliation.

Taurtepetl reacted instantly, his ears flattening as he let out a high-pitched whinny, shifting nervously beneath Tequih. The boy gripped the halter tighter, his eyes wide with fear as he tried to calm the restless stallion.

"Easy," Yordan murmured, his voice steady despite the adrenaline surging through his veins. He raised one hand slowly, palm outward, while his other hand lingered near Tlamashta's hilt. His gaze darted around the group, noting the fluidity of their movements and the discipline in their formation. These were not mere bandits; their confidence and cohesion suggested a deeper purpose.

From among them, a man stepped forward, his presence commanding. He was tall, his broad shoulders draped in a cloak of dark green fabric that blended seamlessly with the forest. His armor bore the same intricate carvings as the others, but his mask was different, painted in stark white with red accents, its angular design resembling the sharp beak of a bird of prey.

In his hand, he held a sword, its polished blade catching the faint light that filtered through the canopy. The weapon was unadorned but flawless in its craftsmanship, the kind of blade forged not for show but for war.

The man approached Yordan with deliberate steps, his movements slow but purposeful. The forest seemed to grow quieter with each step, as though holding its breath. When he stopped, he raised his sword, the point hovering just inches from Yordan's face.

"Who are you?" the man demanded, his voice low and commanding, each word carrying the weight of authority. "What are you doing here?"

Chapter Seventeen

Yordan stood frozen, his breath shallow as he stared into the piercing eyes behind the mask. Taurtepetl shifted uneasily, his hooves stamping against the ground, while Tequih remained silent, gripping the halter with white-knuckled hands.

The forest seemed to close in around them, the presence of the armed figures and their drawn bows suffocating. Yordan swallowed hard, his mind racing as he tried to think of how to answer without provoking the man—or the arrows still trained on them.

Yordan raised his hands slightly, palms outward, his voice calm despite the tension tightening around him like a noose. "We are just refugees from Aralonis," he said, carefully choosing his words. His gaze met the man's behind the mask, the sharp angles of its design making it difficult to read any expression.

The man—silent for a moment—stepped closer, his sword still in hand, his piercing eyes scanning Yordan from head to toe. The proximity was unnerving; Yordan could feel the weight of his scrutiny, as though the man could see every thought and secret laid bare. After a moment, the man shifted his gaze to Tequih, who sat stiffly atop Taurtepetl, his grip on the halter trembling.

The man narrowed his eyes and finally spoke, his tone decisive. "Bind their hands," he ordered, his voice carrying an authority that left no room for question. "And blindfold them."

One of the figures stepped forward immediately, their movements quick and practiced. Yordan felt rough hands seize his wrists, pulling them firmly behind his back. The bite of the rope against his skin was sharp and unforgiving, but he didn't resist. Beside him, Tequih gasped softly as his own hands were bound, his face pale with fear.

"Put this one on the horse," the man continued, gesturing toward Yordan. "He can't know where we're going."

Before Yordan could react, he was hoisted up onto Taurtepetl's back. The stallion shifted uneasily under the added weight, his ears pinning back. A strip of cloth was tied around Yordan's eyes, plunging him into darkness.

Yordan felt the distinct pull of the halter as the man took hold of it. The horse began to move, its steps steady but cautious as it followed the lead. Yordan's heart pounded in his chest, his senses hyper-aware as he strained to hear what was happening around him. The sound of rustling leaves and soft footsteps filled the air, punctuated by the occasional creak of leather and the faint clink of weapons.

"Wait," a woman's voice called out sharply. Yordan felt the shift in attention before he heard her approach. There was a pause, and then he heard her speak again, her tone cold and calculated. "The sword."

Yordan's stomach dropped as he felt the weight of Tlamashta leave his side. The woman had unsheathed it with a practiced motion, the hiss of steel cutting through the air.

"This one travels armed," she remarked, her voice laced with suspicion. "Interesting choice for a 'refugee.'"

There was a moment of silence before she tossed the sword to the man, who caught it with a single hand. "Ueuejtlakatl," she said, her tone shifting to one of deference, "let's get moving."

Yordan tensed at the name, committing it to memory even as his thoughts raced. The title sounded reverent, almost mythical, and it was clear the others regarded this man with both respect and fear. The sound of the group moving through the forest resumed, the cadence of their footsteps blending seamlessly with the natural rhythm of the woods.

The world beyond the blindfold was a void, but Yordan's senses worked overtime to fill in the gaps. He listened to the faint whispers of the men and women around him, caught fragments of conversation too low to make out. He focused on the feeling of Taurtepetl's movement beneath him, the sway of the horse's gait grounding him in the midst of uncertainty.

Beside him, Tequih was silent, though Yordan could sense the boy's fear in the way his breathing quickened. Yordan tightened his jaw, willing himself to remain calm. Wherever they were going, whatever awaited them, he would face it head-on. For now, all he could do was wait—and hope.

As Taurtepetl's hooves moved steadily beneath him, Yordan's mind churned with unease and questions. The name "Ueuejtlakatl" echoed in his thoughts, stirring something buried in the haze of recent memory. He strained to remember where he had heard it before, replaying the past weeks in his mind. Then it struck him: the refugees. Those weary travelers from Lumina City had spoken the name, voices hushed with reverence, when they debated heading west instead of south. The realization sent a chill through him. Was this the man they had meant? And if so, what had they walked into?

Hours passed as the blindfold kept him in a state of oppressive darkness. Every sound heightened in the absence of sight: the rhythmic clop of Taurtepetl's hooves, the murmured commands of their captors, the rustle of leaves as the forest seemed to swallow them whole. Yordan tried to focus on the movements of the horse beneath him, piecing together what little information he could from the shifting terrain. The ground changed subtly—the soft crunch of earth gave way to the sharper clatter of stone, signaling they had entered a new environment.

An enclave? Nahualis itself? Yordan wondered. He strained his ears, listening for any sounds of civilization, but the voices around him remained too low, too controlled to give anything away.

The journey ended as abruptly as it had begun. Taurtepetl came to a halt, letting out a sharp snort as he shifted his weight. Yordan felt a hand grip his arm roughly, dragging him down from the horse. He stumbled slightly as his boots hit the ground, the sudden change in position leaving him momentarily disoriented. Nearby, he heard the faint scuffle of Tequih being pulled down as well, the boy letting out a soft grunt as he landed.

"Move," came a voice, curt and unyielding.

Yordan obeyed, feeling a firm hand on his shoulder steering him forward. He resisted the urge to pull away, knowing it would do no good. His mind raced as he tried to piece together their surroundings based on the faint sounds and smells that filtered through the oppressive darkness of the blindfold. The scent of damp stone and burning wood suggested a sheltered place, perhaps a hidden settlement or a fortified camp.

When they stopped, Yordan heard the scrape of wooden legs against the floor, a chair being pulled out. He was pushed firmly into the seat, the ropes around his wrists cutting into his skin as he adjusted his balance. The faint creak of another chair followed, and he guessed Tequih had been seated beside him.

"Stay," someone commanded, their tone leaving no room for argument.

Yordan felt the tension around him, a silence filled with the weight of watchful eyes. The air was thick, the kind of stillness that made his skin prickle with unease. He could hear the faint shuffle of boots, the rustle of fabric, the creak of leather armor—all signs that they were not alone.

He shifted slightly, testing the limits of his bonds, but the ropes held fast. His breath was shallow as he tried to steady himself, pushing back the rising tide of frustration and fear. Think, Yordan, he told himself. Stay calm.

Beside him, Tequih was silent, though Yordan could sense the boy's fear in the way his chair creaked slightly as he shifted his weight.

"Where are we?" Yordan dared to ask, his voice steady but low.

No one answered. Instead, the silence deepened, oppressive and deliberate. Yordan gritted his teeth, forcing himself to sit still. He had no choice but to wait, blindfolded and bound, until their captors decided what to do with them.

The darkness vanished suddenly as rough hands pulled away the blindfold from Yordan's eyes. Blinking rapidly, he squinted against the faint light filtering through the canopy above. His surroundings slowly came into focus: a hidden enclave deep in the forest, surrounded by towering trees and thick undergrowth. Makeshift shelters of wood and leather were scattered around, blending seamlessly with the natural landscape. A group of armed figures stood in a wide circle, their masks and armor carved with symbols and patterns that seemed to echo the forest itself.

Beside him, Tequih sat in a chair, his wide eyes darting around nervously. Yordan could see the redness around the boy's wrists where the ropes had dug into his skin, and his heart ached at the sight.

At the center of the group stood the man who had commanded their capture. His presence was undeniable—tall, broad-shouldered, and clad in armor that seemed almost ceremonial, adorned with intricate carvings of nature and geometric designs. His face was partially obscured by a mask painted with bold patterns of red and black, resembling the sharp beak of a predatory bird. He held himself with confidence that spoke of years of command, and in his hand was Tlamashta, its sheathed blade a striking contrast against his earthy attire.

"You are under my protection," the man declared, his voice carrying the weight of absolute authority. "My troop protects this forest from those who seek Nahualis for nefarious reasons."

Yordan remained silent, his gaze meeting the man's through the mask. The weight of the statement hung heavy in the air, but before Yordan could respond, the man tossed Tlamashta onto the ground between him and Tequih. The sword hit the earth with a dull thud, its craftsmanship unmistakable even in the dim light.

The man's tone shifted, becoming more probing. "How did you acquire this sword?" he asked. "It's better than any blade I've wielded in the last decade or two."

Yordan didn't answer immediately. His eyes flicked to Tequih, who sat frozen, his breaths shallow and quick. The boy's tension was palpable, and Yordan could see the fear etched into every line of his face. Tequih's bound hands trembled in his lap, and Yordan knew he needed to act quickly to ease his ward's distress.

"Can you please," Yordan said, his voice steady but carrying a note of urgency, "cut my ward's bonds? We were imprisoned in the Luminar Citadel about a week ago. The boy has been through enough."

The masked man tilted his head slightly, considering the request. After a moment, he made a subtle motion with his hand. A woman stepped forward from the circle of figures, her armor adorned with flowing, vine-like carvings. Her expression was unreadable beneath her mask, but her movements were precise and purposeful.

Drawing a short, curved knife from her belt, she approached Tequih. The boy flinched slightly as she neared, but she worked quickly, slicing through the ropes with a practiced motion. The bindings fell away, and Tequih immediately began rubbing his raw wrists, letting out a shaky breath.

"Thank you," Yordan said, his voice low but filled with genuine gratitude.

The woman stepped back into the circle without a word, disappearing among the ranks of the silent onlookers. The man's gaze—sharp and unrelenting—remained fixed on Yordan.

"Now," he said, his tone cool and probing, "answer my question. How did you come by this sword?"

Yordan hesitated, his mind racing. He wasn't sure how much to reveal to this enigmatic figure, especially when he still didn't fully understand the man's intentions. For now, he focused on steadying his breathing and ensuring Tequih felt secure.

Leaning slightly toward the boy, Yordan whispered, "You're okay now. Just breathe."

Tequih nodded, his eyes flicking nervously between Yordan and their captors as he tried to calm himself. The tension in the air was suffocating, and Yordan braced himself for what might come next, knowing that every word he spoke would be scrutinized.

Yordan straightened slightly in his chair, his wrists still aching from where the ropes had chafed against his skin. He glanced at the sword lying between him and Tequih, then back to the man in the commanding mask. Summoning his courage, he spoke clearly, his voice steady despite the tension in the air.

"I made it," Yordan said, locking eyes with the man. "I am a blacksmith. I'm assuming you must be Ueuejtlakatl?"

The masked man—Ueuejtlakatl—smirked faintly, his lips barely curling beneath the edge of his mask. He reached down and picked up the sword, holding it with the respect and precision of someone who understood its craftsmanship. He turned it slightly, examining the intricate details of the blade and hilt.

"Impossible," Ueuejtlakatl said, his voice tinged with skepticism but not dismissive. "The last known smith capable of crafting such weaponry, whenever he could find the ore, was Ferran of Aralonis."

Yordan allowed himself a small, confident smirk, meeting Ueuejtlakatl's gaze without faltering. "He was my master," Yordan replied. "He taught me."

Ueuejtlakatl lowered the sword slightly, his gaze narrowing behind the mask. His tone became more probing, layered with faint disbelief. "He taught you? A boy barely in his twenties?" Ueuejtlakatl tilted his head slightly, his voice gaining an edge of incredulity. "Ferran didn't master this craft until he was past thirty. Before then, he apprenticed under his own master for years—a man who died in battle while Ferran tried desperately to save him. I was there. I had to pull him back for fear he'd be lost as well."

Yordan blinked, the revelation catching him off guard. "Funny," he said after a moment, his voice laced with quiet defiance. "He never mentioned you."

Ueuejtlakatl chuckled softly, the sound low and almost amused. "Don't be so quick to assume," he said. "Ferran and I share a complicated history. But tell me—" He leaned forward slightly, his tone shifting to something more intense, almost interrogative. "Why did you end up imprisoned?"

Yordan hesitated, glancing briefly at Tequih, who sat tense beside him. Ueuejtlakatl's gaze followed his, and his eyes lingered on the boy. A faint sigh escaped him, as though he had already pieced together part of the answer.

"Sadly," Ueuejtlakatl said, his tone laced with disdain as he gestured toward Tequih, "I can figure out why." He paused, crouching slightly to bring himself closer to Tequih's level. His voice softened just enough to make the boy feel less threatened. "What's your name, lad?"

Tequih swallowed hard, his hands trembling slightly in his lap. But he straightened his posture, summoning enough courage to speak clearly, though his voice still carried a faint tremor. "Tequih," he said.

Ueuejtlakatl nodded, his expression unreadable behind the mask. He stood slowly, sheathing Tlamashta at his side as he turned back to Yordan. The tension in the air was palpable, the weight of the moment pressing heavily on all of them.

Yordan glanced at Tequih, his expression softening briefly before he looked back at Ueuejtlakatl, bracing himself for the next inevitable question.

Yordan took a steadying breath before speaking, his voice calm but resolute. "I was trying to keep Tequih and his family from being imprisoned by Lucien, Prince Joseph's son," he said, his gaze unwavering as he looked at Ueuejtlakatl. "They were accused of being spies. When I spoke up to defend them, it made me a target too."

Ueuejtlakatl's piercing gaze didn't falter as he stepped closer, his hand resting casually on the hilt of Tlamashta, now sheathed at his side. The weight of his presence pressed down on Yordan, but he held firm, refusing to back away.

"And you came into the forest for what?" Ueuejtlakatl asked, his tone sharp and probing. "Surely, you didn't think you'd find safety here."

Yordan straightened, his shoulders squaring despite the tension in the air. "I came to take Tequih to Nahualis," he said plainly. "It's the only place I thought he might be safe. And..." He hesitated for a moment, searching for the right words before continuing, "I hoped to spread the message I carry from Toteko."

At the mention of Toteko, Ueuejtlakatl stiffened slightly, his eyes narrowing behind his mask. The faintest trace of a smirk curled his lips, though it carried no warmth. "Ah," he said, his voice dripping with skepticism. "Just another prophet, huh? One more voice claiming divine purpose. Let me guess—you've come to save us all?"

Yordan clenched his jaw, but before he could respond, Ueuejtlakatl waved a hand dismissively. "The boy can stay here," he said, his tone firm. "But you'll remain as my supervised guest. I've seen too many like you—fanatics spreading chaos in the name of their so-called revelations."

"No," a voice interrupted, trembling but resolute. Tequih stepped forward, his small frame shaking but his eyes locked on Ueuejtlakatl with surprising intensity. "No, I will stay with him. He's the only thing I have left of any family."

Ueuejtlakatl turned his attention to the boy, his expression unreadable. Tequih's voice grew steadier as he continued, his words pouring out in a rush of emotion. "My entire family was imprisoned. I don't know if any of them are still alive. But he—" Tequih glanced at Yordan, his eyes glassy with unshed tears. "He risked everything to try to protect us. I won't leave him."

337

The room fell into a tense silence, the weight of Tequih's words hanging heavily in the air. Yordan felt a pang of guilt and determination as he looked at the boy, his heart aching at the raw pain etched into his face.

Ueuejtlakatl remained still for a moment, his gaze flickering between the two of them. The skepticism in his eyes softened slightly, replaced by something more thoughtful, though he kept his tone guarded. "Very well," he said at last, his voice quieter but no less commanding. "But understand this—you are both under my watch now. Step out of line, and there will be consequences."

Yordan nodded, his shoulders relaxing slightly, though the tension in his chest remained. He placed a reassuring hand on Tequih's shoulder, squeezing gently. "We'll do what we must," he said, his voice steady.

Tequih nodded, his resolve clear despite the fear still lingering in his eyes. Together, they braced themselves for whatever lay ahead in this enigmatic enclave deep within the Teoyojtika Forest.

Yordan glanced down at the sword—Tlamashta—still sheathed at Ueuejtlakatl's side. The intricate craftsmanship of its hilt shimmered faintly in the dappled forest light, and Yordan felt a pang of longing for the blade he and Ferran had poured their souls into forging. He took a breath, steadying himself, before speaking.

"Can I get my sword back?" he asked, keeping his tone calm and neutral. He avoided mentioning the blade's name, not wanting Ueuejtlakatl to sense how much it truly meant to him.

Ueuejtlakatl turned his head sharply, fixing Yordan with a piercing stare from behind his mask. For a moment, there was silence, the weight of the question hanging heavily in the air. Then, with a faint, humorless smirk, Ueuejtlakatl responded, "No."

Yordan blinked, surprised by the bluntness of the reply. Before he could protest, Ueuejtlakatl stepped closer, his voice taking on an edge of scorn. "You look like someone who's lucky he's never been in a real fight. That sword is more likely to get you killed than to save your life."

Yordan's jaw tightened, but he bit back his retort as Ueuejtlakatl continued, his disdain palpable. "Do you even know what you're doing out here? Wandering into the forest with a boy and a horse, claiming you've been sent by Toteko? You sound like every other fanatic who thinks they've been chosen to save the world. You all think you know what Toteko wants." He leaned in slightly, his voice low and biting. "And you know what happens to fanatics? They get people killed."

The words struck a nerve, but Yordan forced himself to remain composed. He met Ueuejtlakatl's gaze, his voice steady even as frustration churned inside him. "I'm not a fanatic," he said. "I just want to help. To stop what's happening to people like Tequih."

Ueuejtlakatl scoffed, shaking his head. "Help? You think spouting a few vague messages from on high will help anyone? Do you even understand the weight of what you claim to carry? Or are you just stumbling into something far bigger than you can handle?"

Yordan's fists clenched at his sides, and he realized he wasn't going to convince Ueuejtlakatl to take him seriously—not here, not now. But something gnawed at the back of his mind, a memory sparked by this man's presence. Taking a breath to steady himself, Yordan decided to pivot.

"Did you serve at the siege of Zetopolis with Ferran?" Yordan asked, his tone even but pointed.

Ueuejtlakatl's body stiffened, the question visibly hitting its mark. For a brief moment, the man seemed caught off guard, but his mask concealed whatever emotions might have flickered across his face. After a tense pause, he spoke again, his tone curt and dismissive.

"No more questions," he said sharply, his voice cutting through the charged air like a blade.

He turned abruptly, gesturing for Yordan to follow. "Let me show you where to get food to feed your horse while we figure out exactly what to do with you."

Yordan exhaled slowly, his shoulders relaxing slightly even as unease settled more heavily in his chest. His gaze flicked to Tequih, who looked just as wary, before he fell in step behind Ueuejtlakatl. Tlamashta remained at Ueuejtlakatl's side, and though the sword was out of reach, Yordan's resolve was far from broken.

Yordan and Tequih finished brushing down Taurtepetl under the fading light of the forest. The blood bay stallion, though still wary of them, seemed slightly more at ease, his powerful muscles rippling as Yordan ran the brush over his flank one final time. Tequih's small, deliberate movements showed his growing confidence, even if his hands still shook slightly.

As they put the brushes away, a Nahuali woman approached, her steps light but purposeful. She was dressed in a flowing tunic of earthy greens and browns adorned with intricate beadwork, and her long black hair was tied back with a braided leather cord. Her features were sharp yet kind, her dark eyes observing them with a mixture of curiosity and warmth.

"I am Naliyo," she said, her voice steady and melodic, carrying a gentle authority. "Come, it is time for food. You both must be tired, and as our guests, you will eat with us."

Yordan exchanged a glance with Tequih, who seemed hesitant but nodded. They followed Naliyo through the camp, weaving between the firelight and shadows, until they reached a large tent-like structure.

Its exterior was made of tightly woven fabric stretched over wooden poles, decorated with painted patterns of animals and celestial symbols that seemed to shimmer in the flickering light of nearby torches.

As they stepped inside, Yordan was struck by the openness of the space. Long, low tables were arranged in rows, surrounded by cushions where people sat cross-legged, sharing food from communal platters. The warm, rich aroma of roasted meats, stewed vegetables, and freshly baked flatbreads filled the air, mingling with the soft hum of conversation.

Yordan's eyes scanned the room until they landed on Ueuejtlakatl. The imposing leader sat at one of the central tables, speaking in low tones with the same woman who had cut Tequih's bonds. She nodded occasionally, her sharp eyes darting toward Yordan briefly before returning to Ueuejtlakatl.

Tequih tugged at Yordan's sleeve, drawing his attention. "Have you ever eaten with the Nahuali before?" Yordan asked, keeping his voice low.

Tequih shook his head. "No," he murmured, but his gaze quickly shifted to the food as it was brought to their table. His hesitation vanished, and he began to eat with an almost frantic energy, shoveling food into his mouth as though he hadn't eaten in days.

Yordan noticed the shift in the atmosphere almost immediately. Conversations at nearby tables grew quieter, and several people paused mid-bite to watch Tequih. Their gazes weren't hostile, but they carried a weight of curiosity and judgment that made Yordan's skin prickle. He set a steadying hand on Tequih's shoulder, hoping to calm him, but the boy continued to eat voraciously.

Thinking quickly, Yordan cleared his throat and raised his voice slightly, keeping it steady and respectful. "My ward, Tequih, and I would like to thank our hosts for their hospitality," he said, projecting his words just enough to carry to those watching.

The room seemed to pause for a heartbeat, the weight of the gazes still pressing on him. Then, slowly, the communal hum of conversation returned, and the people around them resumed eating as though nothing had happened. Yordan let out a quiet breath of relief, turning back to his own food.

As he ate, his eyes drifted again to Ueuejtlakatl. The man leaned back slightly, his arms crossed as he listened to the woman beside him speak. Occasionally, he would nod or respond briefly, but his eyes flickered toward Yordan now and then, scrutinizing him from across the room.

Yordan's thoughts churned as he chewed on a piece of bread, trying to decipher how to earn the man's trust. Ueuejtlakatl clearly saw him as a fanatic, someone who had no real grasp of the dangers or weight of what he claimed. But Yordan wasn't sure how to show him otherwise, how to prove that his intentions were genuine and that he wasn't just another fool with grandiose ideas.

The sound of Tequih's eating grounded him momentarily, and Yordan glanced at the boy, whose energy had waned slightly as his hunger abated. Yordan resolved to tread carefully—for Tequih's sake as much as his own. Whatever it took, he needed to show Ueuejtlakatl he was more than the man's initial impression.

For now, though, he focused on the food in front of him, the communal warmth of the tent, and the faint hope that tomorrow would bring clarity.

As the meal concluded, Naliyo returned, her presence as calm and steady as before. "Come," she said, motioning for Yordan and Tequih to follow. "I'll show you where you can rest for the night."

They walked through the camp, the faint glow of lanterns casting long shadows over the forest floor. The distant murmur of voices and the crackle of firelight added to the quiet rhythm of the night. Eventually, they reached a small, simple shelter made of sturdy wooden beams and canvas, tucked away near the edge of the camp.

Inside, the space was modest but clean, with two simple bedrolls laid out on a floor of woven mats. A small lamp flickered in the corner, casting a soft glow over the interior.

"This will be your place for now," Naliyo said, her tone leaving no room for argument. "Rest well." With that, she turned and left, leaving Yordan and Tequih alone.

Tequih sat down on one of the bedrolls, fidgeting slightly as he looked over at Yordan. After a few moments of silence, he finally spoke. "Is it true? You think you saw Toteko?"

Yordan froze for a moment, his hands pausing mid-motion as he unrolled his bedroll. He looked over at the boy, his expression conflicted. After a long sigh, he answered, "Yes. And trust me, there are days I wish I hadn't."

Tequih tilted his head, his young face scrunched in curiosity. "What were they like?"

Yordan hesitated, closing his eyes as the memory surged forward, vivid and overwhelming. His voice was low when he spoke. "Terrifying. They felt... like something I've never felt before. My entire body felt like it was on fire from the inside."

Tequih blinked, leaning back slightly as he processed the answer. "Sounds like they were rough on you," he said, his tone both curious and slightly cautious. "Have they spoken to you since?"

Yordan opened his mouth, then closed it, unsure how to answer. After a moment, he shook his head slightly. "Get some sleep, Tequih," he said instead, his voice soft but firm.

Tequih looked like he wanted to press further, but something in Yordan's tone stopped him. He lay down on his bedroll, curling up slightly as he pulled the blanket over himself. Yordan sat for a while longer, his eyes fixed on the flickering lamp, his thoughts swirling with doubt and purpose as the forest night deepened around them.

In the dream, Yordan found himself standing at the edge of the River Lumina, its shimmering waters casting a golden glow across the landscape. Before him stood two women, their forms shifting like shadows in the flickering light. One moment, he saw the striking red hair and piercing blue eyes of the woman he had seen in his dreams before—her presence commanding yet mysterious. The next moment, the image shifted, and there stood Aisha, her fiery gaze full of passion and frustration, her every movement laced with the intensity he remembered from their brief encounters.

The two alternated speaking, their voices overlapping yet distinct, weaving together the words his mother had whispered to him as she lay dying by this very river.

"The light within you shall guide your path," said the red-haired woman, her voice firm yet soothing, her eyes locking onto his as though daring him to falter.

"Even when darkness surrounds," Aisha continued, her voice sharp but laced with a deep undercurrent of sorrow, her expression both accusing and pleading.

"Trust in the luminescence of your heart, my son," the two voices said in unison, their tones merging into a haunting harmony that sent chills down Yordan's spine.

"For it will lead you to your true destiny," they finished, the words reverberating through the air like an echoing bell.

Suddenly, the serene glow of the river darkened, the water turning black and still. The golden tree appeared in the distance, its branches reaching toward the heavens like a beacon. Its light pulsed, each flash like a heartbeat, commanding his attention.

"Find me," the tree seemed to say, though no words passed its leaves. The urgency in its presence was overwhelming. Yordan tried to step forward, to draw closer, but the river began to swell, its dark waters rising, threatening to engulf him.

"You must know the path," the voices of the women intertwined again, their tones now filled with urgency. "Or you risk the people of Toteko."

The tree's light intensified, blinding him, and in that instant, Yordan jolted awake.

His breathing was ragged as his eyes darted around the dimly lit shelter. The soft sounds of Tequih's steady breathing reminded him where he was. The boy was still asleep, his small frame curled tightly under the blanket.

Yordan ran a hand through his hair, damp with sweat, his heart still pounding from the vivid dream. He sat up, resting his elbows on his knees, as the guilt began to creep in. Katherine's face, once a constant source of comfort and resolve in his thoughts, felt distant now. He couldn't deny the truth—the red-haired woman and Aisha seemed to occupy his mind more often than Katherine did.

The realization left a bitter taste in his mouth. He hated himself for it, for the way his thoughts seemed to betray Katherine and everything she had meant to him. He clenched his fists, trying to suppress the wave of shame that washed over him.

What is happening to me? he thought, staring at the flickering shadows on the tent's canvas walls. He leaned back against the wooden support beam, closing his eyes and taking a deep breath, trying to steady himself.

The golden tree's light still lingered in his mind, a persistent reminder of the path he had yet to find. As sleep began to claim him once more, he resolved to continue searching, even if it meant confronting the chaos within his own heart.

Chapter Eighteen

Yordan stepped outside the shelter, the early morning light filtering through the thick canopy of the forest. The crisp air carried a sense of quiet, the kind that settled in the depths of the Teoyojtika Forest, broken only by the occasional rustle of leaves and the chirping of distant birds. Near the edge of the camp, he spotted a bridle and saddle resting on a makeshift wooden stand. The leather was well-worn but sturdy, etched with simple geometric patterns that hinted at the Nahuali craftsmanship.

Picking up the bridle, Yordan turned it over in his hands, running his fingers along the leather straps, checking the fit and strength. With a deep breath, he made his way to where Taurtepetl stood tethered to a post. The blood bay stallion watched him approach with an unblinking gaze, his ears flicking back slightly as Yordan came closer.

"Easy, boy," Yordan murmured, his voice low and steady as he untied the stallion. Taurtepetl shifted his weight, pawing at the ground but staying still enough for Yordan to begin fitting the bridle. Yordan moved carefully, taking his time to ensure the straps settled comfortably over Taurtepetl's head. The stallion snorted, tossing his head once in protest, but Yordan held firm, his hands gentle yet insistent.

With the bridle secured, Yordan fetched the saddle. Taurtepetl shifted again, his muscles tensing as Yordan carefully lifted the saddle onto his back. "I know you're not a fan of this, but we need to get you used to it," Yordan said softly, adjusting the girth strap beneath the horse's belly. Taurtepetl let out a loud huff, stamping a hoof, but Yordan didn't back down. Instead, he stepped back, giving the horse a moment to adjust to the unfamiliar weight.

As Yordan began to walk Taurtepetl around, his focus was broken by a familiar voice behind him. "Are you going to leave?" Tequih's voice was cautious, almost timid, as he approached from the shelter.

Yordan turned, his expression softening as he saw the boy standing a few paces away, his dark eyes filled with uncertainty. "No," Yordan answered firmly, shaking his head. He gestured to Taurtepetl, a small smile playing at the corner of his lips. "Today, you're going to learn how to ride."

Tequih's eyes widened in surprise. "Ride? On him?" he asked, pointing at the imposing stallion.

"Yes," Yordan said, his tone resolute. "We'll stay close to camp, but if something happens and we get separated, I want to know you can ride. Taurtepetl is your best chance to escape if there's danger."

Tequih hesitated, glancing between Yordan and the stallion. "He 's... big," he admitted.

Yordan chuckled softly. "He is. But he's strong and smart. You just have to earn his trust."

Guiding Taurtepetl back to where Tequih stood, Yordan showed the boy how to hold the reins and explained the basics of mounting. After a few tries and some stifled laughter from Yordan as Tequih struggled to swing his leg over, the boy finally managed to settle into the saddle.

"Good," Yordan said encouragingly, adjusting the stirrups for Tequih's shorter legs. "Now hold the reins gently, like this," he demonstrated, guiding the boy's hands.

Taurtepetl shifted under the unfamiliar rider but didn't protest too much. Yordan walked alongside them, holding the bridle as Tequih practiced sitting upright and balancing. With each step, the boy grew more confident, a tentative smile replacing his initial nervousness.

"See? You're getting the hang of it," Yordan said, stepping back slightly to let Tequih guide Taurtepetl on his own.

Tequih grinned, gripping the reins tightly as he urged the stallion forward. "This isn't as bad as I thought," he admitted, his voice filled with cautious excitement.

Yordan nodded, a sense of pride swelling in his chest. "Told you. You're doing great."

They spent the rest of the morning practicing, Yordan walking alongside Taurtepetl, offering tips and encouragement as Tequih gained more control and confidence. By the time they returned to the camp, both of them were tired but in good spirits.

As Tequih dismounted, his legs wobbly but his grin wide, Yordan patted Taurtepetl's neck. "Good job, both of you," he said, guiding the horse back to the post.

Tequih looked up at Yordan, his expression thoughtful. "Thanks," he said quietly, his voice carrying a rare note of gratitude.

Yordan nodded, his gaze lingering on the boy for a moment. "You'll be ready if anything happens," he said simply. But inwardly, he hoped that day would never come.

Yordan sat astride Taurtepetl, the blood bay stallion's muscles rippling beneath him as the horse moved gracefully across the open clearing near the edge of the camp. Yordan loosened the reins slightly, letting Taurtepetl find his rhythm. The horse broke into a brisk canter, his strides smooth yet powerful. Yordan leaned forward slightly, adjusting his balance and grip, feeling the strength of the animal beneath him.

As they rounded the clearing, Yordan noticed a thin sheen of sweat forming on Taurtepetl's neck. Not wanting to overwork the stallion, he tugged gently on the reins, slowing him to a trot and then a walk. Finally, Yordan dismounted, patting Taurtepetl's flank as he led him toward a bucket of water resting near a shaded area. The stallion dipped his head eagerly, lapping at the cool water, his ears flicking back and forth.

As Yordan stood by Taurtepetl, his gaze wandered toward a group of figures moving through the trees. Ueuejtlakatl and several of his troops were gathered in a nearby clearing, their swords glinting in the dappled sunlight as they moved in precise, fluid formations. The rhythmic clash of steel against wooden posts and the occasional barked commands echoed faintly through the forest.

Curiosity got the better of Yordan, and he began to approach, keeping a respectful distance. He spotted a rack of wooden training sabers leaning against a tree at the edge of the clearing. One in particular caught his eye, its simple yet sturdy design reminding him of the practice swords Ferran had used to teach him basic strikes and stances back in Aralonis.

Unable to resist, Yordan picked up the wooden saber, feeling its weight in his hand. He stepped back into the shade and began mimicking the movements he saw the troops performing. His strikes were hesitant at first, his footing slightly off, but he quickly adjusted, his muscles remembering the drills Ferran had taught him.

"Not bad," he murmured to himself as he executed a sweeping slash, feeling the satisfying arc of the blade through the air.

A sudden shadow loomed over him, and Yordan turned to see Ueuejtlakatl standing mere steps away, his arms crossed and his expression unreadable. Without a word, the man reached out and took the wooden saber from Yordan's hand, his grip firm but not aggressive.

"You don't belong here," Ueuejtlakatl said, his voice low but sharp. He stepped back, holding the wooden saber as if inspecting it, then glanced at Yordan. "Tomorrow, you will leave this forest and never return, fanatic."

Yordan blinked, stunned by the blunt dismissal. He opened his mouth to respond, but no words came out. Before he could gather his thoughts, Tequih appeared at his side, his face breaking into a mischievous grin.

"You got in trouble," Tequih teased, nudging Yordan with his elbow.

Yordan frowned, the sting of Ueuejtlakatl's words lingering as he looked at the boy. "I wasn't doing anything wrong," he muttered, more to himself than to Tequih.

Tequih only smirked, clearly enjoying the rare moment of Yordan being put in his place. Meanwhile, Ueuejtlakatl returned to his troops, leaving Yordan standing in the clearing, a mixture of frustration and confusion swirling in his chest. He looked back at Taurtepetl, still drinking from the bucket, and sighed deeply.

"Come on," Yordan said to Tequih, gesturing for him to follow. "We'd better get back."

Yordan hesitated outside Ueuejtlakatl's tent, the faint sounds of murmured words drifting through the air. As he stepped closer, he realized the voice was Ueuejtlakatl's, reciting something lyrical yet incomplete:

"Among the trees, their roots run deep, Through whispered winds, their secrets keep. Beneath their shade, life finds its hold, Yet how to speak what can't be told..."

The voice paused, followed by a frustrated grunt. "It doesn't fit. Curse these words," Ueuejtlakatl muttered, the sound of a quill being set down hard echoing faintly from inside.

Summoning his courage, Yordan stepped into the tent, and Ueuejtlakatl's sharp gaze immediately found him. His eyes narrowed, but there was no surprise—only a cold curiosity.

"Let me guess," Ueuejtlakatl said dryly, leaning back slightly. "You're here to convince me to let you stay under my protection."

"Well, yes and no," Yordan began cautiously, standing tall despite the intensity of the older man's stare. "I don't want to stay under your protection. I want to learn how to wield the sword you took from me."

At this, Ueuejtlakatl raised an eyebrow, clearly intrigued but skeptical. He leaned forward, resting his elbows on his knees. "And you are so certain of your path that you must know how to use that blade?"

Yordan shook his head, his voice steady but honest. "No. It's because I'm unsure if I'm on the right path. I don't know if I'm doing the right thing, and I still have much to learn despite the mission I've been given. I'm not even sure I'll ever achieve it."

The tension in the room hung like a weight between them as Ueuejtlakatl studied him, his piercing gaze seemingly reaching into Yordan's very soul. Yordan shifted slightly, feeling the intensity of the silence. Then Ueuejtlakatl spoke, his voice low and deliberate.

"Are you willing to humble yourself to my teaching?" he asked, his tone carrying both challenge and expectation.

"Yes," Yordan replied without hesitation, his voice resolute.

Without a word, Ueuejtlakatl stood and reached for a wooden training saber from a nearby rack. With a casual flick of his wrist, he tossed it to Yordan, who caught it awkwardly. The older man gestured toward the entrance of the tent.

"Follow me," Ueuejtlakatl commanded.

Outside, Yordan saw several Ojtlists gathered near a training area. Among them was the same woman who had cut Tequih's bonds. She stood tall, her braided hair tied tightly, and her piercing eyes regarded Yordan with cool indifference.

"This is Xochitl," Ueuejtlakatl said, nodding toward the woman. "She is one of my most skilled fighters. If you truly wish to learn, prove you have the will to face defeat."

Xochitl stepped forward, taking her own wooden saber from the rack. "This will be quick," she said, her voice laced with quiet confidence.

Yordan took his position, gripping the wooden saber tightly, his heart pounding in his chest. Xochitl moved first, her steps fluid and precise. Yordan tried to block her initial strike, but her movements were far too quick. Her blade twisted under his guard, disarming him in a single, clean motion. His wooden saber clattered to the ground.

"Pathetic," Xochitl said bluntly, stepping back as she rested her weapon against her shoulder. "He's going to embarrass himself in real combat."

Laughter rippled through the nearby Ojtlists, but Ueuejtlakatl raised a hand, silencing them. He approached Yordan, who picked up his saber, his face flushed but his grip steady.

"Every warrior starts with defeat," Ueuejtlakatl said, his voice calm but firm. "The question is whether you rise after you fall. Tomorrow, we begin again." He glanced at Xochitl. "He's yours until I say otherwise."

Xochitl sighed, her gaze flicking back to Yordan. "Try not to waste my time," she said flatly before walking away.

Yordan stood there, his breath heavy and his body tense, but his resolve was unshaken. He tightened his grip on the saber, silently vowing to prove he was more than what they saw.

Over the next few weeks, Yordan's world became a cycle of bruises, exhaustion, and frustration. Each morning, before the sun fully rose over the forest canopy, Xochitl would summon him to the training grounds. Her movements were a relentless barrage of strikes and counters, her skill a constant reminder of his inexperience.

"Again," she would command after disarming him for what felt like the hundredth time, her tone devoid of sympathy. Yordan would grit his teeth, pick up his wooden saber, and try to anticipate her next move. Yet no matter how hard he tried, Xochitl's blade found its mark, her footwork too swift, her counters too precise.

At times, Xochitl didn't even bother sparring with him herself. Instead, she handed him off to younger warriors under her command—Ojtlists with less experience but still leagues ahead of Yordan in skill. They, too, defeated him with ease, their strikes landing with a sting of humiliation that felt heavier than the physical pain.

Meanwhile, Tequih had taken to the composite bow like he was born with it in his hands. His slight frame and steady hands allowed him to draw and release arrows with remarkable accuracy. Watching Tequih hit target after target, Yordan couldn't help but feel a pang of frustration. The boy, barely fourteen, was flourishing, while Yordan could barely keep his feet under him in a fight.

One day, after yet another sparring session, Yordan found himself flat on his back, the breath knocked out of him. Xochitl stood over him, the tip of her wooden saber pressed lightly against his chest.

"You're too predictable," she said, shaking her head as she walked away, leaving him on the dirt.

As he pulled himself up, brushing off the dust and trying to catch his breath, a loud, mocking whinny came from the edge of the training grounds. Yordan turned to see Taurtepetl, his blood bay coat gleaming in the sunlight, standing near the paddock. The stallion's ears twitched, his head bobbing slightly, as if he were laughing at Yordan's predicament.

"Oh, you think that's funny?" Yordan muttered, wiping sweat from his brow. He raised his hand and gave the blood bay a very pointed middle finger. Taurtepetl let out another whinny, this one softer but still laced with an unmistakable sense of smugness.

Nearby, Tequih, who had been watching from a shaded spot, stifled a laugh. "I think he's trying to tell you that you're not very good at this," he said, grinning.

"Thanks for the vote of confidence," Yordan grumbled, stretching his sore shoulder. "You're supposed to be on my side, not the horse's."

Tequih shrugged, standing to retrieve his bow. "At least Taurtepetl is honest," he said, the grin still on his face as he walked toward the archery range.

Yordan sighed, turning his gaze back to the stallion. "Yeah, yeah, I'll show you," he muttered, picking up his training saber once more. He could feel every muscle in his body protesting, every joint stiff from weeks of unrelenting training, but he couldn't stop now.

One of these days, he thought, gripping the wooden blade tightly. One of these days, I'm going to land a hit on her. And then we'll see who's laughing.

The sharp clamor of the training grounds fell silent as Yordan spotted the commotion at the edge of the clearing. Ueuejtlakatl and his troops strode into view, their steps deliberate, the air around them tense. Trailing behind them was a figure Yordan never thought he'd see again in this place, Sam.

Yordan's heart skipped a beat as recognition hit him. Sam's steady, deliberate movements betrayed no fear, but his blind stick tapped softly against the ground, a testament to his vulnerability. Relief flooded Yordan as he dropped the wooden training saber he'd been practicing with, his hands instinctively flexing with pent-up emotion.

Xochitl glanced toward Ueuejtlakatl, her arms folded as she asked, "Who is this?"

Ueuejtlakatl's gaze was sharp as ever. "A blind man wandering the forest," he said curtly. "Claims he's looking for a friend—a man who left with a boy several weeks ago." His voice carried both suspicion and curiosity, making it clear he was unsure of what to make of the situation.

Yordan didn't wait for more details. He stepped forward, his voice breaking with a mix of disbelief and joy. "Sam!"

Sam turned his head slightly toward the sound, his expression softening as a relieved smile spread across his face. "Yordan?" he called out, his tone almost playful despite the tension in the air.

Yordan closed the gap quickly, pulling Sam into a tight embrace. The familiar comfort of his best friend's presence overwhelmed him for a moment. "I thought you had been stabbed," Yordan whispered urgently in Sam's ear, his voice trembling.

Sam chuckled softly, patting Yordan on the back. "Well, it's good to know you had such high hopes for me," he teased quietly.

Ueuejtlakatl, his patience clearly wearing thin, stepped closer. "How do you know this man?" he demanded, his sharp tone breaking through their reunion.

Yordan released Sam, steadying his breathing as he turned to meet Ueuejtlakatl's stern gaze. "He's my best friend," Yordan said firmly. "He's been with me through everything, he's the reason I made it this far."

Sam tilted his head slightly in Ueuejtlakatl's direction, his voice measured but confident. "I'm thankful I found him. This forest is no easy place to navigate, but I wasn't going to stop until I did."

Tequih, standing a few steps behind, finally spoke up, his voice cautious. "You're really his friend?" His guarded tone betrayed his lingering doubts.

Sam turned toward Tequih, his expression softening. "I am. And you must be Tequih," he said. "We've met before—back at the Ferran's forge."

Tequih blinked, his brow furrowing slightly. "I didn't realize you were blind," he admitted, almost shyly.

Sam smiled, his voice carrying a gentle humor. "You were going through quite a bit when we last met. I didn't expect you to notice."

Tequih's shoulders relaxed slightly, and a faint smile tugged at his lips.

Ueuejtlakatl finally sighed, rubbing the bridge of his nose as though this reunion was testing his limits. "He stays under the same rules as everyone else," he declared sharply. "No special treatment. And if either of you causes trouble, you'll both be sent out—no exceptions."

"Understood," Yordan said, nodding quickly. He gave Sam's shoulder a reassuring squeeze before stepping back.

As the tension eased, Yordan looked around, a fresh wave of gratitude washing over him. Sam's presence felt like a much-needed anchor in the storm, even if his arrival raised questions about what might come next under Ueuejtlakatl's wary watch.

Yordan and Tequih helped Sam settle into the small tent that had been prepared for him, carefully arranging his few belongings while ensuring he had a place to sit and rest. Sam ran his hands over the fabric of the cot, feeling its roughness, and then the small, carved wood stool nearby.

"So, this is Nahualis?" Sam asked as he felt around the tent, his tone curious but hesitant.

Yordan shook his head, glancing at Tequih. "No," he said quietly. "We're just at an enclave in the forest. They haven't taken us to Nahualis. I don't think they trust us enough yet."

Sam's brow furrowed, and he tilted his head toward Yordan. "Interesting. They certainly seem like the type to keep things close to the chest."

Yordan hesitated before sitting on the cot opposite Sam. "So...what happened? Back in Aralonis," he began, his voice faltering slightly. "I...had a dream—men armed with knives came to my house. They turned you over while you were lying in my bed, and they were about to stab you."

Sam's face fell, the calm facade he usually wore slipping for a moment. He leaned forward, clasping his hands together as he took a deep breath. "Um..." Sam started, his voice quiet. "I don't know how your dream got that detail so right, but yes." He paused, rubbing the back of his neck before continuing. "There were nine of them. They came in during the night. They must've thought I was you because they pulled me over like they were going to attack." His voice wavered slightly. "But then...when they realized I wasn't you, they just left. I think they didn't know I was blind, they probably assumed I was still asleep. But yeah...they left."

Yordan's heart sank, and his hands trembled slightly as he gripped the edge of the cot. "And Ferran?" he asked, his voice whispering. "Was he murdered...in his forge?"

Sam exhaled deeply, his face heavy with sorrow. "I'm so sorry, Yordan," he said softly. "But yes. Ferran...he's gone. They killed him in his forge. They didn't make it easy on him."

The weight of Sam's words crushed Yordan, and silent tears began to fall. He didn't sob, but the grief etched across his face was unmistakable. Sam leaned forward, wrapping an arm around him in a comforting embrace. Tequih, who had been standing nearby, stepped closer and hugged Yordan from the other side, his smaller frame doing his best to offer solace.

After a moment of shared silence, Tequih spoke gently. "Sam...was there any word on my brother Ayome? Or the rest of my family?"

Sam shook his head, his expression hurt. "I'm sorry, Tequih," he said softly. "I didn't hear anything about them. It's like they...vanished."

Tequih's face tightened, but he didn't cry. Instead, he tightened his grip on Yordan's arm, his silent support a small yet significant gesture.

It was then that Yordan found the strength to ask the question that had been clawing at the back of his mind. "What about Katherine?" he asked, his voice barely above a whisper. "Is she safe? Is she...alright?"

Sam hesitated before answering, his tone careful. "She came to the funeral for Ferran," he said slowly. "But she didn't say anything to me. She left some flowers at his gravesite and then left."

Yordan's heart twisted with a mix of relief and longing. He nodded slowly, wiping his face and taking a deep, steadying breath. The grief and confusion lingered, but he knew he had to keep moving forward—for Ferran, for Tequih, for the message he carried, and for all those he had yet to protect.

Yordan lay on his cot, staring at the dim, flickering light of the campfire outside the tent. His mind churned with guilt and grief, a heavy weight pressing against his chest. Ferran was gone—murdered—because he had vouched for Yordan. The man who had been his protector, his mentor, and the closest thing to a father he had after his grandfather's death had paid the ultimate price for his loyalty.

Yordan clenched his fists against the coarse blanket, the words his mother had whispered to him all those years ago surfacing in his mind like a haunting echo:

"The light within you shall guide your path, even when darkness surrounds. Trust in the luminescence of your heart, my son, for it will lead you to your true destiny."

How was he supposed to trust in anything now? The light within him felt dim, like a flickering candle struggling against a relentless wind. He reached into his bag, pulling out the carefully folded piece of paper he had written the Kamanali on.

He unfolded it slowly, staring at the words he had written, now blurred slightly by smudges from travel. They were meant to be a beacon of hope, a guide for the people of Anakuatl to unite and rise above the hatred and division tearing them apart. But now, in the quiet of the night, the message felt so distant, so far from the reality of the bloodshed and cruelty he had witnessed.

"Will this even matter?" he whispered to himself, his voice barely audible over the night sounds of the forest. "Will anyone even listen?"

His eyes drifted to Tequih, who was curled up a few feet away, his small frame barely shifting with his soft breaths. Tequih's face, even in sleep, bore a faint shadow of sadness and fear. The boy had lost everything—his family, his home—and was now clinging to Yordan as his last semblance of safety.

If Yordan gave up now, how many more like Tequih would face the same fate? How many more children would be orphaned, left to fend for themselves in a world that showed them no mercy?

He let out a slow breath, folding the paper carefully and tucking it back into his bag. The doubt and guilt still gnawed at him, but as he lay back down, staring at the roof of the tent, a new resolve began to simmer beneath the surface.

Tomorrow, he would train harder. He would face Xochitl again, and maybe this time, he would last more than a few minutes. He had to. He couldn't afford to falter, not for Ferran, not for Tequih, and not for the message he carried.

Sleep came eventually, though it was uneasy. His dreams were a swirl of guilt and faint glimmers of hope, like the first rays of dawn struggling against the night.

The crisp morning air was heavy with the sounds of training—wooden swords clashing, grunts of exertion, and the occasional bark of orders from Xochitl. Yordan tightened the straps on his gloves and stepped into the sparring circle. Across from him stood one of Xochitl's subordinates, a wiry but solidly built woman with sharp eyes and an even sharper stance. She twirled her wooden training sword effortlessly, smirking at Yordan.

"Ready?" she asked.

Yordan nodded, gripping the training saber with sweaty palms. Sam and Tequih watched from the edge of the circle, their expressions varying from curiosity to mild concern. Sam leaned on his stick, tilting his head slightly as if tuning into the sounds of the upcoming match.

The match began with a sharp bark from Xochitl. The subordinate lunged forward, her movements fluid and decisive. Yordan stepped back, clumsily deflecting the first swing but losing his footing in the process. The next strike came too fast, and her blade clipped the back of his knee, sending him tumbling face-first into the dirt.

A burst of laughter erupted from Sam. "Oh, Yordan, I could hear that fall from the other side of the forest!" he teased, his grin wide.

Yordan groaned, spitting out a bit of dirt as the subordinate extended a hand to pull him up. Her grip was firm but not unkind.

"You're thinking too much," she said, her tone calm but firm. "In a fight, there's no time to think. You need to anticipate and react—everything else has to leave your mind."

Yordan wiped his face and nodded, her words echoing in his head. He stepped back into the circle, gripping the wooden sword more deliberately this time. His breathing steadied as he tried to block out the world around him—the laughter, the pain from his previous fall, the weight of expectations.

"Focus," he whispered to himself.

The spar began again, her movements just as fast as before. But this time, Yordan didn't overthink. He watched her shoulders, her hips, the way her weight shifted. When she swung, he sidestepped, her blade slicing through empty air. She swung again, and he parried, the clash of wood against wood ringing through the clearing.

He stepped in, delivering a quick strike to her side before stepping back to avoid her counter. She stumbled slightly, surprised by his sudden speed and precision. Seizing the moment, Yordan moved forward, feinting left before delivering a clean strike to her chest. The subordinate staggered, then dropped her sword, signaling her defeat.

The clearing fell silent for a moment, save for the sound of Yordan's heavy breathing. Sam's mouth hung open slightly, and Tequih blinked in disbelief. Even Xochitl, who had been observing from a distance, arched an eyebrow, her arms crossed.

The subordinate picked up her sword, nodding at Yordan with a small smile. "Better," she said. "Much better. You're starting to get it."

Sam broke the silence with a low whistle. "Well, I'll be damned. You actually won one, Yordan."

Yordan couldn't help but grin, his chest swelling with a mixture of pride and relief. He glanced at Tequih, who gave him an encouraging nod, his usual stoicism momentarily broken by a hint of a smile.

Xochitl approached the circle, her sharp gaze fixed on Yordan. "Don't get cocky," she said, though there was a glimmer of approval in her eyes. "One win doesn't make you a warrior. But... it's a start."

Yordan nodded, still catching his breath. For the first time since arriving in the forest, he felt like he was beginning to prove himself—not just to the Ojtlists, but to himself.

The following morning, Yordan found himself blindfolded, his hands tied loosely in front of him as Ueuejtlakatl led him deep into the forest. The crisp morning air carried the earthy scent of moss and bark, with faint birdcalls breaking the otherwise eerie silence. Yordan could feel the uneven ground beneath his boots, the crunch of twigs and leaves reminding him of how far they'd gone from the familiar training areas.

"Where are we going?" Yordan asked, his voice tinged with curiosity and a hint of irritation.

"You'll see soon enough," Ueuejtlakatl replied curtly. "Focus on your steps and your breathing. That's all you need for now."

They walked for what felt like an eternity before Ueuejtlakatl finally stopped. Yordan heard the faint rustle of leaves as the blindfold was untied and slipped off. His eyes squinted as they adjusted to the filtered sunlight peeking through the dense canopy. When his vision cleared, his breath caught.

Before him lay Nahualis, the hidden heart of the forest. The city was a seamless blend of human ingenuity and nature's grace. Buildings, no taller than the surrounding trees, were crafted from smooth adobe and intricately carved stone. Their walls bore vibrant murals of mythic beasts, sacred symbols, and depictions of Nahuali life. Wooden beams jutted gracefully from rooftops, adorned with hanging vines and colorful cloth banners that swayed gently in the breeze.

Pathways, paved with smooth river stones, wove between the structures, leading to open courtyards where people gathered to trade goods, tell stories, and perform rituals. Elevated wooden walkways connected parts of the city, weaving between the massive trunks of ancient trees that seemed as much a part of Nahualis as the buildings themselves.

The entire city felt alive streams of clear water flowed through channels carved into the streets, feeding lush gardens of wildflowers, herbs, and vegetables. The architecture was practical yet stunning, painted in earthen tones of ochre, turquoise, and deep red. Circular plazas served as communal spaces, their centers often marked with fire pits or carved totems depicting the Teoyojtika Forest's guardians.

In the distance, Yordan caught a glimpse of a grand temple-like structure, its base made of polished stone with a staircase winding upward to a platform that did not breach the canopy. The sacred geometry of its design seemed to echo the celestial patterns that Nahuali elders likely read in the night sky.

"Turn around," Ueuejtlakatl ordered sharply, breaking Yordan's awe-stricken reverie.

"What?" Yordan asked, confused.

"You've seen it. Now turn around. You'll never get more than a glance in battle—learn to make it count."

Yordan hesitated but did as instructed, turning his back on the breathtaking view. A brush, a small jar of natural pigments, and a piece of coarse parchment were shoved into his hands.

"Paint it," Ueuejtlakatl commanded.

"Paint the city?" Yordan asked, incredulously. "I've barely seen it for five seconds!"

"Exactly," Ueuejtlakatl snapped. "That's all you'll get when your life depends on it. Now paint."

Yordan sat on a nearby stump, frowning in concentration. He dipped the brush into the pigments and began working, his mind scrambling to recall every detail—the vibrant murals, the winding pathways, the flowing water, and the harmony of the city with the forest around it. His strokes were hesitant at first, but gradually he found a rhythm, blending colors and shapes to recreate the fleeting image burned into his memory.

An hour later, Yordan wiped sweat from his brow, handing the completed painting to Ueuejtlakatl. His fingers were stained with pigments, and he felt as though he'd just fought a battle of his own.

Ueuejtlakatl examined the painting silently, his sharp eyes scanning every stroke. His lips pressed into a thin line as he exhaled a long, low sigh.

"It's... acceptable," he said finally, handing the parchment back. "But acceptable won't keep you alive. Work on your observation skills—your eyes must become your strongest weapon."

Yordan took the parchment back, staring at his work. It wasn't perfect, but it captured enough of Nahualis' essence to make him proud, at least for a fleeting moment. Still, Ueuejtlakatl's words stung, and the weight of his expectations felt heavier than ever.

"Come," Ueuejtlakatl said, already turning away. "We have more to do, and this forest doesn't forgive the distracted."

Chapter Nineteen

Yordan awoke to the sound of Naliyo's voice, firm yet calm, outside his tent.

"Wake up, blacksmith. We're breaking camp today and heading to Nahualis."

The words jolted him from a restless sleep, and he rubbed his eyes, disoriented. The air was still cool, the first rays of sunlight struggling to pierce the dense canopy overhead. The camp was already alive with movement—footsteps, the soft nickering of horses, and the rustle of supplies being packed.

Yordan stepped out of his tent, catching sight of Naliyo, who had already moved on to wake another group. He turned to Sam's tent next, crouching to gently nudge his best friend awake.

"Sam, wake up," Yordan said softly. "We're packing up to leave."

Sam stirred, his hand instinctively reaching out to find his stick. He sat up, his blind eyes scanning in Yordan's direction, a habit that always seemed to unnerve those unfamiliar with him.

"Where are we heading now?" Sam asked groggily, rubbing his temples.

"To Nahualis," Yordan answered. "Finally."

Sam raised an eyebrow. "About time. I was starting to think this elusive place was just a myth."

Yordan chuckled lightly but didn't respond. As Sam stretched and began to gather his things, Yordan glanced toward Tequih, who was still asleep, his form curled up beneath a thick blanket. Yordan decided to let the boy rest a little longer and quietly whispered to Sam what they were doing, ensuring their movements wouldn't disturb him.

By the time Tequih woke, the camp was nearly dismantled, and the golden light of the sun had begun spilling over the treetops. The troop's mounts were being saddled, and the forest was alive with the sounds of preparation. Yordan helped Tequih pack his belongings before leading him toward the horses.

Tequih was assigned a sturdy forest horse, smaller than Taurtepetl but strong and nimble—its coat was a dappled gray that blended seamlessly with the forest surroundings. The boy looked unsure at first, hesitating to climb into the saddle, but with a little encouragement from Yordan, he managed to mount.

Nearby, Ueuejtlakatl stood at the head of the column, his commanding presence impossible to ignore. He surveyed the assembled group with a sharp, assessing gaze. When he saw that all were mounted and ready, he gave a curt nod.

"Move out," Ueuejtlakatl ordered.

The column began to move, the sound of hooves muffled by the soft forest floor. Yordan felt Sam shift slightly behind him as they shared Taurtepetl's saddle. The blood bay stallion seemed to sense the importance of the moment, his steps measured and deliberate as he carried them forward.

The group rode in near silence, the only sounds the occasional creak of leather, the snort of a horse, or the distant calls of forest birds. Shafts of sunlight pierced through the canopy, casting dappled patterns on the ground. The forest felt alive, as though it were watching their passage, its ancient trees towering like silent sentinels.

Yordan occasionally glanced back at Tequih, who clutched the reins tightly but seemed to be adapting well to riding. The boy's face was a mix of determination and lingering unease, but he managed to keep pace with the troop.

"Doing alright back there?" Yordan called to him.

Tequih nodded, his voice steady. "I think so. It's easier than I thought, but I don't think I'll ever ride like you."

Yordan grinned faintly. "Give it time. Taurtepetl makes it look easier than it is."

Ueuejtlakatl led the troop with quiet confidence, his figure cutting an imposing silhouette against the backdrop of the forest. The journey felt both tense and exhilarating as they moved deeper into the heart of the Teoyojtika Forest, each step bringing them closer to the legendary city of Nahualis.

The morning passed swiftly, the rhythm of the horses lulling Yordan into a contemplative state. With Sam behind him and Tequih close by, he felt a fragile sense of unity, though the weight of their mission and the uncertainty of what lay ahead pressed heavily on his mind.

As they emerged from the dense embrace of the Teoyojtika Forest, Yordan felt his breath hitch. Before them lay Nahualis, its presence more magnificent and enigmatic than he had imagined. The city seemed to rise organically from the forest itself, its structures blending seamlessly with the natural surroundings. Towering, spiraled stone buildings were adorned with intricate carvings of animals, celestial symbols, and Nahuali glyphs. The roofs of the dwellings were layered with woven bark and thatch, camouflaged among the trees. No structure rose above the canopy, ensuring Nahualis remained hidden from the untrained eye.

Sam shifted slightly behind Yordan on Taurtepetl. "What does it look like?" he asked, his voice soft with curiosity.

Yordan paused, taking it all in before speaking. "It's... incredible. The buildings are carved from stone, but it's like the forest grew them instead of them being built. There are these symbols everywhere, etched into the walls—animals, stars, things I can't even describe. The roofs blend into the trees like the city doesn't want to be found. It's alive, Sam. The air feels different here."

Sam smiled faintly. "Sounds like something worth seeing."

As they drew closer, the streets came into view—narrow pathways paved with smooth river stones, their edges lined with moss. Nahualis bustled with activity, yet it was a quiet sort of liveliness. Nahuali men and women moved with purpose, dressed in garments that mirrored the colors of the forest—deep greens, browns, and subtle blues. Their clothing was woven with intricate patterns that reflected their culture's deep connection to nature.

In the center of the city stood the largest structure, a grand, circular building that seemed to pulse with significance. Its stone walls were covered with glyphs and murals depicting the history and teachings of the Nahuali people. Vines and flowering plants cascaded down its sides, adding a vibrant contrast to the ancient stone.

Ueuejtlakatl dismounted his horse and motioned for his troops to disperse. As he strode toward the central building, Yordan moved to follow, his curiosity outweighing his sense of decorum.

But before Yordan could take another step, Ueuejtlakatl turned sharply, his expression stern yet tinged with amusement. "You have no place in this meeting, blacksmith. Wait outside. Besides, it's usually stuffy with old men arguing over things better solved in the field."

Yordan clenched his jaw but said nothing, stepping back as Ueuejtlakatl disappeared into the building.

Sam, still astride Taurtepetl, broke the tension. "Well, we're here. What now?"

Yordan sighed and glanced at Tequih, who was taking in the sights with wide eyes. "We should at least explore the city. Get a sense of the place."

Naliyo, ever watchful, fell in step with them as they began their walk. Her presence was quiet but commanding, her hand resting lightly on the hilt of her blade. The streets were alive with Nahuali vendors selling woven goods, carved trinkets, and food that smelled earthy and rich. Children darted between the stalls, their laughter mingling with the hum of quiet conversation.

As they walked, Yordan turned to Naliyo. "Does Ueuejtlakatl not trust us?"

Naliyo's sharp gaze flicked toward him. "He trusts few. Trust is earned, not freely given. Especially here."

Yordan nodded, taking her words to heart. As they wandered through the streets of Nahualis, the weight of their journey and the significance of this hidden city settled over him. The intricate beauty of the city's design and the harmony between its people and their environment was awe-inspiring, but it also served as a reminder of how much he still had to learn and prove—not just to Ueuejtlakatl, but to himself.

As they continued their exploration of Nahualis, Yordan noticed a group of Ojtlists sitting in a circle near a serene pool of water, their eyes closed in deep meditation. The surrounding area was quiet, save for the rustle of leaves and the occasional birdcall. Their stillness radiated a sense of peace, starkly contrasting with the bustling streets they had just passed.

Curious, Yordan turned to Naliyo. "Those people... are they meditating? Do they believe in Toteko, or is their faith... different?"

Naliyo raised an eyebrow, her expression sharp. "Why does it matter to you, blacksmith? You're a self-proclaimed fanatic for Toteko, aren't you? Shouldn't you think you already have the answers?"

Yordan hesitated, then replied calmly, "When Toteko spoke to me, they said to care for all their people in Anakuatl—not just the Lumites, Aralonites, or Zetians. All their people. If I'm to follow this mission, I need to understand everyone, not just assume I know them."

For a moment, Naliyo scrutinized him, her gaze piercing, as though she were weighing the truth of his words. Then, to Yordan's surprise, her expression softened. "You've got a lot to learn. Come, I'll tell you about the Ojtlists."

They found a quiet spot by a low stone wall, away from the bustling paths. Tequih and Sam listened intently as Naliyo began to speak.

"The Ojtlists don't reject Toteko outright," she began, her voice steady and measured. "But they don't see Toteko as a singular figure either—not in the way the Lumites or Aralonites do. To us, the divine isn't a being sitting on high, commanding and judging. The divine is woven into everything—the trees, the rivers, the stones beneath your feet. Toteko is not above us; Toteko is within us and around us."

She gestured toward the meditating Ojtlists. "What you see there isn't worship in the traditional sense. It's a practice we call Tlakatilistli, or 'finding the balance.' We believe the world is in a constant dance of harmony and chaos, and it's our duty to maintain balance, both within ourselves and the world around us."

Sam leaned forward slightly, his interest piqued. "So, it's more about self-awareness and connection to nature?"

Naliyo nodded. "Yes, but it's deeper than that. We believe every living thing has a spirit, and those spirits are interconnected. When we meditate, we're not just centering ourselves, we're listening to the voices of the world, to the whispers of Toteko within the earth and sky."

Tequih, who had been quietly absorbing her words, asked softly, "Do you think Toteko speaks to everyone?"

Naliyo tilted her head, considering the question. "I think Toteko speaks to those who are willing to listen—but not in words, not always. A storm might be Toteko's voice. The rustling of leaves, the howl of a wolf. The Ojtlists learn to interpret these signs, to understand the language of the world."

Yordan, his brow furrowed, asked, "But what about the message Toteko gave me? How does that fit into your beliefs?"

Naliyo met his gaze, her expression unreadable. "If Toteko truly spoke to you, then perhaps it's not for me to decide how it fits. But I will say this—balance is not achieved by forcing others to see things your way. Balance requires understanding, patience, and sometimes, letting go of your own certainty."

Her words struck a chord in Yordan, leaving him thoughtful and quiet as they walked back toward the meditating Ojtlists. The peace radiating from the group seemed to resonate more deeply with him now, even if he didn't fully understand their ways.

Sam broke the silence with a faint smile. "Well, that's a refreshing take. I might not believe in Toteko, but I think I could get behind the idea of balance."

Tequih nodded. "It... makes sense. I think I like it too."

Yordan, still processing, glanced back at Naliyo. "Thank you. That helped me understand more than I expected."

Naliyo gave a small, almost imperceptible smile. "Good. Maybe there's hope for you yet, blacksmith."

As Yordan stood with Sam, Tequih, and Naliyo near the meditating Ojtlists, the sound of hurried footsteps broke the calm. Turning, Yordan saw Xochitl rushing toward them, her sharp eyes scanning the group. "Naliyo!" she shouted, her voice carrying a mix of urgency and relief.

When Xochitl reached them, her expression softened as she grasped Naliyo's arm briefly before planting a quick, affectionate kiss on her cheek. "Finally! I've been searching everywhere for you."

"What's wrong?" Naliyo asked, concern flashing across her face.

Xochitl exhaled heavily, placing a hand on her hip. "We're to head back now. Ueuejtlakatl wants everyone settled into the quarters for the night. Come on, we shouldn't keep him waiting."

With that, the group began their journey back toward the center of Nahualis, winding through the intricate pathways between low stone buildings and towering trees that concealed the city. The sky above was painted in shades of amber and violet as the sun began to set, casting long shadows over the streets.

As they walked, Yordan's thoughts wandered. He realized that, despite everything he had learned from the Lumites, Aralonites, and even the Ojtlists, he had never actually spoken to a Zetian about their beliefs. He turned toward Tequih, who was walking beside him, and asked curiously, "Tequih, what do Zetians believe? I've spent my life surrounded by Lumites and Aralonites, but I've never really learned about your people's faith."

Tequih blinked at the question, clearly surprised. He glanced ahead, his expression pensive, before answering. "Well... I don't know if I can speak for all Zetians. My brother, Ayome, was an Ant—he didn't believe in Toteko or any god, really. But my mother... she believed strongly in Toteko."

Tequih's voice grew quieter as he continued, as though recalling long-forgotten lessons. "My mother and grandmother always said that Toteko's presence is in every act of kindness, every shared meal, and every moment of love. To them, Toteko wasn't a distant figure, but someone who walked among us in spirit, experiencing our joys and pains."

Yordan tilted his head. "So, how did that shape how you live?"

Tequih thought for a moment. "My mother said that Toteko's greatest commandment to Zetians is to endure and remain strong in our suffering. She believed that every trial we face is a test, not of our faith, but of our ability to find light in the darkest moments. She used to say, 'The shadows are only proof of the sun's presence."

His voice faltered slightly as he added, "My grandmother said that our prayers aren't just words—they're woven into the acts we do every day. When she made bread, she would say it was a prayer for nourishment. When she mended clothes, it was a prayer for warmth. To her, even silence could be a prayer if it came from the heart."

Yordan felt a pang of guilt and admiration as he listened. The depth of resilience and quiet strength in the Zetian faith was humbling. "It sounds like your family found their faith in the simplest things."

Tequih nodded. "They did. My grandmother used to say Toteko doesn't need grand temples or golden altars. Toteko needs open hands and open hearts."

Sam, who had been quietly listening, added, "Sounds a lot more grounded than most beliefs I've heard."

Tequih glanced at Sam, his lips twitching into a faint smile. "It had to be, I think. Life's never been easy for us."

As they neared the heart of Nahualis, Yordan found himself contemplating Tequih's words. For all the grandeur and rituals he had known through the Lumites and Aralonites, the Zetian faith seemed rooted in survival and connections, something he couldn't help but respect.

As the group settled into their new quarters in Nahualis, Sam ran his fingers along the walls, his head tilted slightly as though sensing the atmosphere. The house was constructed of cool, smooth stone with accents of intricately carved wood, tucked under the shadow of the surrounding trees. The thick foliage above filtered the sunlight, casting the room in a dappled green glow.

"It's surprisingly cool in here," Sam commented, pausing by the doorframe. "Feels like they've built these places to resist the heat. Sun's beating down outside, but in here? Almost comfortable."

Yordan nodded absently, glancing out the small window toward where Taurtepetl was stabled nearby. The blood bay stallion had already made his displeasure at being cooped up known with a loud whinny, but Yordan knew the stable would keep him safe and cool for now.

Turning back to his companions, Yordan took a deep breath. He had been holding onto the Kamanali since the night in the Sitlali Mountains, and though uncertainty plagued him, he decided it was time. Sitting cross-legged on the floor, he reached into his pack, pulling out the carefully folded piece of paper where he had written the message.

"I think it's time I share this," Yordan said, his voice low but steady. "This is what Toteko's messenger asked me to deliver to the people of Anakuatl."

Sam, leaning against the wall, raised an eyebrow. "This should be good."

Yordan unfolded the paper, the words still as vivid in his mind as the moment Tlanextli spoke them to him. With a deep breath, he read aloud the Kamanali, the guiding principles he had been tasked to spread.

When he finished, silence hung in the air for a moment. Sam broke it with a wry chuckle. "Well," he said, crossing his arms, "if I didn't know you claimed to have gotten this from a messenger of Toteko, I'd think you pinched it from the Ants."

Yordan frowned. "What's that supposed to mean?"

Sam smirked faintly, gesturing vaguely in Yordan's direction. "All this talk about justice, accountability, and compassion? Ants aren't about wiping out faith, contrary to what some believe. We're about challenging the corrupt, exposing the immoral, and holding people—including so-called religious leaders—accountable for their actions."

Tequih, who had been listening intently, looked between the two. "Wait," he said, his voice hesitant but curious. "So Ants don't want to ban religion?"

Sam shook his head. "Not at all. We know people will always believe in something—Toteko, the stars, themselves. Belief isn't the enemy. It's when leaders use that belief to exploit, harm, or control others that we step in. Faith should be personal, not a tool for oppression."

Tequih absorbed this, his expression thoughtful. "So... you're not trying to make people stop believing. You're just trying to make sure no one uses belief as a weapon."

"Exactly," Sam said with a nod. "We want a world where people can believe—or not believe—freely, without fear of being manipulated or oppressed. That's all."

Yordan leaned back, processing Sam's words. "And you think this... message," he gestured to the paper, "aligns with that?"

Sam shrugged. "Depends on who you're asking. Some might call it divine wisdom. Others might call it common sense. Either way, you've got a tall task ahead of you if you're going to make anyone listen."

Tequih, still mulling over Sam's explanation, finally spoke again. "It's... a good message," he said softly. "If Toteko—or whoever sent it—really wants people to follow it, maybe it could bring some hope."

Yordan glanced down at the paper in his hands, the weight of the task pressing heavily on him. "Hope," he echoed. "Maybe that's the first step."

As the evening fell, Yordan glanced out at the setting sun, its light casting fiery streaks across the sky and painting the tops of Nahualis' trees in gold. After their quiet dinner, he turned to Sam and Tequih, who were already settling into their spots for the night.

"I'll be back in a bit," Yordan said, pulling on his cloak as he stepped toward the door. "Just... want to stretch my legs."

Sam tilted his head, a hint of suspicion flickering across his face, but he said nothing. Tequih just nodded, already distracted by one of the Ojtlist wood carvings he'd been admiring earlier.

Yordan stepped out into the cool night air, the buzz of Nahualis humming faintly around him. The city had an almost magical quality at this hour, with lanterns hung in intricate patterns along paths and homes. Shadows danced beneath the towering trees, and faint music floated on the wind from a distant gathering.

His curiosity pulled him away from their quarters and toward the heart of the city. Yordan had hoped to observe more about the Ojtlists—to learn something that might aid him on his mission. He turned a corner near a secluded alley and, just as he thought he was free to roam unnoticed, he collided with someone.

"Oh, my apologies," a woman's voice said softly, steadying herself.

Yordan instinctively started to mutter his own apology, but the words caught in his throat as he looked up. She was stunning. Her vibrant red hair, loose and flowing like a river of fire, framed a heart-shaped face. Her striking blue eyes met his, locking him in place.

She wore layered garments unlike anything common in Nahualis, rich in deep hues and intricate detailing. A long, flowing outer robe draped over a fitted tunic, its wide sleeves embroidered with swirling patterns of wind and flame. The high collar wrapped snugly around her neck, lined with soft fur, adding both warmth and an air of quiet authority. A wide, woven sash cinched the layers at her waist, its intricate knots and embroidered symbols hinting at meaning beyond mere decoration. Over this, she wore a sleeveless coat reinforced with subtle stitching, its hem adorned with elaborate geometric designs. Her boots laced high, their thick soles made for travel, yet her every movement carried the grace of someone equally at home in courtly halls or on the open road.

Everything about her spoke of precision and elegance, a balance between function and artistry, marking her as a stranger to this land possibly from Siranthia—and utterly unforgettable.

In his head, he reeled. Her... I've seen her before. His mind raced, piecing together fragments of his dreams. This was the woman—the woman—who had haunted his visions.

She gave him a small smile, perhaps noticing his stunned expression. "It seems I bumped into you," she said, her tone polite but detached. "Forgive me."

She turned to leave, her cloak billowing behind her, but Yordan's voice called after her before he could stop himself. "Wait! Please!"

She paused, looking over her shoulder with an arched brow. "Yes?"

Yordan scrambled for words. "I—I mean, can I at least get you a dessert or a drink?" His heart hammered in his chest as he stepped toward her. He knew it was foolish—impulsive—but he couldn't let her vanish like a fleeting shadow.

Her lips quirked into an almost amused smile, but her gaze darted past him. "I think your bodyguard might have other plans," she said dryly.

Yordan blinked, confused, until he turned to look behind him—and froze. Ueuejtlakatl stood a few paces away, arms crossed, his expression a mix of irritation and disbelief. His piercing gaze locked onto Yordan like a hawk eyeing its prey.

"Well," the woman said, her tone casual but with a sharp edge. "It seems you have enough company for the evening." With that, she turned on her heel and disappeared into the shadows of Nahualis, leaving Yordan standing there, caught between wonder and dread.

As Yordan turned back to face Ueuejtlakatl, the older man stepped closer, his voice low and cutting. "What, exactly, do you think you're doing?"

As Yordan stood in the shadowed streets of Nahualis, he crossed his arms in frustration. "I just wanted to see the city without someone breathing down my neck," he defended, meeting Ueuejtlakatl's sharp gaze.

Ueuejtlakatl didn't look convinced. "While you're under my vouch, if you do anything wrong, I am the one who answers for you," he said firmly, his voice a low growl of authority.

Yordan ran a hand through his hair, his temper barely contained. "I wasn't doing anything wrong. I just bumped into her."

"Well," Ueuejtlakatl said, pointing in the direction of Yordan's quarters, "don't mess with her. She's not for you to trifle with. Now, get back to your quarters."

Yordan paused, his curiosity piqued despite his irritation. "Do you know her? Is she trouble or something?"

For the briefest moment, Ueuejtlakatl's eyes flickered with something Yordan couldn't place, but the older man didn't answer. He simply gestured for Yordan to move along. The silence only deepened Yordan's confusion, making him feel like he was chasing shadows.

As they walked back through the quiet city, the soft murmurs of Nahualis nightlife swirled around them, but Yordan barely noticed. His thoughts churned, frustration bubbling beneath the surface. He couldn't understand Ueuejtlakatl, couldn't figure out why the man guarded his words like a precious treasure. Why wouldn't he say anything about her?

When they reached the quarters, Ueuejtlakatl turned without a word, his figure disappearing into the night. Yordan stared after him, fists clenched, before heading inside. The others were already asleep, the faint sound of Sam's steady breathing and Tequih's restless shifting filling the quiet room.

Yordan threw himself onto his cot, exhaustion tugging at his body, but his mind refused to settle. Every time he closed his eyes, her image burned behind his lids—those piercing blue eyes, that cascade of vibrant red hair. He didn't even know her name, but she had haunted his dreams before he ever met her. Why? What connection did she have to him, if any?

Eventually, sleep claimed him, and his dreams took hold.

Yordan found himself running through a vast forest, its trees looming tall and ancient. The air buzzed with a golden light, and in the distance, he saw her—the red-haired woman. She stood just beyond his reach, her figure shimmering like a mirage.

"Wait!" Yordan called out, his voice echoing through the trees as he ran toward her. "Please, tell me your name!"

She turned, her piercing blue eyes locking onto his, but her lips moved soundlessly. No words came to him, only the faint rustle of leaves and the hum of the golden light.

Yordan ran faster, his breath hitching as the distance between them seemed to stretch endlessly. Every time he thought he might reach her, she turned away, her hair glowing like a fire against the darkened forest.

"Why won't you answer me?" he shouted, desperation clawing at his chest.

Suddenly, the scene shifted. The forest melted into a radiant clearing where a golden tree stood, its branches reaching up to touch the heavens. The woman faded away like mist, and in her place, the tree's voice boomed, deep and resonant, filling the space around him.

"You wish to chase for your passions," the tree intoned, "then seek the knowledge I carry for you. Until you come to me, you will be doomed to fail."

The light from the tree grew blinding, searing into his eyes as the voice repeated its command, echoing endlessly in his ears. Yordan dropped to his knees, shielding his face, until the light consumed him completely.

He jolted awake, sweat clinging to his skin, his breath ragged. His heart pounded in his chest as the dream lingered, vivid and disorienting. He looked around the room. Sam and Tequih were still asleep, their forms bathed in the soft glow of the moonlight filtering through the window.

Yordan ran a hand over his face, trying to calm himself. His mind reeled. Why her? Why does she haunt me so? And the golden tree—it was always there, waiting, commanding him to find it, demanding he follow its path.

He lay back down, staring at the ceiling, the weight of the dream pressing on him like an anchor. For the first time in weeks, doubt whispered to him, sharp and insistent. Was he losing his way? Or was he already lost?

As the midday sun filtered through the towering trees of Nahualis, the city buzzed with its usual energy. Yordan stood near the central building, its modest but commanding presence marking it as a focal point of the community. Ueuejtlakatl strode inside without hesitation, his demeanor sharp and deliberate.

The calm was interrupted by the arrival of a group unlike any Yordan had seen before. Their clothing alone set them apart, rich in earthy tones and intricate embroidery, the patterns told a story that Yordan couldn't quite read but found fascinating. Their armor was practical yet elegant, with reinforced leather adorned by metallic accents. Flowing sashes of muted gold tied the look together, and the group moved as a single, cohesive unit, exuding quiet confidence.

At the head of the group was her—the red-haired woman Yordan had encountered the night before. Her fiery hair caught the dappled sunlight, almost glowing as it framed her striking blue eyes and composed features. Her presence commanded attention without effort, and even the breeze seemed to pause in deference.

Yordan's feet moved before his brain caught up. He took a step toward her, wanting to say something, anything, to connect the puzzle of their encounter. He was barely halfway when two of her guards swiftly intercepted him.

"Step back," one of them said firmly, his voice like the edge of a blade. "You will not approach Abbeba, daughter of High Chief Jethro."

Yordan froze, the title ringing in his ears. He had no idea who Jethro was, but the mention of a high chief suggested importance.

"I—" he began, fumbling for an explanation.

Abbeba turned her gaze toward him, her blue eyes sharp yet unreadable. Her lips curved into a faint, almost imperceptible smile.

"Release him," she said, her tone calm but authoritative. "He means no harm."

The guards hesitated before stepping aside, though their hands remained close to their weapons.

Nearby, Xochitl had been watching the scene unfold. She stepped closer, her hand resting on her sword, ready to intervene. Her glare at the guards was fierce, protective, and unyielding.

"Xochitl," Yordan said quickly, trying to diffuse the tension. "It's fine."

The red-haired woman studied Yordan for a moment longer before turning her back on him. Her movements were fluid, every step purposeful as she walked toward the central building. Half her troop followed her inside, their boots clicking softly on the stone path, while the remaining guards stood sentinel outside, their expressions stony.

Xochitl relaxed her grip on her weapon but remained tense, clearly displeased. "You're lucky they didn't skewer you," she muttered, shooting Yordan a sharp look.

Yordan didn't respond, his eyes fixed on the entrance where Abbeba had disappeared. He couldn't shake the feeling that he was meant to cross paths with her, even if the how and why were still a mystery.

Sam stepped up beside him, his expression unreadable. "I don't know what you were thinking, but you might want to think a little harder next time," he said dryly.

Tequih stood quietly nearby, his brows furrowed in confusion. "What was that all about?" he asked, his voice soft.

Yordan scratched the back of his neck as he shuffled his feet. "I, uh... bumped into her last night while I was wandering through Nahualis," he muttered.

Tequih arched a brow, his curiosity piqued. "Bumped into her in a...?"

"No!" Yordan quickly interjected, waving his hands in dismissal. "We just bumped into each other. I wasn't looking where I was going, and that's all it was."

Sam chuckled, the sound light but teasing. "Sure doesn't sound like it was 'just' anything, from the way you're all flustered about it."

Yordan glared at him, though there was no real heat in it. Sam's amusement only deepened, but Yordan decided to let it slide. Instead, his focus shifted to the guards Abbeba had left stationed outside the building. He took a steady breath and approached them, keeping his hands open and visible.

"I wanted to apologize for earlier," Yordan began, his tone measured and respectful. "I wasn't trying to cause trouble. I was just curious—where are you all from, and why is this meeting so important?"

One of the guards glanced at the senior member of their group, who gave a small nod of approval. The guard who had been addressed took a step closer, their face stern but not unfriendly.

"We hail from Sarathia," the guard replied, their accent smooth but distinct, lending an air of formality to their words. "This meeting concerns the fate of many, including those fleeing to our lands. King Benjamin has grown bold. Reports speak of Aralonis following suit with arbitrary detainments of Zetians. Word has reached us that Zetopolis fears an all-out offensive, and that enclaves harboring Zetians across Anakuatl are being razed."

The words hit Yordan like a hammer to the chest. He felt his breath catch, his mind racing as he tried to process the implications. The thought of enclaves—places like Nahualis—being burned to the ground chilled him. The atrocities he had already seen replayed in his mind: Tequih's family torn apart, the man nailed to a tree outside Lumina City, the graffiti scrawled across his own home.

He nodded absently, his face solemn as he thanked the guard and turned to rejoin Sam and Tequih. His steps felt heavier, as if the weight of this new information bore down on him with each stride.

As he reached them, his resolve hardened. He couldn't stay hidden in the forest much longer. Whatever safety Nahualis offered, it wasn't enough—not with the storm gathering across Anakuatl. He had been chosen to deliver the Kamanali, to speak a truth that could unite Toteko's people.

But the longer he waited, the more people suffered. The longer he hesitated, the harder it would be to bring change.

As the sun dipped lower in the sky, Yordan clenched his fists. The time to act was coming, and he couldn't ignore it much longer.

Yordan approached Xochitl, her sharp eyes catching him even before he cleared his throat to get her attention. "Xochitl, may I seek out a fellow blacksmith here in Nahualis?" he asked carefully. "And could I take Sam and Tequih with me?"

Xochitl raised a brow, her expression as unreadable as ever. "A blacksmith?" she echoed, arms crossing. "What business do you have with one?"

Yordan hesitated before responding. "I have something in mind. Something important. It might take some time, but I'd like to work on it myself."

After a long pause, Xochitl gave a slight nod. "Fine. But stay within the city. And don't cause trouble. You three are still outsiders here, even if Ueuejtlakatl tolerates you."

"Understood. Thank you," Yordan said, motioning for Sam and Tequih to follow.

The trio wandered the streets of Nahualis, their curiosity growing with each turn. Sam tilted his head towards Yordan as they walked. "What's so urgent about finding a blacksmith all of a sudden?" he asked.

Tequih added, "You've been talking about the Kamanali nonstop. Now you're focused on armor?"

Yordan didn't respond immediately, his lips pressed into a thin line. Eventually, they came across a modest forge near the city's edge, its warmth spilling into the surrounding street. A blacksmith, an older man with broad shoulders and soot-stained hands, glanced up as they entered.

"Welcome," the blacksmith said, though his tone carried a trace of confusion. "You don't look like Ojtlists. What can I do for you?"

Yordan stepped forward. "I'm a blacksmith myself," he said, gesturing towards his hands, still bearing the calluses of his trade. "I was wondering if I might use your forge. I'd like to craft some armor for myself and my companions."

The blacksmith raised a brow, clearly intrigued. "You want to craft armor? Here? Why not have it done by someone more experienced?"

Yordan smiled slightly. "Because I know what I need, and I know how to make it."

The blacksmith studied him for a moment before shrugging. "Fine. You can use the forge. Just don't ruin anything, and clean up after yourself."

"Thank you," Yordan said, setting to work immediately. He took quick measurements of both Sam and Tequih, muttering to himself as he calculated dimensions. When he wrapped a measuring strip around Sam's chest, Sam wrinkled his nose.

"Why do I need armor?" Sam asked, his tone half curious, half incredulous. "I'm blind. It's not like I'm going to be on the front lines."

Yordan glanced up, meeting Sam's gaze squarely. "Because I don't want you to die easily from an arrow," he said simply.

The room fell quiet for a moment, the weight of Yordan's words sinking in. Tequih shifted uncomfortably, glancing between the two men.

"Well," Sam finally said, his voice softer, "when you put it that way, I guess I can't argue."

Yordan nodded and turned his attention back to his work, already visualizing the armor pieces he would forge. Each one would be a layer of protection—not just for their bodies, but for their shared mission. As the forge roared to life, Yordan felt a flicker of determination reignited within him.

Over the next week, Yordan poured every ounce of his energy into the forge. The heat became a second skin, the hiss of molten metal a familiar melody. By day, he hammered and shaped, combining the elegance of Ojtlist craftsmanship with the sturdier, more practical designs of Aralonite armor. By night, he maintained his grueling training routine with Xochitl. Each swing of the wooden training saber brought fresh bruises, and each failure stoked a quiet determination in him to improve.

Abbeba's departure two days into the week haunted him like an unspoken question. He hadn't even had a chance to try speaking with her again, and her sudden absence gnawed at his focus in unexpected ways. If anything, it fueled him. He channeled his frustration into every strike of his hammer, every careful notch and groove he etched into the metal. The mixed armor began to take shape: sleek and flexible but undeniably strong, a blend of two traditions that mirrored the path Yordan found himself walking.

On the last day of the week, with his armor completed, Yordan dragged himself to the training grounds, exhaustion heavy in his limbs.

The entire group was there—Sam, Tequih, Naliyo, and even a few other Ojtlists—curious to see how far Yordan had come. Xochitl stood in the center, her expression as unreadable as always, the familiar training saber in hand.

"Ready?" she asked, spinning the wooden blade with casual ease.

Yordan took a deep breath, nodding as he raised his own saber. The sun hung low in the sky, casting long shadows over the training area. His body ached, his hands still raw from days at the forge, but his mind felt unusually clear.

They began to circle each other, the soft crunch of dirt under their feet the only sound. Xochitl struck first, a fast, sweeping blow aimed at his left side. Yordan blocked it cleanly, the wooden blades cracking together. She moved seamlessly into her next attack, but this time, Yordan anticipated it. He shifted his weight, deflecting her strike and stepping back just out of reach.

"You're focused today," Xochitl noted, her tone almost approving.

Yordan didn't respond. He kept his eyes on her, his movements fluid but deliberate. She came at him again, faster this time, her strikes relentless. But where he had faltered before, hesitated or overthought, today he moved with purpose. He sidestepped her lunges, parried her blows, and even forced her to take a step back—something he had never managed before.

A faint smile tugged at the corners of Xochitl's mouth as she launched a feint, only to twist her blade at the last second and aim for his shoulder. Yordan caught the shift in her stance and brought his saber up just in time, countering with a sharp, decisive strike that knocked her blade from her hand.

The training ground went silent. Xochitl stared at him, then at her fallen weapon, before letting out a short laugh. She stepped forward, clapping him on the shoulder.

"Not bad," she said, the closest thing to praise Yordan had ever heard from her.

Tequih let out a cheer, and even Sam gave a small, approving nod. Yordan stood there for a moment, his chest heaving as he processed what had just happened. For the first time since he had begun this journey, he felt like he had truly earned a victory.

As the dust settled on the training ground, Yordan turned to Xochitl, still catching his breath but with a glint of determination in his eye.

"Can we go again?" he asked, his voice steady despite his exhaustion.

The Ojtlists gathered around exchanged glances, some smirking, others nodding in approval. It was clear that Yordan was finally beginning to understand the discipline and perseverance required. Xochitl raised an eyebrow, studying him for a moment before giving a curt nod.

"Alright," she said, retrieving her training saber. "Let's see if that wasn't just a fluke."

Later that evening, back in their quarters, Yordan leaned against the wall, his arms crossed as he addressed Tequih and Sam.

"Tequih," he began, "how fast can you be saddling your horse?"

Tequih looked up from where he sat sharpening an arrowhead. "Maybe ten minutes, if I'm rushing," he replied, his tone cautious.

"Good," Yordan said, nodding. "Tomorrow night, we're leaving. We're going to stop what's happening to these Zetian enclaves before it gets worse."

Tequih froze, his hand gripping the arrowhead tightly. Sam, sitting nearby with his cane resting across his lap, tilted his head toward Yordan.

"You sure about this?" Sam asked, his tone even but carrying an undercurrent of concern.

"I am," Yordan said firmly. "But before we go, I need to do one thing—I have to get my sword back."

Sam let out a slow breath, shaking his head. "Yordan, if Ueuejtlakatl or anyone else catches you sneaking around, they'll shut this whole thing down before we even have a chance to leave."

"I won't get caught," Yordan replied, his voice edged with confidence.

Sam's lips pressed into a thin line. "Just don't do anything reckless." He exhaled sharply. "I'll be waiting with Taurtepetl."

Yordan smirked faintly. "Don't worry about me."

The next morning, Yordan carried on as usual. He trained, helped with camp duties, and even exchanged a few words with Xochitl and the other Ojtlists. But beneath his calm demeanor, he was laser-focused on his plan.

In the early afternoon, he returned to their quarters, his arms laden with the armor he had painstakingly crafted over the last week. He set it down carefully, piece by piece, ensuring everything was in order.

"Here," he said, gesturing toward the armor. "Make sure it's fitted properly. We'll need it."

Sam and Tequih exchanged glances, the weight of what they were about to do settling heavily on the room. Outside, the forest whispered in the afternoon breeze, a stark contrast to the storm brewing in Yordan's heart.

The quiet of Nahualis enveloped the city as the stars began to emerge, their light barely reaching through the thick forest canopy. Yordan moved silently, slipping from shadow to shadow, his heart pounding as he approached Ueuejtlakatl's quarters. The air was cool, and every creak of wood beneath his boots felt deafening, but he pressed on, determined.

He reached the modest structure where he knew Tlamashta was kept. After what felt like an eternity of careful searching, his eyes finally fell on it, the sword's brown leather hilt looked almost luminous in the dim light, a beacon of familiarity. As he grasped it, a sense of peace, sharp and sudden, washed over him, silencing the chaos in his mind. For the first time in months, Yordan felt steady.

He carefully secured the sword at his side and slipped out, making his way to the stables. When he arrived, Tequih was already there, standing beside his forest horse, its coat glinting faintly in the starlight. Taurtepetl stood nearby, saddled and ready, his blood bay coat dark against the night. Sam, perched on Taurtepetl's back, tilted his head slightly, his cane resting across his lap.

"Took you long enough," Sam said in a low voice, his tone teasing but with an edge of concern.

"Had to make sure I wasn't followed," Yordan replied, mounting Taurtepetl in one fluid motion.

Tequih swung onto his horse, his nervous energy evident in the way he adjusted the reins. Yordan gave him a reassuring nod before urging Taurtepetl forward. Together, the three of them rode out of Nahualis, their figures swallowed by the dense forest.

The forest seemed alive with sound—the rustling of leaves, the occasional hoot of an owl, and the soft thud of their horses' hooves against the mossy ground. Yordan pulled a star chart from his pack, studying it by the faint light of the moon filtering through the tree-tops.

"This way," he murmured, pointing ahead.

They moved cautiously, the weight of their departure heavy in the air. Yordan's hand rested on Tlamashta, his fingers brushing its hilt for reassurance. Tequih occasionally glanced around, his youthful face etched with both fear and determination. Sam sat quietly behind

Yordan, his demeanor calm but his ears keenly attuned to the sounds around them.

After hours of travel, they came upon a small clearing, its openness offering a moment of respite. Yordan dismounted and tethered Taurtepetl to a tree, allowing the horse to graze. Tequih followed suit, his movements were slightly clumsy but earnest.

"We'll rest here for the night," Yordan said, his voice low but commanding.

They quickly set up a small camp, a modest fire crackling in the center, its light dancing across their faces. Yordan leaned against a fallen log, his hand instinctively returning to Tlamashta's hilt. Tequih sat nearby, fidgeting with the edge of his cloak, while Sam reclined with his head tilted back, appearing more at ease than the others.

"You should sleep," Yordan said, his gaze fixed on the fire. "We'll need to leave early."

Tequih nodded and wrapped himself in his cloak, his breathing evening out as he drifted to sleep. Sam remained still for a moment before shifting slightly, his voice soft.

"Yordan, you sure about this?" Sam asked.

Yordan didn't answer immediately. He looked toward the stars visible through the canopy, their light faint but steady. Finally, he spoke, his voice quiet but resolute, "We don't have a choice."

Sam nodded, his faith in Yordan unspoken but clear. The camp eventually fell silent save for the fire's occasional crackle. Yordan stayed awake a while longer, his mind racing with plans and possibilities. When sleep finally claimed him, it was filled with images of the path ahead.

Chapter Twenty

Yordan awoke to the faint sound of leaves rustling nearby. As he blinked into consciousness, he noticed a lone forest wolf standing just beyond the edge of their camp. Its silver-gray coat shimmered faintly in the soft pre-dawn light, and its intelligent amber eyes were fixed intently on him. The wolf tilted its head slightly, as though questioning his presence, its gaze calm but curious.

Yordan slowly stood, careful not to wake Sam or Tequih, his hand instinctively resting on Tlamashta's hilt. The wolf held his gaze for a moment longer, its head tilting further, almost as if asking, What are you doing here? Then, with a quiet huff, it turned and darted silently into the depths of the forest, vanishing among the trees.

Yordan exhaled and shook his head, brushing off the strange encounter. The forest had always felt alive, but this moment made him feel like it had a watchful guardian observing their every move.

With the camp packed up, the three prepared to ride out. Yordan mounted Taurtepetl and glanced at Tequih, who was checking his pack. It was then Yordan noticed a composite bow attached to the side of it.

"Tequih," Yordan said, his voice a mix of surprise and approval as he rode closer. "You've been busy."

Tequih turned to him, a hint of pride in his youthful face. "Figured we might need it. The Ojtlists taught me well enough, didn't they?"

Yordan clapped him on the shoulder, a smile breaking through his usual focus. "Good thinking. It might just save our lives."

Sam, already seated behind Yordan on Taurtepetl, tilted his head slightly at the exchange but didn't comment. With their gear secure and the fire extinguished, they set off into the forest once more.

The days that followed were marked by steady travel, the dense foliage of the Teoyojtika Forest providing cover and serenity. They passed through sections where the trees grew so tightly together that only slivers of sunlight broke through, casting shifting patterns on the forest floor. Tequih, riding his forest horse, occasionally pointed out tracks or landmarks he recognized from his time with the Ojtlists, while Sam listened intently, using the details to map their journey in his mind.

By the fourth day, the forest began to thin. The air grew warmer, and the light seemed harsher without the canopy above to diffuse it. As they emerged into a clearing, the sight that greeted them made Yordan's stomach drop.

Several large trees had been felled, their trunks lying haphazardly across the ground, scorched and blackened as though by fire. The grass and undergrowth were charred in patches, and the acrid smell of smoke lingered heavily in the air. Tequih reined in his horse, his face a mix of confusion and alarm.

"What happened here?" Tequih asked, his voice barely above a whisper.

Yordan scanned the area, his hand once again drifting to Tlamashta. "It looks like this part of the forest was cleared out—and burned. But why?"

Sam sniffed the air, his face tightening. "I can smell it—burning wood and something else... something foul. What do you see?"

Yordan hesitated, then described the scene in grim detail. "It's like someone wanted to carve through the forest with no care for what they left behind. The trees aren't just cut—they're destroyed. It's wasteful. There's no sign of new growth or any attempt to make use of what they've taken."

Tequih's voice quivered slightly as he added, "And it's not just the trees. The ground is scarred, too. It's like they wanted to make sure nothing could grow back here."

Yordan frowned deeply, his gaze following the devastation. "This isn't near Zetopolis. We're closer to Lumina City—and Aralonis. Whoever did this wasn't just cutting wood. This was deliberate."

The realization sent a shiver down his spine. Whoever was responsible had no respect for the forest's sanctity—or its people. He exchanged a grim look with Tequih, who nodded silently.

Sam shifted slightly, sensing their unease. "What's next?" he asked, his tone steady despite the tension in the air.

Yordan turned Taurtepetl toward the faint trail leading beyond the clearing. "We keep moving. We need to find out exactly what's happening—and stop it."

As they rode southward, the sound of distant marching filled the air. Yordan, Sam, and Tequih reined in their horses and steered them off the narrow path, seeking cover behind a thick cluster of trees. From their concealed vantage point, they saw the unmistakable sight of a large troop—about 200 men—advancing steadily.

Banners fluttered in the breeze above the marching soldiers. Yordan's sharp eyes immediately recognized the symbols etched into the fabric. The dominant banners were unmistakably Lumite, their golden lion heads gleaming even in the fading sunlight. Interspersed among them were banners bearing the emblem of Aralonis, the familiar crest tugging at something deeply personal within Yordan.

"Lucien," Yordan muttered under his breath, gripping the reins of Taurtepetl tightly. His voice was low and tense as he continued, "He's leading them south. Mostly Lumites, but some of them are from Aralonis."

Tequih, seated atop his forest horse, tensed beside him. His young face hardened with determination as he slowly reached for the composite bow strapped to his back. "I could hit one of them. Maybe take out Lucien himself from here," he whispered, his voice sharp with anger.

Yordan's hand shot out, gripping Tequih's arm firmly. "No," he said, his tone brooking no argument. "We can't risk it. They'd spot us in an instant, and there are too many. We have to be smart about this."

Tequih frowned but lowered his bow. "So what do we do? Let them march south unopposed?"

Yordan shook his head. "We head south, but ahead of them. We warn every enclave we come across. If they're marching like this, they won't spare anyone who stands in their way."

Sam, perched behind Yordan on Taurtepetl, spoke up, his tone practical but concerned. "What if they don't believe us? What if they think we're just stirring panic?"

Yordan exhaled deeply, the weight of responsibility pressing on his shoulders. "We'll just have to try our best. Even if just one enclave listens, it could save lives."

He turned his gaze south, where the troop was steadily making its way. The sight of Lucien's banners made his blood boil, but he tamped down the anger, focusing instead on the urgency of their mission. "Come on," Yordan said, nudging Taurtepetl forward. "We've got no time to waste."

The three rode carefully, sticking to the cover of the forest while keeping an eye on the marching soldiers in the distance. Yordan's heart pounded as he thought about the task ahead. Finding the right words to warn people of the impending danger seemed as daunting as the danger itself. But he knew one thing for certain: they had to try.

The enclave came into view as the forest thinned. Makeshift tents and crudely built shelters huddled together in a clearing, their occupants clearly weary but alert. As Yordan, Tequih, and Sam approached on horseback, a sharp whistle pierced the air. Refugee lookouts, perched on the edges of the camp, called out for them to stop, their voices loud and urgent.

"Stop right there! Don't come any closer!" one lookout shouted, his hand on the hilt of a worn blade.

Yordan immediately raised a hand, signaling for Tequih to halt behind him. "Stay here," Yordan murmured to Tequih, who reluctantly reined in his forest horse. Dismounting from Taurtepetl, Yordan approached on foot, keeping his hands visible and his posture non-threatening.

"I'm sorry for scaring you," Yordan began, his voice calm but firm. "We mean no harm. But I need to warn you—Lucien, Prince Joseph's son, is leading a band of about 200 soldiers south. They're just two days' march behind us. Their target is clear: Zetian and Ojtlists enclaves like this one."

The crowd murmured anxiously, some clutching loved ones or stepping closer to their makeshift homes. From the center of the camp, a woman stepped forward, her gray-streaked hair tied back, and her eyes sharp with both wisdom and suspicion. It was Sira, the leader of this group of refugees. Her gaze locked onto Yordan with recognition.

"I remember you," Sira said, her voice steady but cutting. "You're the Aralonite who told us we misunderstood what the Lumites were doing. You doubted us then. Why should we trust you now? What proof do we have that you aren't here to trick us?"

Yordan hesitated, her words striking deep. The memory of that earlier encounter, the skepticism in his voice, the dismissal of their warnings, hit him like a blow to the chest. Swallowing his pride, he took a deep breath and stepped forward. Then, to the surprise of everyone, he knelt before her in the dirt, bowing his head.

"I was wrong," Yordan said, his voice carrying across the clearing. "I didn't listen when I should have. I doubted your cries when I had no right to. And for that, I am deeply sorry."

Sira's sharp eyes narrowed, but she remained silent, letting him continue.

"It took meeting a Zetian woman in Lumina City—seeing first-hand the suffering you endure—to open my eyes. And after that moment, Toteko spoke to me. They gave me the Kamanali, a message meant for all the people of Anakuatl, not just the Lumites, Aralonites, Zetians, or Ojtlists, but for everyone."

A hushed murmur spread through the gathered refugees. Some folded their arms skeptically, others exchanged uncertain glances, while a few seemed to soften, curious despite themselves.

"What is this 'Kamanali'?" Sira asked, her tone still guarded.

Yordan raised his head to meet her gaze, his hands resting on his thighs in supplication. "It is a call for unity and compassion, a reminder that we are all interconnected. One of its principles is 'Interconnectedness and Community,' to embrace a global ummah—a community that transcends borders and divisions. It calls on us to take collective responsibility for each other, prioritizing the most vulnerable among us."

Sira's expression remained unreadable, so Yordan pressed on.

"Another principle is 'Compassion and Ethical Leadership.' It is a call to lead with integrity, wisdom, and empathy, rejecting cruelty and manipulation. It challenges us to alleviate suffering and work for the happiness and well-being of all people."

Some refugees began nodding subtly, their rigid stances softening as they took in his words. Others still looked doubtful, their suspicion evident in their narrowed eyes and crossed arms.

"You expect us to believe this?" one man called from the crowd. "What proof do we have that you're not just another fanatic with pretty words?"

Yordan turned to the man, his expression earnest. "I can't prove it. All I can do is try to show you through my actions. That's why I'm here—to warn you, to stand with you. Whether you believe me or not, Lucien and his men are coming. You have two days to decide what to do."

The camp fell silent, tension thick in the air. Some whispered among themselves, weighing his words. Others remained wary, their skepticism unwavering.

Finally, Sira spoke, her voice measured. "We'll see if your warning holds true, Aralonite. But if it doesn't, you'll answer to me."

As the tension lingered in the enclave, Yordan stood up, his mind racing for a way to convince the skeptics. Taking a deep breath, he stepped closer to Sira, keeping his tone steady and measured.

"If you don't believe me entirely, leave my best friend Sam here with you. My ward, Tequih, and I can take two of your most trusted people to see for themselves. They can decide whether what I'm warning you about is true."

Sira raised an eyebrow, her sharp gaze flicking to Tequih and then back to Yordan. "You're willing to leave your friend behind to prove your case?"

Yordan nodded. "Yes. If it's the only way to gain your trust, I'll do it."

Sira studied him for a moment before turning to the crowd. "Lalina, Xeni—step forward."

Two women emerged from the gathered refugees. Lalina, a tall woman with piercing eyes and a calm demeanor, and Xeni, shorter but muscular, both carried themselves with the quiet confidence of seasoned fighters. Each had a knife strapped to their belts, and their expressions revealed their cautious but resolute nature.

"You trust them?" Yordan asked, glancing at Sira.

"With my life," Sira replied. She fixed her gaze on Lalina and Xeni. "If you feel your lives are in danger, don't hesitate to use your knives. Stay sharp."

The two women nodded. Lalina adjusted her knife, while Xeni gave Yordan and Tequih a scrutinizing look. "Lead the way," Lalina said simply.

Tequih mounted his forest horse while Yordan swung himself back onto Taurtepetl, who snorted softly as if sensing the urgency of the moment. Lalina and Xeni climbed up behind them, and the group set off, leaving Sam behind with the enclave.

The ride northward through the plains was tense and silent. The wind carried the faint scent of smoke, and the occasional distant call of a bird broke the stillness. The horizon was vast and empty, but as they neared a slight rise, Yordan pulled Taurtepetl to a stop and pointed.

"There," he said, his voice grim.

Below them, torches illuminated a column of marching soldiers, their banners flapping in the wind. The golden lion of the Lumites and the twin stars of Aralonis were unmistakable. The soldiers moved with grim purpose, their armor catching the moonlight, and their numbers confirmed Yordan's warning—200 men strong.

Lalina cursed softly under her breath. "By Toteko... you weren't lying."

Xeni's jaw tightened. "We have to warn the enclave."

Yordan nodded. "Let's ride."

They turned and galloped back to the enclave, the urgency of their mission driving them forward. By the time they arrived, the night was thick, and the refugees were anxiously awaiting their return.

Sira stood at the edge of the enclave, her arms crossed. Lalina and Xeni dismounted swiftly, their faces grim.

"He's right," Lalina announced. "The soldiers are real, and they'll be here by tomorrow night at the latest."

The refugees erupted in panic, their voices overlapping in fear and confusion. Some clung to their children, while others began gathering their meager belongings.

Sira silenced them with a raised hand and turned to Yordan. "Where should we go?"

Yordan stepped forward, his voice steady but urgent. "My name is Yordan Arano, and I think you should head south toward Zetopolis. It's the safest place for now. We can warn other Zetian enclaves along the way and gather strength in numbers. But we must leave at dawn."

Sira nodded reluctantly. "Pack everything you can carry. We move at first light."

The refugees scattered, their movements frantic but purposeful. Yordan stepped back, the weight of responsibility heavy on his shoulders. He glanced at Tequih, who was helping guide some of the younger children, and then at the stars above.

There was no turning back now.

As the morning sun rose over the plains, Yordan walked at the front of the group, his eyes scanning the horizon for any signs of danger. The refugees moved as quickly as they could, their pace steady but urgent. Sam rode atop Taurtepetl, the blood bay stallion appearing regal even in such dire circumstances. Tequih, ever resourceful, had offered his forest horse to an elderly woman who struggled to keep up, leading the animal gently as the woman clung to its mane.

Yordan periodically checked on the refugees, ensuring their path was clear and their morale stayed strong. The rhythmic creak of carts and the murmur of hushed conversations filled the air. Yordan glanced back to see Tequih adjusting the reins for the elderly woman, his composure beyond his years. Yordan gave him a nod of approval.

"Put on your armor," Yordan called back to Tequih and Sam. "All of us. If a scout party finds us, we need to be ready."

The three of them donned their armor, the mix of Nahualis and Aralonite craftsmanship shining faintly in the morning light. The sight of them, prepared for battle, reassured some of the refugees, though others looked nervously at the gleaming blades and protective plates.

Sira walked alongside Yordan, her sharp eyes catching every detail. Her gaze fell on the armor, her brow furrowing. "That's not Aralonite armor. Where did you get it?"

Yordan glanced down at the armor before meeting her gaze. "I made it," he said simply. "I used what I had available in Nahualis and combined it with what I knew of Aralonite armor."

"You were a blacksmith?" Sira asked, her tone curious, almost skeptical.

"Yes," Yordan replied without elaborating.

Sira studied him for a moment before nodding. "May the echoes of Toteko keep you steady indeed," she murmured, her voice carrying a touch of respect.

Her eyes shifted to Tequih, who was walking alongside the forest horse, his small frame a stark contrast to the older woman riding atop it. "And the boy?" Sira asked, her voice softer. "How did he come into your care?"

Yordan hesitated, glancing at Tequih, who was busy helping the woman stay secure on the horse. "I saved him from the Luminar Citadel prison," Yordan said finally. "I intervened when they tried to imprison his family. I... couldn't save them all. His brother, Ayome, and the rest of his family were taken. We have no word on what's happened to them."

Sira's expression darkened, her steps slowing as she absorbed his words. "You risked yourself for them?" she asked, her tone tinged with disbelief.

"I had to," Yordan said firmly. "No one else would."

Sira nodded again, though her eyes remained clouded with thought. "You've seen more than most Aralonites," she said quietly. "Perhaps your Kamanali isn't as hollow as I first thought."

Yordan didn't respond, his focus already back on the horizon. He couldn't afford to dwell on whether people believed in him or not. The safety of the refugees was his priority, and with Lucien's forces still in pursuit, every step south brought them closer to both danger and hope.

As the group continued to move, Yordan found himself repeating the principles of the Kamanali in his mind, grounding himself in their guidance. The road ahead was uncertain, but he was determined to see it through.

As the group pressed onward, Yordan couldn't help but notice how much smaller this enclave seemed compared to when he and Sam had first seen them near the Lumina River months ago. The absence of familiar faces weighed on him, a grim reminder of the harsh realities facing the Zetian refugees.

When they came upon another enclave of Zetians scattered across makeshift tents and carts, the reception was far from welcoming. The refugees stood guarded, their eyes narrowed with suspicion as Yordan's group approached. Lookouts raised crude weapons, and some whispered amongst themselves.

Before Yordan could speak, Lalina and Xeni dismounted, stepping forward to address the wary crowd. "We saw the troops," Lalina said, her voice firm yet urgent. "They're less than a day behind us if we're lucky. We need to move now."

The enclave erupted into hushed but frantic murmurs. A few nodded, trusting Lalina and Xeni's word, while others hesitated, fear etched on their faces.

"We don't have time to argue," Sira said sharply, stepping forward. "We've combined our numbers, but if we don't leave now, none of us will stand a chance."

Reluctantly, the Zetians began to pack their meager belongings and join the group. The combined caravan grew larger, a mix of children, elders, and weary travelers. The larger group meant more protection in numbers, but it also meant slower movement—a risk they couldn't afford with Lucien's soldiers so close behind.

Yordan rode up beside Sira, keeping an eye on the refugees as they prepared to move again. "How far are we from Zetopolis if we sent a rider ahead?" he asked, his tone measured but urgent.

Sira furrowed her brow, calculating. "A rider on horseback? Maybe a day and a half, but at this pace, walking, we're looking at another week—if we're lucky."

"Then we don't have time to waste," Yordan said, his jaw tightening.

Sira nodded and turned to Lalina. "You'll ride to Zetopolis with another rider. Plead for help and warn them of what's coming. If we don't make it there in time, they'll need to be ready."

Lalina straightened, her face resolute. "I'll go."

Sam, overhearing, protested immediately. "Send someone else. I'll stay with Yordan. He needs me."

Yordan turned to him, his expression soft but resolute. "Sam, I need you to go. I can't leave these people, and you're the only one I trust to be my voice in Zetopolis."

Sam's face twisted in frustration, his grip tightening on Taurtepetl's reins. "I won't leave you behind," he said, his voice low but firm.

"You're not leaving me," Yordan replied, his voice steady. "You're helping me. These people need someone who can speak for them when we're not there. Support Lalina. Do your best to get help."

Sam hesitated, his lips pressed into a thin line, before finally nodding. "Fine," he said, his voice reluctant but resolved. "But you better make it to Zetopolis."

"I will," Yordan promised, gripping Sam's shoulder firmly. "Just get there and tell them what's coming."

With that, Sam and Lalina mounted their horses, their forms silhouetted against the fading light as they rode off toward Zetopolis. Yordan watched them disappear into the horizon, his heart heavy but resolute.

As the caravan began to move south again, Yordan felt the weight of responsibility pressing down on him. Each step brought them closer to Zetopolis—and closer to the soldiers hunting them.

Two days after sending Tequih to scout the rear, Yordan's tension grew as the group trudged southward, the combined enclaves moving as quickly as their weary bodies allowed. When Tequih returned faster than expected, his horse panting hard, Yordan rushed to meet him.

"How far back?" Yordan demanded, steadying the exhausted horse.

Tequih dismounted, his face pale. "A couple of hours at most," he said, breathless. "We don't have time. We need to find a place to defend ourselves."

Yordan cursed under his breath and turned to Sira. "The terrain ahead—anything defensible?"

Sira squinted toward the horizon. "There's a rise just beyond that stand of trees. It's not much, but it's better than nothing."

Yordan nodded and relayed orders for the group to move quickly. They reached the rise within minutes, and the refugees began stacking loose rocks and positioning themselves for a last-ditch stand. Yordan's stomach churned as he looked around. Their defenses were meager at best.

Then, faintly, the sound of galloping hooves echoed through the air. It wasn't coming from behind but from the south.

Yordan's pulse quickened. He strode to the front of the group, his hand resting on Tlamashta's hilt. Were they being flanked? He scanned the horizon, his heart sinking. The glint of armor and the silhouette of riders emerged.

"Riders approaching!" someone shouted, panic lacing their voice.

"Hold your positions!" Yordan called, his voice steady despite the dread tightening his chest.

But as the riders came into view, Yordan froze. These weren't Lucien's soldiers. The group of about forty mounted warriors bore a different air—disciplined but not menacing. At the forefront, riding a single horse, were two familiar figures: Sam, gripping Lalina's waist tightly, and Lalina guiding the reins with calm confidence.

Taurtepetl, Yordan's blood bay stallion, gleamed in the midday sun, his powerful stride carrying them effortlessly across the plains. Yordan's heart surged with relief.

Sam looked up as they approached, his head turning slightly, as if listening for Yordan's voice. Lalina guided Taurtepetl to a halt before him, her expression firm but carrying a glimmer of reassurance.

"You didn't think I'd let you handle this on your own, did you?" Sam said, his tone teasing but resolute as he steadied himself with Lalina's arm.

Lalina slid off Taurtepetl first, then reached up to guide Sam down. "Zetopolis sent us," she said to Yordan. "We couldn't bring the whole army, but we have reinforcements. These soldiers are ready to fight."

Yordan scanned the mounted warriors, their numbers few but their presence invigorating. Turning back to the refugees, he raised his voice. "Help has come! But we still need to be ready. Let's not waste this chance."

The refugees, many clutching makeshift weapons, straightened their backs. The sight of armed allies reignited hope in their tired faces.

As the riders prepared themselves alongside the refugees, Yordan placed a hand on Taurtepetl's neck, leaning close to the stallion. "Looks like we'll need all the strength you've got."

But as he turned his gaze south, where Lucien's forces loomed just hours away, Yordan knew their greatest challenge was yet to come.

Yordan approached the commander of the mounted reinforcements, his boots crunching against the dry earth as the soldiers parted.

At their center stood a tall, commanding figure, her posture exuding authority. Her armor gleamed in the sunlight, and her sharp eyes swept over Yordan as if measuring him for both worth and weakness.

"You," the woman—Aisha—said coldly as she drew her sword with a practiced hand. The blade pointed directly at Yordan's throat, halting him mid-step. "An Aralonite. Why are you here? Are you a spy for Prince Joseph?"

Sira hurried forward, alarm flashing across her face as she placed herself partially between Aisha and Yordan. "Commander Aisha! Lower your weapon," she demanded firmly. "Do you know this man?"

Aisha's gaze didn't waver as she replied. "We've crossed paths. He dismissed the plight of my people as misunderstandings back in Lumina City. And now he shows up here, of all places."

Yordan raised his hands slightly, showing he meant no harm. "We've never officially met," he said, his voice steady despite the tension in the air. "But yes, we had a disagreement. That said, I am not your enemy. My name is Yordan and your's is?"

Aisha's eyes narrowed, her grip tightening on her sword. "Not my enemy? You stand here asking for trust, but I remember your ignorance."

Before Yordan could respond, Sira stepped closer. "Commander," she said with quiet authority, "he has changed. Yordan warned us of danger approaching and fought to protect us. He even risked his life to save Tequih, a Zetian boy who was imprisoned in the Luminar Citadel. Whatever he once believed, he has proven he is not an enemy."

Tequih dismounted nearby, his presence drawing Aisha's gaze. She studied him for a moment before shifting her attention back to Yordan.

"You vouched for this boy?" she asked skeptically.

Yordan nodded. "I did, and I would again."

Aisha's jaw tightened as she glanced at Uriah, her trusted advisor, standing beside her. "What do you think, Uriah?" she asked, her tone less harsh but no less serious.

Uriah stroked his beard thoughtfully before answering. "Princess, until proven otherwise, it seems he has acted honorably. Perhaps his presence here is not as suspect as you fear."

Aisha sheathed her sword with a sharp motion, her expression still hard. "Fine," she said tersely. "But if you betray us, Yordan, I will not hesitate to deal with you myself."

Yordan exhaled slowly, lowering his hands. "Understood," he said simply.

Sira stepped in, her tone brisk. "We don't have time for distrust. Lucien's forces are close. Commander Aisha, we need you and your riders to hold the line while the rest of us continue south to Zetopolis."

Aisha nodded, her focus shifting to Sira. "We'll hold them off as long as we can," she promised. Then her eyes flicked back to Yordan. "But don't think I trust you."

Yordan gave a faint nod. "You don't have to trust me. Just trust that I'll do what's right."

As Aisha turned to rally her troops, Tequih leaned toward Yordan and whispered, "She really doesn't like you, huh?"

Yordan let out a quiet, dry chuckle. "That's putting it lightly." He adjusted his armor, his resolve hardening. "Let's make sure we all survive this, Tequih. That's the only thing that matters."

Tequih's voice trembled with frustration as he faced Yordan, the weight of the situation pressing heavily on his young shoulders. "I can fight, Yordan," he insisted, his hands balled into fists. "I can help! You don't have to protect me, I'm not a kid anymore."

Yordan sighed, placing a firm but gentle hand on Tequih's shoulder. "Tequih, listen to me. This isn't just about this fight, it's about the future." He reached into his tunic and pulled out the carefully folded piece of paper, the one on which he had written the Kamanali. Yordan placed it in Tequih's hands. "If I don't make it through this, you're the one who has to carry this message forward. Toteko's message. I wouldn't be a good guardian if I let you stay here when the odds are so heavily against us."

Tequih's face fell as he stared at the paper. "But—"

"No buts," Yordan interrupted firmly. "Your task is bigger than this fight. Spread this message. Protect it. Live it." He softened, lowering his voice. "I trust you, Tequih. You have strength in you—more than you realize."

Sam stepped forward, resting a comforting hand on Tequih's arm. "He's right," Sam said, his voice calm and steady. "We need you to keep going. Come on, I'll ride with you."

Tequih hesitated, his knuckles white as he gripped the paper. Finally, he nodded reluctantly. "Fine," he muttered, his voice barely above a whisper.

With that, Sam climbed aboard Tequih's forest horse, settling behind the boy to guide him. Tequih cast one last look at Yordan, his eyes filled with worry and regret, before urging the horse forward. Yordan watched as they descended the hill, their figures growing smaller as they joined the refugees on the road south to Zetopolis.

As the sound of hooves faded, Yordan turned back to the makeshift defenses, throwing himself into the work alongside Aisha's soldiers. He hefted a pile of sharpened stakes and began positioning them in the ground, sweat dripping from his brow.

"You don't look like a soldier," Aisha remarked, her tone sharp as she approached him. She adjusted the strap of her armor, her movements fluid and practiced.

Yordan glanced at her, still hammering a stake into the dirt. "I'm not. Just trying to survive."

Aisha snorted, leaning against the wooden fortifications. "Figures." Her eyes scanned the defenses, and she added bitterly, "Do you want to know why I only brought forty soldiers?"

Yordan paused, straightening up to meet her gaze. "Why?"

Aisha's lips curled into a wry smile, but there was no humor in it. "Because my father didn't think this was important enough. He figured it would be a lost cause. So I gathered the people I trusted and came on my own—dragging your friend Sam and Lalina along with me."

Yordan frowned, anger flickering in his chest. "And he let you leave with so few?"

Aisha shrugged, her expression hardening. "He didn't stop me. Maybe he hoped I'd fail. Maybe he didn't care."

Yordan let out a long breath, his hands resting on his hips. "Then I guess it doesn't matter if I tell you Toteko sent me," he said, his voice quiet but firm.

Aisha's sharp eyes locked onto his. "Toteko sent you? To do what, exactly?"

"To save all their people in Anakuatl," Yordan replied, his voice steady despite the weight of the words. "Not just Lumites or Aralonites or Zetians—all their people."

Aisha stared at him for a long moment, her expression unreadable. Finally, she turned away, her voice cutting through the tense air. "You'd better fight like Toteko is watching. Because if we lose this, it won't matter who sent you."

Aisha's voice carried a mixture of frustration and determination as she turned to Uriah. "You should go with the refugees, Uriah. Head south, get to safety with them. They need a steady voice and someone they trust."

Uriah, standing tall despite his age, shook his head with a gentle but firm smile. "Aisha, I've protected you since you were five years old. I'm not going to stop now just because you might throw your life away. No matter how far down the line of succession you are, you are still my princess, and I will always protect you."

Aisha's lips tightened, but she nodded, realizing there was no arguing with him. "Fine," she muttered. "Just don't do anything stupid, old man."

As the sun dipped below the horizon, a creeping darkness enveloped the plain. Yordan peered out over the tall grass, noticing the flickering lights of Lucien's campfires about 500 yards away. His force had stopped to make camp for the night, their movements barely visible through the shifting shadows. Yordan worked silently to set up a fire with the others, the tension in the air palpable.

Aisha crouched near a makeshift table, sketching rough battle plans on a scrap of parchment. Her brow furrowed in concentration as she tried to devise a strategy to buy the refugees enough time to reach Zetopolis. Yordan glanced at her, then at the tall grass that surrounded their position, an idea forming in his mind.

Clearing his throat, he spoke up, "What if we leave Uriah here with ten of your soldiers to make it look like we're still in camp?"

Aisha looked up sharply, her eyes narrowing. "And then what? Sacrifice them to buy time?"

Yordan shook his head. "No, we use the tall grass and the cloud cover rolling in. It's dark enough to sneak down through the grass, circle behind their camp, and set up a surprise attack. We wait until both lines are ready, then hit them hard from behind. They won't expect it."

Uriah raised an eyebrow but didn't speak, waiting to see how Aisha would respond. Aisha crossed her arms, her gaze locked on Yordan. "And what makes you so sure this will work? Did Toteko advise you of this brilliant plan?"

Yordan smirked faintly, shaking his head. "No. My swordmaster in Nahualis taught me to take in the terrain quickly. This is a one-night opportunity, and the cloud cover makes it possible. If we wait until morning, they'll have the advantage of numbers and daylight. This gives us the best chance to cause chaos in their ranks, maybe even force them to retreat."

Aisha let out a slow breath, her eyes scanning the grass and the distant campfires. "I hate that I like this plan," she muttered. "But you're right. It gives us the best chance. Let's do it."

She turned to her soldiers, issuing sharp, efficient commands. Uriah placed a reassuring hand on her shoulder, nodding his approval. Yordan felt a surge of determination as he tightened the straps on his armor, gripping the hilt of Tlamashta.

Aisha stepped forward, addressing her troops. "Ten of you will stay here with Uriah. The rest, follow me. Move silently, stick to the grass, and wait for my signal. Tonight, we strike for the refugees and for Anakuatl."

Chapter Twenty-One

T he night was shrouded in an eerie stillness, broken only by the rustling of tall grass in the soft breeze and the muffled steps of boots pressing into the dirt. Yordan followed Aisha's lead, his heart pounding as he kept low, moving cautiously through the cover of the plains. The cloud cover overhead added to the darkness, a blessing and a curse as it concealed their movements but also made it harder to see their path.

The grass stretched up to Yordan's shoulders, brushing against his armor and face. He tightened his grip on Tlamashta's hilt, the leather familiar and grounding in his palm. Around him, the other soldiers crept forward in near silence, their forms barely visible through the thick vegetation. Each step was deliberate, careful to avoid snapping twigs or crunching dried leaves beneath their boots. Any sound, no matter how small, could give away their position to the sentries stationed on the fringes of Lucien's camp.

Aisha led the group with practiced precision, her eyes scanning the horizon like a hawk. She moved with a confidence born of experience, every motion purposeful. She raised a hand, signaling for the group to halt. The soldiers froze instantly, the tension in the air palpable. Yordan's breath caught as he squatted lower, peering through the grass.

Ahead, a faint silhouette moved near the edge of Lucien's camp—a sentry pacing back and forth. The faint glow of a distant fire illuminated the figure, their weapon glinting briefly in the flickering light. Aisha waited, her hand still raised. Yordan could feel the soldiers around him holding their breath, the weight of the moment pressing down on them.

The sentry paused, their head tilting as if they heard something. Yordan's stomach clenched, sweat beading on his forehead despite the cool night air. He watched as the sentry scanned the area, their movements slow and deliberate.

After what felt like an eternity, the sentry turned and continued their patrol. Aisha's sharp eyes tracked their movements, and after a few more tense seconds, she gestured for the group to move forward again. Her hand signals were precise pointing to the right for a slight change in direction, then downward to signal the need for absolute silence.

The group pressed on, their pace slow but steady. Yordan's legs ached from staying crouched, but he pushed through discomfort, focusing on each step. His boots brushed against the grass, and he felt every inch of his surroundings: the dampness of the soil, the cool air against his exposed skin, and the rhythmic pounding of his own heartbeat.

Aisha suddenly stopped again, raising her hand higher this time. The soldiers froze in unison, their training and discipline evident. Yordan followed her gaze, spotting another sentry in the distance. This one was further into the camp, their figure partially obscured by the glowing embers of a fire.

Aisha signaled for them to crouch lower and wait. Yordan obeyed, gripping his sword tightly. He felt the tension ripple through the group, every soldier hyper-aware of the risks they were taking. The sentry lingered near the fire for a moment before moving further into the camp. Aisha waited several more seconds, ensuring the coast was clear, before giving the signal to move again.

The group continued their slow crawl through the grass, inching closer to the rear of Lucien's force. Yordan's mind raced as he thought of the refugees they were protecting. The stakes of this operation felt heavier with every step. If they failed, it wouldn't just be their lives, it would be the hundreds of lives depending on their success.

As they neared their target, Aisha raised her hand one final time, signaling for the group to stop. She turned and made a circular motion with her hand, indicating that they were to spread out and prepare for the ambush. Yordan nodded, his muscles taut as he moved into position, readying himself for what was to come.

The faint glow of Lucien's campfires was now just a short distance away, the sounds of the soldiers settling into their camp growing louder. Yordan's grip on Tlamashta tightened as he steadied his breathing, preparing for the signal that would ignite the chaos.

Aisha crouched low, her sharp gaze scanning the rear of Lucien's camp. The faint glow of firelight flickered on the horizon, casting shadows that danced across the tall grass. She turned to the soldiers, her face resolute and voice a hushed whisper.

"We need to make a single line, spread wide enough to make it seem like we're more numerous than we are," she instructed, her tone calm but urgent. "When I give the signal, we charge and yell. Take down as many as you can before they regroup."

She paused, meeting the eyes of each soldier in turn, her intensity unwavering. "May the Echoes of Toteko keep you steady."

The response came in unison, a low murmur that carried a solemnity Yordan hadn't expected. "And may they bring you harmony and peace."

Yordan glanced at the others, their resolve palpable. He couldn't bring himself to echo the phrase—it wasn't yet his to say—but he nodded silently, drawing strength from their unity.

Aisha gave a quick signal with her hand, and the group began to spread out into a single line, their movements careful and quiet. Yordan found his place among them, crouching low in the grass. He could feel the tension in the air, a quiet storm building within the hearts of those around him.

His hand moved to the hilt of Tlamashta, gripping the leather-bound handle with purpose. Slowly, carefully, he drew the blade, ensuring it didn't catch or scrape loudly against the scabbard. The faint moonlight caught the damascene pattern of the sword, its folded steel shimmering like ripples in water. Around him, the other soldiers did the same, the faint glints of steel barely visible in the darkness.

Yordan's heart pounded, each beat echoing in his ears. The cool night air felt sharper now, the scent of burning wood and damp earth mingling in his nostrils. He shifted his weight, testing the firmness of the ground beneath his boots. Every muscle in his body was taut, ready to spring into action.

He glanced down the line, catching glimpses of faces illuminated by slivers of moonlight. Some were expressionless, their focus entirely on the task ahead; others wore grim determination, their lips moving silently in prayer or final preparation. Aisha stood at the center, her form a shadowy silhouette against the backdrop of the campfires. Her sword was unsheathed but still held low, her figure poised like a coiled spring.

Yordan's gaze drifted back to the camp ahead. The flickering fires revealed outlines of tents and resting soldiers. He could hear muffled voices, the occasional clink of armor, and the shifting of restless horses. The camp was alive but unsuspecting. He could feel the seconds dragging on, each one stretching endlessly as the weight of what was about to happen bore down on him.

His grip tightened on Tlamashta, his knuckles whitening. This was it. There was no turning back. Yordan felt the blade almost hum in his hand as if it shared his anticipation. He exhaled slowly, his breath misting in the cool night air. Every nerve in his body screamed for action, yet he remained still, waiting for the signal.

Aisha raised her hand high, her figure sharp and commanding in the dim light. The soldiers around him shifted slightly, their tension palpable. The moment stretched thin, the air crackling with the weight of unspoken words and unfulfilled motion.

Then, Aisha dropped her hand, and with it, the night erupted into chaos.

The signal dropped, and the night split with the thunderous roar of their battle cries. The soldiers surged forward as one, swords flashing in the dim light as they stormed Lucien's camp. Their yells echoed across the plains, a cacophony of defiance and fury that shook the air.

Yordan's voice joined the cry, a raw, guttural sound that tore from his chest as he charged alongside the others. His grip on Tlamashta was firm, the sword feeling like an extension of his arm as he rushed headlong into the fray. The tall grass whipped against his legs, the ground pounding beneath his boots, and then they were upon the camp.

The first strike was instinctual. A soldier turned toward him, startled and unarmored, barely raising his weapon before Yordan's blade sliced clean through his defense. The man fell with a groan, and Yordan moved on without pause, adrenaline surging through him like fire.

Around him, chaos erupted. Soldiers scrambled from their tents, some barely dressed, their weapons haphazardly drawn. Yordan struck another, Tlamashta cutting with precision through minimal resistance. The sword gleamed in the faint firelight, its damascene pattern catching the glow with each swing.

A shout came from his left, and Yordan spun just in time to meet the blade of an Aralonite soldier. The clash rang out, a sharp, metallic scream that vibrated up his arm. The soldier's eyes were wide, and his strikes were frantic. Yordan parried, sidestepped, and drove his sword through the man's side, the force sending him stumbling to the ground.

More soldiers poured into the melee, but their lack of armor left them vulnerable. One rushed Yordan, swinging wildly, his blade glancing off Yordan's shoulder plate with a dull thud. The armor held, the impact barely bruising, and Yordan retaliated with a swift, decisive slash. The soldier fell, clutching at his wound, and Yordan pressed on.

The deeper he plunged into the camp, the more resistance he encountered. Some soldiers were better equipped, wearing piecemeal armor that offered more protection but limited their mobility. Even so, Tlamashta bit through them, its edge unyielding. The weight of the sword was perfect, its balance allowing Yordan to keep moving, keep striking, keep surviving.

Around him, the sounds of battle roared—shouts of pain, the clash of steel, the thudding of bodies hitting the ground. Fires spread, licking at the edges of tents, casting an orange glow over the chaos. The air grew thick with smoke and the metallic tang of blood.

Yordan's muscles burned, his breaths coming in short, ragged gasps, but he didn't stop. Every swing of Tlamashta felt heavier, yet every enemy that fell fueled his determination. He had to give the refugees time to escape. He had to keep going.

Then he saw her, amid the chaos, Aisha stood locked in combat with Lucien. She moved like a storm, her strikes precise and powerful, but Lucien met her blow for blow. His chest plate gleamed in the firelight, the only armor he wore, but it was enough to turn aside her slashes. His swordwork was disciplined, his movements calculated.

Yordan froze for a moment, caught by the intensity of their battle. Aisha's face was set in fierce determination, her red hair wild and fiery in the flickering light. Lucien's expression was cold, a predator savoring the challenge. Their swords clashed again and again, sparks flying with each collision.

"Aisha!" Yordan shouted, his voice hoarse from exertion.

Lucien's eyes flicked toward Yordan for a brief second, a smirk tugging at his lips. It was all the opening Aisha needed. She feinted left, then drove her blade toward Lucien's exposed side. But he twisted at the last second, the tip of her sword glancing off his chest plate with a screech.

Yordan pushed forward, cutting down a soldier who tried to block his path. He had to reach them. He had to help. But the battle swirled around him, each step forward met with resistance. His grip on Tlamashta tightened as he fought his way closer, every muscle in his body screaming with effort.

Lucien and Aisha's duel raged on, their blades a blur of motion. And Yordan, bloodied and determined, pressed on through the chaos, driven by the desperate need to tip the scales.

Yordan cut down the soldier in front of him with a swift slash of Tlamashta, the blade cleaving through the unarmored man as if he were air. Blood sprayed against his armor as the soldier crumpled to the ground, and Yordan barely paused to catch his breath before charging toward Aisha and Lucien.

Lucien, already engaged in a fierce duel with Aisha, turned just in time to meet Yordan's blade. Their swords clashed with a deafening ring, the force of the impact jolting up Yordan's arm. Lucien's expression remained composed, a chilling smirk on his face as he smoothly sidestepped and countered with a lightning-quick strike.

Yordan barely managed to block, Tlamashta shuddering under the blow. The momentum drove him back a step, and Lucien advanced, his blade a blur as he pressed the attack. Yordan's focus narrowed to the rhythm of parry and dodge, his chest tightening with every calculated strike Lucien delivered.

Aisha darted in from the side, her sword aiming for Lucien's flank. He pivoted fluidly, catching her blade with his own and forcing her back with a powerful shove. Yordan took the opportunity to thrust forward, but Lucien anticipated it, twisting his torso to deflect Tlamashta with the flat of his blade. His counterstrike came in a flash, slicing across Yordan's shoulder armor.

The impact sent Yordan stumbling, the sting of the strike reminding him how close he had come to being gutted. He gritted his teeth and steadied himself, gripping Tlamashta tighter. Lucien's skill was undeniable—his movements were precise, his strikes deliberate, his composure unshaken despite fighting two opponents.

"You're slower than I expected, Yordan," Lucien sneered, his blade arcing toward Yordan's side.

Yordan blocked, barely, but the force of the strike sent him reeling again. Lucien followed with a thrust aimed for Yordan's midsection, only for Aisha to intercept. Her blade slammed into Lucien's, the clash sending sparks flying between them. Her face was set in grim determination, sweat matting her fiery hair to her forehead.

"You'll have to do better than that!" Aisha snarled, stepping into her strike and forcing Lucien to backpedal.

Lucien recovered with a spin, his blade sweeping in a wide arc that forced both Aisha and Yordan to step back. He moved like a predator, his eyes sharp and calculating as he sized them up.

"You think two against one gives you an advantage?" Lucien mocked. "You only double your mistakes."

Yordan lunged, trying to capitalize on Lucien's distraction. But Lucien parried with infuriating ease, turning the attack aside and slashing upward in a single fluid motion. The tip of his blade scraped across Yordan's breastplate, the impact knocking the wind out of him and forcing him to his knees.

Lucien raised his sword to deliver a finishing blow, but Aisha leapt into the fray. Her blade lashed out, forcing Lucien to redirect his strike toward her instead. Their swords locked, the strength of their clash sending tremors through the ground.

"A little help here!" Aisha barked, her voice strained as she fought to hold her ground.

Yordan pushed himself back to his feet, his muscles screaming in protest. Blood trickled from beneath his armor where Lucien's strike had grazed him, but he ignored it, focusing all his energy on the duel before him.

Then Yordan spotted a discarded spear lying in the dirt nearby. His mind raced as he realized the opportunity. "Aisha, hold him for one second!"

Aisha gritted her teeth, her blade pressing against Lucien's in a desperate lock. Yordan dove for the spear, grabbing it and spinning on his heel just as Aisha twisted her blade to unbalance Lucien.

The opening was brief, but it was enough. Yordan hurled the spear with all his strength, the weapon hurtling toward Lucien. It struck true, piercing his side with a sickening crunch. Lucien let out a strangled gasp, his grip faltering.

Aisha seized the moment, her blade flashing as she slashed at Lucien's exposed chest. The wound wasn't deep enough to fell him, but it staggered him, forcing him to drop his sword and clutch at the spear embedded in his side.

With a roar, Yordan surged forward, Tlamashta raised high. His blade came down in a sweeping arc, slashing across Lucien's chest and sending him collapsing to the ground. Blood pooled around him as he gasped for air, his smirk finally gone.

Yordan staggered back, his chest heaving, his vision swimming from exhaustion and pain. Aisha stood beside him, her sword still raised, her expression unreadable as she stared down at Lucien.

As the first rays of dawn spilled over the battlefield, Aisha stood amidst the wreckage of Lucien's camp, her almond-shaped brown eyes scanning the horizon with an intensity that belied her exhaustion. Stray tendrils of her raven-black hair framed her dirt-smudged face, while the long braid down her back swayed slightly in the morning breeze. She planted her sword tip into the ground, leaning on it briefly as she steadied her breath.

Yordan, standing beside her, felt the ache in his muscles with every passing moment. His armor bore the marks of battle—scratches, dents, and the blood of enemies—and Tlamashta still rested heavily in his hand, its once-pristine blade dulled from the night's violence. He glanced at Aisha, who, despite her graceful demeanor, showed the toll the fight had taken on her. Her jaw was set with resolve, and her posture, though steady, hinted at weariness.

"They've gone," Aisha said, her voice quiet but firm. "We held them off."

Yordan nodded, letting out a breath he hadn't realized he'd been holding. Around them lay the remnants of Lucien's force—abandoned tents, scattered weapons, and the bodies of the fallen. The silence was heavy, broken only by the groans of the wounded and the rustling of soldiers beginning to regroup.

Hoofbeats echoed in the distance, and both turned toward the sound. Uriah appeared, leading the ten riders who had stayed behind. His weathered face lit with relief as he dismounted and strode toward Aisha.

"Princess," Uriah said, his voice trembling with emotion. "Thank the echoes, you're alive."

Aisha's hard expression softened at the sight of him. "I told you I wouldn't fall, Uriah," she said, clasping his forearm firmly. "You should've stayed with the others."

Uriah chuckled, his eyes glinting with pride. "An old man like me isn't about to let his princess fight alone. You should know that by now."

Yordan watched the exchange with quiet admiration. Uriah's loyalty to Aisha was palpable, a bond forged over decades of shared struggles. Around them, the remaining soldiers began the somber task of burying the dead. Their movements were methodical, their expressions reverent as they dug graves for friends and foe alike.

Yordan turned his gaze to the fallen Aralonite soldiers, scanning their faces with a heavy heart. To his relief, none of them were familiar, but their deaths weighed on him nonetheless. These were men who had followed orders, caught in the endless tide of conflict that ravaged Anakuatl.

The scene pulled Yordan back to a memory that had haunted him for months—the man nailed to the tree by King Benjamin's orders, his broken body a testament to the depths of cruelty the world could reach. Yet here, amidst Zetians honoring even their enemies in death, Yordan saw a glimmer of what humanity could aspire to.

Aisha stepped closer to him, her eyes softening slightly. "We honor the dead," she said, her voice quieter now. "It's what separates us from men like Lucien. Even our enemies deserve dignity in death."

Yordan nodded, his voice subdued. "What your people are doing here... it's humbling. It's a reminder of what we're fighting for."

She tilted her head, studying him for a moment before offering a faint smile. "You fought well last night, Yordan. But don't let victory make you complacent. This was just one battle."

Yordan looked toward the rising sun, the warm light slowly casting away the shadows of the night's carnage. His grip on Tlamashta loosened, and he allowed himself a weary smile.

"I'm not complacent," he said, meeting her gaze. "But I know we did what had to be done. And now... we keep moving forward."

The soldiers worked in silence as the graves were dug, their collective energy focused on honoring the dead. Aisha's commanding presence guided them, ensuring that each fallen Lumite, Aralonite, and Zetian was given the dignity they deserved. Yordan labored alongside the others, sweat dripping from his brow as he used a borrowed spade to carve out the earth. The weight of what they were doing wasn't lost on him. Every grave dug was a reminder of the cost of hatred, war, and division.

When the last grave was filled and marked, Aisha stood at the head of the group. Her brown eyes glistened as she raised her hands, palms upward, in the Zetian style of prayer. The soldiers and refugees alike bowed their heads, and a hush fell over the field.

"Toteko," Aisha began, her voice clear yet filled with solemnity, "guardian of the light and life of Anakuatl, we offer these souls into your embrace. May they find peace beyond this world, free of the burdens and strife that bound them here. May the echoes of your love guide them to harmony, and may their sacrifice remind the living of the cost of hate."

Yordan, bowing his head, found himself struck by the prayer's familiarity. It mirrored the words spoken over his mother's grave so many years ago, following Aralonite traditions. The shared reverence for life, the hope for peace—it resonated deeply within him. For a brief moment, the lines between Zetian and Aralonite seemed to blur, united in their grief and aspirations for a better world.

As the prayer concluded, Yordan wiped his hands on his pants and reached for Tlamashta to sheath it. His mind, distracted by the prayer, caused him to slip, nicking his fingertip on the blade's edge. He hissed softly, shaking his hand, when Aisha noticed and approached him.

"Yordan," she said, her eyes narrowing slightly as they fell on the blade in his hand. "Is that... is that Tzilkarit steel?"

Her tone carried a mix of wonder and suspicion. The soldiers around them glanced over, clearly intrigued. Uriah, who had been overseeing the recovery of supplies, straightened up and listened closely.

"How did you get one of those?" Aisha continued, her voice lowering. "Uriah once told me the method to forge them was lost."

Yordan hesitated, his gaze shifting to the gleaming surface of the sword. Finally, he said, "My master taught me. It was the last thing he did for me before he died."

Aisha's expression softened. "I'm sorry," she said simply, her voice carrying an unexpected warmth.

Yordan gave a small nod, wiping the blood from his finger. "He gave me more than I ever deserved."

The moment passed, and the group returned to their work. They salvaged what they could from Lucien's decimated forces—food, water, weapons, and any usable supplies. By the time they returned to the camp, the sun was high in the sky, casting long shadows over the field of graves.

The remainder of the day was spent recovering, tending to wounds, and reinforcing their supplies for the journey ahead. Yordan sat by the fire later that evening, running a whetstone along Tlamashta's edge, the events of the day weighing heavily on his mind. The dead were honored, but the war was far from over.

As the camp settled under the deepening hues of twilight, Yordan tended to Taurtepetl with quiet care. The blood bay stallion, his coat gleaming in the soft glow of the firelight, nickered softly as Yordan ran a brush along his side. The rhythmic motion of grooming helped calm Yordan's mind after the day's events. He checked the feedbag, making sure Taurtepetl had enough to eat, and murmured soothing words to the horse as he worked.

The sound of approaching footsteps pulled Yordan's attention momentarily. He glanced up to see Aisha, her figure framed by the flickering light of nearby torches. Her raven-black hair was braided neatly, but loose strands framed her face, softening the resolute determination in her eyes.

"Yordan," she said, her tone measured but curious. "What happened after I yelled at you back at the Restless Respite in Lumina City?"

Yordan hesitated, focusing on brushing Taurtepetl's coat as if the act would somehow shield him from the weight of the question. After a moment, he sighed and answered, "I saw things, Aisha. Observed things. You were right—I didn't really see any Zetians, and though I never confirmed the restricted streets... well, no Zetian would talk to me. Still, I saw enough to know your words weren't just complaints."

He paused, running the brush down Taurtepetl's flank. The stallion snorted softly and shifted, but Yordan steadied him with a gentle pat.

"I saw things that only make sense if what you were saying was true," Yordan continued. His voice was low, almost as though he were confessing. "The signs, the silences, the way people avoided even mentioning Zetians in certain quarters. It wasn't just fear—it was something deeper, more deliberate."

Aisha crossed her arms, her eyes narrowing slightly. "So Toteko sent you to free us Zetians from oppression?" she asked, her voice tinged with both sarcasm and a flicker of curiosity.

Yordan set the brush down and leaned against Taurtepetl's side, his hand resting on the horse's sturdy frame. He shook his head. "No," he replied, his gaze fixed on the stallion's coat. "They spoke of something much larger. They said this obsession with destroying Zetians wouldn't just consume your people—it would consume everyone in Anakuatl. Lumites, Aralonites... all of us. It was like they were warning me of a fire that would burn unchecked unless I did something."

He let out a deep breath, his fingers absently tracing the grain of the leather straps on Taurtepetl's bridle. "But I can't even explain what happened that day. It still feels like my skin is on fire in a way I've never felt before. And now... I just hope I'm doing what they wanted me to do."

Aisha stepped closer, her expression softening slightly. She reached out to run her hand over Taurtepetl's coat, her fingers brushing through the stallion's smooth fur. In the dim light, her features looked less sharp, more contemplative. The stallion shifted slightly, and her hand moved over Yordan's, their fingers accidentally meeting.

The touch froze them both. Yordan looked up, startled, his green eyes locking with Aisha's deep brown gaze. For a moment, the world

428

seemed to narrow, the distant sounds of the camp fading into the background. There was something unspoken in her expression, something conflicted but unyielding, mirroring the storm within him. They stood like that, their hands touching, their eyes locked, as the weight of unspoken words hung heavy in the cool night air.

Aisha's hand trembled slightly beneath his, but she didn't pull away. Instead, she stepped closer, her body drawn to his like a moth to a flame. Yordan's heart pounded in his chest, each beat a thunderous echo of the desire that coursed through his veins. He could feel the warmth of her skin, the softness of her touch, and it ignited a hunger within him that he had never known before.

Slowly, hesitantly, Yordan raised his free hand to brush a stray lock of hair from Aisha's face. His fingers lingered on her cheek, tracing the curve of her jaw with a gentleness that belied the strength of his calloused hands. Aisha's eyes fluttered closed at his touch, her lips parting slightly as if in invitation.

And then, as if drawn by an irresistible force, their lips met. It was a kiss that shattered the world around them, a collision of passion and need that consumed them both. Yordan's arms encircled Aisha's waist, pulling her flush against him as he deepened the kiss. Her hands tangled in his hair, clutching him closer as if afraid he might disappear.

Their bodies molded together as if they were two halves of a whole, finally reunited. Yordan could taste the salt of Aisha's tears on her lips, could feel the pounding of her heart against his chest. It was as if every moment of his life had been leading to this, to the feel of her in his arms, to the fire that burned between them.

When at last they broke apart, both were breathless and trembling. Yordan rested his forehead against Aisha's, his eyes closed as he savored the lingering taste of her on his lips. Aisha's hands slid down to rest on his chest, her fingers splayed over the steady beat of his heart.

"Aisha," Yordan whispered, his voice rough with emotion. "I..."

Aisha pressed a finger to Yordan's lips, silencing his words before they could form. Her eyes, dark and intense in the flickering firelight, held his gaze with unwavering purpose. Without a word, she took his hand in hers, her touch electric against his skin, and tugged him gently towards her tent.

Yordan hesitated for a moment, glancing around the camp to see if any of their fellow soldiers had noticed their intimate exchange. The sounds of the camp—the crackle of fires, the low murmur of conversation, the occasional whinny of a horse—seemed distant, muffled by the pounding of his own heart.

"Aisha," he whispered, his voice hoarse with uncertainty, "shouldn't we talk about what this means? About us?"

Aisha paused at the entrance to her tent, the canvas flap partially open. She turned to face him, her expression softening. In the warm glow of the torches, her raven-black hair seemed to shimmer, the loose strands framing her face like a halo.

"Yordan," she said, her voice low and earnest, "I am a woman who just survived a battle she thought she would die in. I don't need to talk. I need you to get that shirt off."

With a fluid motion, Aisha reached up and tugged the leather tie that held her braid in place. Her hair cascaded down her back in a dark, silken wave, the loose curls brushing against her shoulders. Yordan's breath caught in his throat at the sight, his fingers itching to run through those soft tresses.

Aisha stepped backwards into the tent, her eyes never leaving his. Yordan followed as if in a trance, ducking beneath the canvas flap and letting it fall closed behind him. The interior of the tent was lit by a single lantern, its soft light casting dancing shadows on the walls. A simple bedroll lay on the ground, a blanket of deep blue wool folded neatly at its foot.

Yordan's heart raced as Aisha stepped closer, her hands reaching for the hem of his shirt. Her fingers brushed against the bare skin of his stomach, sending a shiver down his spine. Slowly, deliberately, she tugged the fabric upwards, her knuckles grazing his chest as she pulled the shirt over his head.

The garment fell to the ground, forgotten, as Aisha's hands explored the planes of Yordan's chest. Her touch was feather-light, tracing the scars that marred his skin, the muscles that rippled beneath her fingertips. Yordan's own hands found her waist, pulling her closer until their bodies were flush against each other.

Aisha tilted her head up, her lips hovering just a breath away from his. "I want you, Yordan," she whispered, her words a caress against his skin. "I want to feel..." Aisha's words trailed off as her hands trailed down Yordan's chest, her fingertips grazing the sensitive skin just above the waistband of his pants. Yordan's muscles tensed beneath Aisha's touch, a sharp breath catching in his throat as her fingers trailed lower. Heat flared through him, his senses narrowing to the point of contact. Then—her palm pressed against him, firm and deliberate. A shock of pleasure coiled through his spine, his body instinctively responding. His breath left him in a slow, shuddering exhale, his grip tightening slightly where his hands rested.

Yordan groaned, his hand snapping to her wrist and stilling her movements. "Not yet, princess," he rasped, his voice low and rough with need. "I want to savor every moment of this."

In one swift motion, Yordan grasped the hem of Aisha's tunic and pulled it over her head, tossing it aside. His eyes roamed hungrily over her newly exposed skin, drinking in the sight of her like a man dying of thirst. Aisha felt her cheeks flush under the intensity of his gaze, but she made no move to cover herself.

Yordan's strong arms encircled her waist and he lifted her effortlessly, pulling her tight against his bare chest. Aisha wrapped her legs around him instinctively as he carried her the few short steps to the bedroll. He lowered her gently onto the soft blankets, following her down and covering her body with his own.

Their lips met in a searing kiss, all tongues and teeth and desperation. Aisha arched beneath him, pressing herself closer, needing to feel every inch of his skin against hers. Yordan's hands roamed her body, caressing and kneading, leaving trails of fire in their wake.

Aisha gasped as his lips left hers to blaze a path down her throat. He nipped and sucked at the sensitive flesh, no doubt leaving marks she would have to hide come morning. But in that moment, she couldn't bring herself to care. All that mattered was his touch, his taste, the delicious weight of him pressing her into the bedroll.

"Yordan," she breathed, tangling her fingers in his hair to pull him back up for another hungry kiss. She could feel the evidence of his arousal, hot and hard against her thigh, and it sent a fresh wave of desire coursing through her veins.

Rolling her hips, Aisha ground herself against him, reveling in the low groan that rumbled through his chest. Yordan's hand slid down between their bodies to the laces of her pants. With a deft tug, he loosened the ties and slipped his fingers beneath the waistband.

Aisha whimpered as he cupped her mound, his touch sure and purposeful even through the thin fabric of her undergarments. He stroked her gently, teasingly, until she was writhing beneath him in frustrated need.

Yordan's fingers hooked into the waistband of Aisha's pants, tugging them down slowly, reverently, revealing inch after tantalizing inch of smooth, tawny skin. Aisha lifted her hips to aid him, her breath coming in shallow pants as cool air kissed her newly bared flesh. With aching gentleness, he slid the garment down her long, toned legs until she could kick them free.

His reverent gaze drank in the sight of her, clothed now in nothing but her thin undergarments. The sheer fabric did little to conceal the dusky peaks of her breasts or the enticing shadow at the apex of her thighs. Yordan licked his lips, his eyes darkening with undisguised hunger.

"You're so beautiful," he murmured, his voice rough with awe and desire. His hands skimmed up her calves, over her knees, caressing the silken skin of her thighs. Aisha shivered at his touch, her back arching slightly off the bedroll.

Slowly, teasingly, Yordan's fingers curled into the delicate fabric of her undergarments. He drew them down with excruciating care, exposing her to his ardent gaze inch by torturous inch. Aisha held her breath, fighting the urge to squirm under the intensity of his stare.

At last, she lay bare before him, her skin glowing like burnished bronze in the lantern's soft light. Yordan sat back on his heels, just looking at her, his expression one of reverent wonder.

"Aisha…" he breathed, and the raw emotion in that single word made her heart clench.

Then he was moving over her, his lips blazing a trail of fire down her throat, across her collarbone. He paused at the gentle swell of her breasts, each one no bigger than a ripe nectarine. Cupping the delicate mounds in his calloused hands, he brushed his thumbs over the dusky peaks, coaxing them to tight, aching buds.

Aisha gasped, her fingers threading through his hair as he lowered his head to lave one sensitive nipple with the flat of his tongue. He suckled her gently at first, then with increasing pressure, drawing the peak deep into the wet heat of his mouth. His teeth grazed the tender bud and Aisha cried out, her nails digging into his scalp.

He lavished the same sweet torture on her other breast, suckling and nipping until Aisha was certain she would combust from the sheer pleasure of it. Her nipples felt as hard as diamonds, almost painfully sensitive as he worked them relentlessly with lips and tongue and teeth.

"Please," she whimpered, though what exactly she was begging for, she couldn't say. Yordan's lips blazed a fiery trail down Aisha's taut stomach, his tongue swirling around her navel before dipping inside. Aisha gasped, her back arching off the bedroll as sparks of pleasure radiated outward from his ministrations. Lower and lower he went, mapping every curve and hollow of her body with single-minded focus.

His hands continued their sweet torment of her breasts, kneading the soft mounds and rolling the pebbled peaks between his fingers. Each pinch and tug sent jolts of sensation straight to Aisha's core, stoking the aching need that burned there.

At last, Yordan settled between her thighs, his breath hot against her most intimate flesh. He pressed a tender kiss to her glistening folds, and Aisha nearly sobbed with relief and anticipation. Gently, reverently, he parted her lower lips with his fingers, exposing the glistening pink of her innermost secrets.

"So beautiful," he murmured again, his voice husky with desire. "So perfect."

Then his mouth was on her and Aisha's world narrowed to nothing but delicious, mind-melting sensation. His tongue swept through her folds, parting her delicate petals and lapping up the honey that dripped from her core. He explored her with long, slow strokes, savoring her essence, learning the contours of her most secret places.

When the tip of his tongue found the sensitive bundle of nerves at the apex of her sex, Aisha keened, her hips bucking up into his face. Yordan growled his approval, the vibrations making her toes curl. He sealed his lips around the sensitive nub and suckled gently, flicking the tip of his tongue against her in maddening circles.

Aisha writhed beneath him, her fingers fisting in his hair as she held him to her. Each lap and swirl of his tongue stoked the fire building low in her belly, winding the coil of tension tighter and tighter. He seemed to know instinctively how to touch her, alternating between broad, flat strokes and precise flicks, keeping her balanced on a knife's edge of pleasure.

Just when Aisha thought she could take no more, Yordan slid one long finger into her dripping heat. Her slick walls clenched around the welcome intrusion, drawing him deeper. He pumped the digit slowly, curling it to stroke a spot inside her that made stars burst behind her eyelids.

"Yes," Aisha gasped, rocking her hips to meet his thrusts. "Oh gods, yes, right there..."

Yordan added a second finger, stretching her exquisitely as his tongue continued its relentless assault on her clit. Aisha could feel her peak fast approaching, the tension coiling tighter and tighter in her core. Her thighs began to tremble, Yordan's fingers pumped faster, plunging deep into Aisha's dripping core as his tongue swirled mercilessly around her throbbing clit. The dual sensations were almost too much to bear, and Aisha felt herself hurtling towards the precipice of ecstasy.

"Don't stop," she panted, her voice high and breathy with need. "Please, Yordan, I'm so close..."

He growled against her sensitive flesh, the vibrations sending shockwaves of pleasure rippling through her. Aisha's back bowed off the bedroll as he curled his fingers inside her, stroking that secret spot that made her see stars. His tongue flicked rapidly over her clit, circling and teasing the swollen nub until Aisha thought she might go mad from the intensity of it all.

And then, with a final hard suck, Yordan sent her flying over the edge. Aisha's orgasm crashed over her like a tidal wave, stealing her breath and causing her vision to white out. Her inner muscles clenched rhythmically around Yordan's fingers as pulse after pulse of pure, unadulterated bliss radiated outward from her core.

Aisha cried out, a wordless, guttural sound of raw ecstasy. Her body shuddered and convulsed, wave after wave of pleasure crashing over her until she thought she might drown in the force of it. Through it all, Yordan continued his sweet torment, prolonging her climax until she was boneless and spent.

As the last aftershocks rolled through her, Aisha felt Yordan pressing tender kisses to her trembling thighs, his touch gentle and soothing now. She lay there, panting, her body humming with satisfaction even as a new hunger began to stir in her belly.

Almost of their own accord, her legs shifted, her toes finding the waistband of Yordan's pants and pushing insistently. He chuckled, low and deep, the sound sending shivers down Aisha's spine. Lifting his head from between her thighs, he met her heavy-lidded gaze, his eyes dark with promise.

"Impatient, are we?" he teased, even as he shifted to aid her in her efforts.

Together, they worked his pants down over his hips, freeing his straining erection. Aisha's mouth went dry at the sight of him, long and thick and pulsing with need. A pearly bead of moisture glistened at the tip, and she felt a fresh gush of wetness between her thighs.

Using the strength in her legs, Aisha drew Yordan toward her until the broad head of his cock nudged against her slick folds. They both groaned at the contact, Yordan's hips flexing instinctively to slide his length along her slit, coating himself in her juices.

Aisha pulled Yordan down for a searing kiss, their tongues tangling as she savored the taste of herself on his lips. The hard length of him pressed insistently against her core, and she rolled her hips, desperate for more contact. Breaking the kiss, Yordan gazed down at her with an expression of pure reverence, his eyes dark with desire.

"Aisha," he breathed, his voice rough with emotion. "Are you sure?"

In answer, she reached between them and grasped his thick shaft, guiding him to her entrance. The broad head parted her glistening folds, and they both groaned at the exquisite sensation. Slowly, carefully, Yordan began to push forward, sinking into her tight heat inch by delicious inch.

Aisha's breath caught at the stretch, her body accommodating his girth. He filled her utterly, touching places inside her she didn't know existed. When at last he was seated to the hilt, they stilled, savoring the feeling of being joined so intimately.

Yordan's forehead dropped to rest against hers, his breath mingling with her own. "You feel incredible," he murmured, nuzzling her cheek. "Like you were made for me."

Aisha's heart swelled at his words, and she clenched her inner muscles around him, relishing his sharp intake of breath. "Then take me," she whispered, her lips brushing the shell of his ear. "Make me yours."

With a low growl, Yordan withdrew until only the tip remained inside her, then surged forward in a smooth, deep stroke. Aisha gasped, her nails digging into the hard planes of his back as he began to move in earnest. Each thrust sent sparks of pleasure racing up her spine, stoking the fire that burned anew in her core.

Yordan set a steady rhythm, his hips rolling and undulating against hers in a sensual dance as old as time itself. Aisha met him stroke for stroke, tilting her pelvis to take him even deeper. The wet sounds of their joining filled the tent, punctuated by their harsh breathing and soft moans of pleasure.

Lowering his head, Yordan captured one taut nipple between his lips, lavishing it with attention. Aisha keened, her back arching off the bedroll as he suckled and nipped at the sensitive bud. His hand came up to palm her other breast, kneading the soft mound and plucking at the pebbled peak.

The dual sensations sent Aisha's pleasure skyrocketing, and she could feel a second climax fast approaching. Yordan seemed to sense it too, for he redoubled his efforts, pistoling his hips faster and harder against hers. The thick ridge on the underside of his cock dragged deliciously along her front wall with every thrust, hitting that secret spot that made her toes curl.

Aisha's climax hit her with the force of a lightning strike, stealing her breath and causing her inner walls to clench rhythmically around Yordan's pistoning length. She cried out, her voice a keening wail of ecstasy as wave after wave of pure bliss crashed over her. Her body shuddered and convulsed, fingernails raking down Yordan's sweat-slicked back as she held on for dear life.

Yordan groaned at the exquisite sensation of her fluttering around him, his thrusts becoming erratic as he chased his own release. But even in the throes of her pleasure, Aisha sensed his hesitation, his restraint. He was holding back, not wanting to overwhelm her, to push her too far too fast.

With a burst of strength, Aisha flipped them over, rolling Yordan onto his back without breaking their intimate connection. He stared up at her in awe, his hands coming to rest on her hips as she straddled him. The change in angle made them both gasp, his thick length somehow sinking even deeper into her still spasming sheath.

Aisha braced her hands on Yordan's chest, her hair cascading around them in a dark curtain as she began to roll her hips. She rode him slowly at first, savoring the delicious drag of his hardness against her sensitive inner walls. Yordan's grip tightened on her hips, his jaw clenching as he fought to maintain control.

Leaning down, Aisha captured his lips in a searing kiss, nipping at his bottom lip before soothing it with her tongue. "Let go, my love," she murmured against his mouth. "I need to feel you come undone inside me."

Yordan groaned, his hips flexing instinctively to meet her downward thrusts. Aisha sat back up, changing the angle once more, and they both moaned at the exquisite sensation. She began to move faster, rising and falling on his thick shaft, chasing the building pressure low in her belly.

Reaching for Yordan's hands, Aisha guided them to her breasts, shivering as his calloused palms cupped the sensitive mounds. "Touch me," she breathed, her voice husky with need. "Make me come again."

Yordan obeyed with reverence, kneading her soft flesh and rolling her pebbled nipples between his fingers. Each pinch and tug sent lightning bolts of pleasure straight to Aisha's core, stoking the fire that burned ever brighter. She threw her head back, her movements becoming more frenzied, more desperate as she chased her impending climax.

"That's it, princess," Yordan rasped, his own voice strained with the effort of holding back. "Ride me. Take what you need."

His words inflamed Aisha as she rode Yordan with wild abandon, her hips undulating in a primal rhythm as old as time itself. The wet sounds of their joining filled the tent, punctuated by their harsh breathing and guttural moans of ecstasy. Sweat glistened on their skin in the lantern light, their bodies moving as one in a sensual dance of give and take, push and pull.

Yordan's hands roamed Aisha's body, caressing every curve and hollow, stoking the fires of her desire. He plucked at her taut nipples, rolling the sensitive buds between his fingers until she keened with pleasure. His touch was electric, igniting sparks beneath her skin that coalesced into a raging inferno at her core.

Aisha could feel her climax building, the coil of tension winding tighter and tighter in her belly with each roll of her hips. She chased it with single-minded focus, angling her pelvis to take Yordan's thick length deeper, harder. The broad head of his cock kissed her womb with every thrust, sending shockwaves of bliss rippling through her.

"Yordan," she gasped, her nails digging into the hard planes of his chest. "I'm so close. Don't stop, please don't stop..."

He growled low in his throat, his grip on her hips tightening as he pistoned up into her with renewed vigor. The force of his thrusts made Aisha's breasts bounce, and Yordan watched, enraptured, as the dusky tips jiggled and swayed. Leaning up, he captured one rosy peak between his lips, suckling hard.

Aisha cried out, her back arching as the added stimulation sent her hurtling towards the edge. She could feel Yordan's cock pulsing inside her, his release fast approaching. Desperate to feel him come undone with her, she clenched her inner muscles around him, rippling along his length like a velvet vice.

"Fuck, Aisha!" Yordan grunted, his hips faltering for a moment before redoubling their efforts. "You feel incredible. I can't...I'm go nna..."

"Yes," Aisha hissed, bearing down hard and grinding her clit against his pubic bone. Bright sparks of pleasure burst behind her eyelids, her toes curling as her climax finally crested. "Now, Yordan. Come with me now!"

As if on command, Yordan's body went rigid beneath her, his cock jerking and twitching as he erupted deep inside her. Aisha felt the hot rush of his seed filling her, prolonging her own release. Her inner walls fluttered and clenched around him, milking him for every last drop as they shuddered and moaned through the aftershocks.

Finally spent, Aisha collapsed against Yordan's chest, her body still trembling with the aftershocks of her intense climax. Yordan's arms came around her, holding her close as their racing hearts gradually slowed. They lay there, limbs entangled, reveling in the profound intimacy of the moment.

Yordan's hand traced lazy patterns on the damp skin of Aisha's back, his touch feather-light and reverent. Aisha nuzzled into the crook of his neck, breathing in the musky scent of their lovemaking that clung to his skin. In that moment, the rest of the world fell away - the war, the death, the uncertainty of what tomorrow might bring. There was only the two of them, cocooned in the warmth of each other's arms.

As their breathing evened out, Aisha propped herself up on one elbow to gaze down at Yordan. The lantern light played across the chiseled planes of his face, casting his features in a warm, golden glow. His hazel eyes were soft with adoration as he looked up at her, a small smile tugging at the corners of his lips.

Aisha reached out to trace the line of his jaw, marveling at the contrast of her tawny skin against his olive complexion. Yordan turned his head to press a tender kiss to her palm, his lips tickling her sensitive skin and sending a shiver down her spine.

"That was..." Aisha started, her voice husky with emotion.

"Earth-shattering? Life-changing? The most incredible thing you've ever experienced?" Yordan supplied with a grin, his eyes twinkling with mirth.

Aisha laughed, a pure, joyful sound that filled the tent. "All of the above," she agreed, leaning down to brush her nose against his.

Yordan's hand came up to tangle in her hair, his fingers sifting through the silky strands. He guided her mouth to his, capturing her lips in a slow, sensual kiss. Aisha melted into him, savoring the taste and feel of him. What started as a tender exploration quickly ignited into something hungrier, more urgent.

Aisha nipped at Yordan's bottom lip, soothing the sting with a swipe of her tongue. He groaned, his hands roaming the curves of her body with renewed purpose. Aisha could feel him stirring against her thigh, his cock twitching and hardening as their kiss deepened.

Breaking away with a gasp, Aisha stared down at him with heavy-lidded eyes, her lips kiss-swollen and glistening. "Already?" she teased, rocking her hips against him meaningfully.

Yordan smirked, his hands coming to rest on the globes of her ass and squeezing. "What can I say? You inspire me."

Aisha laughed again, fading into a contented sigh as she nestled against Yordan's chest, her body molding to his like two puzzle pieces finally sliding into place. Despite the renewed stirring of desire between them, a sense of languid satisfaction suffused her limbs, making her eyelids grow heavy.

Yordan seemed to sense the shift in her energy, his hands gentling their exploration to trace soothing patterns along her spine. Aisha shivered at the feather-light touch, goosebumps rising on her cooling skin. As if reading her mind, Yordan reached down to tug the soft woolen blanket over their entwined bodies, cocooning them in warmth.

"As much as I'd love to explore this further," Aisha murmured, her words muffled slightly against his chest, "I think sleep is calling louder right now."

Yordan hummed in agreement, the sound of a deep rumble beneath her ear. "Rest, my fierce warrior princess," he said softly, pressing a tender kiss to the crown of her head. "We've earned a moment's respite."

Yordan lay on his back, his arm cradling Aisha as she rested against his chest. Her raven-black hair spilled over his shoulder, the soft scent of earth and faint floral notes clinging to her from the day's march. The steady rhythm of her breathing, soft and calm, contrasted with the racing thoughts tumbling through Yordan's mind.

He stared at the ceiling of the tent, tracing the flickering patterns made by the firelight. His hand gently rested on Aisha's back, feeling the rise and fall of her breaths. The weight of the moment pressed on him, both grounding and disorienting.

This can't be real. The thought struck him like a whisper in the dark, tinged with disbelief. His eyes moved down to the curve of her form nestled into his side, her warmth a stark reminder of the battle they had fought and survived. He felt the ghost of her touch, the fervent connection they had shared just moments ago, still igniting his skin like the embers of a campfire.

When I fall asleep, he thought, his chest tightening, this moment will vanish. I'll wake up back in my own tent, alone, and this will have all been some cruel dream. He exhaled softly, careful not to disturb Aisha. His fingers lightly brushed a strand of her hair from her face, marveling at how someone who exuded such fierce strength in battle could appear so peaceful now.

The memory of his first battle replayed in his mind like a haunting melody. The chaos, the blood, the desperate shouts of warriors locked in the struggle for survival, it all felt like another lifetime. He had survived. Somehow, against the odds, he was still here, breathing, holding someone who had become more than just a fellow fighter. The surreal nature of it all left him questioning whether he deserved this fleeting solace.

His gaze softened as it lingered on Aisha, her face serene and at rest. The hard edges of her features, so often set in determination or fiery resolve, were now relaxed, vulnerable in a way he had never seen before. As his own exhaustion began to pull him under, he whispered silently into the stillness of the tent, a promise to himself as much as to her. If this is real, I will carry it with me. If it's a dream, I will make it my purpose to ensure this connection, this fight, this mission—everything—is worth remembering.

Chapter Twenty-Two

Yordan found himself at the serene banks of the Lumina River. The sunlight danced on the water's surface, casting ripples of light onto the surrounding rocks and foliage. Laughter filled the air—his own, carefree and unburdened, joined by Aisha's melodic laugh. She stood barefoot near the riverbank, her raven-black hair catching the golden glow of the sun as she splashed him playfully.

He chased after her, his steps light and unencumbered. Her brown eyes gleamed with mischief as she dodged his attempts to catch her, darting around like a shadow in the midday sun. When he finally caught her wrist, pulling her close, their shared laughter subsided into a moment of stillness. The gentle breeze carried the scent of the river, the sound of its flow underscoring the intimacy of the moment. Yordan thought, perhaps, this is what peace could look like—a future where battles were memories, and the Lumina River flowed freely for all of Anakuatl.

But then, without warning, the golden tree erupted into his vision, stark and jarring against the tranquil scene. Its massive, radiant form loomed above them, its branches twisting as if alive with fury. A deafening screech reverberated through the air, shattering the idyllic moment.

"You fool," the tree's voice boomed, shaking the very ground beneath him. "Chasing after the women you lust after, you risk all of Anakuatl's destruction for this fleeting moment. Find me soon, or you shall see it all come to an end."

The dream dissolved into chaos, the river's shimmering waters turning to ash, the laughter swallowed by the tree's echoing screeches. Yordan tried to reach for Aisha, but she faded from his grasp as the golden tree's light consumed everything.

Yordan awoke with a start, his breathing labored and his body tense. For a brief moment, he thought he was in his tent, alone with only his racing heart and the echoes of the dream. But as he shifted, he realized something was different. Looking down, he saw Aisha nestled against him, her arm draped over his chest, her breathing soft and steady. Her hair spilled over the blanket that covered them both, and he could feel the warmth of her bare skin pressed against his.

Blinking, he tried to piece together his thoughts. His fingers brushed against the blanket, feeling its coarse texture, and the realization hit him. What happened last night was not a dream. It was real—every touch, every whispered moment, and every shared breath.

Yordan's chest tightened as conflicting emotions coursed through him. Relief, confusion, guilt, and an overwhelming sense of uncertainty churned together. He had thought the dream with Aisha at the river was a vision of a possible future, but the golden tree's words haunted him. You risk all of Anakuatl's destruction...

Aisha stirred against him, her breathing changing as she began to wake. Yordan braced himself, unsure of what to say or how to navigate the fragile and complicated reality they now shared. Aisha stirred, stretching lazily as the soft morning light filtered into the tent. Yordan tried to steady his breathing, his eyes darting to the edges of the tent, as if hoping to find something to anchor his scattered thoughts. Then her voice broke the silence, warm and content. "Good morning," she said, her tone carrying a hint of mischief.

Yordan turned to her, his face heating as he became acutely aware of her lack of clothing. She sat up, her hair tumbling over her shoulders, and casually began reaching for her clothes, seemingly unbothered by his self-consciousness.

"I have to say," she continued, slipping into her undershirt, "I've never felt this good after a battle. Maybe I should yell at you more often—it seems to work wonders."

Her words pulled a nervous chuckle from Yordan, but his awkwardness only grew as she stood to finish dressing. Aisha glanced at him, her sharp brown eyes locking onto his expression, and then a playful smirk tugged at her lips. "Oh, Yordan, was that... your first time?" she asked, raising an eyebrow.

Yordan's face flushed a deeper shade of red as he sat up quickly, tugging the blanket around his waist. "No! What virgin do you know that knows how to do all of that on the first go?"

Aisha let out a hearty laugh, slipping into her breeches and fastening them. "Oh, thank Toteko," she said with exaggerated relief, her smirk widening. "Because if that was your first time, I was about to think, woah, he's absolutely unbelievable."

Yordan shook his head, a small smile tugging at his lips despite himself, but then his expression turned serious. "Aisha," he began, his voice softer, "what are we now?"

Pausing mid-motion as she reached for her belt, Aisha looked at him. She seemed caught off guard by the question, her confident demeanor faltering for just a moment. She picked up his shirt from where it was draped on the tent floor and handed it to him, her gaze flickering away briefly. "Here," she said, as if the gesture could give her the time she needed to form a response.

Finally, she sighed and sat on the edge of the cot, her tone more measured. "Right now," she said, looking directly at him, "let's say we're regular lovers. Maybe in a week, we'll realize we don't work at all. But right now? I can't say I don't want to fight beside you again. Whatever we are... I don't want to define it yet, Yordan."

Yordan nodded, slipping on his shirt, still feeling a mixture of uncertainty and relief. He could respect that answer, even if it didn't ease all the questions swirling in his mind.

"Let's get camp packed up," Aisha continued, standing and slipping on her boots. "We've got refugees to catch up with before they make it to Zetopolis."

Yordan stood as well, grabbing his gear and shaking off the lingering weight of his thoughts. Whatever they were, whatever was ahead, he knew there wasn't time to dwell on it. They had a mission, and that was something he could focus on, for now.

As the morning sun climbed higher into the sky, Yordan felt a newfound energy settle over him. With his gear packed and Taurtepetl saddled, he mounted the blood bay stallion, settling into the rhythm of the horse's powerful stride. Aisha, exuding her usual commanding presence, barked orders for the troop to fall out, her voice sharp and steady as the soldiers fell into formation behind her. Yordan, glancing back at the disciplined line, felt a rare sense of unity with the group. They were battered but victorious, and the air seemed lighter despite the lingering scent of ash and blood from the battlefield.

The ride through the plains was peaceful compared to the chaos of the past days. Taurtepetl's hooves thudded against the soft earth, and Yordan allowed himself to enjoy the ride, the wind brushing against his face and carrying with it the faint smell of wildflowers from the distant grasslands. Then, on the horizon, he spotted the group of refugees. The sight of their huddled figures stirred a deep relief within him. Despite everything, they had made it this far.

Without a second thought, Yordan nudged Taurtepetl into a gallop, breaking formation and rushing ahead of the troop. The blood bay's muscular frame stretched into each stride, and the thundering hooves drew the attention of the refugees. Gasps rippled through the crowd as Yordan approached, and for a moment, fear flickered in their expressions, but it melted away when they recognized him.

As Taurtepetl skidded to a halt, Yordan leapt from the saddle, the impact of his boots kicking up a small cloud of dust. His eyes immediately locked onto Tequih and Sam, who were standing near the edge of the group. Tequih's expression lit up with a mix of disbelief and joy, and Sam, hearing the commotion, instinctively turned his head toward the sound of Yordan's voice.

"Tequih! Sam!" Yordan called, his voice cracking slightly with emotion.

Tequih sprinted toward him, and Yordan caught the boy in a fierce embrace, gripping his shoulders tightly before pulling him into a proper hug. "I missed you, kid," Yordan muttered, ruffling Tequih's hair before turning to Sam.

Sam reached out cautiously, but Yordan pulled him into a strong embrace as well. "You made it," Sam said, his voice carrying equal parts relief and pride. "Of course I did," Yordan replied, his voice steady despite the lump in his throat. "We all did."

The cheers of the refugees grew louder as Aisha and her troop rode into view, their shining armor and steadfast expressions signaling a hard-won victory. The refugees waved and clapped, some crying openly at the sight of the princess and her soldiers. For the first time in what felt like forever, hope seemed to return to their faces.

Aisha dismounted gracefully, her raven-black hair catching the sunlight as she surveyed the gathered crowd with a calm yet authoritative gaze. She exchanged a quick glance with Yordan, her lips curving into a faint, almost private smile, before turning her attention to the refugees. The soldiers behind her began to dismount as well, helping to distribute water and supplies.

The atmosphere among the refugees shifted, relief mingling with cautious optimism. Yordan stood among them, his hand resting lightly on Tequih's shoulder. He felt a deep sense of accomplishment but also a renewed sense of purpose. They had overcome one battle, but the journey was far from over. As he looked at the faces of those they had fought to protect, Yordan knew they had no choice but to keep moving forward, one step—or one gallop—at a time.

As the refugees continued their southward journey toward Zetopolis, the plains stretched endlessly under the clear sky. The group moved at a steady pace, their spirits lifted somewhat by the presence of Aisha and her soldiers. Yordan, riding atop Taurtepetl, looked over the procession. Tequih was walking alongside his forest horse, keeping close to the elderly woman he'd been helping for most of their trek. Seeing the boy's quiet demeanor, Yordan dismounted and walked his stallion over to him.

"You doing okay?" Yordan asked, his voice gentle.

Tequih glanced up at him, his eyes clouded with something Yordan couldn't quite place. The boy hesitated, then reached into his pack, pulling out the folded piece of paper Yordan had given him two days earlier—the Kamanali.

"I've been carrying this, thinking you were dead," Tequih said, his voice wavering slightly. "And I kept asking myself... if you didn't come back, what would I even do with this?"

Yordan stopped walking, the reins of Taurtepetl loosely held in his hand. He watched as Tequih unfolded the paper, smoothing it out with trembling fingers. The boy's gaze lingered on the handwritten words, his voice growing steadier as he continued.

"When you handed me this... I thought it was just a way to make me feel useful. Like, if I had something important, I wouldn't feel so small or scared. But when you didn't come back, Yordan, I started to really read it. And I thought... what if this is all that's left of you? What if this is the only way anyone will remember you?"

Yordan's throat tightened. He crouched down slightly to meet Tequih's eyes, placing a reassuring hand on the boy's shoulder. "Tequih," he said softly, "I didn't give you that because I thought I wasn't coming back. I gave it to you because I trust you. I trust that if something happened to me, you'd carry this message forward."

Tequih shook his head, his voice breaking. "But I didn't want to carry it, Yordan! I wanted you to come back! I wanted you to be the one to tell everyone about Toteko's message—not me, not some kid who doesn't even know what half of it means."

The boy's words hit Yordan harder than he expected. He knelt fully now, letting Taurtepetl's reins drop to the ground. "Tequih, I... I'm sorry," Yordan said, his voice thick with emotion. "I didn't mean to put that kind of weight on you. I didn't think... I didn't think about how much it would hurt you to think I was gone."

Tequih looked down at the paper, his fingers gripping it tightly. "I don't even understand all of this," he admitted. "But I read it over and over because I thought... if this is all I have left of you, I have to make it matter."

Yordan took a deep breath, his hand still on the boy's shoulder. "Tequih, this message—it's not just mine. It's not just Toteko's. It's for everyone. And maybe I didn't explain that well enough, but it's not about one person carrying it all. It's about all of us trying to live it, together."

Tequih's eyes glistened with unshed tears, and he finally looked up at Yordan. "Do you really believe it? Do you really think it'll change anything?"

Yordan hesitated. He thought about everything they'd been through—the battles, the loss, the doubts that still gnawed at him. But then he thought of the refugees, of Aisha and her soldiers, of the way people had come together despite their differences.

"I think it has to," Yordan said firmly. "If we don't try, then nothing will ever change. But if we do—if we live by these principles—maybe we can start to make things better. Even if it's just a little."

Tequih stared at him for a long moment, then nodded slowly. He handed the paper back to Yordan. "Then you carry it," he said. "It's your message. But if you ever need me to help, I will."

Yordan smiled faintly, taking the paper and tucking it safely into his pack. "Thanks, Tequih. That means a lot."

As they resumed walking, Tequih glanced over at Yordan. "You know," he said, his voice quieter now, "I really thought you were dead. And I didn't know what I'd do if you were. You're... kind of all I have left."

Yordan's heart ached at the boy's words. He reached out, pulling Tequih into a brief, one-armed hug. "I'm here," he said softly. "And I'm not going anywhere."

The two of them walked in silence for a while after that, the weight of their conversation settling between them. But for the first time in days, Yordan felt a sense of clarity. The Kamanali wasn't just a set of principles. It was a promise—to Tequih, to himself, and to everyone who dared to hope for a better Anakuatl.

About a day away from Zetopolis, Yordan found Sam sitting quietly near a low-burning fire, Taurtepetl resting nearby with his tail swishing lazily. The soft glow of the flames danced across Sam's face, his sightless eyes fixed forward in quiet contemplation. Yordan approached, his boots crunching softly against the dry plains grass, and settled down next to his best friend.

Sam turned his head slightly, his acute hearing picking up the familiar sound of Yordan's footsteps. "Yordan," he said, a small smirk forming on his lips. "You finally took a break from doting on Tequih?"

Yordan chuckled, shaking his head even though he knew Sam couldn't see it. "Figured it was your turn to endure my company. Speaking of which..." He shifted his weight to face Sam. "How was it, being Tequih's guardian these past few days?"

Sam let out a soft laugh, leaning back on his hands. "Honestly? Exhausting. That kid's got more questions than a philosopher on a sleepless night. But..." His expression softened. "He's a good kid. Just needs some stability in his life, and maybe someone to remind him it's okay to trust people again. You've been that for him, Yordan."

Yordan stared at the fire, the flames reflected in his tired eyes. "I don't know if I've been anything good for him. Sometimes I feel like I'm just dragging him into more chaos."

"Chaos, sure," Sam said with a grin. "But you're dragging him through it with a purpose. There's a difference."

The words hung in the air for a moment before Sam leaned forward, his tone shifting to something more teasing. "You know, you really are insane, though. I mean, I knew you were a little off when you first dragged me to Lumina City, but this... this is a whole new level."

Yordan laughed, shaking his head. "Yeah, I've been thinking about that. Did you ever imagine this? When we left Aralonis together, did you ever think we'd end up here? On our way to Zetopolis, exiled from the only home we've ever known?"

Sam tilted his head, a thoughtful look crossing his face. "No," he admitted. "I thought we'd see the sights, maybe get into a little trouble, and then go home to Ferran and his forge. Never did I imagine we'd be fighting battles, leading refugees, or dodging armies. But..." He paused, his voice softening. "I guess that's what makes life unpredictable, doesn't it? We can plan all we want, but the world has its own ideas."

Yordan nodded, staring into the fire. "It's just... sometimes I wonder if I made the right choices. If dragging you, Tequih, and all these people into my mess was worth it."

Sam turned to him, his expression serious. "Yordan, look at me. Well... you know what I mean." He gestured vaguely toward Yordan's direction. "You've always been the one to jump into the fire, to try and fix things when no one else will. It's maddening, sure. But it's also why I'm proud to call you my best friend."

Yordan's throat tightened at Sam's words, the sincerity in his voice cutting through the doubts that had been plaguing him. "Thanks, Sam. That... that means a lot."

Sam reached out, his hand landing lightly on Yordan's shoulder. "You're still here, Yordan. We're still here. And maybe we've lost a lot along the way, but you're fighting for something bigger than yourself. That's not nothing."

Yordan exhaled, leaning back and staring at the stars. "Sometimes it feels like too much, though. Like the weight of it all is crushing me."

Sam smirked. "Good thing I'm here to keep you grounded then, huh?"

Yordan chuckled, shaking his head. "Yeah. You always have been."

The two of them sat in comfortable silence for a moment before Yordan finally spoke again. "You know, Sam... I don't know what's waiting for us in Zetopolis. I don't know if we'll even make it there. But whatever happens, I'm glad you're here with me."

Sam's smirk softened into a warm smile. "Right back at you, Yordan. Just... try not to get yourself killed, okay? I'd hate to have to explain that to Tequih."

Yordan laughed, the sound carrying softly into the night. "I'll do my best."

As the sun climbed higher in the sky, the sprawling city of Zetopolis came into view. Yordan stood at the crest of a gentle hill with Tequih on one side and Sam on the other. The sight before them was breathtaking, even for Yordan, who had heard tales of the city but never imagined its grandeur.

Sam tilted his head toward Yordan, his sightless eyes searching for some hint of the reaction on his friend's face. "What does it look like?" he asked quietly, his voice tinged with both curiosity and hope.

Yordan took a deep breath, his words coming slowly as he tried to encapsulate the sight before him. "It's... it's unlike anything I've ever seen. The city is enormous, sprawling across the plain with its outer walls rising high, like a shield for its people. The stone is a deep, warm gray, but sunlight glints off the edges of its towers, almost as if they've been dusted with gold.

"Closer to the center, there's a massive temple—it looks like it was carved straight out of the earth itself. It's surrounded by intricate terraces filled with greenery and fountains, their water catching the light as if Toteko's essence flows through them. The buildings inside the walls seem to glow with life, painted in earthy tones but adorned with bright, vibrant patterns. It's like the city itself is alive, thriving despite everything that's happening beyond its walls."

Tequih let out a soft, amazed breath. "It's beautiful," he murmured.

"It is," Yordan agreed, his voice low, as if afraid to disturb the moment.

Behind them, the group of refugees began to murmur, their voices rising in waves of relief and joy. Families clung to one another, some falling to their knees to offer prayers to Toteko, others simply standing in awe at the sight of the city that promised them safety. The weariness of their long journey seemed to lift, replaced by hope.

Sam, standing silently, let the sounds wash over him. "It sounds... incredible," he said softly. "Like a place where things could finally get better."

Yordan reached out, placing a reassuring hand on Sam's shoulder. "It feels that way," he said. "For the first time in a while."

Just as Yordan let the moment sink in, Aisha approached from behind. Her raven-black hair, tied back in a simple braid, swayed slightly with her steps. Her eyes, sharp and discerning, moved between the three of them, noting the stillness in their posture as they stared at the city.

"This is just the beginning," she said, her voice steady and resolute. "Getting here is one thing. But keeping everyone safe, making sure the promises this city represents aren't broken? That's the real battle."

Yordan turned to her, his expression firm. "Then we'll fight that battle too. Whatever it takes."

Aisha's lips curved into a small, knowing smile. "I hope you're ready for it, Yordan Arano. The path ahead isn't going to get easier."

"It hasn't been easy so far," he replied, his hand still resting lightly on Sam's shoulder. "But we're here now. That has to mean something."

Tequih, still staring at the city, nodded silently. The determination on his young face mirrored the resolve in Yordan's heart. Together, they would face whatever came next.